A Healing Kiss

"'Tis only a bruise," Rand said.

"Earned on my account," Florie muttered.

He flashed her a mischievous grin. "Ye know, my mother always gave my bruises a kiss. She assured me 'twould speed the healin'."

"Did she?"

"Oh, aye," he assured her with mock solemnity.

Her eyes were drawn instinctively to his mouth—his wide, elegant, sensual mouth with its seductive upward curve. Faith, she wanted to kiss him. She'd wanted to kiss him for days now.

He turned his head aside, presenting his injured cheek. Though she'd hoped for more, the playful innocence in his eyes was irresistible. With a brief smile, she inclined her head to bestow upon his cheek a chaste kiss of healing.

Her lips had scarcely grazed his cheek when he captured her face of a sudden between his hands. His touch was not ungentle, but 'twas uncompromising. A glimmer of danger gleamed in his eyes.

She gasped softly. Their mouths inches apart, she felt his intent as if 'twere a living thing.

"Ye want it as well," he whispered, and there was no need to clarify. "Ye want this."

MacFARLAND'S LASS

Copyright © 2010, 2014 by Glynnis Campbell
Previously published as "Captured by Desire" by Kira Morgan
By Hachette Book Group, Inc.

Cover design by Tanya Straley
Cover photo courtesy of Armstreet, makers of medieval clothing, http://www.armstreet.com. If you like the outfit, you can own it! Formatting by Author E.M.S.

Glynnis Campbell – Publisher
P.O. Box 341144
Arleta, California 91331

ISBN-10: 1938114396
ISBN-13: 978-1-938114-39-7
Contact: glynnis@glynnis.net

Published in the United States of America

MACFARLAND'S LASS

The Scottish Lasses, Book 1

GLYNNIS CAMPBELL

DEDICATION

For Sarah and Kira,
sisters of my heart...

R. I. P.

OTHER BOOKS BY GLYNNIS CAMPBELL

THE WARRIOR MAIDS OF RIVENLOCH
The Shipwreck (novella)
Lady Danger
Captive Heart
Knight's Prize

THE KNIGHTS OF DE WARE
The Handfasting (novella)
My Champion
My Warrior
My Hero

MEDIEVAL OUTLAWS
Danger's Kiss
Passion's Exile

THE SCOTTISH LASSES
The Outcast (novella)
MacFarland's Lass
MacAdam's Lass

THE CALIFORNIA LEGENDS
Native Gold
Native Wolf

ACKNOWLEDGMENTS

Special thanks to...

Brynna, Dylan, and Richard Campbell,
Lauren Royal, "America,"
Winona Ryder, Karl Urban,
and Carol and Velera from Celebrate Romance

CHAPTER 1

SPRING 1545
SELKIRK, SCOTLAND

"Thief! Thief! Stop her!"

Lady Mavis Fraser's sharp shrieks cut through the noise of the Selkirk Fair like the blade of a claymore.

Luckily for the thief, clutching tightly to her prize as she raced through the crowd—bumping a pie man, dodging a lady with a monkey, and passing perilously close to a fire-eater—most of the afternoon revelers were too drunk on bayberry mead to pay her much mind.

But the shrill screams of outrage jangled Florie's nerves and doubled her panic, spurring her to run faster. Her heart pounded with fear and amazement and, to her shame, a warped thrill of triumph.

She had what she wanted now. The precious gold pomander rested safely in her palm. But at what price?

Florie Gilder, respected apprentice of the goldsmith to

the Princess Mary herself, with one reckless act of passion, had become a common outlaw.

"Catch her!"

Florie knew she should stop running. She should never have bolted in the first place. A wise lass would calm herself, use diplomacy. 'Twas only a simple misunderstanding, after all.

But panic propelled her past stall after stall of tailors, potters, jewelers, glovers, and cobblers, wreaking chaos as she went. She elbowed aside a lad playing an hautboy, making a discord in his music, and earned hisses from a cluster of children as she barged between them and a puppet play. She scattered a flock of tethered hens, then trod upon the hem of a lady's velvet gown.

Fortunately, Florie's small size, which made her tiny fingers perfect for crafting the most intricate gold filigree, served her here as well. She was able to slip easily under the noses of the Selkirk guards, now alerted to the presence of a thief in their midst.

She scurried past the vendors of roast capon and oatcakes, gingerbread and umble pies. But then, sparing one quick glance over her shoulder, she spied a pair of determined men-at-arms clearing a path toward her.

Lord Gilbert's constables!

Her heart jabbed against her ribs.

Lady Mavis must have reported the crime to her husband's men, who were naturally everywhere, since 'twas Gilbert Fraser, the lord sheriff, whose amber-colored glove was displayed atop the pole at the fair's entrance, signifying his permission for the event.

"Ballocks," she whispered.

At that moment, one of the constables locked gazes with

her. Florie, unable to hide the culpability in her wide eyes, spun and bolted away.

She crashed through a circle of dice-casting peasants who yelled at her in anger, careened past an old woman selling ribbons, and wriggled through a knot of spectators wagering on a wrestling match.

She really had to stop. Running was a sure sign of guilt. Besides, what did she know about the countryside of Selkirk? She'd get lost, and the men-at-arms would catch up with her in no time.

But she could no more fight her instincts for self-preservation than a vixen could keep from fleeing a pack of slavering hounds.

Ahead, the way parted—leather goods down one lane, kitchenware down the other. Deciding in haste, she bolted to the right. The toe of her boot caught on an upright pole hung with iron pots, knocking the lot over with a clamoring like alarm bells.

"Shite!" she hissed, tearing away while the merchant shook his fist at her.

At last she reached the end of the fair, where the crowd began to thin and the trees to thicken.

She didn't dare look back. She knew the guards pursued her. Her only hope was to head for the forest and pray they'd lose track of her in the afternoon shadows.

Just past the last stall, she darted into a copse of trees overhanging a narrow deer trail. Fortunately, when she'd gone to the privy earlier, she'd taken off her bright blue apprentice's smock. Now, clad in her gown of fawn-colored brocade, Florie practically vanished among the shedding sycamores as she moved swiftly down the path.

The cacophony of the fair gradually receded, yielding to

the still of the forest. But Florie's jagged breathing and the rapid beat of her heart seemed deafening as she scurried through the wood.

The path constricted as it angled through the brush. Branches reached for her like a brazen cutpurse, one of them snagging her black velvet French hood and snatching it from her head. She cursed as her dark waist-length hair tumbled helter-skelter out of its pins, half blinding her. Her heavy skirts seemed to plot against her as well, dragging through the mulch, catching on twigs, slowing her progress.

But she hurtled along as best she could, guided by spots of sun that flashed through gaps in the thicket.

Before long, her mouth grew as dry as chalk. Strands of her loose hair clung to her damp face. And a javelin of pain began to stab at her side, making her wince at every limping tread. It seemed to Florie as if she'd run forever...that she'd never stop. And she began to regret taking that first fateful step.

Then she tripped over an exposed root, dropping the precious pomander and landing hard on her hands and knees.

She knelt there, gasping for breath. Her cheeks were flushed with heat. Runnels of sweat trickled down her neck. Her lungs burned. Her palms stung. She had no idea where she was. For a fleeting moment, the temptation to surrender—to collapse onto the ground and simply wait for destiny to take its course—was great.

Then she remembered the disparaging men of the goldsmith's guild. They'd belittled Florie when she'd taken over her foster father's trade, claiming that a lass was too frail and weak-willed for the work. They'd admonished the master goldsmith, saying he should have apprenticed a lad instead.

She wasn't about to prove them right.

With a determined oath, she scooped up the pomander, secured it quickly to the girdle of gold links about her hips, and forced herself up again, staggering forward.

Anger and despair warred within her as the gorse thickened and the trail narrowed, thwarting her escape. Then, just as she began to fear the path would dwindle to nothing, it blessedly opened up again. She plunged forward down the gradual slope, faster and faster, tripping along moss-covered stones, slipping through the sycamores, and skidding on the leaf-fall.

So quickly did she descend the hill that she almost broke through the trees when the path emerged unexpectedly upon the main thoroughfare. Somehow she managed to slew to a halt soon enough to avoid running into the open road and revealing herself.

Leaning against an oak to rest, she pressed at the sharp stitch in her side. Curse her luck! This close to the road, she was no better off than when she'd set out an hour ago.

Maybe she should just surrender herself to the authorities. Perhaps Lord Gilbert would be more reasonable than his wife. She'd seen him earlier when he'd passed by her stall, a comely man of forty winters or so, and his face had not seemed unkind. His neatly clipped dark beard revealed a penchant for order, his carefully selected jewels a preference for restraint—things Florie admired.

Perhaps he'd grant her mercy. After all, she was a respected merchant. And she hadn't precisely stolen the pomander. She'd only *reclaimed* it.

But she doubted that even the guild would concur with her reckoning of the incident. As her foster father oft complained, Florie's uncompromising nature might serve her well when it came to crafting exquisite jewelry, but 'twas a curse when it came to marketing what she made.

This incident was certainly proof of that.

Yet what else could she have done? The pomander was too important to let it fall into the hands of a spoiled noblewoman. Within the precious piece dwelled the secret of Florie's past and the key to her future.

From the very first, when she'd decided she could no longer live in the shadow of her dead mother, her foster father had warned her against going to Selkirk, against opening old wounds.

But she hadn't listened to him. He wasn't her *real* father, after all, and she had to find the one who was.

It didn't matter that 'twas the first fair she'd been to on her own, did it?

Or that her bargaining skills weren't quite polished yet?

Or that her uncompromising nature would drive her to commit a seemingly criminal act where a noblewoman screamed at her and lawmen chased her through the woods?

She blew out a breath of dismay, shaking her head.

'Twas hard to believe that only a fortnight ago, Florie had been welcomed into the queen's private solar at Dumbarton Castle. There, surrounded by the ladies of the court, she'd had the honor of presenting a gold pendant to young Princess Mary.

As always, Florie hadn't been allowed to take credit for the work, even though she'd designed and crafted every part of it, from the brightly jeweled bouquet of flowers to the filigree butterfly that perched upon them. She was, after all, only a lowly apprentice. 'Twas her foster father who claimed the title of master goldsmith to the princess.

But Mary's delighted cooing and the gleeful squeals of her companions, the Four Maries, had been reward enough. The queen had expressed her appreciation with a nod and an approving smile that promised future commissions.

Now the memory made Florie wince. She wondered what future a known felon could possibly have in the royal household. And as far as finding her real father now...

How could things have gone so wrong so quickly?

Curse Wat! This was *his* fault. She wouldn't have brought the servant along at all if her foster father hadn't insisted on his coming for her protection. Protection? He might be as brawny as an ox, but what Wat possessed in the way of intimidating bulk he made up for by a lack of wits.

Only moments ago, Florie had left the booth to answer the call of nature at the public jakes, trusting Wat to watch over her goods. Somehow, in her brief absence, he'd managed to *sell* her mother's pomander, the one piece she'd handed to him for safekeeping.

As for Florie, she'd simply attempted to secure the pomander's return...which was only reasonable.

She'd been more than fair in her dealings with Lady Mavis. She'd explained in civil tones how the sale of that particular piece had been an error. She'd managed to conceal her impatience, offering to substitute a beautiful girdle—one with a lovely little jeweled looking glass attached—in an equal exchange, even though the girdle was worth much more than the pomander.

But the nasty woman had rejected her generous offer. Naturally, Florie had no choice but to take the pomander back by force. To her credit, as she snatched it and turned to flee, she even tossed back to Lady Mavis the coins she'd laid out for the piece.

Now Florie was branded a thief and a fugitive. And contrary to her foster father's belief in Wat, she knew the servant was unlikely to rush to her defense. Considering the tongue-lashing she'd given him for selling the pomander in the first place, he'd probably retreated somewhere to lick his wounds.

While Florie stood there, catching her breath and wondering how she'd ever restore her reputation in the guild, a soft rumbling sounded in the distance.

Horses. At a gallop. Coming nearer.

As the thrumming grew louder, she peered cautiously down the road from behind the oak. And gulped.

The amber-colored crest of the snapping pennant was unmistakable. Lord Gilbert Fraser himself charged down the lane with a half-dozen men. She whipped back behind the oak trunk, frozen in breathless waiting while they passed in a flurry of flapping cloaks and horseflesh, close enough to choke her on the rising silt.

Only when they were well past the bend in the lane did she dare peek again through the branches to the road beyond. That road was the same western passage she'd come in on three days past. She tried to remember what shelter lay along the route—an inn, a tavern, a crofter's cottage, anyplace she might hide until tempers cooled and the incident faded in memory. Damn, where could she go?

A stream ran along the south side of the road for several miles, she recalled. At one point it deserted that course to pass through a sunken lea, opening up into a large round pond. Up the rise from that pond, near the crossroads, stood an old wayside church.

Sanctuary.

She could claim sanctuary. By law, churches were obliged to protect outlaws, weren't they? She'd take shelter inside until tensions settled and reason prevailed.

Bolstered by hope, she pushed off the tree and hastened forward, skirting the edge of the main road. How far was it? A quarter of a mile? Half?

Lord Gilbert would pass this way again, realizing his prey couldn't go far on foot. How long would he ride before he wheeled about?

She didn't dare wait to find out. Dismissing the painful throbbing in her chest, she sprang forward like the quarry in a foxhunt, racing her pursuers and the setting sun.

Rane MacFarland stood motionless behind the cluster of elms. His bow lay at rest across his thigh, but an arrow was nocked at the ready. 'Twas almost sunset. Soon they'd arrive.

Invisible flies nipped at the quiet water of the deep pond, making tiny ripples across its surface. A squirrel had come to drink its fill, and a fox, fooled by Rane's masking scent of rosemary, had fearlessly approached the water, unaware that a hunter lurked not ten yards away.

Rane wasn't interested in the fox. He saved his talents for edible game, chiefly deer.

The lowering sun winked through the elm branches, and Rane shifted the slightest bit to the left to keep his eyes in shadow, imperceptible. The fair hair he owed to his

Viking forefathers blended perfectly with the pale bark of the elms. Garbed in the muted greens and browns of the forest, he was nearly invisible. Now he had only to watch and wait.

And brood.

'Twas a dangerous game he played, poaching in Ettrick Forest, the royal wood guarded by Lord Gilbert Fraser, sheriff of Selkirk.

After all, Rane was Gilbert's own huntsman, well-respected in the nobleman's household. Chosen for his keen eye and steady hand, he'd put food on the Fraser table for seven years.

'Twas a point of pride with Rane that, unlike other archers, who crippled prey with wounds that were grievous but not mortal, he almost always felled game instantly with a single arrow through the heart.

Still, only years of practice steadied his arm now, for the peril of committing such a crime would have set most men's limbs to trembling.

He scanned the trees on the far side of the pond, at the narrow break that marked the end of the deer trail. No creature stirred the brush yet. But he knew they'd come. They always came to the water at twilight.

The shadows grew long. Soon the Selkirk Fair would close. He swallowed down the acrid taste of apprehension, a taste to which he was unfortunately becoming accustomed. By the grace of Odin and his own fleet hand, he'd have a stag slain and dressed and be gone by the time the first burghers passed by on the main road.

For if he didn't, if anyone caught him with his prize…

He frowned. 'Twas too late to think about the penalty for poaching. He'd already weighed the consequences when he'd decided he had to do something to feed the starving crofters.

Between King Henry VIII's years of relentless razing of the Borders and the massacre done by the English at the River Esk last fall, Scotland had suffered wounds from which it might never recover, wounds that were felt most deeply by the helpless poor. Yet the Scots nobles had done little to relieve the suffering of their subjects. Even now, Lady Mavis was likely ambling through the Selkirk Fair, wasting her husband's coin on some frippery or other.

As for Rane, he refused to let perfectly good game roam the forest, awaiting the pleasure of plump-bellied royals, while Scottish children starved to death.

But anger ruined a man's aim as readily as fear. So he banished everything from his mind but the task at hand. His gaze flitted over every leaf twisting in the receding sunlight. His ear remarked upon every sparrow and mouse that stirred the brush. All the while, he stood as still as the elm trunk beside him.

Still no deer approached the pool. And as the forest darkened, growing more and more inhospitable to his sharp eye, he began to believe he might fail the good peasants depending upon him.

Then, from far off in the wood, he heard a noise. 'Twas more lurching than the usual timid footfall of a stag coming to drink. But the turmoil of the fair had likely left the woodland animals skittish. Wary deer were more challenging to hunt. But not impossible. Never impossible.

His fingers circled with practiced ease around the leather grip of the longbow. He slowly raised it to eye level, hooking in and drawing back on the sinew until the bow arced and his thumb rested against his cheek.

The thrashing grew louder. He narrowed his eyes against the fast-fading light, straining to see into the deep shadows of the wood.

'Twas reckless to hunt this way, he thought, cursing the desperation that drove him to do so. Not only did he risk his life by poaching on royal lands, but 'twas also foolhardy to use a bow when he could barely discern his prey, much less get off a clean shot.

Still, the animal was almost out in the open now. He heard the snap of twigs as it slowed, cautiously approaching the widening of the trail. Through the drooping branches, by the failing light, he at last caught a glimpse of what he thought was the broad side of a deer.

The instant before he released the arrow, the creature moved forward out of the shadows, and he saw 'twas not a deer at all.

But 'twas too late to prevent his shot, and only his lightning-quick reflexes prevented the bolt from landing with deadly accuracy.

Still it sank with a sickening thud into flesh, and the piercing cry that followed staggered him as if he'd taken the arrow himself.

CHAPTER 2

The pain was shocking, intense. Florie's first thought was that a wolf had sprung at her from the brush, sinking its fangs into her thigh. She screamed, but the sound was cut off as she twisted and fell, colliding hard with the earth.

Knocked breathless, for an instant she lay stunned. Then, fearing to be devoured, she kicked desperate heels into the decaying leaf-fall, scrambling, clambering, scraping dirt beneath her nails as she struggled to escape the unrelenting burn of the teeth embedded in her flesh.

No beast snarled or sprang to finish her, but neither did the stabbing pain in her leg subside. She wrenched about to see what demon had her in its jaws.

The sight left her faint with horror.

An arrow pinned her through a trailing link of her gold girdle and her skirts, its steel head buried in her flesh, its thick shaft bobbing as she writhed in pain.

The edges of perception blurred then. She felt herself tilting, fading, falling into a cavern of seductive oblivion.

Rane's bowstring was still vibrating when the blood

drained from his face and his arms dropped limp at his sides.

"Bloody hell," he breathed.

Casting off the bow, he charged forward into the open meadow, his heart hammering. He bolted for the trail, toward his fallen prey, hurtling along the pond's edge, around its perimeter, whipping past reeds and fern, snapping off bracken as he ran. When he reached his victim, he dropped his quiver to the ground and fell to his knees with a bitter cry.

Guilt threatened to unman him, and he ground his teeth against a wave of self-loathing.

Curse his hands, he'd shot a child.

Then he peered closer by the fading twilight. Nae, not a child. A slight, slender lass.

Though she lay as still as death, she wasn't dead. Thank Odin, he'd been able to redirect the arrow at the last moment, thus sparing her life.

He turned her carefully toward him, and she revived with a wheezing gasp, reflexively scrabbling at the outside of her thigh, where his arrow obscenely protruded.

"Nae!" he cautioned. "Leave it be!"

Her eyes widened, and he instantly withdrew his hands, trying not to panic her, raising his palms in what he hoped was a placating gesture.

The last thing he expected was the sting of a sharp needle through his open hand.

He grunted in pain, drawing back his wounded palm. Blood welled from the puncture. He sucked a sharp hiss through his teeth.

The needle had pierced him deeply. But he supposed he should have known better. After all, only a fool approached a wounded animal.

Her left arm arced toward him again with whatever vicious weapon she wielded.

He lunged aside. "Nae, lass! I mean ye no—"

His words were cut short as her right fist clipped his jaw.

"Ach!"

The needle returned to graze his bare neck, leaving a stinging trail.

"Son of a... Lass, cease! 'Twas an acci—"

She ignored his command, attacking him again and again, as if she intended to fight him to the death. Damn! If she didn't stop thrashing about, she'd drive the arrow deeper into her thigh.

"Woman!" he finally bellowed, startling her into momentary submission. "Put away your weapon. I'm friend, not foe."

Florie didn't believe him for an instant. Whether he was Gilbert's man she couldn't tell. 'Twas too dark to make out his face or the color of his cloak. But the villain had shot her. *Shot* her!

She'd managed to wound him with her brooch pin. She'd heard his grunt, felt the point sink into his flesh. But she hadn't inflicted enough damage to stop him. And if she didn't... If he turned her over to the law...

Fighting for her life, she stabbed forward with the brooch again. This time he was prepared for her attack. He caught her wrist in a steely grip.

Thrashing against his punishing hold, she tried to pry his fingers away with her free hand. But he gave her wrist a sharp flick, and the brooch flew loose, skittering out of reach.

"Lie still," he commanded. "Ye'll only make it worse."

Worse? What could be worse? Florie wasn't about to surrender, regardless of the wave of dizziness that assailed her...regardless of the dire stain widening on her best brocade skirts...regardless of the drops of blood, her blood, dripping onto the leaves of the forest floor.

Summoning up one last, desperate burst of power, she reared back her closed fist and swung forward as hard as she could, aiming for his jaw. But he ducked easily out of the way, seizing that hand as well.

"For the love o' Frigga, lass, lie *still!*"

The edges of her vision dimmed, darkening as her bones dissolved into submission, and she vaguely wondered who the devil Frigga was.

God have mercy. Maybe the archer had dealt her a mortal wound and she was dying, for she felt as weak as a bairn, with neither the strength nor the will to move.

"Nae, nae, nae, nae, NAE!" he shouted, giving her wrists a reviving shake. "Not *that* still!" His voice, for all its vehemence, sounded distant, dreamlike. "Stay awake, do ye hear me?"

"Ye go to hell," she mumbled.

He cursed under his breath, returning her arms to her sides, where they lay as limp and useless as empty sleeves.

"Ach, lass," he murmured, as if to himself, "what were ye doin', stealin' through the thicket like that?"

"Leave me alone."

"If I leave ye alone, ye'll bleed to d—" He shook his head. "I'm not leavin'."

From beneath eyelids growing heavier by the moment, Florie could faintly discern the man's silhouette as he crouched nearby. He was unbuckling his belt.

Ballocks! Did the monster mean to swive her while she lay helpless?

"Get the hell away from me," she managed to croak.

He ignored her.

She heard the sound of fabric being shredded. The brute must be tearing her clothes from her. Tears of rage and frustration and anguish welled in her eyes. "Bastard," she whispered.

"Aye, I know. But 'twill be over in a moment. Lie still."

"Nae!" she groaned. She wasn't about to let the lout have his way with her. She tried to curl her weak fingers into lethal fists. "Don't touch me."

A dark fog crept in at the sides of her vision like a closing curtain. She fought to keep her eyes open.

"I'll be swift as I can," he promised, "but ye have to hold still." He positioned himself beside her injured leg. "I'll carry ye to shelter afterward. There's a priest up the rise from here, not far—"

A priest! That brought her instantly alert. "The church!" she blurted.

Sanctuary! By strength of sheer will, she seized his wrist in one hand with such ferocity that she almost knocked him off his haunches.

"Aye!" she cried, though her command came out on a weak wheeze. "The church... Go... Now..." If she could make it to the church... Pain gripped her again, and she winced, digging her fingers into the leather bracer around his forearm.

"Soon." He clasped a restraining hand over hers, his fingers sticky with blood.

"Now," she groaned. Leveraging against his wrist, she began to creep forward, determined to drag herself bodily up the hill if need be.

"Lass, be still! Ye'll drive the arrow—"

"Sanctuary!" she beseeched him.

"What?"

"Take me...to sanctuary." Lord Gilbert couldn't be far away. "They're comin'," she mumbled.

"Who?"

She gasped as searing lightning shot up her leg.

He squeezed her hand. "All right. I'll hurry, lass," he promised, "but the shaft's got to come out first." The cloth he'd torn he now rapidly wadded into his hand. Then he offered her his leather belt. "Hold this in your teeth."

She turned her head aside. She didn't want his belt. All she wanted was sanctuary.

But he pulled her jaw down with his thumb anyway, wedging the thick belt between her teeth. "Bite down."

She scowled. No one told Florie what to do. Then a strong wave of pain washed over her as he pressed the wad of linen against her wound, and she reflexively clamped down.

Blowing out a forceful breath and kneeling above her, the man curved his right hand around the shaft so 'twas braced under his arm. "Ready?"

Nae, she wasn't ready. But Lord Gilbert was coming. And this knave wouldn't let her go until the arrow was out. Praying the brute wouldn't betray her, that he'd keep his word, she ground her teeth into his belt and nodded.

"One...two..."

She fainted before he reached three.

Rane clenched his jaw. 'Twas probably best the maid was unconscious. He made quick work of extracting the arrow, and then compressed the cloth against the wound to stop the bleeding.

Shite! How could he have shot a woman? How could he have made such a grievous error in judgment? His face burned with shame. 'Twas the sort of mistake a lad of twelve might make, not a seasoned hunter. By Thor, if he'd lamed the lass, he'd never forgive himself.

His palm stung where she'd stabbed it, and his jaw ached from her punch. The lass, for her small size, had as much fight in her as a cornered wildcat.

But she'd grown quite still now, and her silence troubled him. If she slumbered too deeply, she might not wake.

"Nae!" he ordered. "Don't ye be nappin' on me!" He freed one hand to jostle her jaw, leaving a bloody smudge there. "Come on, wee one! Ye cannot claim sanctuary without confessin'. Wake up!"

Letting up on the pressure briefly, he pushed her skirts up to her thigh, baring the puncture in her flesh. She tried to force his invading hands away, murmuring vaguely in protest. But this was no time for modesty. Her lifeblood was seeping away. He pushed her hands aside and lifted her leg slightly, circling his leather belt around her upper thigh twice to cinch it tightly.

Damn! He had to keep her from drifting off again, at least till he got her wound properly bandaged.

"Pay heed, lass!" he barked. "Recite for me the Saint's days." He tore the stained linen into long strips. "Come on!"

She frowned in confusion. "Nae."

By Odin, she was a stubborn lass. "Aye! Now! Be a good lass," he commanded, "or I won't take ye to the church."

'Twas an outright lie, of course. After what he'd done, he'd carry her to St. Andrews if she liked. But the lass didn't know that.

She moaned in protest, then conceded on a breathy rasp. "Saint... Saint Valen..."

"That's it, darlin'. Saint Valentine." He wrapped the cloth quickly about her limb. Faith, her skin was softer than a hart's. To think he'd marred that flesh...

"Saint Swith..." she murmured.

"Saint Swithin's, right." He knotted the bandage over the wound. "And next?"

"Sain..." She started to drift off.

He patted her cheek. "Come on, sweetheart, stay with me."

He reached under her then and carefully scooped her into his arms. She was lighter than the stags he was accustomed to packing. He prayed she wouldn't bleed to death before he could get her to safety.

"Wait!" she cried. "My pomander."

He frowned, scanning the ground. A long chain of links lay coiled there like a golden serpent, its neck broken where his arrow had bent the metal. An ornament the size of a small apple hung from it. He tucked the damaged treasure into her hands, and she clasped it to her bosom in relief, instantly relaxing toward slumber again.

"Nae! Stay with me!" he commanded, giving her a shake. "Where were we? Saint Swithin's. What comes next?"

She groaned.

"Don't ye faint again. Don't ye dare faint. Saint Swithin's."

"Cris..."

"Saint Crispin's, aye." Rane's long strides served him well as he rounded the pond. "Hold on, lass," he murmured, though her head already fell limp against his shoulder.

Her long tresses spilled over his arm like a dark waterfall. By the day's last faint light he saw that her face, beaded with sweat, was as fair and sweet as a newborn fawn's. She was hot and damp, as if she'd been running a long while.

Climbing the rise, he studied the strange golden girdle she clutched to her breast. 'Twas cleverly worked, very expensive. Indeed, she was adorned all over with ornaments and chains and rings of gold. The lass was obviously a maid of not only considerable beauty, but considerable wealth.

Why such a lass would require sanctuary, he couldn't imagine. Maybe she was fleeing a cruel father or a brutal lover. Or maybe she'd crossed paths with one of the rabid packs of English soldiers that plagued the Borders. He shook his head. To think she might have escaped one danger only to fly into another...

"Come, wee fawn," he said, jostling her. "What's after Saint Crispin's?"

She tried to answer, though her eyes were closed. Her forehead creased, and her lips moved, but no sound came out.

He furrowed his brow, wondering who she was and what she was doing in the middle of the forest.

If she died, he'd never know.

He would have preferred to take her to Father Conan's cottage. The abandoned church could hardly be called a sanctuary. When he reached the steps, he frowned up at the rotting door with misgiving.

The Church at the Crossroads had been constructed before Rane was born, but it hadn't been used in four years. A victim of King Henry's raiding, the church had been desecrated by a band of English soldiers who'd robbed the sanctuary and murdered the resident priest, leaving a missive pinned to the door, *Thank your Cardinal for this.*

Since then, people claimed the place was cursed by King Henry himself. Indeed, misfortune had befallen all five priests who'd presided over the church since. Father Conan, the most recent, had been struck blind and lived in seclusion now, leaving nothing but vermin to inhabit the sanctuary—vermin and, some whispered, evil spirits.

Rane didn't believe in such nonsense. Vermin might dwell within, but surely they were only the earthly sort. With a dismissive snort, he mounted the steps.

The door creaked open under his shoulder. Rane swept through the entrance, past the cobwebbed narthex, and into the dim nave. The faint scent of sweet incense had long ago faded under the musty odor of decay, and the vivid colors of the arched window above the chancel were dulled beneath a patina of dust.

Suddenly something streaked like a dark shadow across the altar dais.

"Shite!" he hissed in surprise, wincing as the oath echoed among the rafters.

'Twas only Methuselah, Father Conan's cat. The ragged old creature hunkered down in fear and squeezed through a crack in the vestry door while Rane silently cursed his rattled nerves.

He carried the lass forward, placing her gently upon the stones before the altar. He cast off his cloak, removed his leather jerkin, and then pulled his outer shirt over his head, rolling it into a makeshift pillow, which he tucked carefully beneath her head.

A fat candle slouched in an iron holder beside the altar. He blew the dust off, then trimmed the wick with his gutting knife and used his flint to light the tallow. As the candle sputtered to life, shadows danced like devils along the crumbling plaster walls and over the blackened beams above.

Now the belt had to be loosened. Rane prayed the maid would lose no more blood. He blew out a bracing breath and knelt beside her. Easing her skirts up, he bared her slim leg, which was now deathly pale. The bandages had stanched the flow, but whether they would hold...

Slowly, cautiously, he unbuckled the belt.

Almost at once, fresh blood oozed through the linen. The lass groaned, but didn't fully waken, as sensation returned to her limb.

He muttered an oath, wadding a fistful of her chemise and pressing it firmly against the wound. She'd rail at him for ruining her fine garments, he supposed, but he'd gladly bear her temper later if it meant her survival now.

While he waited for the flow to cease, his gaze roamed over her features again. Who was this lass thrust into his path?

She wasn't from Selkirk. He knew the maids of Selkirk. Such a bonnie face he'd remember. In the candlelight her skin had an ethereal sheen, almost as if she weren't human, but some fey creature. Her face was heart-shaped, and her pointed chin had a dimple. Her dark brows and long lashes had a distinct upward tilt to them. Her mouth was small, and her lips looked soft enough to kiss a wee bairn without waking it.

He lowered his gaze to her slim throat, from which hung a delicate gold filigree pendant, and the fine collarbone above her bosom, where her pulse beat. Her gown dipped low upon her shoulders, revealing the gentle swell of her modest breasts. The well-made garment hugged her snugly, delineating her tiny waist and the subtle flare of her hips. Below, where his hands pressed, touching her as intimately as a lover, her skin was silky smooth.

Under different circumstances, he might have wished to pursue such a lass. But at the moment, all he could think about was saving her life. Besides, he doubted she'd harbor any tender feelings for the man who'd shot her.

If only she hadn't wandered into his sights... And if only he hadn't been so desperate for game...

Now he held her life in his hands.

The bleeding finally slowed, to his relief, sealing the injury. The narrow-headed shaft had gone deep but straight, thankfully leaving a wound that would require no stitches. Still, blood stained her skirt, the flagstones, her face, and his hands. Anyone stumbling upon the scene at the altar would think some unholy sacrifice had been made on the spot.

He blew out a weighted breath. One more task remained. He needed a priest to grant the lass sanctuary.

Could he convince Father Conan to come? Almost a hermit, the blind old priest lived closeted within his cottage nearby, seldom venturing out. Indeed, if Rane hadn't made a habit of bringing him food once a week, he doubted the man would see himself properly fed. As for getting him to set foot in the cursed church again...

He glanced at the lass, noticing the way her dark lashes lay gently upon her cheek, how her sweet lips parted in slumber. She looked so tiny, so defenseless. He dared not abandon her to fetch the Father, not while she lay helpless and danger lurked outside.

Rane was not a man to turn aside from those in need. Indeed, 'twas his own soft heart that had gotten him into this plight from the beginning. He'd already failed the hungry crofters. He'd not add to his faults by failing the lass.

Still, a huntsman couldn't hear her confession or grant her the right of sanctuary. Only a priest could do that.

A faint commotion outside interrupted his thoughts and brought him to his feet.

Riders. Several of them.

Were they the lass's pursuers?

He lunged for the candle, extinguishing its flame between thumb and finger, throwing the sanctuary into darkness again.

In a single movement he drew his knife and faced the door, his legs braced apart. 'Twas a pity he'd left his bow in the grass—'twas a far more formidable weapon. Outside, men's voices rose and fell on the air, their speech indistinct.

They rode past a number of times but never breached the door, probably because they believed in the curse of the church. Eventually they rode off. Still, Rane doubted they'd give up the hunt. The lass was a prize worthy of pursuit.

He frowned, sheathing his knife. With mounted trackers on the maiden's scent, venturing into the dark woods tonight was out of the question.

Rane would have to see to her safety himself. He might have no authority to grant her the protection of the church, but till morn he could at least offer her the defenses of his sharp ear and his keen eye.

To one side of the chancel sat the fridstool, the low stone chair that served as the seat of refuge. Surely she'd be safe enough there for the night. None would dare drag her from such a holy place. Not with Rane standing guard.

And he intended to stand guard. Piercing a woman's flesh with his arrow had shaken him more than he cared to admit. Now that he'd borne the lass to safety, a nausea born of shame grew in his gut. The sooner he could put this mortifying episode behind him, the better.

He'd hardly be missed. Rane spent half his nights betwixt the willing thighs of some maid or other in the burgh anyway, dragging back to Lord Gilbert's tower house in time for breakfast and some good-natured jesting from his fellows. No one would question his absence.

As he placed the lass gently beside the fridstool, she shivered in her sleep. He tucked her skirts in around her. Rane's Norse blood served him well against the cold, but the abandoned church was a chill and heartless place. On the morrow he'd bring plaids for the lass's comfort. Until then, his wool cloak would have to suffice.

After she was snugly cocooned in his garment, he pulled out his leather costrel of ale, took a hearty swig, and then sat back against the fridstool to watch over her. Retrieving his belt, he ran his thumb over the dents her teeth had made in the leather. They'd serve as a bitter reminder of what his carelessness had cost.

In silence, he watched and waited until the deepening sky beyond the stained windows grew completely black...until Methuselah emerged from the vestry to go on his evening hunt...until distant wolves howled at the stars. The lass's pursuers never returned.

He must have drifted off after that, for he was startled awake in the middle of the night by the sound of rough breathing. He leaned close to the lass sleeping beside him. She was quivering. He reached out, found her hair, and traced his way to her forehead. She wasn't fevered, thank Odin, just cold.

Unfortunately, he had no more spare garments to give the lass. He'd lent her his shirt and cloak already, and he'd torn a good portion of his linen undershirt to make bandages. There was only one way to keep her warm.

He slipped beneath the cloak and stretched out beside her. Careful of her wound, he drew her small body back against his chest, enclosing her in his arms, stopping her shivers with the steam of his breath.

Despite their disparate size, she fit perfectly into the circle of his embrace. Her hair, soft and fragrant under his chin, grazed his chest where his shirt gapped away. Her body felt lissome and yielding beneath his arm, and where her buttocks were nestled against him, his loins, oblivious to his honorable intentions, warmed and stirred of their own accord.

There was nothing like the comfort of a lass in one's arms.

Still, Rane wasn't a man to be ruled by the beast betwixt his legs. He'd sworn to take care of her, to protect her. And he intended to do just that.

He tightened his arms about her. For now he'd shield her from the cold. Then, when the time came, he'd protect her against whatever whoresons had chased her into sanctuary.

Lady Mavis Fraser, quivering with frustration and rage, paced her drafty solar. The leather soles of the new shoes she'd bought at the Selkirk Fair clapped against her heels. She clenched her fists in her ocher velvet skirts as she wheeled, making them swirl about her like a swarm of angry hornets. She couldn't stop reliving her harrowing ordeal at the fair earlier with that horrid wench, an ordeal that her husband had refused to address with the proper concern at supper.

Her anger, of course, only masked a far more vulnerable emotion—nerve-racking dread. She'd recognized that pomander at the goldsmith's booth, not because she'd seen it before, but because she'd heard something about such a piece months ago from her husband's most trusted maidservant. At the time, Mavis had discounted the woman's account as the ramblings of an old crone bent on destroying her marriage. But today, there the thing had been, as real as her own hand, the entwined letters on the lid as familiar to her as the lines in her face. And Mavis had suddenly realized that if, by some chance, the owner of the pomander were still alive...

She'd wasted no time in purchasing the piece, not even quarreling over the price. She intended to have it melted down at once, so that no one would ever know it had existed.

But that damned wench had arrived then, and the instant Mavis caught sight of the dark-haired lass with the hauntingly familiar brown eyes, she realized the danger was even more immediate and grave than she'd imagined. The possessive brat and her bauble could well be the undoing of all Mavis's ambitions.

Of course, Gilbert mustn't learn any of that. One's past indiscretions had no bearing on the future. He must be told only that a gold piece had been stolen from Mavis. He was a simple man who saw only black and white, right and wrong. He hated to be bothered by what he deemed trivial.

And at the moment, with the boy King Edward sitting on the English throne, Princess Mary avoiding his advances in Scotland, and the Borders under frequent attack because of it, a gold trinket seemed indeed trivial.

But for Mavis, it meant everything.

She twisted the wedding ring upon her finger, and the topaz flanked by gold initials appeared to wink at her with bemused scorn. Frowning, she turned it inward, clenching her fist around the gem as if to crush it.

Once, she'd been naive enough to believe she was untouchable. For years she'd been the secret darling of King Henry himself—a beloved spy who'd managed to charm her way into the Scots court, returning to Henry to appease his appetite for bed sport and information about the Scots royals. In the folly of her younger years, Mavis had even imagined one day bearing Henry a son and convincing him to take her to wife.

'Twas not unthinkable. The king flitted like a bee from flower to flower, after all, and Mavis had been beautiful and beguiling once.

But that had never happened.

Her fingers fluttered up to her throat, remembering what had befallen a few of his other wives. She supposed she should be glad the king had slipped her grasp and that she'd had the foresight, upon Henry's death, to let the Scots queen marry her off to the newly widowed Lord Gilbert Fraser.

Unfortunately, Gilbert, while a respectable catch, was also lord sheriff of the remote and savage burgh of Selkirk, which meant Mavis was effectively exiled from the Scots court. She'd lost not only Henry's protection, but also her contacts.

She shivered, silently cursing the crude tower house she was forced to live in now. Its only saving grace was its location along the Borders, which helped Mavis from becoming completely useless. There were a few ambitious Englishmen who'd made use of what bits of information she could pry out of her husband about the movements of the Scots royals.

But when that information led to a few well-planned English attacks, Gilbert became more tight-lipped, claiming he did so for Mavis's protection. After all, he'd told her with a loving kiss, she couldn't be held accountable for what she didn't know.

She remained unmoved by his gesture, as she'd learned to be with any overtures of affection, because last year, when King Henry had died, Mavis had discovered the bitter truth about men. She'd been little more than a cog in Henry's machine. He'd never acknowledged her service to the Crown. He'd left her no coin, no title, not even a bastard to raise.

She enjoyed precious little royal protection now. Once the favorite of a king, she'd been reduced to the lowly wife of a sheriff. Mavis had learned a painful lesson: if she wanted anything in this world, she'd have to seize it herself.

Starting with that gold pomander.

A soft knock on the door interrupted her thoughts.

"My lady?" Gilbert called.

She straightened. Perhaps her husband was finally ready to give her the attention she deserved.

Improvising, she snatched off her gable hood, loosening a few strategic strands of her honey hair. She withdrew a soft lawn napkin from her bodice and unlatched the door, letting it swing slowly open.

"Aye?" she said with a sniff, dabbing at invisible tears.

Gilbert frowned and entered the solar, closing the door behind him. "Do not weep, love," he said gently. "If ye can describe the piece, I'll have another made for ye."

"But I don't want another," she said, pursing her lips into a pout. "I want *that* one."

He sighed and came up behind her, placing placating hands upon her shoulders. "My men could not find the lass."

She twisted away from him. "Then they didn't look hard enough."

"They scoured the grounds. She just disappeared into the woods." He shook his head. "Maybe the English got her."

Mavis rounded on him, curling her lip. "She's a thief! Ye cannot let her...disappear!"

"Be reasonable, darlin'." He spoke to her in patronizing tones. "'Tis only a bauble."

"'Tisn't the point!" she cried, wadding the napkin in her fist. She was seething now with desperation, but she dared not let him know. She turned her back and let her shoulders droop, feigning hurt. "They were laughin' at me, Gilly," she said on a sob. "Ye should have seen them. The entire fair saw her snatch that girdle away from me as easy as stealin' a sweet from a bairn."

This time when Gilbert came up behind her, she let him comfort her while she wept softly into her napkin. She knew her husband's weaknesses all too well. If there was one thing he couldn't abide in his domain, 'twas disharmony.

"The folk here don't like me, Gilly. They've never liked me."

"Ach, 'tis not true, darlin'."

But she knew 'twas true. And with good reason. She didn't like *them*.

These vile Scots were as rough and stubborn as jackasses. If they would simply give up Princess Mary to be wed to King Edward, the killing would stop, no one would go hungry, and Mavis could focus on securing her future.

"*'Tis* true," she countered. "They hate me, and now they don't respect me either."

That touched a nerve. Gilbert's hands tensed upon her shoulders. "O' course they do."

"Not if a thief can get away with stealin' from me and pay no consequences." She drove the knife deeper. "And if they don't respect me, Gilly, how long will it be before they don't respect *ye?*"

That did the trick. And after a long and pensive silence, Gilbert gave her shoulders a decisive squeeze. "My men will find her. I'll round up my constables and have them look for her in the morn."

"The morn?" Mavis blurted out, turning to him, then carefully tempered her voice. "But she may be halfway to Edinburgh by then."

"They'll find her," he vowed, giving her a light kiss on the brow.

Mavis bit her lip as he exited the solar. Gilbert's promise wasn't good enough. Immediate action was necessary. Though she had few friends among the Scots here, there were still those among the English who were interested in Mavis's connections, who valued the unique usefulness of her position, who would, for a price, come to her aid *tonight*.

CHAPTER 3

Emerging from dark, swirling veils of dreams, Florie grew aware of strange sensations. A deep throbbing in her thigh. Intense thirst. Sunlight upon her closed eyes. Hard stone beneath her hip. A profound silence. And the subtle scent of rosemary.

With great effort, she lifted her eyelids. Slowly the world came into focus, a world strangely familiar, yet unfamiliar. Vivid colors—ruby and amber and sapphire—streamed into her eyes like flames bouncing off the facets of gemstones. And then, out of the glowing light, a figure clad in white descended to welcome her.

Her breath caught.

One of God's seraphim gazed upon her. His long hair was as pale as winter wheat, his head haloed in soft gold. His face was radiant, his features bold. And when his aquamarine eyes captured her own, they seemed to delve deeply into her spirit. The eyes of an all-knowing angel of heaven.

"Am I," she whispered, "dead?"

"Dead?" A crease touched the angel's brow as he

reached out to brush a stray lock of hair back from her face.

She flinched, expecting his fingers to be cool and otherworldly. But they felt warm and callused and human upon her cheek.

"Nae," he said with a soft chuckle. "Ye're safe. Ye're in sanctuary, darlin'. Remember?"

Sanctuary. And that voice. Wisps of memory blew past her now as she gazed beyond his shoulder at sunlight leaching through the panel of dingy stained glass. Snatching the pomander. Evading the sheriff's guard. Fleeing through the woods. Discovering the pond. Then a sudden excruciating pain in her leg. Someone had...

She let her gaze drift back to the man's angelic face. Christ's thorns, 'twas *him!* He was the devil who'd shot her.

Her breath quickened. Was he one of Lord Gilbert's men? Had he confiscated her pomander? Frantically seeking the precious piece, she struggled up to her elbows, sending a spike of pain shooting through her leg. But, thank God, the girdle and pomander were still there, within arm's reach.

"Easy there, wee lamb," he bade her, misunderstanding the source of her fear. "No one can harm ye here. Ye're safe."

Safe? There was no reason to trust him. She'd been a merchant long enough to doubt the promises of strangers. He might speak with a calming voice. He might be pleasant to look at. And others might be fooled by the reassuring sincerity in his eyes—eyes that were the complex shade of chrysolite, as lustrous as a polished gem, rich, intense, compelling...

She gave herself a mental shake. Others might be fooled

by such things, but not Florie. So far the man had kept his word, bearing her to sanctuary, staying with her through the night.

But that was *after* he'd shot her with a bow and arrow.

He frowned at the doubt in her eyes. "Ye don't trust me. I don't blame ye." He placed a hand over his heart. "But I swear, my lady, 'twas only an unfortunate accident."

His expression was earnest and concerned. And he was so handsome that she found it difficult to tear her gaze away. The man could easily charm a greener maid out of her sense.

But Florie was wiser than most maids, wise and sensible. Whichever the man truly was, saint or sinner, she dared not linger long enough to learn, let alone trust him.

'Twas already daylight. Surely the lord sheriff had more important things to do than chase after a petty thief. He must have given up his search for her—after all, she hadn't seen any riders follow her to the church. Florie even persuaded herself that by now Lady Mavis had forgotten about the pomander. In any event, Florie must return to the fair, for God only knew what else Wat might have bungled in her absence.

"Ye must be thirsty," the archer murmured, loosening the leather costrel from his hip.

She reflexively licked her lips. Aye, she was. She'd stay long enough to take a few sips, but then she'd be on her way. She dared not linger here, for by the look of the sorry place, the nave might well collapse at any moment.

The man uncorked the costrel with his straight white teeth, which likely afforded him a dazzling smile when he wasn't scowling in concentration as he did now. No wonder she'd mistaken him for one of God's heavenly host.

But his angelic image disappeared when he made the mistake of boldly reaching an arm about her shoulders.

She reacted out of pure instinct, rearing back and jabbing her elbow hard into his belly.

Rane collapsed forward with a wheeze. The blow didn't hurt. Not really. After all, she was a wee creature, and his stomach was hard with muscle. But the shock of a woman clouting him for nothing served to knock Rane's world awry.

Women never clouted Rane.

Women *adored* Rane.

He was kind and gentle to them. He was their friend, their lover, their champion. Father Conan claimed there wasn't a female in all of Selkirk who didn't harbor some wee measure of affection for Rane MacFarland.

"What was that for?" he asked.

"Do not...touch me," she said stiffly.

He frowned, perplexed. 'Twas the first time a maid had said *that* to him. Said it and *meant* it. He didn't know what to make of it.

Then he narrowed his eyes. "Ye're still afraid o' me, aren't ye?"

"Nae." She raised her charmingly dimpled chin a notch, though she didn't meet his gaze. "I'm not afraid of anyone."

He resisted the urge to remind her that she'd been running from someone last night of whom she was clearly quite afraid. "Be at ease, my love. I only mean to help ye."

"I don't need your help."

"Indeed?" He raised a dubious brow.

"I can manage on my own."

"I see."

"And I'm not..."

"Aye?"

"Your love." She said it under her breath, as if it were an embarrassing epithet.

Rane was dumbfounded. "Huh. So ye're done with me, then?"

She nodded.

Rane frowned. Was she seriously asking him to go away? He supposed he understood her mistrust—how could he blame her, when he'd so grievously wounded her?

But 'twas not in Rane's nature to abandon the helpless. He couldn't pass by a bird with a broken wing, much less leave a wounded maid to fend for herself. If the lass had known him better, she would have realized he had no intention of leaving her alone and defenseless.

"Fine," he bluffed.

"Fine."

He popped the cork back into the costrel, noting the fleeting look of dismay that flickered over her face. "I suppose ye'll give and take your own confession as well?" He lifted a brow.

Her lips were parted as if she meant to say something, but couldn't think of the words. By Freyja, she had a lovely mouth. He wondered if she knew how tempted he was to kiss her, her protests be damned.

Instead, he rose to his feet.

"Wait!"

She would doubtless recant and beg for his aid now.

"I'll have that drink," she murmured.

His mouth twitched with amusement. 'Twas hardly the humble supplication he'd expected. "Ye will?"

She nodded.

Astounding, he thought, shaking his head. Earlier, as he'd watched the lass sleep, he'd thought her sweet and helpless. He'd planned to explain his unfortunate negligence to her when she awakened, to implore her forgiveness. He'd imagined her blushing, then placing one of her delicate hands upon his forearm, reassuring him with a gentle smile that she absolved him of his sin, murmuring her thanks for bringing her to sanctuary, for seeing to her wound, for protecting her. Maybe she'd offer him a soft kiss as reward, maybe more...

"Sometime before Lent, if ye please," she quipped.

He blinked. What a saucy lass she was. Rane was accustomed to maids flushing and stammering around him, stumbling over their words, scarcely able to string one thought to the next. This lass seemed neither intimidated nor awestruck, which was both disconcerting and perversely attractive.

A bemused smile tugged at the corner of his lip as he surrendered the costrel to her.

She was weak, probably weaker than she realized. Though she managed to twist off the cork, letting it drop into her lap, her arms began to tremble as she brought the costrel to her lips. She tried to take a sip but tipped it too far and choked instead. Ale dribbled out of her mouth, down her chin, and onto her gown as she alternately coughed and cursed.

Hunkering down before her, he confiscated the costrel. "Let me help ye, lass."

He saw her swallow uncertainly as she wiped her mouth with the back of one shaky hand. She might not fear him, but she clearly resented his help. She eyed the costrel, weighing her options, and finally gave him a curt nod.

He felt he'd won a bit of a victory. Still, he approached her slowly, the way he did a felled animal.

This time the lass kept her elbows in check. But when he curved his arm about her narrow back, gathering her against his shoulder, she definitely stiffened. Indeed, Rane thought, as he tried to make her comfortable, he'd felt wooden posts more yielding.

Florie fought to maintain her calm. She wasn't used to being touched. 'Twas overwhelming. Too intimate. Too invasive.

Once, long ago, she might have enjoyed it. Indeed, she seemed to recall her mother holding her thus when she was a child. But after her death, when Florie had craved comfort the most, her foster father had turned away from her, more at ease with his arms wrapped 'round a keg of ale than his own daughter. And over the years, she'd grown accustomed to the lack of contact.

Florie told herself she was no longer a child to be coddled and cuddled. She was almost a grown woman, practically a goldsmith in her own right, destined for the guild. She needed no consoling, nor did she want it.

Especially since her foster father, who wandered about in a drunken fog most of the time, had begun to mistake her for her dead mother. He'd never abused her, but he'd received a sobering slap for his improper advances more than once, and Florie had blackened his eye a fortnight ago when his straying fingers began fumbling at the ties of her gown.

'Twas that final offense that had convinced her to leave his household altogether to seek out her real father. 'Twas only natural then that she should be mistrustful of anyone laying hands upon her.

Still, Florie had to admit that the archer's tender overtures were nothing like the frenetic groping to which she'd been exposed. When he eased her upright against his broad chest, surrounding her small body like some oversized throne, his warmth was not unpleasant. And his gentle strength could hardly be called threatening.

But her heart was definitely pounding, and a powerful surge of strange emotion washed over her. Resisting the urge to lunge away, Florie instead held herself rigid as he brought the costrel to her parched lips.

The drink was cool and sweet and refreshing. He showed patience, never letting a drop spill, as she slaked her thirst, sip by slow sip.

Whether 'twas the effect of the ale on her empty belly or simply surrender to the inevitable, she gradually grew accustomed to the intimacy of his embrace. Her pulse calmed, her breathing slowed, and her muscles relaxed into a pleasant languor.

After a few more pulls from the costrel, she had to concede that resting within the archer's imposing arms wasn't nearly as disagreeable as she'd first imagined. His shoulder was firm and reassuring, warm beneath the thin shirt of linen. He smelled surprisingly favorable, much better than the stagnant air of the church, rather like the forest—all evergreen and moss and rosemary.

She reached up to tip the costrel further, letting the liquid soothe her throat, and her fingers tangled briefly with his. She couldn't help but notice they were long and sun-bronzed and supple, plainly more human than angelic.

They were also, she noted, stained with blood. *Her* blood.

She choked on the ale.

"Slowly," he bade her, withdrawing the vessel and wiping away a drip at the corner of her mouth with his thumb, a far too personal gesture. "Better?"

Florie felt weak and battered, as if a company of soldiers had ridden their warhorses over her. She was also beginning to get a wee bit tipsy and confused. The man had shot her. She should despise him. Or at least fear him.

But whether 'twas the comeliness of his face, the persuasion of his voice, the welcome yet unwelcome tenderness of his touch, or simply the ale, there was definitely something intriguing about the man who'd come to her rescue...after, of course, he'd ruthlessly wounded her with his bow and arrow.

Before she could sort out her tangled thoughts and demand of him how he could have shot her, mistakenly or not, his hand roved brazenly over her face, settling upon her brow.

"No fever. Good. I'll fetch the priest, clean your wound, change the bandages. Then we'll see about findin' somethin' to eat and—"

"Nae!" Florie tensed. The man, like a naughty lad stealing a horse, seemed to have seized the reins of her fate to steer her in a direction she didn't wish to go.

"Nae?"

"Nae." Remembering the manners her mother had taught her, she added, "Thank ye." She had neither the need nor the time for his help. No matter how handsome he was. "I have to go back to the fair. I have accounts to settle." She nudged back the green wool garment that had been placed over her. "Thank ye for..." For what? she wondered. Shooting her? "For the ale. And the sanctuary. But I cannot tarry. I have—"

"Ye won't get far with that wound, lass."

She furrowed her brows. Surely twasn't that bad. After all, the bleeding had stopped. She threw back the covers.

When she beheld the extent of the gory stains on her clothing, she paled and felt suddenly queasy. She'd lost far more blood than she'd imagined. And to make matters worse, 'twas clear by the bandage that this man, this *stranger,* had already tended to her. Marry, he'd glimpsed her bare thigh, touched her bare flesh.

As she sat in stunned silence, he shifted to clasp her under the arms, completely disregarding her propriety. Then, with no more effort or ceremony than if she were a cloth puppet, he dragged her backward until she sat propped against the squat fridstool.

Her horror must have shown on her face, for when he crouched before her, meeting her gaze, his eyes softened slightly. "Don't be afraid, love. I mean ye no harm."

Florie stiffened. He misunderstood. Harm or no, she didn't want to be at his mercy. Her wound already left her feeling at a disadvantage, weak and vulnerable. There was nothing she hated more than feeling helpless. She didn't need his aid. She could take care of herself. She'd done so since the day her mother died.

Already, this stranger had trespassed upon her person. She wouldn't allow it again...no matter how her pulse quickened at the thought.

He took her hand between his two, not tightly, but firmly enough that she couldn't snatch it back without force.

"Listen, lass," he said, suddenly serious, his shadowed eyes locking with hers, gentle and commanding all at once, as if they might swallow her soul as surely as his palms swallowed her hand. "I don't want ye to be afraid o' me. I may be unworthy o' forgiveness, but pray hear me out," he murmured. "I never meant to harm ye. I was huntin' in the forest. 'Twas truly an accident. God's truth, I'd sooner cut off my own hand than hurt a maid."

She gulped as she stared into his beautiful beryl-bright eyes...breathless...speechless...

Suddenly the church door creaked open, admitting a narrow shaft of sunlight. Florie gasped.

The archer turned and rose in one smooth movement, drawing his knife and planting himself like a guard between her and whoever violated the sanctuary.

But between her champion's widespread, towering legs, Florie spied only a tattered old striped cat slinking along the wall. For one horrible instant she wondered if the man might hurl his knife and skewer the animal, the way he'd fired his arrow at *her.*

But he lowered his weapon and scolded, "Methuselah! Ye wayward beast." With an exasperated sigh, he sheathed his knife and turned to her, explaining, "I thought it might be the riders who passed by last evenin'."

Florie's breath caught. "Riders?" She'd been so sure Lord Gilbert had forgotten about her. Had his men followed her, after all? Was she still in danger? Dread squeezed her heart. "What riders?"

He shrugged, then lifted his brows. "Maybe *ye* can tell *me.*"

Maybe not, she thought, swallowing hard. She didn't fully trust the archer. For all she knew, he might be an accomplice to Lord Gilbert. Nae, the less he knew, the better. "I'd rather confess to the priest."

"As ye like." He swept up his discarded shirt from the flagstones. Lord, was *that* what she'd slept on all night? "Ye should be safe enough here for a bit if ye stay by the fridstool. The Father doesn't live far. I'll be back in a wink."

Indeed, she was surprised there was a priest who belonged to this church at all. The crumbling nave looked abandoned by man and perhaps by God as well.

The archer slipped the crumpled shirt down over his head, followed by his leather jerkin, and Florie only halfheartedly tried to avert her eyes. As he moved, his shirt clung to the defined contours of his back and strained at his wide shoulders, delineating an impressive array of muscle, and when he strode away, 'twas with the elegant strength of a cat. He was the sort of man to turn the heads of ladies and ladies' maids alike—virile, feral, and well-favored. She shivered, deciding 'twas best to avoid such a tempting and dangerous man.

Just as he reached the door, he turned and fixed his gaze upon her, a gaze that brooked no rebellion. "Stay here."

Florie blinked. No one ordered her about, and 'twas on the tip of her tongue to tell him so. But for once, she bit off her words, instead turning up the corners of her mouth in what she hoped resembled a smile of compliance.

No sooner did the door close behind him than she flung his cloak off and began examining her wound, calculating her chances of escaping before he returned.

CҺAPTER 4

Rane wasn't fooled for a moment by the lass's foxy grin. He'd seen the mutinous glint in her innocent brown eyes. She might not be able to limp far enough to place herself in real danger before he returned, but he never doubted she'd try. And a lass so beautiful, lame, and helpless was as tempting a target to an outlaw as a crippled fawn was to a wolf.

At the church well, Rane washed his face from the bucket, welcoming the sobering slap of cold water. He needed the bracing chill to clear his thoughts, which had gone lustfully astray. The lass's elfin eyes, that tempting mouth, her delectably carved body, and the resulting ache in his braies reminded him that he'd been almost a week without a wench. Even his shirt, rumpled from the weight of the maiden's slumber, smelled of her—earthy, sweet, womanly.

He rattled his head, scattering droplets, and took a deep breath. He needed the fresh air to chase her scent from his nostrils and rouse him from his amorous stupor.

He also needed to retrieve the discarded weapon he'd

left in plain sight, while keeping his senses sharp for the lass's tormenters, who no doubt still ranged somewhere in the forest.

'Twas more than his natural affinity for helpless females that drove him to protect the maid, more even than his need to assuage his guilt and make amends. Maybe 'twas the challenge of her saucy tongue. Or the memory of her body nestled for warmth against his all night. Or her strange, skittish nature, reminding him of a wild kitten that needed, yet feared, to be stroked.

Whatever 'twas, that silken skin, those lustrous brown eyes, that curving mouth enchanted him, moved him, and left him feeling as uneasy as a stag catching scent of a hunter.

This lass intrigued him more than most. If he were inclined to fantasy, he'd almost believe she was one of the impish woodland sprites rumored to live in Ettrick Forest, garbed in the pale pelt of a deer and bejeweled with gold treasure, or perhaps a daughter of the Norse goddess Frigg, playing mischief upon his wits.

He shook his head as he tromped down the hill toward the pond, scooping up his discarded bow as he went. 'Twas his Scottish blood that made such absurd fancies creep into his brain. Nae, the lass was only human, no matter how difficult 'twas to purge her image—her gentle curves, her trembling mouth, her compelling gaze—from his mind.

He found his quiver, undisturbed except for a beetle crawling over the fletching of his arrows. He coaxed the bug onto his finger and set it upon the trunk of a laurel, then slung the quiver over his shoulder.

A spot of maroon among the fallen leaves caught his eye, and Rane realized with a guilty pang that he looked upon a drop of spilled blood, the lass's blood.

He carefully picked up the stained leaf. Over the last several years he'd hunted scores of deer, shot them, dressed them out. Never had the sight of blood troubled him. But as he looked upon the leaf, his mouth dried and his fingers began to quake.

"Loki's teeth," he muttered angrily, crushing the leaf in his fist. What if shooting the lass had spoiled him for hunting altogether?

Steeling himself against that fear, he searched for the quarrel he'd removed from her thigh. But though he looked high and low, he never found it. And while he deemed himself well rid of the damning shaft, he couldn't help believing some mischief or magic had made it go missing.

Armed now, Rane hastily loped along the weed-choked path from the church to the priest's cottage, though doubt dogged his heels every step of the way. 'Twould be a miracle if he could get the priest to set foot in the sanctuary after all these years.

As always, Father Conan welcomed him warmly. The two were old friends, despite Rane's preference for Viking gods, and Rane visited his humble cottage often. The white-haired priest offered him a cup of ale and a seat at the hearth, inquiring about his health and asking whether he'd picked out a wife yet. Rane chuckled at that. Everyone knew Rane was in no hurry to settle down.

But the old man's hospitality only extended so far. As Rane had expected, after a bit of friendly banter, when he confronted Father Conan with his request, misgiving reared its head. Despite the cheery fire flickering on the hearth, a cool gravity descended upon the cottage, distancing the two men.

The aged priest seemed to shrink within his already

withered frame. "I won't go back there. Do not ask it o' me, lad."

Rane hated haranguing the poor fellow. He understood the priest's fears. Like the holy men before him, Father Conan believed in the curse. In the old man's mind, something evil in the church had ruined him, slowly destroying his eyesight until he could no longer fulfill his priestly duties.

"'Tisn't for my sake, Father," Rane said, hunkering down by the fire to stir the coals and adding another log. "'Tis for a lass."

The priest rocked forward on his three-legged stool with a knowing frown. "Why does that not surprise me?"

"This one's in grave danger. Someone chased her through the wood. If ye don't grant her sanctuary—"

The priest shivered visibly. "That church is hardly a sanctuary," he said bitterly. "I'd imagine the devil himself has taken up residence there by now."

"Then all the better for her," he countered. "No one will dare enter the sanctuary to seize her."

"Nor will I. I crawled out o' that cursed nave four winters ago. I have no intention o' goin' back. The place is filled with evil." He crossed himself. "Ye should remove her before it works its sorcery upon *her.*"

"Ach! I don't believe in sorcery."

"Five priests, Rane, *five.*" He recited the history almost like an incantation. "One by English dagger. One by fire. One by water. One fallen to drink. And one..." He gestured to his sightless eyes.

Rane supposed there was no shaking the priest's conviction that the premature demise of the holy men was somehow orchestrated by the devil. Father Conan found it unthinkable to blame his god or fate for the cruel irony of robbing a priest of his sight.

But in Rane's eyes, the priest's refusal to return to the church meant that King Henry had won when he'd attacked the sanctuary four years ago. And that was unthinkable to Rane. He wanted Scotland to reclaim the church, to forever dispel the myth of Henry's curse.

With a sigh, Rane crossed to the pantry shelf, perusing the nearly depleted stores. A week ago he'd brought the priest a haunch of venison. 'Twas gone, yet the Father looked as gaunt and frail as ever. Rane unwrapped a block of cheese, carving away the mold with his knife.

"Ye've been givin' your food away to beggars again, haven't ye?"

"There are those less fortunate and more hungry."

Rane shook his head. Blind, old, and feeble, Father Conan still believed he was privileged among men.

"By Loki, ye're as shrunken as a grandmother's teat," he scolded. "Ye'll starve yourself to death. Then where will the beggars go for food?"

"Rane," the Father chided, "ye know I cannot turn away one in need."

"And what about this lass in need?"

The priest's mouth turned down, and his face closed like the visor on a yeoman's helmet.

Rane wrapped and replaced the cheese, then crouched beside the priest, resting a hand upon the man's shoulder. "She's not well, Father. She's wounded and—"

Father Conan grumbled, "Then she has need of a doctor, not a priest."

"Her first need is for protection."

"Ye have a bow. *Ye* protect her."

"Father, she's asked for sanctuary." Rane's patience was dwindling. "I cannot take her confession."

"Then find another church. Find another priest," the Father muttered. "But do not ask me to go into that devil's den again."

Rane rose, mouthing a silent oath. Indeed, he couldn't blame the Father. King Henry's men had left their mark. *No one* had entered the place in four years. Even the most devout of priests wouldn't take up residence there. Nor did he imagine the nasty, ill-tempered priest who presided over the church at nearby Selkirk could be persuaded to travel to hear the confession of a lone maiden in a moldering church purported to be cursed.

As for conveying her elsewhere, the nearest sanctuary was miles away. Though Rane supposed he could carry her the distance if he heaved her across his back like a deer, 'twas too dangerous to move her.

Rane clenched his fists, frustrated. "Father, I pray ye... There's no one else."

The priest's chin quivered, partly with fear, partly with irritation. "I will...pray for her."

Rane blew out an exasperated breath. "Evil spirits," he muttered, his patience at an end. "Curses. The devil. If ye ask me, every one o' those priests was the victim of his own human frailty or the simple cruelty o' fate."

The Father blinked in surprise.

"Aye, even ye," Rane continued, unable to halt his tirade, harsh though 'twas. "'Tis far too easy to blame your misfortune on the devil. Maybe your *god* gave ye this affliction. Maybe he blinded ye to test your faith."

'Twas the first time Rane had ever voiced his opinion on the matter, and perhaps later he would regret his candor.

But at the moment he didn't have time to smooth the priest's ruffled feathers. He didn't trust the lass to stay where he'd left her. Every moment he was away, the threat to her grew. And he wasn't about to abandon the lass he'd wounded by his own hand.

So with a pointed slam of the priest's door, he trudged back along the overgrown path from the cottage to the old church.

What was he to do now? How would he explain to the lass that of all the wayside churches dotting the road from Falkirk to Selkirk, she'd managed to choose the one with the threshold no priest would cross?

"Ballocks." Florie perched on the low fridstool with her bare legs stretched out before her. Damn her chemise! 'Twas stuck to her bloody bandages, stuck in such a way that when she tried to get up, it pulled painfully at the scab. And all her tugging at the linen had caused her only more pain and frustration. As she bent over the injury, she saw 'twas bleeding again.

"Ye're not worryin' that wound, are ye?"

She yelped in surprise. She hadn't even heard the stealthy hunter come in. She hastily tossed her skirts back down over her legs, but not, she noted, before he got a good, long look at them.

He closed the door behind him. "*Are* ye?"

She gulped guiltily. How long had he been watching her? She should have left while she had the chance, her wound be damned. And aye, she was worrying it, with good reason.

"Nae," she lied.

The arch of his brow said he didn't believe her. "If ye worry at it," he said, resting his bow and arrows against the wall, "the wound won't heal."

"I'm not," she insisted.

One corner of his lip drifted up in a dubious smirk, and he started inexorably forward. "Let me see."

"'Tis fine."

She was sure she'd seen a lusty gleam in his eye a moment ago. 'Twas doubtless a dangerous thing to let him anywhere near her bare flesh. And yet here he came.

"The cloth is stuck fast to the wound, isn't it?" he guessed, hunkering down far too closely beside her.

"Nae," she hedged.

"Show me."

She drew her leg up out of his reach. She refused to be cowed into submission, no matter how her heart quivered with the powerful giant so near. "I can take care of it myself."

To prove her point, she braced her hands on the arms of the fridstool, preparing to get up despite the painful consequences.

He stopped her with a single hand on her shoulder. "Sit."

She had little choice. Her strength was no match for his.

"I vowed to take care o' ye, love," he told her with a wink. "'Tis what I intend to do."

She bit at her lip. Despite his casual endearment and coy wink, his words sounded more like a threat than a vow, and her heart skittered at the thought of him sliding his fingers along her thigh. "I don't need your help. I'll be fine."

He ignored her words, nodding toward her leg. "Let me see."

Heat crept into her cheeks. "I'll find a doctor in the burgh."

"I wouldn't advise it. We've only one doctor in Selkirk, and he's a crack-pated butcher." He took hold of the hem of her skirt and started to tug it upward.

"Wait!" She clapped her hands over her knees to hamper his progress. "What about the priest ye promised to fetch?"

He lowered his gaze. "In time, wee one." He tugged again on her kirtle. "First your wound."

"Nae!" She tightened her grip on her skirts. She was fast running out of excuses. "Nae... I..."

He paused and studied her, absently rubbing the fabric of her skirt between his thumb and finger. "Are ye blushin'?" A half smile lurked at the corners of his mouth. "Ach, darlin', I assure ye, 'tis nothin' I haven't seen already."

She swallowed. He needn't remind her of that fact. She clung fiercely to the last bit of cloth guarding her modesty as her gaze darted over his sinewy forearms and broad shoulders. She wondered if he might resort to bodily restraining her. If he did, she'd fight, but she knew she hadn't a breath of hope against him.

After a long moment of impasse, to her immense relief, he withdrew, shaking his head and settling himself patiently on the floor beside her. He snagged the costrel from his hip and uncorked it. "Ale?"

She nodded, uncertain of his game, yet grateful for any reprieve from his physical attentions.

But the knave didn't immediately offer it to her. Instead, he swirled the ale lazily around in the costrel. "Ye're a merchant, aye? I'll tell ye what I'll do. I'll make a bargain with ye," he said, a faint sparkle in his shrewd gaze. "Ye let me look after your wound, and I'll give ye a drink."

She lowered her brows. "That isn't a bargain," she told him. "'Tis extortion."

He gave her a maddening shrug.

She bit the inside of her cheek. The rogue might think he'd gotten the best of her, but she'd learned a trick or two from her foster father about haggling. One way or another, she'd get her way.

"Give me my drink first," she said. "Then I'll let ye look at it."

He thoughtfully stroked his chin. "Fair enough. One swallow. More later." He passed her the costrel.

She took one swig. Then stole another. But just as she would have nervily downed the rest of its contents, he wrested the vessel away.

"Enough, darlin'," he chided, popping the stopper in.

Darlin'. Did he have to keep calling her that? Nobody called her that. Every time he did it, her silly heart fluttered inexplicably, which only increased her discomfort.

"With no food in your belly, lass," he added, "ye're likely to drink yourself into a stupor."

He'd likely prefer that, she thought. "Then ye could paw me at your leisure," she murmured under her breath, though apparently not *enough* under her breath.

"Paw ye?"

She blushed. "'Twould seem to be your wont."

"Indeed?" By the subtle crinkling of his eyes, her words appeared to entertain him. "I assure ye I've never pawed a lass in my life." He tucked the costrel back into his belt. "Caressed maybe. Fondled. But pawed?"

Florie's ears burned. The last thing she needed to hear was a full accounting of the knave's debauchery.

"Maybe," he whispered, leaning far too close to her, close enough that she could see blue crystals in his pale green eyes as he arched an amused brow, "ye're afraid ye might enjoy it."

The blood rushed to her face, and her mouth made an "O" of outrage.

He was spared her reply when a sharp cough came from the direction of the church door. Her guardian's knife was out and flipped backward in his hand, poised for throwing, before Florie could even look up. Faith, did he always attack first and identify his target later?

'Twas but a hunched old man in a ragged brown cassock. A ring of rusty keys hung from his belt, and he hobbled in with the aid of a long, gnarled stick. The priest pushed back his cowl, revealing a wrinkled face, a shock of white hair, and a milky stare that marked him as a blind man.

"Father," the archer said, sliding his knife back into its sheath. "Ye came."

The priest shivered once, then crossed himself. "Even old fools can mend their ways, Rane."

Florie glanced up at her meddlesome defender, who rose to meet the priest. Rane. So that was his name. It suddenly seemed appalling that, before this moment, she couldn't even name the man taking such liberties with her person.

The old priest took a slow breath of musty air and croaked, "I fear I've been away too long."

He extended his wrinkled hand, and Rane took it, drawing the old priest into a hearty and completely irreverent embrace. Florie's eyes widened. Did the archer treat no one with the proper decorum?

"Bless ye for comin', Father," he said.

The wizened priest somehow managed to extricate himself from Rane's smothering hug. "So where's the lass who seeks sanctuary at this forsaken place?"

"Here, Father," Florie replied, hastily adding, "but I no longer need sanctuary. I'm sure I'll be safe enough now. I just want to go back to the fair."

Rane frowned. "Back? Ye cannot go back. Not yet."

"I beg your pardon," Florie said, bristling at the archer's tyrannical nature, no matter how handsome he was, "But I may go wherever and whenever I will."

"Not while ye're under my protection."

"I didn't ask for your protection. I don't want your protection."

"Ye need me."

"I don't *need* anybody."

"Is that so? Well, ye seemed to need me badly enough last night."

The Father's brows shot up in astonishment at the possible implication of the archer's words. "Rane, do ye hold the lady here against her will?"

"Nae," Rane said.

"Aye," Florie interjected.

The priest shook his head. "I'm told a dozen maids asked after ye last evenin' at the fair, Rane. Leave it to ye to tumble the one who doesn't favor ye."

Florie's jaw dropped. "Tumble? I didn't—"

"Ye misunderstand, Father," Rane said, rushing to her defense. "'Tis not the way of it at all." He grimaced, then rubbed at the back of his neck, as if trying to decide how to proceed. Finally, he lowered his shoulders with a deep sigh. "'Tis in truth a very grave matter."

A shadow drifted across his eyes, liked a grim cloud eclipsing the sun. His hand tightened subtly into a fist at his side, and a muscle twitched once along his cheek. The cocksure knave vanished.

The priest, blind though he was, detected Rane's darkening mood. He crept closer, his brow furrowed with concern. "What is it, lad?" he whispered, resting a fatherly hand upon Rane's forearm.

Rane covered the priest's hand with his own and spoke so softly, she had to strain to hear. "I was huntin' last night."

"Indeed?" The priest raised one snowy brow. "Well, 'tis your trade, after all, Rane."

Rane exhaled heavily. "Without sanction."

Florie stilled.

The priest let his breath out on a soft whistle. "Poachin'."

"Aye."

Florie gulped, staring at the archer in horrified awe. She remembered crow-ravaged corpses of poachers twisting from the gallows at Stirling. If Rane was a poacher, maybe he was seeking sanctuary as well.

"I see," Father Conan said thoughtfully.

"I've been doin' so for weeks," Rane confessed.

"But why, lad? Surely ye're well provided for."

"I am, aye. But some o' the crofters..." He shook his head.

"Ye give the meat to them," the priest guessed, "and to me." Then he gave a dry chuckle. "And ye scolded me for *my* soft heart."

Rane gave the priest back his hand, turned rueful eyes upon Florie, and then furrowed his brows. "There's more." His mouth was grim as he lowered his gaze to her wounded leg, and she saw him swallow back shame. "Last night, while I was huntin', I..." He steeled his jaw and spoke gruffly, but his voice still cracked. "God forgive me, I..."

Florie didn't want to feel sorry for the varlet. But when she heard that crack in his voice, she couldn't help herself.

The hunter clearly was not the sort of man to go about shooting maidens for sport. It had been an accident, an accident both appalling and unforgivable to him. He'd never meant to hurt her. God's mercy, the man had shot her while hunting to feed starving crofters.

Worse, he seemed the kind of person to torment himself over the misdeed for the rest of his life. And as much as her leg throbbed from his lapse of judgment, or lack of sense, or dearth of skill, she couldn't let him do that. 'Twasn't fair.

Florie prized fairness. 'Twas the hallmark of a good goldsmith. The man had done his best to make amends. He'd extracted the arrow. He'd dressed her wound. And he'd carried her to sanctuary. The least she could do was ease his guilt.

"What is it, lad?" the priest asked.

"I—"

"He found me lost in the forest," Florie interrupted, "and brought me here." 'Twasn't a lie, not exactly. Wetting her lips, she explained, "Ye see, there was a...a mite of a misunderstandin'...and a mob o' men chased me a great distance through the wood. I scarcely escaped them."

The anxiety of deceiving a priest made Florie rattle on

like a milkmaid with a fresh rumor. "At the edge o' the forest, I...I fell, and *this* kind man helped me to the church. Since there was no priest within to grant me sanctuary, he offered to watch over me for the night."

She glanced up at Rane. He was staring at her as if she'd grown horns.

The priest turned to him. "Is this true, lad?"

The archer lowered his brows. "Nae."

"Aye," she replied, glaring pointedly at Rane. "O' course 'tis true. Ye brought me here, didn't ye?"

He grunted assent.

"And ye watched over me."

"Aye, but—"

"There. Ye see?"

"Rane MacFarland," the priest chided him, clucking his tongue at the perplexed archer, "ye're too humble for your own good." He inclined his head toward Florie. "Have no fear, my child. All are welcome in the house o' the Lord. 'Tis a decrepit old church, nearly as decrepit as myself, but surely ye shall have sanctuary here. Lad, there's a fridstool here somewhere, as I recall. I'll unearth my books from the vestry." Then he waddled off.

"Pray do not trouble yourself, Father," Florie called after the priest. "I cannot stay here much longer. As soon as I'm able to walk, I'll just be on my way and—"

"Nonsense, lass," he replied, unlocking the vestry door with one of his keys and disappearing within. "O' course ye'll stay. Never let it be said that the charity o' the..."

As the priest's words dwindled out of hearing, Rane whirled about, sinking onto his haunches beside Florie. "Ye lied for me," he accused. His eyes were suspicious and entirely too penetrating. "Why?"

She shrugged uneasily. "Ye didn't mean to shoot me." Then she gave him a sharp glance. "Did ye?"

His brows came together, as if she'd dealt him a bewildering blow. "I told ye before," he whispered passionately, his gaze—more piercing than his arrow—leaving her breathless, "I would not for the world harm a maid."

For a moment, she could only stare back. She'd been wrong about his eyes. They were far richer than chrysolite. They were as fathomless and crystalline as the most precious aquamarine beryl. The silence grew strained. His proximity and the way her heart was wobbling began to unsettle her. She wiped sweating palms on her skirts and gave a brittle little laugh. "How ye mistook me for game, I cannot imagine."

He reached out, startling her by gathering a fistful of her skirt. "Your garments. They're a most unfortunate shade."

'Twas true, she realized. Her gown was pale beige. Half hidden in the branches, she must have looked like a ranging buck.

"Aye. Well. The next time I flee into the forest," she said with nervous humor, "I shall be certain to dress in bright scarlet."

He released her skirt, and she released her breath.

But he wasn't finished with her. Without warning, he caught her under the arms and lifted her effortlessly up onto the low fridstool. While she was reeling from that shock, he propped up her chin with his finger to peer at the scratch on her cheek. She tried to draw away, but he held fast with his thumb and finger, apparently intent on scrutinizing her every scrape.

"Thank Odin ye're all right," he murmured.

Her face grew hot under his stare, her nerves strained. "Thank God ye're a terrible shot," she retorted.

His gaze held hers then, and he released her chin, but his mood was far from light. Indeed, he met her eyes with chilling sobriety.

"I never miss," he told her. "If I hadn't turned the bow aside at the last instant, ye'd be dead."

CHAPTER 5

The priest returned at that moment, thumping the dust from his Bible, to hear her confession. "Vermin in the vestry, and Methuselah's gone missin'. Lad, will ye meander outdoors and see if ye can find him?"

"Missin'? But I saw him only—"

"Lad," the Father interjected pointedly, "I'm certain he's somewhere *outside* the church."

"Ah," Rane nodded, taking the hint. "Aye."

Florie was glad to see him go, for the man was definitely a distraction, and his uninvited touch had left her as bristly as a kitten in a lightning storm.

Now that the priest stood beside Rane, she saw how improbably tall the archer was. Taller even than Wat, who, when he wasn't slouching, stood a full head over Florie. Rane's legs were long, his hips narrow, yet he possessed no dearth of muscle. Still, for all his clearly mortal flesh, he was as handsome as an angel.

Out of habit, she began to consider what jewels would best suit his build and coloring. A simple wide cuff of hammered gold about his wrist, she decided, and a medallion set with chalcedony upon his chest.

"M'lady?" the priest prompted.

She watched Rane swoop up his discarded cloak, shake out the wrinkles, and whirl it about his shoulders. It needed a gold cloak pin in the form of a bow and arrow, she thought, to set off his hair, which shone like a sheet of gold leaf.

"M'lady?" Father Conan repeated.

Rane tightened his leather belt, the one that bore the marks of her teeth, and Florie noted again how nimble his fingers were, probably from years of hunting with the longbow. The belt, of course, would have looked better with a heavy buckle of gold. She studied him as, giving her a nod of farewell, he swaggered down the length of the sanctuary—confident, agile, splendid. By the rood, he was magnificent, the perfect foil for a goldsmith's wares.

"M'lady!"

The church door closed behind him. Only then did Florie whip her head toward the priest. "Aye?"

She would have sworn the Father's filmy eyes sparkled. "Do I have your attention now?"

She cleared her throat, painfully aware he'd been addressing her for some time. "Aye."

"Poor lass, ye must be a victim o' the curse," he said enigmatically.

She frowned. "Curse?"

"Indeed." He leaned forward. "Hearken, m'lady, and I'll tell ye the tale." He rubbed his palms together, warming to his subject like a well-traveled bard.

Now that Rane had gone, Florie couldn't help feeling impatient. What would become of her goods at the pavilion? Was there any chance she could return to Wat if she hobbled like a hunched old crone all the way back? She planted her hands on the low arms of the fridstool and started to push up. "I really should be—"

"'Tis a short tale," he promised, "and worth the hearin'."

"But—"

"Long, long ago," he intoned, undaunted by her protest, "a Viking warrior came to the Highlands to claim a Scots bride. He was a strong and stalwart man, generous in manner, but iron hard in his ways."

Florie sighed, settling back onto the fridstool. Apparently the Father was iron hard in his ways as well. She supposed there was no way to politely evade the man's story. He was a priest, after all, and Florie, unlike Rane, had been taught to respect men of God.

The Father continued. "He wedded and bedded his new young wife and soon got her with child." He frowned, shaking his head. "But she despised her foreign husband. So spiteful was she o' his Viking seed that she prayed the bairn would die ere 'twas born."

Florie scowled. She hoped this wasn't one of those long Norse sagas. Time was a-wasting.

"When the Viking learned o' her prayers, he grew livid with rage. He damned the wicked wench and all her ilk with a powerful curse. For all eternity, he swore, no lass born on Scottish soil would be able to resist the charms of a son sprung from his Viking loins."

The priest lifted expectant brows then, and Florie furrowed her own. Was that the tale? All of it? 'Twas not a very good one. It didn't have much of an ending. Well, no matter, she decided. She might as well take advantage of the lull.

"A charmin' tale, Father. Thank ye for your charity," she said, pressing up from the fridstool once again.

"Rane MacFarland," the priest interrupted, "is such a son."

Florie froze. Rane? The spawn of Vikings? That explained the size of him and his fair hair. But cursed with charm? Irresistible?

Faugh! Florie didn't believe in bewitchery. Nor was she charmed by the archer, despite the way her heart stumbled in his presence. She only found him…unsettling. "I don't hold much with curses," she muttered, "nor, should I think, would a man o' God."

The priest quickly crossed himself. "Nae. Nae. Certainly not. 'Tis but a legend, after all. Only the Lord God steers the fate o' man."

But though he spoke the words with solemn haste, as if he feared lightning might strike him at any moment, Florie suspected Father Conan preferred such fanciful tales to his usual Gospel fare.

He also insisted upon hearing her confession. He wanted to know every detail of what had transpired, which she painstakingly related…except for her real reason for coming to Selkirk.

And the truth about the pomander's significance.

And the bit about Rane shooting her.

About that, she told him merely that she'd injured herself in a fall…which was partially true.

Afterward, he made her swear to the customary conditions of sanctuary—to remain peaceful, to carry no sharp weapons, and to aid if the church caught fire.

She restlessly endured the procedure, while the priest penned the tedious record of her confession in a book. He dipped his quill in a vial of black ink and, using one finger as a guide, scratched words across the page with such meticulous sloth that Florie was sorely tempted to snatch the quill from him and do it herself.

The morn grew later and later. Meanwhile Wat, back at the fair, was surely wondering where the devil she'd gone.

As he scribed, the priest spoke to her of thievery, as she supposed he must in good conscience, advising that she trust in God's will and surrender herself to His judgment, for only then would her sins be erased. Only then might she leave sanctuary after the allotted forty days.

Of course, Florie had other ideas. She intended to leave sanctuary the instant she was able to walk.

At long last the Father made his halting way toward the door, muttering something about fetching supper, assuring Florie that she would be safe with Rane nearby, extolling the archer's selfless attributes as if the man were a saint.

Florie wondered what the priest would say if she revealed that his saintly archer had shot her. It didn't matter, she decided. She never would reveal it.

Now was her chance, she thought. With the priest gone, she could test her leg and see if it could hold her weight without reopening the wound.

But to her chagrin, no sooner did the Father close the church door than it swung open again, admitting Rane.

Her heart quickened when she saw him again, this time with the knowledge that he was the son of savage Vikings. Indeed, she found it far too easy, as he strode toward her, to conjure up visions of him in warrior garb, mounting an invasion, his jaw set, his ax in hand, his mind fixed on ravishing and plunder.

The fact that he wielded not a war ax but a bucket of

water did nothing to ease her fears, for she knew why he'd returned. He'd come to collect his end of the bargain—the dubious privilege of tending to her wound. Already she could imagine him sweeping her skirts aside with his bold Viking hands to touch her wherever he willed.

Before her wits could completely crumble she rattled out, "Well, now that I've been absolved o' my sins, I should practice walkin' so that I can make my way to the fair before too long. I'm certain my servant is wonderin' what's become o' me. The fool can hardly tell his left foot from his right, let alone display wares without upsettin' both the goods and the buyers." The closer he got, the shriller her voice became. "Please give the Father my thanks and—"

"If I didn't know better," he said, lowering the bucket to the flagstones next to her, "I'd say ye were tryin' to worm your way out of our bargain, merchant."

Against her better judgment, she rose to the bait. "Worm my..." She straightened her spine. "I'll have ye know I'm apprenticed to a member o' the guild and a woman o' my word. I do not worm my way out o' bargains."

Still, when he crouched beside her and rolled up his sleeves, she instinctively drew her leg back.

He cocked an eyebrow at her.

Florie's mind raced. "Ye'll...ye'll rip the bandage loose all at once," she blurted. "I know ye will. Or...or ye'll poke about and cause more damage. Maybe if ye were a light-fingered artisan, I'd not mind. But ye...fightin' men with your bows and arrows and swords and pikes, ye have little finesse. And less patience."

If 'twasn't quite the truth, Florie thought, 'twas close enough. She'd die before she'd admit that her pulse raced when he looked at her...that she couldn't breathe properly when he drew near...that she warmed dangerously when his fingertips brushed her skin.

Still, she considered she must be daft to give insult to a man twice her size, a man whose veins ran with the blood of Vikings, a man upon whom, at least for the moment, her welfare depended.

But to her astonishment, he didn't rage at her. Instead, surprise registered on his face, and he gave a bark of laughter. And aye, as she'd imagined, his smile was indeed brilliant. Not that it mattered. She wasn't some callow maid to swoon over a man's smile.

"Never fear," he said. One side of his mouth still curved upward, turning his grin devilishly coy and undeniably charming. "I'm not, as ye seem to believe, a fightin' man. I'm a huntsman. And if it puts your mind at ease, I'm told I have quite a soothin' touch."

It didn't ease Florie's mind in the least. She wondered who'd told him *that.* Likely one of those Scotswomen who had fallen under the spell of that ridiculous Viking curse.

Still, whatever her reservations, she *was* a woman of her word. She'd told him she'd allow him to look after her wound, and she supposed she must. The sooner she let him do so, the sooner she could take her leave. "Ach! Do your worst, then."

He grinned and crouched beside her, peeling off his jerkin and pulling his outer shirt free of his belt to tear yet another patch from his undershirt. As he rent the linen, her breath suddenly stuck in her throat, for beneath the cloth she briefly glimpsed the narrow strip of his stomach. Unlike Wat's plaster-white belly, which she'd unfortunately seen on occasion when he hitched up his hose, Rane's stomach was firm and flat, lightly gilt by the sun.

For a fleeting moment her mind was assailed by another image of him as a Viking of old, leaping from his dragon ship, swinging a broadsword, charging bare-chested across the shore, his long hair blowing back over his broad, golden shoulders. The vision brought an inexplicable giddiness to her head and swift heat to her face.

"Do ye feel well?" he asked with a concerned frown, brazenly planting his palm upon her forehead again and startling her from her thoughts. "Ye look fevered."

His words irked her. She nervously knocked his hand aside. Curse her childishness, she was blushing like an infatuated maid.

"Nae, I'm not well," she said, her heart racing. "I've been chased into sanctuary. I have a gapin' hole in my leg. And 'tween the hard floor and the chill o' the night, I hardly slept a wink."

"Indeed?" If she expected sympathy, she didn't get it. In fact, she would have sworn he smiled as he dropped a linen square into the pail of water. "Your sleepless squirmin' didn't trouble me in the least."

"What?"

He only smiled enigmatically, then nodded toward her leg. "Let's see how the wound fares."

Still blushing, she nonetheless acquiesced, consoling herself with the fact that soon she'd leave and never have to face him again. She eased aside the cloak to reveal the unsightly dark red stain marring the pale brocade. Then she carefully pushed up her outer skirt. The linen skirt beneath was still stubbornly stuck to the wound.

She jerked when his fingertips touched her knee, and he glanced at her sharply.

"Does that hurt?"

She shook her head, mortified. Nae, it didn't hurt at all. His hand felt warm, welcome, yet deliciously forbidden upon her skin. She tried not to think about it.

As it turned out, to Florie's great chagrin, the Scotswomen were right. Rane *did* have a soothing touch, and far more patience than she. He soaked the rag in the pail again and again, sponging the dried blood from the wound, rinsing it, easing the cloth away bit by bit. And not once did he hurt her.

On the contrary...

She swallowed hard as the backs of his fingers swept her calf, grazed her knee, brushed the inside of her thigh. Each caress became less threatening and more arousing. The silence between them grew heavier and heavier, until she thought she might suffocate if she didn't speak.

"I'm...Florie," she finally ventured, her voice cracking.

He lifted his eyes to hers. They sparkled, translucent aquamarine and full of light. For a moment they held her entranced, speechless, the way a flawless gem sometimes could.

"That's my name," she finally managed. "Florie, from Stirlin'."

A smile touched his lips as he lowered his eyes once again to her injury. "Pleased to meet ye, Florie." God help her, even his voice wrapping around her name felt like a caress. "Stirlin'. Ye're a long way from home."

"I came to sell my wares at the Selkirk Fair."

"And what wares are those?"

"Gold. I'm a goldsmith. Well," she corrected, "a goldsmith's apprentice."

He glanced at her jewelry and nodded.

She added, "My foster father is the goldsmith." 'Twas

not precisely true. Her foster father *had* been a goldsmith, but since he passed most days in a besotted blur now, Florie did the bulk of the work, or at least repaired his mistakes.

He looked up. "So he traveled with ye?"

"Nae, I came with his servant, Wat."

"He entrusted this servant to watch over ye?"

She blinked. Why did he make it sound as if she were someone's flock of sheep? "I don't need watchin' over. I'm a grown woman."

"Oh, I can see ye're a grown woman." His eyes sparkled unnecessarily. "But ye wouldn't have been runnin' like the devil was after ye last night if ye didn't need watchin' over." Before she could digest his words enough to be insulted, he asked, "Where is this servant now?"

She presumed Wat still tended the goods—after all, they carried a baron's ransom with them. But then she'd presumed the dolt wouldn't be so careless as to sell her heirloom. "Likely still at the fair."

"I'll have the Father ask after him."

"I can go there myself."

"Ye're not goin' anywhere," he told her, "not for a while."

She bristled. "I most certainly—"

Rane suddenly whipped out his dagger, eliciting a gasp from her. But he only chuckled and slipped the blade carefully between the bandage and the skin of her thigh, slicing swiftly and cleanly through the linen.

She steeled herself not to flinch, averting her eyes as he teased the bandage loose with the tip of his knife, and tried to think of anything but the sharp blade so near her tender flesh.

Eager for the diversion of conversation, she asked, "Did ye find the cat?"

He smirked as he squeezed the linen rag, drizzling cool water over the wound. "Nae. He was in the church. There's a crack in the vestry door. He sleeps among the altar cloths and holy vessels." He looked up long enough to give her a wink. "But don't tell the Father." Then his brows lowered as he inspected the wet bandage. "He only sent me on a fool's errand to be rid o' me. The Father prefers no distractions when he hears a confession."

"Distractions? Hmph. I suppose ye believe that silly curse, then." She paled, realizing what she'd blurted.

"Curse?" he said casually as his fingers inadvertently grazed the back of her thigh in a far too familiar caress. He smirked again. "Which one?" Apparently the priest had a collection of them.

"Oh..." she fumbled, aghast at her blunder and unsettled by the strangely pleasant touch of his hand. "Just...some bit o' nonsense the Father was blatherin' about..."

The bandage came loose then, providing a timely interruption. She gasped as her gaze was drawn to the injury. 'Twas an ugly thing.

"It looks good," he pronounced cheerily, gently swabbing at the bloodstains. "If the bandage is changed daily, it should heal in a few weeks."

Even as her stomach turned, her heart plummeted. She'd planned to leave behind this sordid mess as soon as possible and be back in the queen's solar in Dumbarton in a few days. She forced her gaze away from the wound, trying to pretend 'twasn't so bad. "I told ye, ye needn't look after me. I'll not be stayin' that long."

He raised a skeptical brow. "Ye're jestin', right? What o'

73

those who hunt ye? Are ye goin' to race away from them like a cracked snail?" He didn't wait for her reply. "Nae, I swore I'd take care o' ye." He began to wrap the fresh bandage around her leg. "This is my fault. I cannot in good faith let ye leave until ye're whole."

She opened her mouth to launch a vehement protest, but just at that moment his fingertips chanced to tickle the back of her thigh again, and her leg jumped reflexively. His gaze darted to hers, catching the spark of pleasure in her eyes, and in that brief meeting his eyes flared with a like fire. Breathless, she glanced away, discomfited by the intense heat of his gaze.

An uncomfortable silence followed as he wrapped and knotted the bandage, yet Florie's mind was anything but quiet. 'Twas as if her senses had been awakened after a long sleep. She grew shockingly aware of his wooded scent, his golden skin, the warmth of his body. She noticed the broad contour of his shoulders beneath his shirt, the silken fall of his hair, like liquid sunlight, and most of all, the brush of his fingers, smooth and nimble, upon her tingling flesh.

At last he spoke, without looking up, rinsing the rag in the bucket. "'Tisn't true, ye know."

"What?" she purred. God's bones, what ailed her? Her voice felt thick in her throat, as if she'd been drinking cream and honey. She coughed. "What isn't true?"

"That curse."

She stiffened, then tried to feign indifference. "Curse?"

He draped the linen rag over the edge of the pail. "The Viking curse Father Conan likes to tell, that no Scotswoman can resist—"

"O' course not," she broke in, wondering if he could hear

the edge of panic in her voice. "A lass would have to be addled to believe any man could be irresist…" She trailed off as the blue light from the window hit his eyes suddenly, refracting in a burst, spraying teal across the pale green like the most irresistible gem she'd ever seen.

"Aye?"

She scowled in self-reproach. What was wrong with her? If she were superstitious, she'd say there *was* a curse at work.

Just to prove she was still master of her own emotions, she announced, "I don't find ye irresistible at all."

"What's this?" The church door swung wide, admitting Father Conan, his back bowed beneath the weight of a parcel.

Though Florie knew the priest couldn't see her, she snatched her skirts back down and looked aghast at Rane. Bloody water still dripped from his fingertips. Lord, it looked as though they'd been engaging in some sacrificial pagan rite.

The priest waddled forward, oblivious to the spectacle. "Are ye losin' your touch, Rane?"

Rane rose to help the priest with his burden. "Ye know, Father," he sighed, shaking his head, "I believe ye invented that curse to torment me."

"The curse is true enough, m'lady," the priest insisted. "Not a day goes by when I don't hear the name o' Rane MacFarland sighed on some lass's lips."

Rane smirked. He hefted the bundle. "What have ye brought, Father?"

"Mead. Hard cheese. A bit o' mashloch, though 'tis o' poor grain. Thank the Lord for acorns and weeds, or we'd have no bread at all."

Florie wanted to try walking, but her belly convinced her to eat first. A meal would help sustain her as she exercised her leg, she reasoned, and 'twould be ungracious, after all, to refuse what the Father had brought. She supposed another quarter hour would make little difference. Besides, she was famished.

As it turned out, 'twas wretched fare indeed. The bread was bitter, the cheese so hard that Florie feared she might break a tooth on it. But the mead proved sweet and strong, and to her surprise, whether from the turmoil of the past day or the calming effects of the drink, soon after their simple meal, she found herself nodding with fatigue.

CHAPTER 6

"Feverfew," the Father whispered to Rane, showing him the vial of the powdered plant he'd slipped into Florie's mead.

"Ye didn't."

"Just a wee bit."

Rane frowned. He didn't approve of such sinister tactics, no matter how peaceful Florie looked, snoring lightly beside the fridstool.

"She mustn't leave sanctuary," Father Conan explained. "Ye were right, Rane. She's in grave danger."

The back of his neck bristled. "What kind o' danger?"

"Ye know I cannot violate the sanctity o' confession, lad," he murmured. "Suffice it to say the lass has very powerful enemies."

Rane glanced at the slumbering maiden—so small, so helpless. Whoever her enemies were, he'd wager they were after her gold. That servant of hers was a blockhead to allow her to wander loose so richly bejeweled. 'Twas fortunate that Rane had happened upon her when he did, despite the unfavorable circumstances of their meeting.

"Did she tell ye she's a goldsmith?" Rane asked. "She left goods and a servant back at the fair."

Father Conan sighed. "That's the other piece o' bad news I bring. I didn't wish to worry the lass, but I'm afraid the merchants have fled."

"Fled?"

The Father shook his head. "The English are back."

Rane's heart sank. "Hertford."

"He's loosed his hounds again."

Rane mouthed a silent curse.

"A pack o' them ransacked the fair late last night, lootin', stealin' livestock, wreakin' their usual havoc. The merchants scattered to the four winds."

Rane's heart dropped. "Was anyone...?"

"Killed? Nae. The burghers are salvagin' what they can. But with so much o' their goods and provender gone, 'twill mean hard times come winter."

Rane scowled, muttering under his breath. "Damned English bastards. Why do they plague Princess Mary with this brutal courtship?"

The Father shrugged. "They cannot afford her alliance with France."

"Hertford's a fool if he believes he can turn her affections to this new king by threatenin' her. That never worked for Henry."

Father Conan gave a dry laugh. "Not all men are as handy with the lasses as ye are, Rane. Hertford's even more brutish than King Henry was. He imagines he can win by force what he cannot by favor."

Rane shook his head. "'Tis a fool's game the English are playin', and we're the pawns that are sufferin' in their chess match."

"Faugh!" the Father said. "We Scots are a hardy lot. 'Twill take more than a few English torches to scorch the mane o' the Lion o' the North." He toddled off toward Florie, murmuring, "Meanwhile, until I can discover what's become o' her servant, I think 'tis best not to trouble the lass with bad tidin's."

Rane glanced at the sleeping beauty and nodded. She'd been fortunate indeed. God only knew what might have befallen her, had she not fled the fair last night.

If King Henry's temper had been short, Hertford, the agent of the new king, was even less discriminating in his violence, putting to the sword any who got in his way, whether priest or lass or bairn.

Still, the Father had a point. The Scots were a tough breed. Rane might not be able to fend off the entire English horde, but he could at least help the Border folk survive against their attacks. And he could begin with this lass.

"She'll need garments," Father Conan whispered, "plaids against the chill, perhaps a comb." He dug in his pouch to discover what silver he had. "Forty days is a long while."

Rane clasped the Father's wrist. "Put away your coin. I'll see what I can forage from the burghers."

As Rane expected, the people in the burgh were more than generous, despite their own poverty. The lasses, in particular, seemed pleased to donate their best things to Rane, as if he were a knight upon whom they bestowed a lady's favor.

Of course, when he made his requests, he carefully omitted the fact that the items were intended for the sustenance of a comely maiden under his intimate care. After all, he was no fool.

Agnes the alewife blushed as she gave him a comb made of horn, and Meg Cockburn donated a kirtle she claimed to have outgrown, jutting out her ample breasts as proof. Redheaded Effy slipped him a chunk of soap, hardly used, she said with a wink. Bessy the leatherworker's daughter sighed wistfully as she cut one of the clumps of fragrant sage from the beam of her cottage. And with a broad, brazen smile, Nanne Trumbel tossed him a pair of well-worn hose.

Hefting the bundle that had cost him little more than a kind word, a smile, and, in one instance, a friendly pat to his arse, Rane made his way back to the church.

By the time he returned, the sun had nearly completed its slow journey across the sky, beginning to slip behind the west hills like a departing paramour, still warm from bed.

Rane sighed. He knew well that warmth, knew it and missed it. He was unaccustomed to abstinence. Indeed, any other day, he might have answered Nanne's bold flirtation. But thoughts of the fey lass awaiting him at the church kept interfering with his lusty intentions, almost as if Florie bewitched him, compelling him instead to return to her.

When Rane entered the sanctuary, relieving the Father of his watch, he discovered that Florie was still asleep, curled up at the base of the fridstool. He frowned, wondering how careful the priest had been with the feverfew. The old man *was* blind, after all.

Placing his satchel on the stone seat, he tucked the coarse plaids in around her. Then he found and lit a long taper to place in a sconce beside her, should she waken in the night.

The candlelight flickered over her delicate features. 'Twas difficult for Rane to believe anyone would wish harm upon such a beauty. But he knew that even while she claimed sanctuary, the heathen English would readily violate it for such a prize. Florie was still in danger. He needed to remain watchful for her foes.

He'd prefer to sleep with her in his protective arms again, both for her safety and his satisfaction. Yet he knew he'd have no true satisfaction tonight. 'Twas needless torment for a man to bed down with a lass he couldn't have.

Besides watching for her enemies, he had to keep watch for Hertford's marauders, in case they decided to make a return visit to the church to finish the damage Henry had begun four years ago. So, arming himself with his bow and arrows and a cloak against the night, he whispered good night to the tempting lass and bedded down upon the steps of the church, under the starlit spring sky.

'Twas close to midnight when the soft knocking on Lady Mavis's solar door finally came. Mavis, too anxious for sleep, had spent the last several hours peering out her shutters, wringing her hands, watching for her maid's return in the impossible darkness.

Now, expelling a relieved sigh, she rushed to the door, snatching it open. Before the maid could speak, Mavis dragged her inside by her elbow and closed the door again.

There was no time for pleasantries. "Do ye have it?" she whispered.

The maid lifted the corner of her cloak. She was dressed as a lad, her braid tucked under a floppy bonnet, her knobby legs disguised by baggy slops and knee-high boots. She loosened the laces of the satchel hung across one shoulder and pulled out a rolled parchment.

Mavis's gut tightened. "What's that?"

"'Tis what he gave me, m'lady."

"But where is..."

Mavis tried to remain calm. She'd expected the maid to bring her the pomander, not a missive. After all, the command she'd sent to the English had been simple and straightforward. They were to ransack the fair, find the gold piece she described, and put it into the safekeeping of her servant.

What could have gone wrong?

Mavis eyed the lass with suspicion. Was her maidservant capable of deceit? Had she kept the piece for herself? "Ye're sure that's all?" she said sharply.

"Aye, m'lady. The man said—"

"What?" she snapped. "What did he say?"

The maid gulped. "He bade me tell ye...he was sorry."

Sorry. Mavis narrowed smoldering eyes. Sorry? For the love of God, she'd just risked her neck, betraying her own husband! She'd kept the lord sheriff distracted this eve, giving the English sergeant unfettered access to the fair and allowing his band of ruffians to fill their purses to their hearts' content. And all the ungrateful bastard could say was he was sorry?

She snatched the parchment from her maid's hands and began to read. According to the missive, the soldiers had located the goldsmith's cart, not at the fair, but on the road heading north, driven by a servant. They'd rifled through the goods, but the pomander was not to be found. The servant volunteered that his mistress had taken the piece with her, but he didn't know where she'd gone. He didn't change his story, even after they used their fists on him, so they took a hefty reward in gold and left the man senseless beside the road.

Tears of frustration welled in Mavis's eyes, blurring the letters on the page. 'Twasn't fair. The piece had been in her possession, in her hands. To be so close...

God, she didn't want her maid to see her crying.

"Go!" she croaked.

The wise lass, accustomed to Mavis's commands, bobbed her head and immediately did as she was told.

When she was gone, Mavis collapsed onto the velvet cushions of her settle. A single hot tear rolled down her cheek as she twisted the parchment in her fists.

She'd been so sure the English sergeant would come through for her, that the pomander would be safely in her hands by now, that she'd be able to melt the piece into oblivion before anyone was the wiser.

But 'twas not to be. That cursed wench still ranged the countryside somewhere with the damned thing. And Mavis wouldn't rest until she saw both of them destroyed.

As if one failure weren't painful enough, this eve, to keep her husband busy, Mavis had bedded with him. And though she'd prayed to God to make her fruitful, 'twas salt in her wound to know that, like all the other times before, she'd prove as barren as a hollowed pear.

In the dark hours before dawn, Florie stirred groggily from her slumber. Her foster father would no doubt be snoring off last night's excesses, she thought, so she'd have to go downstairs and open the shop herself. Her eyes still half-shut with sleep, she threw back the coverlet and prepared to swing her legs over the edge of her goose-down pallet.

The needle-sharp jab of pain in her thigh stopped her, bringing her fully awake. She grimaced, sucking hard through her teeth.

She'd forgotten. She wasn't in Stirling, in the comfortable house of her foster father.

When the pain faded, she rubbed at her eyes, groaning as the memories came filtering back. She was an outlaw now. She was wounded. And she was alone in a dark church outside of Selkirk.

God's bones! What time was it? The last thing she remembered was supping with Rane and Father Conan. How could she have fallen asleep?

Wat must be worried ill. She must get back to him. She had to try hobbling on her injured leg.

"Bloody hell," she whispered.

The floor beneath her felt as frigid and hard as winter ground. Her leg throbbed. Her mouth was dry. And there was a soft scrabbling in the shadowy corner that she hoped was only Methuselah the cat.

Why anyone would call this a sanctuary, she couldn't fathom. 'Twas cold and lonely and dismal. She'd already had to bargain for a swallow of ale and scrounge for food. Relying on the charity of strangers was insufferable. 'Twas a good thing she intended to leave, for she couldn't endure one more day of such dependence.

Only yesterday she'd been a successful craftswoman with a goose-down bed, a fire on her hearth, meat on her table, a clean gown for every day of the week, and an audience with the queen. How she'd come to this, and how anyone could ever live thus for forty days, she couldn't imagine.

'Twas no matter, she told herself. She wasn't going to be here for forty days.

She perused the pile of plaids she'd cast off and frowned. They hadn't been there before. Someone had draped them over her and lit the candle at her side. By its waxy glow, she spied a satchel left on the fridstool.

Her curiosity momentarily outweighed her caution. She opened the cloth sack and pulled out the contents: a wool kirtle, a ragged pair of hose, a horn comb, a bundle of dried sage, and a chunk of soap.

They were far coarser things than she was accustomed to, but more than she had a right to expect. She sniffed at the fragrant clump of sage. Where had the offering come from? Who had been so charitable?

Then a sudden misgiving jarred her. Maybe 'twasn't charity at all. Maybe she'd been charged for the items.

She patted her throat. Her pendant was still there. Her wrist and fingers were still encircled with gold.

Her pomander! Where was her pomander?

Tossing the sage aside, she dug through the plaids, frantic. Surely the Father had not bartered away her heirloom to purchase these trifles. Aye, he was blind, but certainly he could tell that piece was worth far more than the contents of the satchel.

Her fingers finally closed around a familiar link, then the pomander, and she exhaled in relief. She pulled the girdle out from beneath the cloth and fastened it securely about her hips.

Then she perused the gifts again. They were a kind gesture, though she wouldn't be staying long enough to require them.

Using the fridstool to lever herself up, she gradually

struggled to her feet, inch by arduous inch. Her thigh pulsed painfully as she stood, and she feared for a moment the pressure would open the wound again.

Balancing on her good leg and squinting into the dark recesses of the church, she focused on the door, determined to venture outside.

Filching a plaid to bundle about her shoulders, she pulled the candle from the sconce, then took a tentative step forward on her injured leg. Blood surged with excruciating force to her day-old wound, and she fought off a wave of dizziness as she shifted back onto her good leg.

When her vision cleared and the ache diminished somewhat, she tried again. Step by agonizing step, she limped forward, blinking her eyes to keep her light-headedness at bay, biting her lip against the torturous pain. It took an eternity to traverse the twenty yards of the sanctuary, and by the time she reached the doorway, sweat glazed her face and she was exhausted.

Balancing carefully on her good leg, she strained to pull open the door. To her dismay, the moment she managed the feat a mischievous devil's breath of a draft blew in, instantly extinguishing the candle's flame and leaving her in utter darkness.

With a silent oath, Florie dropped the useless taper, then hobbled awkwardly into the doorway, straining to see in the moonless night. The sky was as dark as onyx, the air unseasonably chill. Despite the thick plaid, she shivered as the breeze sighed across her clammy skin.

At her next step, her ankle twisted upon the threshold, sending hot fire streaking up her thigh. She winced, holding her breath until it passed.

Perhaps her imminent departure wasn't so pressing,

after all. Perhaps she could wait till dawn, when she'd actually be able to see where she was going rather than risk tripping and breaking her neck.

But then she mentally scolded herself for her lack of nerve. God's bones! She was the goldsmith to the queen, not some whimpering milkmaid. She could get past her pain and fear and do this.

She took one determined step.

Then something rustled at her feet.

Wolf! she thought at once. She dragged in a huge gasping breath as her toes curled back instinctively in her boots.

"Who goes!" a harsh voice suddenly barked, sending her heart vaulting.

The shock proved too much for Florie in her weakened state. Though she fought to stay conscious, her head began to spin and fog crept in at the edges of her vision. She faltered, then swayed. For an awful moment, she feared she'd topple.

With her last wisp of air, she managed a whisper of surprise. "Ye!"

"Florie?"

As she staggered dizzily forward, two large hands dug into her ribs, holding her upright.

"Florie!"

Her heart pounded wildly in her temples, her eyes rolled, and her bones melted like butter. As she sank, she remembered thinking vaguely that the archer shouldn't be touching her like that. Then she slumped into shadow.

"Come on, wee nightingale. Wake up."

Rane cradled the limp lass on his lap, buffeting her cheeks with soft pats, trying to rouse her. His heart was still lodged in his gullet.

"Ach, lass," he chided, more worried than angry. "Where in Nott's name were ye goin'?"

He knew the answer to that already. The headstrong maid was determined to return to the fair. 'Twas a good thing he'd prevented her. If her "powerful enemies" didn't hunt her down in the dark, the wolves surely would.

He caught her by her adorable pointed chin and jostled her gently. She moaned.

"That's it, love, come on. Wake up. Wake *up.*"

Finally she roused, jerking her head irritably away from his slaps. "I *am!*" Her voice came out on a hoarse squeak, but nothing had sounded so welcome to his ears. "I *am* awake! Stop—"

"Are ye all right?"

She tried to wriggle out of his tight embrace. "I *was,*" she said, "before ye scared the bloody hell out o' me."

"*Ye?*" Lord, the lass had no idea how his own heart pounded. "What the devil are ye doin' out here in the dead o' night?"

She retorted, "What the devil are *ye* doin' out here?"

She attempted to wrench herself away. Wary of her jabbing elbows, he tightened his grip.

"Unhand me, sirrah," she muttered, struggling against his binding arms.

"Hold still."

"Let go o' me!"

"Not until ye hold still."

"If ye don't let go o' me, I'll scream!"

"Ye're *already* screamin'."

She emitted an exasperated growl and began fighting him in earnest. But she'd left her pointy brooch behind, and he'd disabled her dangerous elbows. There was little she could do in her present position, and if Rane's hunting had taught him one thing, 'twas patience. He'd happily wait till dawn with the lovely lass on his lap, her backside squirming warmly atop that part of him that most liked warming.

Gradually she weakened and finally, realizing the futility of her struggles, slumped back against his chest. "I'm holdin' still. Now what the hell do ye want?"

Loki, the lass could curse like a quartermaster. "I'll tell ye what I *don't* want, poppet. I don't want to find your bloody corpse in the woods tomorrow morn because ye decided to flee, wounded and limpin', into a pack o' hungry wolves."

"Who said I was fleein'?"

"Aren't ye?"

"Nae."

"Then where were ye goin'?"

"Just...out, gettin' a breath o' fresh air."

He lifted a brow. Of course she'd been fleeing. This was the same headstrong lass who'd tried to crawl to sanctuary with an arrow in her thigh. Who'd refused to let him tend to her wound. Who'd protested when he'd tried to help her drink. The lass had a streak of willfulness a mile wide.

"Well, I'm afraid I cannot let ye do that."

"Oh?" She whipped her head around, and a hank of her hair slapped his cheek. "And how do ye intend to prevent me?"

"By reason if I can. By force if I must."

He almost felt the hackles rise along her back.

"Heed me well, sirrah," she said. "I'm not your servant, your child, or your dog. Ye cannot tell me where I may or may not go."

The lass had a point. But her stubbornness was overriding her common sense. "'Tis for your own safety, love," he explained. "As long as I'm carin' for ye, ye're just goin' to have to trust me."

"Trust ye? Trust *ye?* The man who shot me?"

He supposed he deserved that.

"Listen," she continued. "I didn't ask ye to care for me. I don't *want* ye to care for me."

Rane blinked, astonished, and a chuff of laughter escaped him.

Perhaps he hadn't explained himself properly. Normally, with a cunning turn of phrase, he could coax a lass out of anything—her bad temper or her clothes. But something about this rebellious wench drove all his usual sweet persuasions straight out of his head.

"Now ye heed *me* well, brat," he told her in no uncertain terms. "Ye've been gravely hurt. God willin', ye'll improve and be dancin' a reel by month's end. But at the moment?" He shook his head. "I'd wager it took all your strength just to cross the sanctuary. In your condition, ye'd be easy prey for the men who are after ye, as well as the beasts."

Florie scowled. 'Twas true. She knew she'd be lucky to walk twenty yards before she fell down in another faint. But curse it all, she didn't want to be beholden to anyone, least of all this knave who was holding her far too cozily on his lap.

"So what are *ye* doin' out here?" she asked. "Poachin'?"

"In the dark?"

She smirked, reminding him, "That didn't stop ye before."

"Ach, lass!" He gave her a chiding squeeze. "Ye cut me to the quick. Such cruel words from such a pretty mouth."

His comment rattled her. A pretty mouth? No one had ever told her she had a pretty mouth.

He clucked his tongue. "This is the thanks I get for watchin' over ye?"

She frowned. Then she realized why he was on the steps of the church. "Ye were guardin' the door."

"O' course."

That took the wind from her sails. "Well," she said with grudging courtesy, "ye needn't go to such trouble."

"'Tis no trouble."

No trouble? That was hardly true. Staying an hour late in the workshop to finish a nobleman's cloak pin was no trouble. But sleeping out of doors on a chilly night...

She shook her head in wonder. "Ye must be mad."

"Mad?"

"'Tis cold enough out here to freeze your ball—" She cut herself off. Living with two men, she'd learned a colorful array of crude expressions, none of which, her foster father constantly reminded her, were appropriate for a young lady.

Rane chuckled. "Ye needn't worry. My thick Norse hide keeps me warm enough."

Heat rushed to her face. His arms were snug around her, and that place beneath her bottom that she feared he'd freeze felt warm as well. Too warm. 'Twas sinful, reclining upon this stranger's lap. While he continued to trap her thus, it seemed as if he hollowed away at some fortress within her, like a stealthy sapper undermining the wall of her defenses.

"Ye, however, my tender Scottish blossom," he said, "should go back inside."

Tender Scottish blossom? Who spoke like that?

Before she could protest, he swept her up in his arms as naturally as if he'd done so all his life. Indeed, to her consternation, she fit in his embrace as snugly as a well-made ring on a man's finger, almost like she belonged there.

Their emotions, however, couldn't have been less matched. He seemed calm, casual, composed, while she fought the urge to leap from his smothering arms.

Still, to her chagrin, when he finally returned her to the sanctuary, bidding her a soft good night, tucking her into her bed of plaids, closing the door behind him to leave her blessedly alone again, by some perverse twist of her nature she felt strangely abandoned. The sanctuary, robbed of his presence, seemed cavernous and desolate.

'Twas absurd.

Florie was accustomed to being alone.

After her mother had died, driving her foster father to spend most days in an intoxicated stupor, Florie had learned to pass the time in virtual solitude. She worked by herself behind her bench, with nothing but gleaming gold and lustrous gems for company, for hours on end.

That solitude had served her well. Without the distractions of friendships, she'd excelled in the craft and managed to keep the goldsmith shop quite profitable.

But now she felt inexplicably lonesome. The archer had touched more than just her body. He'd touched a place inside her, a soft place she'd locked away the day she'd watched her mother's coffin lowered into the earth. Like a burnishing cloth revealing the inner glow of a gem, his touch awakened long-lost emotions in her, emotions that both frightened and intrigued her.

'Twas those unsettling memories that kept her awake,

along with a nagging awareness that while she lay snug in her cocoon of plaids, beyond the door Rane shivered in the cold. And 'twas that, nothing else, she told herself, that compelled her to make the grueling trek across the sanctuary once more to seek out her vigilant guard.

CHAPTER 7

This time the lass couldn't startle him, for Rane lay wide-awake, staring up at the stars, unable to quiet his lusting mind.

'Twas Florie's fault. That wee bit of a wicked faerie had worked some enchantment upon him to rouse his passions. Why else would she excite him so?

She didn't have the blond tresses he generally preferred, nor did she possess voluptuous curves to fill his oversized hands. Her stature wasn't even close to matching his own, which he'd found had certain advantages in bed. In fact, her head barely reached the middle of his chest. Furthermore, she displayed no interest in him and, indeed, seemed to have a curious aversion to his touch.

By Freyja, she should be the last maid on earth to arouse him. But arouse him she did.

Indeed, as she slowly opened the door, he was calculating how many of the forty days 'twould be before he might ease his ache in willing woman-flesh.

"Rane?" Lord, even her soft voice excited him. He liked the way his name sounded upon her tongue.

"Hm?" he grunted, raising up on an elbow.

"I cannot sleep."

She couldn't sleep? Even now his cursed loins kept him awake, chafing within the confines of his braies. "What is it?" he asked tautly.

"I cannot sleep, knowin' ye're out here, freezin'..."

She trailed off, but he remembered her words from before. He wondered how she'd blush if he told her that, while the rest of him might crystallize with frost, his ballocks were in no danger of freezing.

Instead, he said the chivalrous thing. "Ye needn't worry about me. I told ye, I have the blood of a Vi—"

"I won't sleep." She said it like a threat. "I won't close my eyes until ye promise to come inside."

He raised a brow. What a shrewd merchant she must be.

"And if ye refuse to come inside," she continued, shivering, "I'll s-sleep out here. If ye can endure the c-cold, so can—"

"Nae."

He grabbed her wrist before she could make good on her promise. Lord, her bones were frail and feminine, so unlike the determined lass herself, threatening to sleep on the cold steps of a church so he wouldn't have to suffer alone. Of course, he wouldn't let her do it.

"Frigg's bow! Ye're a headstrong lass." He blew out a sigh of feigned irritation. "I'll come in, then," he conceded. "I can see 'tis the only way I'll get any sleep."

He bedded down just inside the nave, bundled under the plaid that the lass stubbornly insisted he take. He stretched out with his weapon beside him and his back wedged against the church door. And he tried to think of anything but the bewitching dark-haired faerie with the sparkling brown eyes, sleeping but a dozen of his long strides away.

Florie stirred faintly beneath the prodding spears of dawn and the sound of men murmuring. Lulled by the warm light and the low hum of voices, she almost let herself drift back to sleep.

"They were countin' on venison for Midsummer's Eve," Rane was saying. "I promised Thomas..."

"It won't be the first year they've done without," the Father said. "Ye cannot blame yourself, lad."

"I cannot let them go hungry," Rane said. "I won't watch them starve."

"But poachin'? By my faith, Rane! In the forest o' your own—"

"Who better to slip under his nose?"

Intrigued by the conversation, Florie pricked up her ears, still feigning slumber.

The priest sighed. "Ye cannot risk your life to fill their bellies. Ye know they wouldn't want that."

"I don't have a choice at the moment. But I can at least make sure they're fed till I can hunt again."

Florie heard the soft jangle of coins.

"That should sustain them for a day or two," Rane said.

"Bless ye, lad. I'll see they get it."

Florie's heart softened. Father Conan was half right. Rane *was* a good man. But 'twas plain to Florie 'twas not some ancient curse that drew maids to the huntsman. 'Twas the man himself and his kind nature, his compassion, his generosity.

Still, the priest's words were troubling. Rane was a poacher who apparently had every intention of continuing his criminal activities. Florie would be a fool to traffic with such an outlaw, particularly in light of her own predicament and her precarious standing with the guild.

She'd already ruined her chances of finding her father, at least on this visit. But if she ever hoped to restore her good name and return to Selkirk, she'd have to distance herself from men like Rane. Besides, 'twas obvious he had more pressing matters to attend to than playing nursemaid to her.

The men wandered out of hearing after that, and when the door opened and closed, Florie made the mistake of thinking she was alone. She threw the plaid back and rose up on her elbows.

"Ye're a naughty lass, spyin' on the Father and me." Rane's voice echoed in the sanctuary.

So did her gasp of surprise.

"Ach, love, did I startle ye?" he said with poorly concealed amusement.

"Nae," she lied. "And I wasn't spyin'."

He clucked his tongue, striding toward her. Faith, did his eyes have to twinkle like that? 'Twas distracting. And the sight of his broad chest brought back all-too-lurid memories of their intimate encounter on the steps last night.

"I have bread and cheese," he said. "Are ye hungry?"

She felt guilty accepting the food in light of what she'd just heard about the starving peasants. But she was ravenous, near dizzy with hunger. And the sooner she could regain her strength, the sooner she could leave. "Aye, a bit."

She scooted upright to make a lap for the breakfast, but he set the fare upon the fridstool instead.

"First we wash," he said, dipping a rag in the bucket of fresh water he'd drawn earlier.

She held out her hand for the rag, but he tipped up her chin to do the task himself.

'Twas entirely discomfiting. Not since she was a child had anyone washed her face for her. She was perfectly capable of doing it herself. She started to tell him so, but he wiped the very words from her mouth. When she tried to pull away, he secured her chin like one would a rebellious lad.

"Hold still, darlin'."

She sat paralyzed between aversion and fascination, unsure whether 'twas torment or amusement to endure his ministrations, silent while he took extra care with the cut on her cheek.

He crouched so close to her as he furrowed his brows over the chore that she could discern each eyelash, as dark as wet wood, the faint stubble across his jaw, and the subtle upward curl at the corners of his mouth. His skin was as warm and tawny as gold, and, out of habit, she began to imagine what kind of worked chain might be worthy of such a setting.

"There *was* a lass beneath that filth," he jested. "Hand." He held out his hand for hers.

She placed her hand reluctantly in his, appalled to discover her nails were so dirty. He turned her hand over. The heel was red, scraped raw. He caught her other hand and turned it likewise.

"Ye fell."

She nodded.

"I have balm that may help," he said.

Balm? 'Twas but a patch of sore skin. 'Twould heal on its own. "Ye needn't bother. I..."

Ignoring her, he carefully swabbed her hands with the wet cloth, then took a jar from the satchel at his hip and daubed a generous amount of its contents onto the injured spots. 'Twas soothing, his touch so gentle it almost tickled. When he finished, her hands, greasy with balm, were rendered useless.

She hungrily eyed the loaf of mashloch. "How will I..."

"I warn ye, wee sparrow," he said, lifting a brow as he broke off a chunk of bread, "don't get accustomed to such coddlin'." He popped the morsel into her mouth. "'Tis only until ye heal."

'Twas pathetic, she decided, having to be fed like a bairn. Yet Rane didn't appear to deem it a burden. Indeed, he seemed to take great delight in serving her as if she were some ancient goddess and he, her adoring slave.

Until her tongue by chance happened to lap at the tips of his fingers. Then a duskier emotion shadowed his eyes, a look that frightened and thrilled her all at once.

Her heart hastened. "Enough," she breathed, unsure herself what she'd had enough of.

'Twas just as well. Though they were meager portions, she'd already eaten half the cheese and more than her share of the bread. He helped her take a drink of ale, and when his thumb grazed her chin to catch a stray drop, she flinched away.

He frowned and looked as if he might say something. Then he shook his head and drank from the costrel himself.

After an uncomfortably long moment where the only

sound was Rane munching on his breakfast, Florie looked past her idle hands at the gory blotch staining her skirt. The garment would never be the same, she was certain, but 'twas worth an attempt to improve her appearance for her return to the fair. Using only the balm-free tips of her fingers, she dipped the rag into the pail and tried gingerly scrubbing at the mess.

Rane watched her without comment until he finished eating. Then he perused her handiwork and took the rag out of her hands.

"I fear ye've made it worse, lass."

He was unfortunately right. Though the water diluted the stain, now it smeared over a greater patch of her kirtle, the way gold could be hammered and spread into thin foil.

"'Twill never wash out completely now 'tis set," he told her.

She supposed he would know. He was a huntsman, after all. Likely all his garments were bloodstained.

"Take it off," he suggested matter-of-factly.

"What?"

"Your gown." He beckoned with a wave of his fingers. "Give it to me."

"I think not," she said indignantly, clutching to her skirts and smudging them with balm in the process.

"I'm sure ye've another." He started digging through the pile of things she'd taken from the satchel. She'd forgotten about that kirtle. "Ah. Here." He held up the garment, a large, shapeless thing of woad wool.

"I don't wish to wear...that. I'll wear my own clothin'."

"'Tis a serviceable garment," he said with a shrug. "Maybe not as fine as your own, but..." He perused her once from head to toe. "'Tis better than lookin' like a slaughtered lamb."

She grimaced. She did look gruesome. But she had no coin on her person to purchase the kirtle. And as she'd learned to neither a borrower nor a lender be, she never took anything without paying for it. "I cannot accept charity."

He chuckled. "Why, lass, how do ye expect to survive in sanctuary for forty days if not for charity?"

"I don't intend to be here for forty days. Once I'm fit to travel, I'll return to the fair."

"The fair?" He narrowed confused eyes. "But lass..." His expression told Florie something was wrong. Gradually, understanding dawned in his face. "I see. Ye're not such a good spy, after all. Did ye not hear what the Father said about the fair?" At the shake of her head he grimaced, rubbing the back of his neck. 'Twas clear there was something he didn't want to tell her.

By the look in his eyes, she wasn't sure she wanted to hear. "Go on."

"He went there this morn to seek out your servant."

"And?"

"There are good tidin's and bad."

Florie steeled herself. "Aye?"

"I'm afraid your servant isn't there."

"What?" Her heart tripped. "What about my goods?"

"Gone as well."

"Gone?" Shock drained the strength from Florie. All her worldly goods, her life's work, a veritable fortune, were on that cart. God's blood, she couldn't lose her gold. If she lost her wares... She managed to rasp out, "Gone where?"

He shook his head. "The Father's tryin' to find out. It seems your servant left the fair yesterday, not long after ye did."

Florie tried to choke down the news. So Wat had apparently wasted no time in abandoning her. But where had he gone?

Wat was simpleminded, as malleable as pure gold. Without a hand to mold him he was devoid of any design, incapable of deception, which was both good and bad. Left to his own devices, he'd carelessly sold her mother's girdle. Now he'd been reckless enough to desert her. Was he so rash as to leave her goods to thieves and scavengers? The thought was staggering.

Bracing herself, she murmured, "What are the *good* tidin's?"

"Those *are* the good tidin's. The bad tidin's are the fair was ransacked by a band of English soldiers in the night."

"What?"

"They robbed the merchants and razed the clearin'. Your servant apparently had the good sense to flee before they arrived."

Not good sense. Good fortune. Wat hadn't the sense to come in out of the rain. Thank God he'd escaped, but the thought of English troops in the area sent a frosty shiver up Florie's spine.

Rane caught her forearm and gave it a reassuring squeeze. His fingers were warm, even through her sleeve. "Don't fret. He was seen headin' north. He's likely on his way back to Stirlin'."

'Twas likely. Wat might not be clever, but Florie could depend on him to be cowardly. He'd probably started packing for home when Lady Mavis drew her first breath to scream.

"Ye, on the other hand," Rane said, "are still in peril. 'Tisn't wise for a wee Scots kitten to be limpin' about while

English dogs are on the loose." He nodded toward the satchel. "In the meantime, accept a bit o' charity."

Florie perused the crude items again while Rane left to fetch fresh water. She supposed refusing the gifts would make her seem ungrateful. But the idea that she might need them...

Was it possible? Was she truly trapped here? And if so, for how long?

She'd boasted to Rane that she was afraid of nothing, but the news of roving English soldiers struck fear in her heart. Last year the English had thrust deep into the belly of Scotland, burning a path of devastation as they marched to the River Esk, killing men, women, and children alike. Even from Stirling she'd seen the smoke of Hertford's massacre. 'Twas the reason Princess Mary had been whisked away to Dumbarton, and why there was talk in the queen's solar about moving her again.

Nae, Florie dared not travel apace while the English army ranged the countryside.

But how long would they remain? What if she were stuck here longer than a week or two? Marry, she couldn't dwell on that possibility. Nor could she rely on her sot of a foster father coming for her, if by some miracle Wat made it to Stirling.

Considering her unfortunate predicament, she'd hoped to return home quietly and soon, before her real father could learn of her presence in Selkirk. The longer she remained, the more likely he'd hear about the thief taking sanctuary in the church. And if he happened to glimpse the pomander...

She shuddered, taking great care as she unfastened the golden girdle and set it beside her. She didn't dare let the pomander out of her sight.

Changing into the kirtle was an awkward feat, even after she managed to stand, and she almost wished she'd had Rane's assistance...almost. The woad garment was bulky and dragged along the floor, and the sleeves fell almost to her fingertips. But she managed to rein in its girth somewhat with the girdle, tucking the excess fabric beneath her when she lowered herself back onto the floor.

When Rane returned with the full bucket, he sat down beside her, cross-legged, close enough that their knees nearly touched. Then, without warning and much to her astonishment, he casually lifted her leg to drape it intimately across his lap.

She tensed instantly.

"Does that pain ye?" His brow creased in concern.

"Nae," she said tightly, averting her eyes. Lord, his thighs were as hard as oak.

"Are ye sure?" His sleeve brushed her ankle.

She clenched her teeth, nodding curtly.

He smiled and shook his head, sweeping her voluminous skirts up to bare the bandage. "Are all men so repulsive to ye, or is it only me?"

She refused to look at him, and her denial was about as sincere as the forced apology of a child. "Ye're not...repulsive."

"Oh? Indeed?" He ran his fingers pointedly along the top of her arch, and she sucked in a sharp breath. His eyes crinkled in rueful humor. "Ye know, ye're just goin' to have to grow accustomed to me touchin' ye. I can't very well change your bandages otherwise."

She sat in blushing silence as he sliced away the bandage and cleaned the wound.

After a while she *did* become accustomed to it, for she

had no other choice. She didn't wince when he lightly pressed the edges of the wound with his knuckle to check for infection. She didn't flinch when he dragged her skirts higher to access the injury. She didn't squirm, even when he rested her heel across the bone of his hip.

But her pulse still quickened, her cheeks flamed, and the breath snagged in her throat. Nae, his touch wasn't repulsive in the least...which made him far more threatening.

Rane felt he'd made some progress. 'Twas something like taming a feral kitten. At least the lass wasn't snatching her limb back in horror.

He wondered how much longer she'd put up with his touch. He wondered how long *he* could endure her feminine calf riding high upon his thigh, so close to the focus of his desire, and not crave comfort for the ache there.

She cleared her throat and tried to make conversation. "Where did ye learn your doctorin' skills?"

He shrugged. "Necessity." He grazed her ankle, lightly but intentionally, each time he payed out a length of bandage. "Accidents are part o' the hunt."

"Accidents?" Her eyes dipped with telltale desire. She was definitely enjoying his touch, no matter how she wished to deny it. Still, she managed to keep her tone even. "I thought ye never missed."

"I don't," he said, running his palm casually up the back of her calf, which made her blush prettily, then added, "but the same can't be said of others."

"Others?"

"My fellow hunters." He pressed his fingertips gently into the soft flesh at the back of her knee.

She bit her lip. "Stop..." she said tautly. "Ye mustn't..."

He froze. "Aye?" he asked, all innocence. "Is somethin' wrong?"

She hesitated, waging some inner battle. Then she shook her head.

He happily resumed his attentions, wrapping the bandage around her thigh, smoothing the linen against her skin with a gently provocative touch. "I stitch up more knife wounds in a year than most doctors do in a lifetime."

Visibly distressed now, Florie could only gulp out, "Indeed?"

Rane battled back a smile. 'Twas highly entertaining, tantalizing her this way. He loved seducing lasses. Almost as much as swiving them. He had to admit 'twould give him great pleasure to gradually arouse the skittish lass, to awaken her passions until she fell hungrily into his arms.

Of course, he wouldn't.

Despite his lascivious reputation, Rane was more protector than seducer. 'Twasn't in his nature to traffic with maidens who couldn't tell the difference between lust and love and gave their hearts too freely. Only experience taught a lass to live for the pleasure of the moment, to enjoy the thrill of the hunt.

'Twas the reason Rane eased his lusts upon seasoned wenches for the most part, who kept their hearts under lock and key. 'Twould be reckless to dally with someone like Florie.

But by Thor, he wanted her. Badly. And if she'd move her heel just a few inches to the left, she'd feel how badly.

Her eyes were closed now. Her lower lip was caught between her teeth. And there was a fretful crease in her brow.

"Don't worry," he whispered. "I've yet to kill anyone."

"What?" Her eyes flew open.

"With my doctorin'," he explained.

"Oh." Florie was definitely distracted, hardly able to think straight. He rather liked her that way.

Yet, inwardly cursing the meddlesome scruples that prevented him from slaking his hunger at once with her kisses, he did the noble thing and tied off her bandage. "There ye are."

The lass wasted not a moment when he was done, extricating her leg from his lap at once and pulling her skirts down over his handiwork. "I suppose ye'll be goin' home soon," she said breathlessly. "Your family must wonder what's befallen ye."

A grin hovered at the corner of his mouth. The lass was all but shoving him out the door with her words. Yet a moment before, her smoky chestnut gaze had sent a completely different message. "I've no family here."

She frowned. "Ye live alone?"

"I have my own quarters," he admitted, washing his hands in the last of the clean water, "though I'm seldom alone. There's always a fellow nearby to share an ale with, an adversary for chess, a—"

"Doxy to warm your bed?" she muttered, then winced as if her tongue had spoken without her consent.

He chuckled. "Sometimes."

She made a moue of disapproval. "Ye should go home to them, then. I hate to think o' the number o' wenches languishin' for your company, what with that curse and all."

He fought back a grin, drying his hands on the hem of his linen undershirt. "I told ye, love, there's no curse." He tucked a lock of hair behind her ear, just to watch her bristle. "But what about ye? Have ye got lovers in Stirlin' languishin' for *your* company?"

She audibly caught her breath, whether from his bold touch or his bold question, he wasn't certain. "I most certainly do not. I'm a goldsmith."

He cocked a brow. "Does one prevent the other?"

"It does if ye want to be a *good* goldsmith."

"And are ye a good goldsmith?"

She proudly lifted her chin. "I'll have ye know I'm the goldsmith to..." She hesitated. "To some very important people."

He smiled. Nothing made a lass more tempting to Rane than a cocky streak. And indeed, he was feeling sorely tempted.

'Twas time to search for something to satisfy a less dangerous appetite.

He rummaged through the satchel Father Conan had brought and pulled out a thick slice of gingerbread and a knob of butter wrapped in a green leaf.

He broke off a morsel of the bread, slathered it with butter, and fed it to Florie. "The gold ye wear, is it from your master's shop?"

Her mouth full, she could only nod. Now that there was space between them, her composure had returned. She reminded him again of a feral cat, all purr and fur at a safe distance, nothing but teeth and claws when you tried to pick her up.

He buttered a piece for himself and bobbed his head toward the intricate chain about her wrist. "He does fine work."

She swallowed the gingerbread and licked her lips. "Oh,

I made this one." She moved her forearms, displaying the various rings and bracelets. "These are all mine."

"Indeed?" he said in surprise, inspecting them more closely. The lass had remarkable talent. The design on one of the gold cuffs resembled the stems of intertwined roses, and where each flower should be, a tiny pearl gleamed. One of her rings featured another pearl cunningly enwrapped in leaves of gold to mimic a rosebud. "Very clever."

The way her eyes lit up at his compliment, one might have thought he'd sworn his undying love to her. "My master, o' course, always had the true talent," she said. "I mostly play at foliage and simple ring brooches, usin' pearls and crystal. But he's worked in enameled gold and cabochon gems and the most beautiful intaglio..."

He grinned, not at what she was saying, for he could understand little of it, but at how he'd finally found a subject about which she waxed enthusiastic. Her pretty brown eyes were as bright as gems themselves. 'Twas apparent she had great zeal for her craft.

"Ye have no idea what I'm talkin' about, do ye?" she asked.

He shrugged. "Huntsmen have little use for gold, unless it comes in the form o' coin."

"But, sir, ye're *made* for gold," she gushed, catching him off his guard. "With your tawny skin and flaxen hair, ye should have a thick gold chain with four-in-one links, like chain mail, and a pendant of sea-green chalcedony to match your eyes—" She stopped abruptly, as if suddenly aware she'd said too much.

He allowed a smile to curve his mouth. The lass had been thinking about this for some time, he could see.

Tawny skin? Flaxen hair? Eyes of sea-green? Aye, she'd given him a lot of thought. He popped another crumb of gingerbread into his mouth.

She shrugged with studied indifference, picking at a nub on her skirt. "Anyway, 'tis a piece I could easily craft for ye."

He stopped in mid-chew. Lasses offered him gifts all the time, mostly flowers and honeycakes and verse he couldn't read. No one had ever offered him a thing of such value before.

Why should they? He was, after all, but a huntsman. He'd worn nothing but leather, linen, and wool his entire life. To have something so precious made especially for him, something crafted by her own hand...

Then he scowled at his own gullibility. She was a merchant. 'Twas in her nature to flatter men into purchasing her wares and then demand a king's ransom for them. 'Twas a foolish notion anyway, he decided, an archer wearing a gold chain. 'Twas frivolous, a waste of coin, not worth considering.

He scoffed, offering her another sweet morsel. "I spend my silver on simpler things."

She ducked around the bite, glaring at him as if he'd insulted her. "I wasn't thinkin' o' chargin' ye."

"A bejeweled huntsman," he grumbled, silencing her with the bite of gingerbread. 'Twas absurd. He nodded toward the gilded girdle that she wore about her hips. "What about that piece? Did ye craft it as well?"

She swallowed, lowering her gaze to the golden links. "This? 'Tis my foster father's work. He made it for a...for my mother."

Rane picked up the pomander, turning it in his fingers. "And *ye* wear it," he ventured, "because your mother's...gone?"

She glanced up sharply, surprised by his guess. "She's dead."

"I'm sorry," he murmured.

She gave him a one-shouldered shrug. "It happened long ago, when I was a child."

He examined the piece. The hinged lid was in the shape of a heart, carved with intertwined letters of gold. "What's this?"

"F," she told him, pointing out the letters, "and G. For Florie Gilder. 'Twas added when I was born."

He nodded, picking up the trailing end of the girdle to examine a jousting scene captured in intricate detail on one of the links. "He must love ye very much."

His words seemed to puzzle her. "Who?" she asked.

"Your master. Your foster father, to let ye wear it."

"Oh. Aye." She absently ran her thumb across the clasp of the girdle. "I suppose."

Rane stared at the young lass. There was much unspoken in her eyes, and maybe one day she'd confide in him, but 'twas not the time to pry. At least he knew the reason she clung so tenaciously to that girdle—'twas likely all the lass had left of her mother.

With a nod of farewell, Rane scooped up Florie's discarded gown. At the church well, he spent nearly an hour trying to loosen the smudge on it with water and a pinch of salt, scrubbing at the cloth. But he feared the garment was permanently stained with her blood...just as her thigh was irreparably marked by his shaft...and just as his thoughts were indelibly scribed with her image.

He held the dripping gown before him. 'Twas simple, plain brocade, straight in cut. And yet it managed to hug the sprite's curves with seductive allure. How could such a thing be? Surely 'twas a bewitched garment to work such magic. Or maybe his eyes were blinded by some enchantment when he looked upon her. He shook his head and hung the thing from an oak limb to dry. Whatever 'twas, his strange attraction to the lass and the way his body stirred at the mere thought of her left him uneasy and convinced him to spend the remainder of the afternoon on the church steps, out of sight of her.

His gaze continued to stray, however, to the gown rippling with the breeze, taunting him with its beckoning sleeves. Eventually, weary from his restless night, he leaned back against the door, his arms crossed over his chest, and dozed.

Even in his dreams, he saw the garment. But this time, it twisted slowly in his mind's eye, and when it turned toward him, he saw with horror that it hung, no longer empty, but draping Florie's pale and lifeless body, from a gallows. A thick hangman's rope bit into her delicate neck, and as Rane watched, mortified, a hungry raven flew to perch on her shoulder, preparing to feast on her flesh.

He wakened with a start, his pulse racing. The sun had crawled halfway to the horizon. No wind stirred Florie's gown now. Nonetheless, with the morbid vision still fresh in his brain, he hastened down the steps to snag the garment from the tree, gathering it against his still-pounding heart.

Then, with a jagged sigh, he slung it over one shoulder and trudged down the hill toward the pond. Maybe a sobering splash of cold water would steady his nerves.

'Twas folly, letting a dream frighten him. But it had seemed so real, like the visions his Scots grandmother claimed to have, visions that transcended the dream world and foretold the future. What did the dream mean? What did it portend?

"Ho! Rane!"

The familiar voice made the breath hitch in his chest. He froze in his tracks. So much for his sharp senses. Curse his wandering mind, he'd blundered into half a dozen mounted men-at-arms watering their horses by the pond. And the dark-bearded man at the fore in the amber tunic, the one clutching Rane's missing arrow in silent question, was the man he most dreaded to see.

CHAPTER 8

R
ane drew a steadying breath. He'd anticipated this inevitable, fateful meeting for weeks. Now that the time had come, 'twas almost a relief. Despite the damning evidence of his crime in Lord Gilbert's hand, he found himself curiously unafraid. He straightened slowly, looking destiny squarely in the eye. "My lord."

But 'twas not poaching Lord Gilbert had on his mind. Indeed, the lord looked relieved to see him. "Ye're safe, then. After the raid last night at the fair, when ye didn't return to the tower house..." He twisted the arrow distractedly between his thumb and finger. "I'll admit I feared perhaps ye'd been run through by an English blade."

Rane forced a levity to his voice he didn't feel. "Why, my lord," he said with a wink, "ye know my Viking hide's too tough for that."

"Well, I'm glad to see I was wrong." Rane glimpsed fleeting fatherly affection in the older man's eyes before Gilbert straightened, dismissing his sentiments with a frown. "Good huntsmen are hard to come by."

Rane acknowledged the compliment with a nod. "Did ye find the culprits, my lord?"

"The whelps are long gone, though I'm sure they'll be back. But 'tis another hunt I'm on at present."

Rane glanced at the arrow Gilbert rolled idly between his fingers.

"Tell me, Rane. Ye know the forest better than anyone. Did ye happen to see a strange lass walkin' in the woods in the last few days?"

"A lass?" The arrow spun slowly, back and forth, back and forth, in Gilbert's glove. Perhaps the lord didn't even realize to whom it belonged.

"Aye. A thief. She was seen fleein' into the forest."

Rane's gaze snapped up to Gilbert's face. "A thief?" he echoed. A prickling began at the back of his neck.

"Maybe ye've seen some trace o' her," Gilbert insisted, "footprints, anythin'."

"A thief," he repeated, absently rubbing the cloth of Florie's gown between his finger and thumb. It couldn't be. Yet Father Conan had warned him that Florie had powerful enemies. Had it been Lord Gilbert's men who'd ridden past the other night?

"Aye. She accosted my wife at the fair, stole a gold bauble o' hers, and somehow managed to elude my constables."

The news hit Rane like a bolt in the chest. Was it true? The girdle Florie guarded with her life—had she stolen it? Had she lied about being a goldsmith, about her dead mother? Had she made up that story about the pomander? Rane didn't know his letters—she might have lied about them as well. Odin's teeth, was she no more than a common thief?

"Ye're sure?" he said tightly.

"O' course I'm sure. There were several witnesses to the incident."

Rane felt ill. It couldn't be. Surely Florie wasn't capable of such deceit. This was the lass who'd shielded him from blame, who'd invited him in from the cold, whose eyes lit up when she talked about gold. Aye, he thought bitterly, the same way a robber's eyes lit up when he spoke of silver.

He didn't want to believe Lord Gilbert. Worse, he didn't want to admit that Florie—faerie-faced, doe-eyed, mouth-watering Florie—had utterly beguiled and deceived him. To think he'd imagined her some unfortunate victim of abuse. What a half-wit he'd been, gulled by her sweet face. The little outlaw had led him a merry chase. And, curse his soft heart, Rane had helped her to escape.

"Well?" Lord Gilbert pressed, reining his restless mount away from the pond.

Rane hesitated. Her betrayal stung, and beneath his carefully controlled expression, righteous indignation began to smolder. The scheming lass had intentionally misled him with her dewy gaze, audaciously lied to him through her soft, sweet lips. He should turn her over to Gilbert at once. She deserved whatever punishment he would dole out.

But despite her outright deception, Rane was still hesitant to expose her. Perhaps because he was riddled with guilt over shooting her, some perverse sense of obligation made him want to protect her. Even now. Even though she'd played him for a fool.

Still, honor would not allow him to speak falsely. Sooner or later, Gilbert would discover that the thief he sought resided in the church. He may as well hear it from Rane's lips. There was no need to add harboring an outlaw to Rane's growing list of crimes. The lass had claimed sanctuary, after all. She was safe enough there, at least for the moment.

"I believe the maid ye seek is in the old church," he said softly. "She said she was seekin' sanctuary." But though Rane wouldn't blatantly lie, he was no martyr. He omitted mentioning that he'd carried the fugitive to the fridstool himself.

Gilbert's eyes flared with surprise. "What? She spoke to ye?" Surprise turned quickly to ire. Lord Gilbert's temper had grown short over the past several months, ever since he'd brought his new wife home. "Ye let her escape, and now she's claimed sanctuary?" He pounded his fist on his pommel. "God's bones! Ye bloody fool!"

Rane's jaw tensed. Aye, he might have let a thief escape, but he took exception to being called a fool. He straightened proudly and scowled. "Escape? I hunt *game,* my lord, not fugitives."

Lord Gilbert's dark beard quivered with rage. "'Twas my wife's gold girdle the wench stole," he bit out. "And Lady Mavis paid a king's ransom for it."

Rane doubted that. He'd never seen Lady Mavis offer a king's ransom for anything. Indeed, Gilbert's petulant bride made a practice of bullying merchants to sell her their wares for far below what they were worth. Rane knew 'twas not only the damaging rains and the English attacks, but the economic devastation Lady Mavis had wrought over the past months, that had left the commoners half-starved...and turned Gilbert's huntsman into a poacher.

"Damn ye, Rane!" Lord Gilbert roared. "Forty days ye've

cost me now! Forty days!" His horse sidestepped nervously as he grumbled, "And forty for the guard I'll have to post against her flight. Sanctuary. Shite!"

He wheeled his horse about to choose a man for the task. Rane noted that none of them would meet their lord's eye. He couldn't blame them. 'Twas an irksome duty to be confined for forty days to the perimeter of a church, guarding a fugitive, knowing that if the felon escaped, the guard would be held accountable for the crime...

When Gilbert turned slowly about again, Rane didn't care for the sly smirk on his lord's face.

"Rane, lad," he said, twirling the quarrel between his fingers as he closely inspected the bloodstains, "this *is* your arrow, is it not?"

A dire chill slithered up Rane's spine. "Aye, my lord."

"Yet I never granted ye leave to hunt in Ettrick."

Rane's fist tightened in the fabric of Florie's gown. "Nae, my lord."

Lord Gilbert stared at him a long while, as if measuring his value, then whispered, "Ye know I could have ye hanged for poachin'."

Rane refused to make excuses, refused to show fear or remorse. He'd done what he felt he must do. "Aye."

For a lengthy moment, neither man looked away. Finally, Lord Gilbert hurled the arrow, burying its point into the ground at Rane's feet. "*Ye* shall stand guard against her escape, forty days and forty nights."

"What?" Rane exploded, his brows drawing down sharply.

Him? Rane? Gilbert's huntsman? He couldn't stand guard over an outlaw. Not for forty days. 'Twas madness. Not only was he unequal to the task, but he couldn't afford to foreswear hunting, lawful or not. The crofters depended on him for food. In forty days the deer would be gone, hunted by spoiled, overfed nobles, and there would be no winter provender left for the peasants.

Muzzling his outrage only by dint of great will, he said evenly, "My lord, I'm not a man-at-arms. With all due—"

"If she escapes, 'twill be upon your head. And at Lady Mavis's mercy."

Before Rane could reason further with him, Lord Gilbert wheeled his mount, and he and his men thundered up the rise toward the main road.

For several moments Rane stood mute, his fists clenched, his thoughts running as wildly as scattering rabbits.

In the distant fields, through the slowly clearing dust of Gilbert's departure, Rane glimpsed the hunched backs of a dozen scrawny peasants planting crops for the lord's table. He steeled his jaw against a current of rage.

The lass, the thief, had just doomed them all.

Her greed had likely cost her not only her limb or her life, but the lives of countless crofters for whom Rane would be unable to hunt, helpless families who'd likely starve come winter without his assistance.

He might have been inspired to pity if he thought she'd stolen the girdle to pay for food. After all, such a crime was no different from what Rane did when he poached deer for the peasants. But *his* motivation was mercy. Hers was greed.

The thought made him tremble with rage. 'Twas apparent from the wealth of gold she already wore about her person that she was in no danger of going hungry. And worse, she'd lied to him, repeatedly.

Knowing all that, the only thing that kept him from coldly exhorting her to vanish into the forest as mysteriously as she'd appeared was his own guilty conscience and the fact that now he himself would have to pay for what she'd stolen. Unfortunately, though his skill with the bow afforded him fine quarters and a place at Lord Gilbert's table, that glittering bauble the lass clung to so stubbornly looked to be worth more than all his possessions together.

He supposed he'd have to take it from her by force, as unsavory as that idea was. Maybe in a few weeks, when she was healed and when he no longer felt burdened by remorse for shooting her, 'twould seem less distasteful.

A few weeks at most. He had no intention of standing guard over her for forty days. Lives were at risk. Every day lost was a day closer to famine for the peasants. He wouldn't let them starve for the sake of one scrawny thief who was blatantly guilty of her crime.

Now he knew what the dream meant. The lass *was* going to hang. Sanctuary or no sanctuary, in forty days, Florie would be tried and found guilty. No witness would dare come forward to testify against Lady Mavis, especially when the careless lass had the stolen goods on her person. She was as good as dead. And Rane was vexed enough by the fact that the lying lass's greed had thwarted his mission of mercy that he told himself he didn't care if she *did* hang.

'Twas what he staunchly maintained until he returned to the church, snatched open the door, and looked toward the chancel to behold the delicate bundle of lass on the fridstool, bent forward over several pieces of parchment and one long, slender, shapely, and quite bare leg.

She sat alone, unaware of him, in a pool of sunlight, her

dark spill of hair illuminated by the rays streaming through the red and gold and blue panes of the altar window, the sweet oval of her face fair and ethereal above his cloak of gray-green wool. She looked like a fallen angel, delivered to the earth upon heavenly beams.

Lost.

Helpless.

Irresistible.

A bolt of unwelcome desire shot arrow-swift through his body, leaving his pulse pounding in his ears.

He frowned at once. Loki's ballocks! What was wrong with him? The wench was a thief, a felon, a fugitive. She wasn't some winsome lass he might court.

Nor was he an untried youth who'd never laid eyes upon a female. Quite the contrary. Now that he was of marriageable age, the lasses of the burgh foisted their attentions upon him at every opportunity. In the last year, he'd swived more maids than he could count.

So why was it *this* lass, this outlaw that made the blood sizzle in his veins?

The oath brewing on his tongue was so vile 'twould have cracked the altar window had he voiced it. Instead, he smoldered silently at the treasonous hardening of his loins...and the damned softening of his heart. The tiny voice of Rane's conscience taunted him, telling him he was sorely deceived if he thought he could stand silently by and watch Lord Gilbert drag the beautiful maiden to the gallows.

No matter how guilty she was.

In a rare fit of pique, he slammed the church door behind him with a satisfying crash.

Florie shrieked. Her heart jerked against her ribs. In a mad scramble, she gathered up the pages of parchment.

"What the devil!" she exclaimed, pressing a calming hand to her heaving chest.

Rane had scared her half out of her wits. And despite everything she'd learned about his generosity and loyalty and compassion, at the present his eyes burned with inexplicable rage. He whipped her gown from off his shoulder, and it snapped in the air. He clenched his hands as he swaggered toward her like the Norse marauder who was supposedly Rane's forbear.

She pulled the cloak subtly, protectively to her bosom. No Scotswoman could resist Rane's charms, the priest had said. At the moment, this son of Vikings seemed anything but charming. What had happened to alter him she didn't know, but she'd seen her foster father change from mouse to monster with only the aid of a few tankards of beer. Nothing surprised her when it came to men.

Rane's eyes narrowed to mistrustful slits as he continued to advance toward her. The sight of his dark, stormy brow inspired in her a powerful urge to clamber in retreat and take refuge behind the altar.

Then she silently chided herself for her foolishness. After all, she'd claimed sanctuary. She was already protected by the church, wasn't she? Still, she wished the priest belonging to the church were here now.

She could scarcely draw breath when Rane halted a yard away, towering over her like a conquering barbarian. Holy saints! The immense archer appeared to have grown several inches since she'd last seen him.

For a moment he seemed to struggle for words. His fists closed and opened, closed and opened, as if they debated whether or not to throttle her. And she dared not speak for fear of assisting them in their decision.

When she could no longer endure the suspense, she burst out, "Slay me, then, or leave me be! But do not hang over me like a bloody executioner's ax!"

Her words seemed to shake him from his silent rage. She glimpsed some momentary flicker in his eyes, some awakening spark of remorse or pain. Then he let out a heavy sigh, and the fire in his gaze slowly diminished to a low flame.

"I mean ye no harm," he told her, though she suspected 'twas a stern reminder to himself as well, for his voice sounded as glum as a priest's giving last rites. "I'm a man o' my word. I've sworn to protect ye, and I intend to do just that."

He didn't sound very happy with his decision, and though he might reconcile himself to keeping his word, Florie knew good intentions often went awry. Her mother had vowed to protect her always, yet she'd died when Florie was but a lass. Her foster father's drunken promises were forgotten as soon as he sobered. She'd learned to trust no one.

"I've said I'll take care o' ye," he repeated, though his tone was so irritable, it sounded as if he'd promised to trim the devil's claws.

"Pray," she bit out, the words simmering off her tongue, "do not trouble yourself over my welfare."

"If I didn't wish to trouble myself," he said with a scowl, "I would have left ye to bleed to death."

Her jaw dropped.

Rane cringed inwardly at his own harsh words. Indeed, he didn't mean them. He would no more leave someone to bleed to death than he'd shoot a birthing doe.

'Twas only that he was frustrated. And vexed. And inexplicably aroused.

He cursed silently and regarded the lass he'd again wounded, this time with words. Her dark eyes smoked with fury, but they were also moist. Her pointed chin jutted rebelliously, yet it quivered. At first he feared she might burst into tears, but soon he realized by the defiant angle of her head and the glitter in her gaze that she trembled more with anger than with hurt. The wayward lass loathed him.

'Twas startling. He was unused to being loathed. Particularly by lasses.

Favored, aye.

Adored, aye.

Revered, sometimes.

Never loathed.

But then, he'd never shot one of them before. Nor had he threatened to let a lass bleed to death.

Suddenly he was filled with self-disgust. This wasn't the Rane the burghers spoke highly of—the huntsman who put meat on their table, the friend who always had a spare coin, the lover who never left a lass unsated. Lust and frustration and wrath had turned him into a brute.

Whether or not he willed it, whether or not 'twas wise, 'twas clear he couldn't simply walk away from the lass. He'd become involved the instant he shot her, committed the moment he carried her to sanctuary. Felon she might be, but he couldn't send her away into the woods to get herself killed.

Later, he told himself, in a few weeks, when she'd healed, when his moral obligations were fulfilled, he'd deal with her crime. In the meantime, his heart demanded he show her the charity for which he was renowned.

Her body was stiff with ire, and she glared at him with

smoldering eyes that would melt iron. If she continued to despise him, she'd never assent to letting him treat her wound. If he didn't treat her wound, 'twould likely fester. Somehow, he had to regain the trust he'd just destroyed.

He crouched beside her, raking his fingers through the locks of hair at the scruff of his neck. "Forgive me," he mumbled contritely. "With the English attacks o' late, I'm not myself. I assure ye, mercy is never a burden. I'm glad o' the chance to make amends." He blew out a harsh breath and placed a gentle hand upon her forearm. "I'll see to your wound now, if ye'll allow me."

She snatched her arm free. "Nae, I will not," she said coldly, staring stonily ahead, her brows slashed downward.

He blinked in surprise.

"Begone!" she said. "I don't need ye. I shall have Father Conan fetch me a doctor to attend my wound," she decided, crossing her arms stubbornly over her small heaving bosom.

He narrowed his eyes. 'Twas clear the young thief didn't fully comprehend her situation. She was in a strange place. She was friendless, as far as he could tell, apparently without coin, and as good as imprisoned here unless her fellow robber Wat returned, if indeed he hadn't abandoned her. From the moment she'd stolen that girdle, she'd put herself in the hands of fate and at God's mercy. He almost pitied her.

"Lass, do ye not understand? 'Twill be difficult, if not impossible, to find a doctor willin' to...a doctor charitable toward a thief."

She speared him with an indignant glare. "I'm not a th..." The reply died on her tongue as she read the knowledge in his eyes, assimilating his words and the larger meaning behind them. "Who told ye I was...?"

"Lord Gilbert has been lookin' for ye."

She paled. "The sheriff? Here?"

"Ye're safe for now. He's gone. And he's a God-fearin' man. He won't violate sanctuary."

But Florie didn't look convinced of that. Maybe now she understood. She was a fugitive of the law with no rights, no sustenance, no wherewithal, nothing but the sheer veil of sanctuary to shield her from her accusers.

Fresh moisture began to well in her eyes, not tears of rage this time, but desperation.

Ah, nae, he thought, don't cry. Nothing reduced him to awkward despair faster than a lass's tears.

"Listen!" he bade her. "I'll protect ye. I've sworn I would. Remember?"

A drop quivered on the rim of her lower lashes, beneath eyes that looked wide and lost. 'Twas hard to believe that so innocent a face harbored so guilty a felon.

He rested a placating hand on her sleeve, but she stiffened, so he quickly removed it again. He ran his hand over his mouth, racking his brain for something, anything he could say to change the course of their conversation, to distract her, to keep her from weeping.

"Maybe..." He studied the half-concealed parchments tucked beneath her knee. She'd been scrawling something with bits of charred wood. "Maybe ye'll show me what ye've been drawin'."

Her chin trembled, but she wiped away the tear with the back of her hand. "'Tis nothin'."

"I'd like to see."

She raised her chin a notch. "Maybe I don't wish to show ye."

He'd learned enough about Florie from their short time

together to know that though she was stubborn, she put a price on everything. He draped her laundered garment over his knee. He decided, perusing her form, that the fawn-colored gown wasn't an enchanted garment, after all. Florie looked just as delectable sitting there in the oversized sack of woad wool.

"Your gown," he bargained, "for a look at the parchments."

"'Tis *my* gown already."

He lifted a brow. "And those are the Father's parchments." She must have pilfered the pages from the storage room.

She bit at her lip, considering his offer. "Is the bloodstain gone?"

"As much as 'twill ever be."

After a long while, she reluctantly withdrew the pages. "Very well."

He offered her the garment as she handed him half a dozen pieces of parchment.

She examined the gown.

He examined the pages.

The drawings were expertly done, as fine as the illuminations he'd glimpsed in Father Conan's Bible. But one stood out among the rest. 'Twas a rendering of a pendant, a noble piece, simpler than those she wore, heavy links woven like miniature chain mail. At the bottom hung a dark oval stone, and crowning the top of the oval were branches shaped like the antlers of a stag. 'Twas the piece she'd spoken about, the one designed for him. And 'twas the most extraordinary thing he'd ever seen.

Guilt shot him straight through the heart. If Florie ever suspected that she now guarded against her escape, she'd likely offer to craft him a *noose* of gold. He scowled.

"Ye don't like it," she said flatly, not bothering to look up.

"Nae," he said, overwhelmed. "Nae. 'Tis brilliant. Magnificent. How did ye...? *Ye* drew this?" How could a common thief design such a thing? Maybe there *was* some truth to her claim she was a goldsmith. "Ye could...craft this?"

She shrugged. "Aye, at my master's workshop."

He narrowed his gaze. Who was this inscrutable lass? Thief or merchant? Trickster or innocent?

She *must* be a craftswoman. No mere outlaw could design such a work of art. Yet she'd obviously stolen Lady Mavis's girdle. It made no sense. Unless she'd pilfered the piece to copy the design. He imagined that the competition between goldsmiths was as fierce as the battle between rival hunters. One had to be an exceptional talent to stand out from the crowd. And the girdle was certainly an exceptional piece. Still, if she'd stolen it...

Maybe now was the time to convince her to remedy her crime.

"Listen. Ye're obviously a lass o' great talent. Ye could make a dozen such girdles. Why don't ye simply confess your misdeed and return the piece? I'm sure Lord Gilbert will—"

"'Tis mine," she said fiercely, closing a possessive hand over the links as if he might wrench it from her. "It belongs to me."

He frowned. Surely she wouldn't risk her life for the thing.

"Indeed," he lied, shrugging, "'tis not such a remarkable design. I've seen the like before in—"

"Upon my faith! Ye've seen nothin' like it in your life," she countered, bristling. "There *is* nothin' like it."

"It hardly seems worth the trouble. You're a lass o' some means. Give the lady back her bauble and buy yourself another."

"I told ye. The piece belongs to me. 'Twas my mother's."

"Then how did Lady Mavis happen to come into possession of it?"

"She...bought it."

He arched a brow at her.

Florie's gaze dipped. "But she wasn't supposed to buy it. 'Twas a mistake. And I gave her back her coin."

Clearly the mistake was Florie's, he thought. Regardless of the girdle's origins, even *she* had to admit Lady Mavis had paid her for it. Florie's only hope for mercy then was to let Mavis have the thing. But that looked to be a long, tough battle...one for which he must fortify himself.

He pulled the costrel of ale from his belt, uncorking it and first offering it to her. "Ale?"

As she reached for it, she intentionally let her fingers close over his. For once, rather than withdrawing her hand, she held it there, meeting his eyes. "I know ye don't believe me, but there are others who were there, who will surely bear witness for me. Ye'll see. I'm no thief."

Her blind faith left him sick at heart. Witness or no witness, Florie was clearly in the wrong. And she sadly underestimated her enemy. Lord Gilbert's justice would be swift and uncompromising, and his cruel wife would demand punishment to the fullest extent of the law.

He couldn't bear to tell Florie how hopeless her situation was. He couldn't bear to explain that no one would dare gainsay Lady Mavis, that the word of a goldsmith's apprentice was worthless, that she'd likely march to her death in forty days.

Most of all, he couldn't bear to reveal that he, Rane, the one man in whom she'd placed her faith, was cursed with the duty of guarding against her escape, a duty he was growing to despise more and more with each passing moment.

Against all reason and against all wisdom, his heart went out to the young outlaw. Rane began to wonder with a fearsome dread if he hadn't the will to hold Florie hostage, even for his lord.

CHAPTER 9

Florie woke the next morn, shivering violently despite the sun filling the sanctuary. But how could she be cold? Plaids swathed her body, and sweat beaded her forehead. Still, she couldn't stop trembling.

She lifted her lead-heavy head, far enough to see that Rane no longer slept by the church door. But then, the hour was late. She could tell by the angle of the light that she'd slept far past dawn.

What was wrong with her? Whatever 'twas, her troubles were multiplied by the urge to relieve herself. She needed to get to the door and outside, with or without Rane's aid, quaking or not.

She managed to prop herself onto her elbows but noticed at once a thick pressure around her leg, as if the bandage were tied too tightly. She frowned. It hadn't felt that way last night.

She struggled slowly onto her good knee, fighting a weighty dizziness that enveloped her like a shroud. Then she tried to stand, and everything went black.

The next thing she saw as she pried open her heavy

eyelids was a head of long blond hair draped across her body. Rane appeared to be listening to her chest. 'Twas strange. How she'd come to be lying flat on the floor, she didn't know, and what ministrations Rane practiced were a mystery. She tried to demand an explanation of him, but all that came out was a groan.

He swung his head toward her. "Florie!" Lunging forward, he took her face between his hands. "Are ye all right? What's wrong? What happened, lass?"

"C-cold," was all she could manage. "S-so cold." She scowled. But that wasn't the truth. She was hot, sweltering, drenched with sweat.

"The wound," he muttered. Without asking her leave, he rooted under her skirts to examine her injury.

"Too t-tight," she scolded him weakly. Lord, where was her strength? Her limbs felt as malleable as molten metal.

Whatever he saw when he loosened her bandages made him curse most foully. And when he pressed lightly upon the edge of her wound, fiery pain streaked up her leg, making her arch up from the ground with a thin cry.

"Bloody hell," he mumbled. "Wait here, Florie. Wait. Don't move. I'll be back."

She caught at his sleeve. She didn't want him to go. She didn't know what was wrong, but if he left her, she'd be alone with the pain and the cold and the fear.

His fingers clasped hers momentarily. "I'll be gone but a moment. Stay here. Promise me."

She wondered where he thought she might run off to. She couldn't stand, let alone walk. She reluctantly let her fingers fall from him, and she closed her eyes for what she believed was a brief moment.

But 'twas full dark when Florie emerged again from her

dreamless slumber. A single wan candle burned at her feet, casting the demonic shadow of Methuselah across the stones as the cat skulked past on his midnight rounds.

Florie's throat was as dry as chalk. And yet she thought she would burst if she didn't empty her bladder soon.

She remembered now. She'd fainted the last time she'd tried to get up. But how could she have slept the day away? Faith, what was wrong with her?

She flung out an arm, banging it on the fridstool.

"Florie?" Rane's whisper sounded, less than a yard away.

There was no time to be delicate. "I need the privy," she croaked.

It seemed as if he vanished then, or she must have drifted off, for she awoke to a sudden bang and the splintering of wood. When Rane returned, he bore a great bowl enameled with vines and various beasts.

She frowned. "Is that..."

Rane eyed her sternly. "'Tis a jordan."

She hadn't the strength to argue with him. She barely had the strength to use it.

For hours afterward, Florie floated between waking and sleeping, recalling only disjointed fragments of the day: the Father bringing fruit tarts, which she had neither the appetite nor the strength to eat, Methuselah sniffing at her wound, Rane chasing him away, a cool cloth bathing her forehead and throat, Rane poking and prodding and pressing upon her wound as if to torment her further, weak ale dribbling down her throat, Rane drizzling her leg with some burning potion... Rane brushing the hair back from her brow... Rane tucking the plaids around her... Rane, Rane, Rane...

She was growing to despise him more with each passing hour. Every time she was about to surrender to the bliss of unconsciousness, he did something to rouse her again. Usually something unpleasant.

He lifted her head, forcing her to drink. Or he loosened the neck of her kirtle, leaving her shoulders bare. Or worst of all, he pinched brutally at the tender flesh of her wound. King Henry's gaoler could not have tortured her more skillfully.

Somehow she managed to drowse, alternately shivering under the plaids and kicking them off when she became too fevered. And by afternoon, despite the agony Rane had put her through, 'twas *he* who looked worn and weary. Stubble darkened his jaw, and shadows ringed his eyes. He looked gaunt in the yellow candlelight, and the corners of his mouth turned down with grim fatigue.

The last image she had of him before she slipped into darkness again was in profile. He sat beside the fridstool, one long leg drawn up, his arms draped over it, his head bowed. His long hair fell forward over his shoulders, and his brow was furrowed anxiously. Now and then, a muscle in his cheek would tense. Florie wondered, just before she succumbed to her own ragged slumber, what troubling thoughts disturbed the archer's repose. Perhaps someone tortured *him* in his sleep.

Like a nagging mistress, a final brilliant shaft of fading sunlight goaded Rane from his afternoon nap after too few hours of rest. Nonetheless, he sat up wearily, his eyes as gritty and raw as shucked oysters, and shook the clinging cobwebs of dreams from his head. He ran his fingers over his bristled jaw, then back through his snarled hair, not because he cared 'twas tangled, but out of worry. Then he sought out the one who caused him that worry.

She dozed fitfully, twitching beneath plaids that bunched beneath her chin but bared her legs. Her brow was pale and glazed with moisture, and her eyes seemed sunken into her wan face. Her hair hung in damp strands over her shoulders like black seaweed on a sandy shore, and the breath she drew harshly between her lips sounded strained.

For two days he'd tended her, mopping her forehead, drenching her thigh in carmine thistle, trying to draw the poison from her festering wound. He'd dozed only briefly, awakening to every hitch in her breathing, every moan she made in her sleep. He'd never forgive himself if she worsened, and so he willingly cared for her, using the herbs he carried and healing skills honed from many a hunting mishap.

Yet for all his pains, she likely abhorred him. After all, 'twas he who kept her from the peaceful sleep she desired, he who bullied her with stinging elixirs and prodding to leach out the infection. And soon he was sure he'd have to embarrass her again with the indignity of helping her with the jordan. He wouldn't blame her if she longed to roast him alive when this was over.

But he didn't dare soften in his treatment of her. If he hoped to heal her, 'twould be only through battle, brutal and ruthless, her hatred be damned.

Gray spots danced before his eyes as he arose, and he realized he'd not eaten in nearly a day. The Father had kindly left a pair of Kate Campbell's apple tarts this morn, but when Florie refused hers, Rane had forgotten about his as well. And last evening's supper, Dame Malkin's cabbage skink in a stale trencher, still sat atop the fridstool. He didn't have the stomach for food, even now. Yet he knew he must care for himself to be of any use to her.

So he devoured the cold skink, washing it down with the watered ale the Father had brought. The apple tarts he saved for Florie. He might not get her to eat cold cabbage, but no lass he knew could resist apple tarts, especially Kate's. Like them or not, she would eat today, if he had to stuff the things down her throat.

Steeling himself for another night of unrelenting warfare, he pushed up her skirts to examine the loosely wrapped wound. She murmured a weak protest but didn't waken as he sliced through the bandage.

Her thigh was still warm to the touch, her body fevered, and the flesh around the puncture was yet swollen with infection. The carmine thistle had done as much as it could. 'Twas time for stronger measures.

His fingers strayed in painful memory to the scar that marked his own flesh in the hollow between his shoulder and his chest. He remembered what needed to be done. He must revive the stoked fire he'd built beside the pond so he could begin boiling water.

He carefully replaced the bandage and spread the plaids over Florie's limbs. Then he ventured outside.

The steel jordan Father Conan had finally thought to bring served Florie better as a vessel for boiling water, and for once Rane was glad of the priest's blindness, for if the Father had seen either of his vessels so misappropriated, 'twould have turned his white hair even whiter.

Once the water was set to boil, he added several cloves of garlic from the Father's overgrown plot of herbs, then returned to the sanctuary to find Florie out from under the plaids and shivering again. He replaced the woolens, leaving her thigh exposed, then drenched a piece of linen with the carmine thistle extract.

She awoke abruptly when he began swabbing the wound, kicking out reflexively and catching him in the ribs. He grunted. By Odin, she had a fierce kick for such a tiny thing.

"Nae!" she cried, thrashing.

"Hold still," he said gently.

"Ah, God," she groaned. "Why do ye torment me?"

Her voice, so puny, so helpless, caught at his heart. But he knew he had to be firm. "I must. 'Tis the cure for your ills."

"Stay away," she commanded weakly. "I'm weary o' your cures."

He tenderly brushed her forehead with the back of his hand. "I know."

To his sorrow, she recoiled from his touch. "Just leave me alone," she breathed.

A muscle jumped along his jaw. 'Twas his doing, all of this. He had shot her. And now he tortured her with painful remedies. But, damn his eyes, he was bound to her. He *couldn't* leave her alone.

"Ach, Florie, I'm sorry," he said. But she was already asleep.

An hour later, trudging back from the pond by twilight, Rane was filled with the same sick feeling he got when he had to finish the work of a careless hunter and put a deer out of its misery. His fingers quaked as he looped the bail of the jordan filled with boiling water over a thick branch to carry it to the church.

Florie still dozed. 'Twas tempting to do what he had to do without preamble. 'Twas the way he hunted. A stag scarcely knew what struck him when Rane let fly his arrow. The lass would awake with a shriek of agony, fighting like a wildcat, but 'twould be over quickly.

Then he remembered the brave lass who'd looked at him with trust in her eyes before he pulled the shaft from her wound. For all her feminine vulnerability, she was a strong lass, a sensible lass, not some unwitting animal he might attack unawares. She'd understand, and she deserved to know.

He set the bowl of still-simmering water on the flagstones, crushed several garlic cloves into it, and dropped in a clean square of linen. Then he unbuckled his belt, the belt that would soon bear two sets of her teeth marks. Finally, swallowing hard, he reached over and gently brushed her cheek with the back of his fingers.

"Florie," he whispered. "Florie."

She moaned.

"Wake up."

Her eyes fluttered open. To his dismay, she averted her gaze as soon as she recognized him. "What do ye want?" Her words were slurred.

"There's somethin'...I must do." He plowed his hand through his hair. "I'll not lie to ye, lass. 'Twill hurt like the devil."

Her chin trembled, whether with fear or anger, he wasn't certain. "Everythin' ye do hurts like the devil."

He supposed she was right. But 'twas for her own good. On impulse, he tugged apart the laces of his jerkin. "I want ye to see somethin'." He dragged his shirt down to reveal the jagged scar beside his shoulder.

She glanced sidelong at the spot.

"I was pierced by an arrow once," he told her. "My wound festered as yours has. Only one thing saved me. 'Tis the same thing I must do for ye." He compressed his lips. He well remembered his suffering. "Florie, I need ye to be brave."

That got her attention. She gulped and stared at him. "Why? What are ye goin' to do?"

He held his belt toward her.

"Nae," she breathed, fear wetting her already fever-bright eyes. Then she saw the bowl of ominously steaming water and stubbornly set her jaw. "Nae. *Nae*."

"I must draw the infection out."

"Nae!"

"It has to be done."

"Ye bastard," she whispered.

Her words cracked his heart. He scowled, dropping his gaze. "Bloody hell, lass," he ground out in frustration. "Do ye not think if there was another way..."

He could hold her down if he had to. 'Twould be little trouble for him to force her. But he didn't want to. Though it might mean the difference between life and death for her, still he wanted her consent. And at the moment, he could think of only one way to get it.

He blew out a long breath and shook his head. "I knew I should have done it while ye were unawares," he told her softly. "Faith, ye're only a wee lass. I cannot expect ye to be as strong as a man, as strong as *I* was. After all, 'tisn't as if—"

"Fine," she bit out, clamping her trembling lips shut and lifting her chin in a show of courage. "I won't be bested by a Viking. If ye endured it...then so can I."

"Ye're certain?"

Her curt nod relieved him and helped steady his hands for the task ahead.

"But," she added, "'twill come at a price."

He stared at her, incredulous. Even under such dire circumstances, Florie bargained like a merchant. "A price?"

"If I hold very still for ye and don't...scream," she said with quiet bravery, "ye must repay me."

"I don't have much coin," he admitted.

"I'm not askin' for coin."

"Then what would ye have?" Anything, he thought. He'd promise her anything, though he was certain she couldn't keep her word. Rane himself had writhed and bellowed in pain from the ordeal. And though she was courageous, she was also frail. "What would ye ask o' me?"

For a long moment, she only stared at him. Then she whispered weakly, "When my leg is healed and the English are gone...if my foster father doesn't come for me...help me escape from this place. Take me home to Stirlin'."

His heart plummeted. He'd expected her to ask for what most maids did—new stockings or a ribbon or the deerskin pouches he liked to make for them. He'd never imagined she'd ask him to betray his lord. Guilt sank over his shoulders like an ox yoke, made heavier by the trust in her eyes, trust he didn't deserve.

He couldn't keep such a promise, no matter how much he wanted to. Treating her wounds, seeing her fed, keeping her safe and sheltered were things he could do. But abetting in her flight...

"I pray ye," she breathed.

He furrowed his brow at her faint entreaty, her wide, vulnerable eyes. Then he cursed silently. Why he troubled himself over the matter he didn't know. The lass wouldn't be able to keep her part of the bargain anyway. The moment he held the steaming cloth to her tender flesh, she'd yelp like a cornered vixen. Surely there was no harm then in giving her a hollow promise. "Agreed."

He proffered his belt again, and now she took it, slipping it between her teeth while tears of apprehension seeped from the corners of her eyes. He blew out a hard breath, steeling himself.

"I'm sorry," he growled. He carefully exposed her wound. Then he slid his arm along her calf to cup the back of her knee with one hand, tucking her leg firmly beneath his arm and against his side. With the stick, he retrieved the steaming rag from the bowl. When he met her gaze, she gave an infinitesimal nod.

Then, clenching his jaw against the brutality of what he had to do, he slapped the scalding linen to her open wound.

Amazingly, she didn't scream, though she arched up in pain. He swiftly lunged against her, holding her down with his weight so she couldn't shake the cloth loose. The skin of her thigh reddened and quivered, and the squeals caught in her throat were like slashes cut across his heart. But she didn't scream.

A half dozen times he repeated the process, each time holding her tightly as the cloth cooled and her squirming subsided.

When he was finished, tears drenched her cheeks, and her chest convulsed with wrenching breaths that shook him to his core.

He felt like a monster. All he could do was take her in his arms and let her sob out her anguish upon his shoulder.

He rocked her, murmured apologies to her, cupped her head in his hand as her silent tears fell unchecked upon his shirt. He curled her hair behind her ear and swept away her teardrops with his fingers. He stroked her back, soothing her the way one would a heartbroken child. Then his lips grazed the crown of her head and lower, to her forehead, the arch of her brow.

For once, likely because she was exhausted, she didn't pull away. Indeed, she rested her head against his chest as if he were her fondest companion. And when his lips moved lower still, touching the bridge of her nose, her head tipped back against his shoulder in surrender.

He never intended to kiss her.

Seduction was the furthest thing from his mind.

But the fiery fever of her skin begged for the cool brush of his mouth, and she made no protest as he pressed his lips upon her closed eyes, then along her cheekbone. Sweeping one hand along her neck, he lifted her chin with his thumb and, hesitating only a moment, kissed her full on the mouth.

It began as a sweet kiss, a kiss of atonement from him, a kiss of yielding from her. But as she melted against him, her fervid lips seemed to sear him with their touch, as if she repaid him in kind for the torture he'd dealt her. He felt her restraint dissolve as she branded his mouth again and again, snagging her fingers in the front of his shirt and making feminine moans.

Her rising passion fueled his own desires, and soon his hands moved with schooled instinct over her body, threading through her hair, caressing her face, tracing the curve of her hip. Her response was so ardent and so unexpected that, like a stag shot through the heart with a hunter's shaft, he was felled by a bolt of raging lust. He felt the most overwhelming, ungentlemanly urge to pin her down again, to toss up her skirts, and sink his aching dagger into her maiden's body.

But, God help him, he was *not* a monster.

And she was not herself.

Breathless, he broke off the kiss.

She gave a soft mewl of protest that he pretended not to hear. Instead, he merely held her against his pounding heart, saying nothing, until her breathing slowed and she succumbed to her fatigue.

His mind, however, was far from silent. Conflicting emotions warred within him: guilt and lust, compassion and self-loathing, shame and wonder.

He hadn't imagined her ardor. Even now his lips tingled from her greedy kisses. She had wanted him. She had reached for him. Her desire, like a flaming arrow fired into a hayfield, had sparked his own, and now unquenched fire raged through him.

He had no right to seduce her. He knew that. Not while she was so weak, so vulnerable. But somehow, for the first time in years of seducing maids, Rane had been almost unable to stop himself.

'Twas irresponsible.

Unforgivable.

And uncouth.

Now all he had to do was to convince that snarling beast betwixt his legs.

He pressed a final kiss to the top of her slumbering head and sighed into her hair, maddened by the snare into which he'd let himself be dragged.

Still, seduction was not the most bothersome quandary

on his mind. The thought that truly troubled him, the thought that shook him to the core, was the fact that through the entire painful ordeal, Florie had never screamed, not once.

And now he owed her a promise he dared not keep.

CHAPTER 10

Soft snoring woke Florie. She cracked open her eyelids and beheld Rane, dozing with his back against the fridstool, his arms crossed, his head nodding on his chest.

He looked terrible. Gone were the tresses that shone like a sheet of satin. His hair hung in dull locks, unwashed and unkempt. His chin was covered in dark stubble, and his eyes were limned with gray shadows.

She wondered if she looked as bad as he did, as bad as she felt. Sweat covered her body, and her own hair was oily to the touch. Her leg burned, but the pressure of the swelling had ceased.

How much of what she remembered was true and how much a dream, she wasn't sure. The events of the past few days were as foggy in her mind as the Stirling moors. She knew neither how long she'd slept nor what day 'twas. She had vivid memories of being awakened again and again to endure the rinsing of her wound. And she recalled the agony of the scalding cloth.

But the thing she remembered most vividly was the

impression that she'd let Rane kiss her, kiss her on the mouth. And she had no idea why.

Florie seldom allowed a man to touch her, much less kiss her. Such a thing seemed...predatory. And yet, in her recollection, Rane's arms had felt, not threatening, but reassuring. The touch of his lips had not offended, but excited her.

She shook her head. Surely 'twas a dream, an absurd delusion of her fevered brain.

She lifted the back of her quaking hand to her brow. 'Twas wet there, but at least the unbearable heat had dissipated. And now she was famished.

She let her gaze drift over to the fridstool. There were two golden tarts there. If she could reach one of them...

She moved a quiet inch toward the pastry.

"What?" Rane burst out, coming alert so quickly that it startled the speech from her. He scrubbed the sleep from his eyes, then looked at her and frowned. "Ye're sweatin'."

'Twas true, though not the most gallant thing to say to a lass. She scowled. "*Ye* need a shave," she countered.

With the curious beginnings of a smile, he lunged forward, grabbing the back of her head and flattening his great palm against her brow. Marry! Did the man ask leave for anything?

"The fever, 'tis gone," he said happily, releasing her. "How do ye feel?"

Giddy. She felt giddy. As if his lighthearted mood was contagious. But that feeling confused her. "Hungry," she said instead.

He immediately retrieved both tarts from the fridstool and offered them to her. "Thirsty as well?"

She nodded, and he handed her his costrel.

Ale had never tasted so good. And when she bit off a flaky piece of tart, the chunks of spiced apple inside were remarkably sweet. Indeed, she was nearly finished with the pastry before she realized he was staring at her.

She looked down at the second tart, guiltily swallowing her last bite of the first. "This must be yours."

He smiled and shook his head. "Take it." Something mysterious shone in his eyes, a strange blend of contentment and relief and amusement that set her heart aflutter.

"But what will *ye* eat for supper?" Though she would dearly love to consume both tarts, her father had not raised a mannerless mop.

"Father Conan will come anon. I gave him coin for more food. Go on. Ye haven't eaten properly for three days."

She nodded and nibbled at the second tart. He was still watching her. His eyes looked bleary and careworn.

"Maybe ye should nap, then," she said. "Ye look as if ye haven't *slept* properly for three days."

He rubbed the backs of his fingers over his jaw, grinning. "That wretched?"

Indeed, she thought, he didn't look wretched in the least. The slight shadow upon his cheek made a stunning contrast to his fair features, the way topaz set off bright gold. Nae, though he appeared tired, he also looked more real, coarser, less like an angel now and more...human.

Lord, had she really kissed him? She wished she could remember.

Screwing up her courage, she picked idly at the tart, dribbling crumbs onto her kirtle. "While I was fevered..."

"Aye?"

"Did I..."

He lifted a brow, waiting for her to finish. When she didn't, he guessed, "Talk in your sleep?" Then he gave her a devilishly coy grin. "Oh, aye. Ye revealed to me the mystery o' turnin' lead into gold. But never fear—your secret is safe with me."

She could not help but smile at his nonsense. Turning lead into gold was the pursuit of alchemists insidious enough to find a way to leech off of foolish noblemen's coffers.

"Nae. I mean, did ye...and I..." She moistened her lips and furrowed her brow, intently studying the tart. "That is...did we..."

"Aye?"

She furrowed her brow at him, like a seer trying to read a particularly cloudy glass. But his expression revealed nothing. She shook her head. "I was fevered. Surely 'twas only a dream."

"What did ye dream?"

A short laugh bubbled out of her. The whole idea seemed daft now. She frowned at the absurdity of it. "Nothin'. 'Tis utter tosh, I'm sure. I dreamt that ye...that we...kissed. Can ye fathom that?"

She waited for his laughter. It never came. She glanced sharply at him, and there was a wistful quiet in his eyes as he smiled at her.

"Kissed? But ye don't remember for certain?"

He leaned toward her suddenly, and for one terrible, wonderful instant, she imagined he intended to prove the truth of it, to kiss her here and now. But instead he reached out to brush a stray crumb from the shoulder of her kirtle. Though he seemed not to notice, his forearm chanced to graze her bosom, and she felt his touch as if 'twas flame.

Were he any other man, she would have clouted his errant hand. But she knew Rane meant nothing by it. He simply attended to her the way he had with the jordan, with a gesture that was casual, functional, pragmatic.

Her response, however, was far from casual. His brief caress left her flustered and fascinated and shamefully aroused. Her breast tingled from the contact, and suddenly she was certain they *must* have kissed before, for her body responded to his touch as if 'twere not the first time.

"I assure ye, lass," he murmured with unabashed cocksureness, staring sensuously at her mouth, "if I'd kissed ye, ye'd remember it."

But she *did* remember it. Or she remembered the dream. Her mind reeled with phantom memories. She recalled the strength of his chest and the comfort of his arms around her as he cradled her against his heart. His mouth, she thought, had tasted like the sweetest ambrosia, cooling her fevered lips, slaking her burning thirst. Her pulse had surged through her ears like the deafening roar of the sea, and his gasps had echoed hers as their breath mingled. She'd felt her spirit rise, as if it floated far from her tortured body, and for the first time she'd not felt panicked by his touch but honestly craved it.

'Twas well and good 'twas a dream, she decided. Those kinds of untamed emotions—reckless desire, unruly passion—were what led a person down the path of self-destruction and dependence.

But despite Rane's denial, despite the wisdom of restraint, when Florie glanced at the inviting mouth she'd dreamt of kissing, her blood flowed like molten gold, and she feared 'twould be perilously easy to lend credence to the dream.

Eager to alter the amorous bent of her thoughts, she searched her mind for some safe subject.

His scar. He'd shown her his scar. She nodded toward his shoulder. "How did ye get your wound?"

He ran a hand over the place. "This? It happened long ago. A baron's son I took on his first hunt. The lad got so overeager, he fired at the first thing that moved." He shook his head. "Unfortunately, 'twas me."

Florie's eyes widened.

One corner of his mouth lifted ruefully. "I'm not certain which was worse, the lad shootin' me or his father praisin' him for his marksmanship."

"Nae."

"Aye."

"What did ye do?"

He shrugged. "I pulled the arrow out and—"

"*Ye* pulled the arrow out?"

"The lad panicked and ran. I couldn't very well lie there, bleedin'."

Florie gulped. What strength Rane must have.

"Like your wound, mine festered. The surgeon drew out the infection with scaldin' garlic water. Now I'm as hale as ever, save for the scar."

"'Tis hardly noticeable." Florie remembered too vividly the small mark in the midst of a glorious expanse of golden skin. And now that she thought about it, she also recalled the way his chest felt beneath her palms, firm but yielding, warm and supple. 'Twas far too tangible a memory to be the invention of her imagination. She'd never had such a lucid dream before.

Oh, aye, she realized, she *had* kissed Rane. And she *did* remember it now. Every inch of her body remembered it.

Yet he denied it. Why?

The answer was obvious, knowing Rane's nature. 'Twas the honorable thing to do. Florie had been feverish, only half aware of her actions. Rane, as always, was protecting her, this time from her own impulsiveness.

Father Conan was right. Rane was a good man.

"More ale?" he offered.

Their fingers interlaced on the costrel, and Florie was suddenly struck by the inextricable connection forged between the two of them. They'd gone to hell and back together. They'd shared not only pain but passion—blood and sweat and curses and kisses. Never had she been so intimately joined with another.

'Twas a heady feeling. And yet it left her dangerously weak...like her foster father, after her mother died.

The memory quickly sobered her. She took a drink and returned the costrel. She couldn't afford to indulge in flighty diversions, no matter how pleasant.

She was *not* like her foster father. She wouldn't make the mistakes he had. Her heart was her own. Her fate might rest in the archer's hands now, but soon she'd stand on her own again.

Independent.

Strong.

Self-reliant.

Aye, there was much she desired of Rane. But there was only one thing she *needed* of him, one thing he owed her.

"Ye know," she reminded him softly, "I never cried out."

He didn't answer immediately, tipping the costrel back for a drink instead. He wiped the foam from his stubbled upper lip with the back of his hand.

"Ye didn't," he finally agreed. "Ye were very brave."

But he said nothing more, and when she summoned the courage to gaze upon him, his face was dark, secretive, his mouth grim, his eyes shadowed.

She glanced away, her heart racing.

The decision to flee Selkirk had not been made lightly. After all, Florie had come here on a mission—to find her father, her *real* father, and escape the drunken nightmare that life with her foster father had become. Though her mother had never disclosed the nobleman's name, Florie knew that he'd once resided in Selkirk. She was certain that, armed with the distinctive gold pomander, she could find him.

Leaving now meant abandoning her quest for him and returning to her foster father, who didn't remember who she was half the time. But she was willing to do that, for there would be another fair in Selkirk after harvest. She could come back then, after all this unpleasant business was forgotten. Better she should return safe to Stirling than linger here for her trial. If she *could* return to Stirling...

God's eyes, did Rane mean to cheat her? The reality of the kiss she may have doubted, but she remembered well his pledge. Could he possibly intend to deny his promise? Betrayal lodged like a hangman's knot at her throat.

But she never learned his thoughts, for at that very instant, Father Conan waddled in through the church door with supper.

Florie, full from the tarts, let the men eat most of the fish skink and oatcakes. She conversed very little, except to reassure the priest that she was feeling much better after her bout with the ague. At heart, however, she felt sick. What if Rane broke his word and refused to help her?

Bloody hell, she hated depending on anyone. She'd seen what it had done to her foster father. He'd devoted himself wholly to her mother, and it had destroyed him. When death took her, he'd crawled into a tankard of ale and never emerged.

And yet she had no choice but to trust Rane, for the more she thought about it, the more she realized how few options she had.

She couldn't leave on her own, not while she was wounded and English blackguards roved the countryside.

She dared not go to trial, for with the merchants scattered, no guildsman remained to speak on her behalf or defend her honor.

She was alone, helpless, doomed to be tried and condemned.

She choked down a crumb of oatcake. 'Twas unthinkable. Rane *had* to help her. She had no other ally.

After supper, the priest groped for his staff and limped toward the door, calling over his shoulder, "Get a good night's rest. Tomorrow is the Sabbath, and I plan to say a Mass o' thanksgivin' in the sanctuary. 'Tis time these old church walls echoed with the word o' God again."

His words jarred Florie from her brooding. When the door closed behind the priest, she whipped about toward Rane with a look of horror. "Mass? I cannot go to Mass like this."

"Like what?"

"Look at me." Her hair hung in strings, her kirtle was rumpled, and she was certain the stink of fever was upon her. She'd never attended church in anything less than her best attire, decked in velvet, tastefully adorned with precious gems. And though her foster father thought it a waste of water, she always took a bath on Saturday evening, just like her mother always had, so that, in her mother's words, she would be sinlessly clean for the Sabbath.

Rane did look at her, a far too thorough perusal that took her breath away and somehow, despite her sweat-stained kirtle and sickly pallor, made her feel impossibly beautiful. 'Twas ridiculous. And yet the appreciation in his eyes seemed genuine.

"I...I must have a bath," she explained.

His eyes widened. "A bath?"

"In Stirlin', I always bathe before the Sabbath."

"Ye're not at your house in Stirlin', lass. Ye're in a church, an abandoned one at that. Here there are no tubs, no bath linens, no servants to heat water."

She frowned in frustration. Sanctuary was becoming damned inconvenient. But she wasn't about to give up. "I'll bathe in the pond."

He snorted. "Darlin', 'tis full night."

She glanced out the west window to the darkness beyond. "I don't care. I won't appear like this on the Sabbath."

"Appear before whom?" He sent her a one-sided smile. "No one worships here, save the mice."

"I've always bathed before the Sabbath," she insisted. "I'm not about to cease just because 'tis...difficult."

"Difficult? 'Tis nigh impossible."

Florie jutted out her chin. "I'll bathe in the pond."

Rane mouthed what she was certain was an expletive, drumming his fingers upon the fridstool, staring at her with mild irritation.

She didn't expect him to understand. After all, he was a

man. Stubble and sweat and mud only made him look more...manly.

He blew out a frustrated breath. "I cannot allow it."

"I didn't ask your permission."

"Nonetheless, I'll not allow it. Ye have an open wound. I didn't labor so hard to cleanse it of infection only to have ye foul it again in pond muck."

She ran a hand through her hair, unwittingly mimicking his favorite gesture. She supposed he had a point. "Then I'll lower myself into the well."

He coughed. "Into the well? Into the water we drink? I'm sure ye're as sweet as clover, love, but—"

"Curse it all!" she cried, at her wits' end. "I cannot live like this!"

"Ye cannot live otherwise, my lady," he said gently. "Indeed, ye should count yourself fortunate to have provender and a plaid against the chill. There are those who perish in sanctuary for want o' food."

'Twas the last thing Florie wanted to hear. That she might starve to death. And that she was helpless to do anything about it. The idea terrified her and made her all the more desperate to secure her escape.

"Well, I won't have long to worry about that, will I?" she asked, glancing sidelong at him. "After all, ye've promised to help me escape, haven't ye?"

He didn't reply. His eyes grew shuttered, just as they had the first time she'd asked him about the promise. An unwelcome frisson of fear skittered along her spine.

She spoke as evenly as she could. "Ye said ye would."

He wouldn't meet her eyes, and she saw him swallow uncomfortably.

She took a deep breath to steady herself, but 'twas

ragged and strained. "Ye promised that if I didn't scream—"

"I..."

He clenched his fists and his jaw, tensing, releasing, tensing, releasing, like a warrior deciding whether to advance or retreat, his scowl growing blacker by the moment.

Finally he shot to his feet. This time she heard his curse. 'Twas most foul. Without another word, he turned and stormed out of the sanctuary, slamming the door behind him.

CHAPTER 11

Even before the echo of Rane's oath died, Florie's chin began to tremble. She stared at the closed door in disbelief, and it blurred through her welling tears as her throat thickened with the urge to sob.

Rane had never intended to keep his word, she realized. He'd lied to her, forsaken her. After all they'd endured together—pain and succor, exhaustion and solace, shame and triumph—he'd ruthlessly betrayed her. Faith, his treachery stung far worse than any broken vows her foster father had made, worse even than her mother abandoning her.

But she fought back the despicable impulse to weep. Weeping was for weakhearted maids who couldn't compete in a man's world. Florie was stronger than that. She gave an angry sniff and whisked away the droplets gathered on her lashes.

Somehow she'd manage. Somehow she'd survive. She always had. She didn't need the archer. And when he came back, she'd tell him so.

If he came back.

It didn't matter, she told herself. She was better off without him.

Still, she couldn't help stealing glances at the church door every few moments. She worried her sleeve between her fingers and chewed at her lip as the candle beside her burned down a quarter of an inch, then half. Another half inch melted away as she adjusted her makeshift pillow beneath her head, scrunching the fabric into a shape more conducive to slumber.

But she couldn't sleep. The hour grew late. Where had the archer gone? To the woods? Home? Now that her leg was improving, had he left her for good? Would he ever return?

She flopped onto her side and pulled the plaids over her shoulders, smearing away a stray tear of self-pity with a furious swipe. She didn't care if he ever came back, she told herself.

After all, he was an arrogant knave.

A vile worm.

A miserable cur.

A black-hearted whoreson who…

The church door swept open abruptly, banging back against the wall, catapulting her heart against her ribs. In staggered Rane, struggling with a steaming cauldron. She rose up on her elbows with a puzzled frown. Muttering irritably, Rane lugged the heavy basin forward, finally setting it beside her on the flagstones.

"Oh," she breathed, suddenly realizing what he'd done. Indeed, so moved was she that she nearly strangled on the lump rising in her throat.

He scowled as if he'd had to travel to the Orient to get

the hot water, but she could tell her response pleased him. He dropped a linen cloth into the basin.

"I haven't any rose petals to sprinkle in, *my lady,*" he said with heavy sarcasm, shaking out his wet hands. "'Tis only a basin, not a full bath. But ye've got soap and a rag. 'Tis the best I can manage."

Florie's eyes teared up again, and she self-consciously brushed away the moisture. "'Tis more than enough," she choked out.

He grunted. "See ye don't get your bandage wet," he said, wagging his finger, "and leave me a little o' the water before it cools." Then he left her to her ablutions.

For Florie, it may not have been the most complete scrubbing she'd had before the Sabbath, but 'twas indeed the most welcome.

As she finished washing behind her ears, she cast a glance up at the cobweb-strewn altar, sending up a word of thanks to God for sending her Rane MacFarland, as well as an apology for all the wretched names she'd called him.

One more prayer remained. 'Twas not precisely a prayer. Indeed, 'twas more akin to a curse, and Florie flushed with chagrin even as she formed the words. She clasped her hands before her and made a silent appeal to Sebastian, the patron saint of archers, that until such time as Rane saw fit to keep his promise to her, his bow arm would tremble and his arrows would fly astray.

Mavis awoke in the dark, roused by the familiar, unwelcome ache, low in her belly, of her courses coming on. She moaned and reached out an arm for Gilbert. But she'd forgotten he was gone, summoned to the queen's court, leaving her alone in her misery. Frustration and anger twisted her mouth as tears filled her eyes.

She'd been foolish enough to hope that maybe this time his seed would take, maybe this time she'd grow fat and happy with a son, and she could forget about everything—King Henry's bitter betrayal, her exile from the Scots court to this miserable patch of land, and, aye, even that pesky whelp at the fair with the incriminating pomander.

But the stars had crossed her again. And now she'd be forced to endure another month of malicious whispers. She despised the gossips, who clucked their tongues, spreading rumors that the sheriff's second wife might do no better than his first and leave their lord childless. Worst of all, in the darkest recesses of her heart, Mavis lived in fear they might be right, that she'd be cast aside like one of Henry's barren queens.

She was getting no younger, and upon Henry's death she'd lost the protection of the English crown. If she didn't secure her future soon with Gilbert's child...

Even now she felt her authority slipping. Her own servants looked at her with pity instead of fear. The English soldiers were not so quick of late to come at her beck and call. Gilbert was away far too frequently on the queen's business, and though the Scots court was not the den of debauchery that King Henry's had been, Mavis wondered what tempting doxies lurked there. Then there had been the nasty surprise at the fair, which had caught Mavis completely off-guard, awakening her to an even more imminent threat.

Mavis's belly cramped. She winced, knowing she'd have to attend to her body's needs soon. But she knew she wouldn't sleep another wink until she decided what to do about that damned goldsmith, the conniving wench who'd managed to claim sanctuary in the old church.

If 'twere up to Mavis, there would be no more sanctuary. Henry had always felt the Pope held too much power, and Mavis agreed, though 'twas heresy here to speak of it. One day, perhaps, all that would change, but until then she'd have to abide by the dictates of the church, which meant that for forty days, no matter how much Mavis wanted to throttle the life out of the wicked trull who'd crossed her, she was untouchable.

But Mavis couldn't afford forty days. Every hour the urchin lingered in Selkirk felt like an hour plucked from Mavis's future. And now that Gilbert was away...

She pursed her lips in thought.

The wench might be untouchable, but perhaps she wasn't unreachable. Perhaps, Mavis mused, managing a weak smile despite the spasm snaking through her belly, there was a way to make the miserable whelp see the error of her ways.

"Shite!" Rane hissed, making Father Conan wince. "Sorry."

"Who is it?" the Father asked. "Can ye see?"

Rane scanned the furthest turn of the road, where the rising sun crested the horizon to be immediately swallowed by a bank of gray clouds. They were definitely coming this way—a retinue of lords, ladies, men-at-arms, maids—dressed for Mass.

"The Frasers. And Lady Mavis."

"Mavis?" The Father squinted with displeasure. "Shite," he echoed under his breath. "What does *she* want?"

Rane spit into the dirt. "Florie."

The priest straightened, as much as his bent back would allow. "She's in sanctuary. She cannot be taken."

"Nae. But now that Gilbert's away, nothin' would please Mavis more than to force a confession from her."

The Father exhaled, his breath making a thin cloud on the chill air. "What will ye tell the lass?"

Rane sniffed. Last night his loyalties had been wrenched between his allegiance to his lord and his vow to Florie. But with the coming of Lady Mavis this morn in force, the balance shifted. 'Twas an underhanded attack, blatantly cruel and utterly ruthless.

"I'll tell her to be strong." As an afterthought he added, "And silent."

"And what will ye tell your lord when he returns?" Father Conan asked gently.

Rane narrowed his eyes at the distant mustard-colored pennants drooping in the damp morn. What *could* he tell Lord Gilbert? That he questioned his own loyalty?

"'Tis a quandary, is it not?" the Father asked. "To serve two masters, one who'd own your soul and one who'd claim your heart."

Rane glanced sharply at the priest. What was he babbling about? Aye, he'd sworn lifelong fealty to Gilbert. But Florie had no claim upon him. She wanted his protection, not his heart.

Still, the priest's words were impossible to forget, and he pondered them all the way back to the church.

Rane prepared Florie for the ordeal as best he could. Predictably, when he told her the news, she thrust out her chin at a rebellious angle. But Rane knew her moods well enough now to recognize the subtle fear behind her feigned bravado.

"I won't have them starin' at me like I'm a two-headed ox," she declared. "I'll wait in the vestry."

"Nae. Ye must stay at the fridstool."

Frustration hardened her features. "Stay here. Drink this. Hold still. Rane, ye're not my master. I'm not some grovelin' hound to do your—"

He unpinned his cloak and whirled it about her shoulders, pulling the hood well over her face, muffling the remainder of her words.

"There," he said. "Now they can't stare. But heed my words, ye must remain on this spot. If Lady Mavis suspects ye've fled, she'll send her men to look for ye," he warned her. "Better ye sit where ye belong than have them drag ye, kickin' and shriekin', through the nave."

He didn't want to frighten her, but he doubted the men would hesitate to lug Florie forcibly out of sanctuary at Mavis's imperious command.

She sulked, folding the cloak about her until nothing was visible but the tip of her stubborn chin. "If she dares utter a word about—"

His hand shot out to snag the folds of the cloak beneath her chin in one fist, commanding her attention. "Heed me well," he told her sternly. "Ye'll say nothin'. Ye'll not speak. Ye'll not whisper. Ye'll not...hiccough."

Her fingers scrabbled at his wrist, trying to pry him loose. "And *ye'll* not command me."

"Thor's thunder, lass!" he hissed, releasing her. "I tell ye this for your safety." He sniffed, straightening the wrinkles his fist had left in the cloak, softening his tone. Why could he not be his normal charming self with her? Maybe because he cared too much what happened to her. "Promise me, Florie. Promise me ye'll be silent for once."

"Ye're a fine one to speak o' promises," she muttered.

He supposed he deserved that. And he supposed, as usual, Florie would do as she willed. With a sigh of defeat, he turned to go.

"Wait!" she said. "Will ye...will ye stay here?" she asked, trying to sound indifferent but failing.

Her sudden vulnerability caught at his heart. "I have somethin' to attend to. But fear not, wee dove," he said. "I won't let them have ye. I swear it."

Then, on impulse, he leaned forward, peeling back the hood of the cloak to press a light kiss to her forehead. 'Twas nothing indeed, only a tender gesture of comfort, and yet it tempted him to so much more. Her skin was fragrant and soft and warm, and he had no trouble imagining brushing his lips across more of it. *She* might not remember their kiss before, but he could think of nothing else. Only with great reluctance did he withdraw, tugging the hood forward over her face again.

He joined the Father, who awaited the arrival of his unwelcome guests at the door. Glancing back at the little felon huddled upon the fridstool, Rane was struck again by how small she seemed, swallowed up by his cloak. Small and defenseless.

"Pray, Father, do not under any circumstances let them take her from this place," Rane said.

The priest frowned. "And where will *ye* go?"

Rane narrowed his eyes slyly. "I suspect there's a deer in the forest who'd like nothin' better than to serve as supper for a certain man o' God and a fugitive in sanctuary."

Father Conan gasped. "Ye'd...poach? On the Sabbath? Right under Lady Mavis's nose?"

Rane's smile was grim. "Can ye think of a more opportune time? The entire Fraser household will be held captive here till the end o' Mass." He propped his quiver and bow in a shadowed corner of the narthex, within easy reach when he decided to slip out of the church. "Just make certain your sermon is...sufficiently thorough."

The old priest tried to look stern, but amusement stole into the wrinkles at the corners of his eyes. "Rane, lad," he confided, "I'd recite the entire Gospel for a bite o' roast venison."

Rane's kiss meant nothing, Florie told herself. 'Twas only a brotherly gesture, meant to lend comfort. She was no fool. Besides, she was vexed with him, wasn't she? He still hadn't addressed the matter of his vow. And yet her forehead tingled with the touch of his lips, and her heart raced as she inhaled the familiar rosemary scent of his cloak.

No one had kissed her like that—softly, tenderly—since her mother died. Oh, aye, men had made advances, usually when they were rutting drunk, but she'd never allowed a man to touch her. Wat, who would have fondled any willing lass, quickly learned how unwilling Florie was. Even her foster father, occasionally mistaking Florie for his lost wife, exhibited no more than a sort of pathetic lust, which was easy to fend off.

But Rane was different. He withheld nothing from her—neither his touch nor his emotions. He seemed to live life more fully, embracing it with body and heart. And for Florie, whose world was the narrow sphere of a goldsmith's shop, Rane offered a taste of adventure.

Lord, she thought, tucking her lip between her teeth, sometimes she longed to take that taste.

But that way lay ruin. She knew better than to let her emotions lead her actions. Every merchant knew the importance of keeping one's wits firmly engaged in any transaction. Her foster father's heartsick decline had proved the wisdom of that advice.

And yet a voice inside her, one that had been silent for years, whispered, *Aye, Florie, aye.*

Or maybe 'twas only the curious whisperings of the Fraser household, now filing into the church. One by one, they stopped and stared, hissing behind their hands and into one another's ears as she withdrew further into Rane's concealing cloak.

For Florie, accustomed to toiling in quiet obscurity at the back of her father's workshop, being on public display was more than unsettling. Before this swarm of murmuring strangers, she felt utterly naked. 'Twas an interminable ordeal of humiliation and disgrace.

"If only she'd confess her crime and surrender the piece," said a woman at the back of the babbling crowd, "she might save her soul."

Florie had met the lady only once, but Mavis's strident drawl was unmistakable. She didn't dare look, but she knew the lady would be wagging her beringed finger, her painted lips pursed in false compassion.

"Wherever are ye keepin' her, Father?" Lady Mavis inquired with false concern. "Where is the poor, misguided wench?"

Florie squeezed her eyes shut as she felt the suffocating press of the crowd. *Do not speak,* Rane had said. *Do not speak.*

"Gads!" Lady Mavis remarked in a loud whisper. "This *is* a rat's nest of a church, isn't it, my ladies? It must be crawlin' with vermin at night. I couldn't stay here a single day, let alone forty." She clucked her tongue. "Why would the miserable wretch abide in such filth, dyin' a slow death, when she could fall into the lovin' arms o' God with a simple confession?"

Florie bit her tongue. How could Rane expect her to be silent? Maybe he intended to speak in her defense. From the shadows of the hood, she scanned the back wall of the church where the archer had retreated. He was nowhere to be seen.

"Father Conan," Mavis inquired, "where have ye put the hapless wench?"

The Father's voice was laced with mild impatience at the stupid question. "On the fridstool, my lady, the seat o' refuge?"

Suddenly, Lady Mavis drew in an enormous gasp that seemed to suck all the air from the sanctuary. "Why, there she is, the miserable darlin'."

Florie stiffened.

Silent. She had promised to be silent.

Mavis widened her eyes at Florie, clasping a hand to her breast in a counterfeit show of sympathy. "Ach, sweetin', ye look half-dead already. Will ye not do the right thing and surrender to God's wi—"

"*Introibo ad altare Dei,*" Father Conan chimed in loudly from the altar, effectively silencing Lady Mavis with the beginning of the Mass.

As soon as the congregation's attention focused on the priest, Florie breathed a relieved sigh. Soon, soothing syllables of Latin wound around the nave, and she let her hooded glance drift along the faces in the crowd until it lit again upon the figure of Lady Mavis.

The lady might have been pretty once, Florie decided, fair of skin and even-featured, just plump enough to be considered ripe. She was dressed with keen taste in garments of richly embroidered ocher velvet, which set off her bright gold hair. The gilt pendant and rings she wore, though neither excessive nor flamboyant, were expensive.

Yet nothing about the lady was pretty anymore. She appeared to have been born into a world that was a grand disillusionment to her, for resentment was etched into every feature. Her mouth was set in a permanent pout, as if nothing could ever please her, as if life had been an enormous disappointment and those around her inadequate to the task of repairing her ills. Even now, beneath brows gathered like the dark clouds of a pending storm, she looked out of eyes as hard as jet.

Somehow, though Lady Mavis could not possibly see through the thick layers of wool, her eyes seemed to fix with hatred upon Florie, as if by dint of will she might expose her, condemn her, curse her soul.

Unnerved, Florie scrabbled beneath the cloak until her fingers closed around her precious girdle, as if to ensure it remained on her person. She would never give the lady her heirloom, never.

The Mass seemed to drone on and on, far longer than any she'd attended in Stirling. The stone fridstool was not nearly as comfortable as her cushioned workbench. Though her thigh felt much improved—Rane had assured her she'd be turning cartwheels down the nave in a fortnight—her hips ached from sitting. She shifted on the fridstool, flexing her feet back and forth beneath the cloak, trying to keep the blood flowing.

Then, just as Father Conan voiced the final amen, all of a sudden her twitching toe was caught in Methuselah's sharp claws, and she shrieked, drawing her foot back. She clapped her hands over her mouth in dismay as her cry echoed over the amen.

The sanctuary fell deathly still. She squeezed her eyes shut in dread. So much for her promise to remain silent.

"By my faith!" Lady Mavis wasted no time filling the silence. "What sort o' godless whelp," she announced with shaking self-righteousness, "would screech in the middle o' Mass?"

'Twas upon Florie's lips to give her answer, but what trouble the naughty cat had started, he unwittingly solved. He trotted from the fridstool with his ears flat, sidling up with ingratiating elegance to the Father's cassock, and meowed loudly in complaint.

"Ah," she heard the priest say, "Methuselah's remindin' me o' two vital matters. First, ye may have wondered about our guest before ye."

Florie gulped.

"As ye know, the church has always been a place o' sanctuary for the oppressed, the outcast, the poor, the misguided—the wretched sinners among us. It happens our fridstool is occupied by one such unfortunate. I intend to pray on her behalf that she may find God's mercy and redemption. And I entreat ye, as well, that ye look upon her not with scorn and contempt," he said pointedly, "but with that same mercy in your heart that is the keystone o' the house o' the Lord."

If Florie's chin rose a bit smugly, she could hardly be blamed.

"Secondly, I have a request o' ye good folk. As ye can surely see, though *my* poor old eyes are unable to appreciate it, this crumblin' church stands in sad neglect. I have, maybe against sound judgment, deigned to return in the hopes o' resurrectin' what has fallen to ruin. But I cannot do so without the help o' generous souls such as yourselves. Our most pressin' need is concernin' the vestry, where are kept the sacred articles o' service. It must be guarded against intrusion. But alas, the vestry door has rotted away."

Florie's brows shot up. Rotted away? Rane had only yesterday confessed to the priest that he'd kicked in the door.

The priest continued blithely on. "The thing must be rebuilt. So I'd ask humbly that any among ye with a timber or two to spare donate it to the church. Our friend Rane has generously offered to perform the labor."

Florie heard a definite collective sigh at the mention of the archer's name, and she noted that several feminine heads swiveled, searching for the elusive Rane. She frowned. Maybe there *was* something to that Viking curse.

'Twas completely unexpected, the sharp pang of envy that gripped her at the thought. And yet 'twas undeniable. Somehow, whether through their mutual adversity or common affection or mere familiarity, she'd begun to think of the archer as *her* Rane. And suddenly she was loath to share him.

How many lasses before her, she wondered, had felt the brush of his gentle hand, tasted his tempting mouth, maybe even shared the warmth of his bed? The thought pricked at her mind like a lad prodding a hound with a stick as she watched the parishioners file out of the church.

Indeed, so preoccupied was she with not only the idea of all those admirers, but also the notion that she should even care, that she almost missed the furious bit of whispering at the church door. There, Lady Mavis accosted Father Conan, pointing vexedly in Florie's direction, and at last loudly demanded audience with the outlaw.

Florie welcomed the opportunity. Mass was over. No one save the lady and a few of her faithful companions lingered in the nave. Let the lady come. After all, Florie was safe in sanctuary. Now was her chance to speak her mind.

Then she remembered her promise to Rane. She'd sworn she'd say nothing. But how could she sit silently by while the lady insulted her, threatened her, accused her of crimes she hadn't committed? Rane, like her foster father, didn't understand. Florie's temper, like ale kept too long in the cask, would explode if she didn't drain it off on occasion.

Still, Florie was a person of her word. She'd vowed she wouldn't speak. Torn between defending her honor and keeping her oath, she at last settled on a satisfactory compromise. After all, there were other ways of making her point.

Lady Mavis gave a simpering smile for the benefit of her ladies. "I only wish to see if I might persuade the lass to return what she stole from me, Father, to erase the stain upon her soul so she may die without sin."

As Mavis cast cunning eyes in her direction, Florie, smiling grimly and raising her chin in challenge, slowly opened the edges of the cloak to reveal her mother's girdle, gold and brazen and winking like a taunt at her hips.

Lady Mavis flushed as purple as amethyst. Her cheeks

quivered, and she sputtered in rage. Were it not for Father Conan's placating grip upon the noblewoman's arm, she might have barreled forward to strangle Florie with her own hands. But despite the lady's apoplexy, or maybe because the priest was blind to it, he didn't bow beneath her demands. Florie saw him smile, shake his head in apology, and make the sign of the cross.

Mavis hissed across the nave, "I'll see ye hang if ye don't starve to death first." She wheeled with a regal sweep of her skirts and slammed the door on her way out, hard enough to crack one of the hinges.

When she'd gone, the priest came to lend Florie reassurance. "Don't let Lady Mavis's overbearin' nature frighten ye, m'lady. She cannot violate the sanctity o' the church."

But his words were meager comfort, and Florie wondered if she hadn't been unwise to goad the lady. She'd seen the threat in Lady Mavis's eyes. She didn't seem the sort to let stone church walls or the slow wheels of justice or even God's will interfere with her thirst for vengeance.

Florie had to escape. Very soon. Aye, she'd wait until she was healed and the English were gone. But then she must flee Selkirk.

Rane's grip wavered as he aimed his quarrel behind the shoulder of the grazing stag. He compressed his lips into a grim line, deciding he must have a wish for death, or an affinity for irony, to flagrantly poach in Ettrick Forest by the full light of day while the Frasers attended Mass not half a mile away.

Yet what could be more favorable? Florie was protected

by a sanctuary full of witnesses, and as long as they stayed within, no one could mount guard over the forest. By God's good grace, Rane would find enough game to feed a few families until next Sabbath.

But there was another reason Rane hunted. He needed to prove to himself that his unfortunate accident with Florie hadn't ruined his hunting skills.

A half mile into the woods, a break in the canopy of trees allowed enough sunlight to keep a patch of meadow growing. A scattering of fresh deer spoor marked the narrow trail running along its perimeter. No doubt the tender clover provided a tasty feast for the forest dwellers.

Climbing a sturdy elm with a split trunk, he chose a vantage point in the crook, rested his bow upon his thigh, and waited.

He heard the soft foraging of the beast long before he saw it—the subtle rustle of reeds nuzzled aside to gain access to the young clover beneath. Rane eased an arrow into the bowstring and slowly pulled back. To his relief, his arms remained as steady as stone.

In another moment the deer's moist nose would emerge from behind the brush, and Rane would be perfectly positioned to take the unwary animal.

Cautiously, the stag appeared, its pale antlers mimicking the branches of the surrounding trees. It stepped cautiously forward, froze, swiveled its long ears about to listen for sounds of danger. But Rane was absolutely silent.

Another step and the creature would be completely exposed. It lowered its head to nibble at the sweet clover.

Now! Rane thought. He should loose his arrow now. One deer could mean the difference between life and death for a crofter's family. The animal was out in the open, a broad target, unaware 'twas being stalked. One well-aimed quarrel would kill it instantly, and he could have it gutted and skinned before it grew cold. Now!

But when the stag lifted its head and looked straight at him, its gaze wide and guileless, its flank smooth and unblemished, Rane saw only Florie, innocent and untouched, and his aim faltered.

He swallowed hard. He could do this. He *must* do this.

He closed his eyes tight, then, with renewed determination, opened them again. The stag's eyes were alert now, its ears forward, its haunches poised to bolt.

But though Rane clenched his jaw and furrowed his brow and cursed silently, demanding it of himself, he could not force his fingers to let the arrow fly. And then his arms began to shake.

"Bloody hell!"

His oath startled the deer, and it bounded away. Horrified and angered by his body's betrayal, Rane dropped the bow to the ground as if 'twere made of molten lead.

"Ballocks!"

He glared down at his trusty weapon, then at his quivering hands. He didn't want to think about what had just happened. Surely 'twas only a passing malady, a short-lived impotence. And yet dire eventualities managed to seep into his thoughts like poison.

If he couldn't hunt, he couldn't eat. 'Twas all he knew how to do. The Fraser household relied upon his talents, as did the crofters for whom he poached this year. If he lost the will to hunt, not only would he go hungry, but he'd doom half the burghers to certain starvation.

Nae, he thought, 'twasn't possible. 'Twasn't tolerable. He couldn't let one small turn of fate unman him. Choking back a lump of nauseating dread, he seized his bow and arrow and tromped back through the forest.

'Twas the lass, nothing else. Like the goddess Frigg, Florie safeguarded the woodland creatures by thwarting his aim. Once she was healed, once she was out of his life, he could purge himself of this debilitating weakness. Hell, then he'd load Lord Gilbert's tables with so much meat, the household would think every day a feast day.

Aye, as soon as Florie returned home, he'd be able to hunt.

Yet a part of him wished the lass wouldn't go.

'Twas admittedly ridiculous. After all, she didn't want to stay in Selkirk. All she spoke of was returning home.

Still, he knew there'd be a hollow place in his heart when she left. Maybe 'twas only that he was accustomed to her company after so many days. Or maybe 'twas the bond her sickness had forged between them. Maybe 'twas but the sorrel shine of her eyes, the rosy cast of her lips, the saucy angle of her chin, the inviting curve of her waist. Maybe, he thought ruefully, 'twas only that he'd been so long away from a wench's bed.

But nae, none of these rang true. He felt things for Florie that he'd never felt for another before. Not just a need to protect her. Not just a desire to take her in his arms. He felt...drawn to her, as if by magic.

A crow cawed at him from the high branch of an alder, as if to mock his superstitions. The bird was right. No faerie spell or Scottish bane or Viking curse bewitched him. He was beginning to sound as fanciful as Father Conan. 'Twas his own heart that took the reins, his *unwise* heart, for only a fool would allow himself to be drawn to that which had the power to unman him.

"Take this," Florie whispered to the priest late that afternoon, after Rane had changed her bandages and she was certain he was out of hearing. She wiggled loose one of her gold rings and pressed it into the Father's palm. "'Twill pay for what I've already eaten and buy our supper for the next several days."

She'd seen Rane return after Mass, his bow across his back, his hands empty, and she'd guessed at once where he'd gone. That his hunt hadn't been successful was no surprise. According to Father Conan, game was scarcer this year than any other in memory.

"Now mind ye," she added, "'tis gold and pearl and o' decent quality. Don't take less than a mark for it. And Father," she said softly, "I pray ye speak not a word of it to Rane. I wouldn't want to insult his pride."

She told herself 'twas because she couldn't *afford* to insult him. Her foster father had reminded her endlessly that one must never give offense to a man from whom one might stand to gain. Certainly she had everything to gain from Rane.

But she knew 'twas only half of the truth. Indeed, she cared for Rane's feelings. Whether she wanted him there or not, the stealthy archer was beginning to steal his way into her heart.

CHAPTER 12

Florie dreamt they were coming for her, Lady Mavis and the whole Fraser household. They had formed an ugly mob, and men-at-arms charged the door with an enormous battering ram. The pummeling was relentless, and the walls of the church shuddered, threatening to collapse about her.

Pound. Pound. Pound.

She started awake and sat up, her pulse racing, glancing toward the door, expecting it to splinter before her eyes. But there was only silence.

'Twas just a dream. An inane dream, she realized. Why would anyone storm the door of a church? 'Twas never barred.

Pound.

She nearly jumped from her skin. Someone *was* pounding at the door. She drew her good knee defensively up to her chest, watching the door shudder.

Pound. Pound.

She twitched again, then cursed her own cowardice. 'Twas ridiculous, she thought. No one had a battering ram at the door. There was a reasonable explanation for the noise.

She struggled to her feet and made her hesitant way across the sanctuary. The pounding grew louder and more threatening as she closed in on the door.

Mustering up her courage, she took a deep breath and snatched open the door all at once.

She startled Rane as much as he startled her. He slipped with the wooden mallet and caught the tip of his thumb.

"Shite!"

She might have cursed back at him, but all the breath had been sucked from her lungs.

Rane the Viking's son, like some ancient warrior, stood before her, filling the doorway, bared to the waist, in all his bronze glory. His hair was pulled back, bound with a leather tie, revealing his massive shoulders and the flexing muscles of his stomach. His skin, as golden as honey, was dusted with a light film of perspiration. And as she stood in open-mouthed awe, a droplet of sweat trickled down the side of his throat, past his arrow scar, and across the wide expanse of his chest.

Flustered, she forced her eyes back up to his face. But at the moment he was sucking on his injured thumb, and something about the sight sent another wave of heat rippling through her, discomfiting her even more.

Now flushed and faint, she dropped her glance to the ground, but the image of Rane standing so close, so naked, so beautiful, would live in her mind forever.

"Sorry," he said, withdrawing his thumb with an audible smack. "Did I wake ye?"

The absurdity of his question helped to sober her, but she was still reeling from the effects of the sensual heat roiling off of him like steam off of a simmering crucible.

"I'm repairin' the door," he told her. "It looks like someone slammed it right off its hinges."

"Lady M-Mavis," she managed to murmur.

Misunderstanding her stammer, he reached out to cup her chin. She held her breath. His hand was rough and dusty from labor, but 'twas as warm as malleable gold. "Ye needn't fear her, love."

She shivered. Lord, what ailed her? 'Twas not the first time he'd called her that. 'Twas not the first time she'd seen a half-naked man—men wrestled every May at the Stirling fair in their hose and boots. Nor was it the first time a man had touched her, though 'twas the first time a man had touched her and not suffered a cracked pate.

"I'm not afraid o' Mavis," she croaked. "Remember? I'm not afraid of...anythin'."

He studied her closer. "But ye're tremblin'. Are ye chilled?"

She gulped and shook her head. It took most of her willpower to keep her eyes trained on the stone steps. It took the rest to fight off an overwhelming desire to wrench her jaw from his grasp...or pitch forward into his warm, golden, naked embrace—she wasn't sure which.

She closed her eyes, hoping to dispel his disturbing image. "I'm just...weak, I suppose...from the wound."

This was ridiculous. She could certainly look at Rane. He was only a man, no different from any other. But when she lifted her eyes to meet those beryl-brilliant orbs, her lids dipped with something other than indifference.

Rane recognized the smoldering in her eyes. Desire. Pure, raw, unadulterated desire. The feminine question for which he always had a ready answer. And this morn that answer came swiftly and with great force, heating his blood and deepening his breath, rising so quickly it dizzied him.

"Ah," he said, realizing the truth. Florie wasn't afraid or cold or weak. She was aroused. He'd forgotten his state of undress and the effect it sometimes had on the lasses.

Not that he let it bother him. Indeed, gazing into Florie's smoky chestnut eyes, limpid yet filled with longing, he wished he'd forgotten his braies as well.

"'Tisn't that at all," he murmured, "is it, wee fawn?"

She swallowed visibly. Still cradling her chin, Rane loosed one finger to rest alongside her throat. Beneath his fingertip, her pulse pounded.

"Your heart's throbbin'," he whispered.

Her nostrils flared with a quick inhalation.

"And your breath is short."

Her eyes drifted shut, and her lips parted infinitesimally, enough to reveal the moist recess within, warm and welcoming.

Rane felt his own pulse race. "'Tis...somethin' else."

He stared at her mouth—her soft, pouting lips that were made for kissing. He was going to kiss them. Soon. And she was going to let him.

"Nae," she breathed, as if she read his thoughts.

"Ye said ye feared nothin'." He brushed his bruised thumb lightly over her lower lip.

"I...I..."

"I remember how ye taste," he murmured. Sweet. Warm. Willing. His loins tensed with the memory.

She made a soft moan, sharpening his lust to a fine point.

"Come, darlin'," he breathed. "Ye want it."

"Do not...call me...that," she said weakly.

He dropped the mallet to the ground with a thud. Then, encircling her with one arm, he tipped her jaw to an accessible angle and let his mouth stop her ineffectual protests.

If Rane had learned anything from a lifetime of hunting, 'twas the art of pursuit. The rules were the same for beasts or maidens. He knew how to steal up on them unawares, to seduce them into complacency, easing gradually closer and closer. He could anticipate their every movement, always controlling the pace, always calculating the moment of attack.

As he did now.

He kissed her lightly, nipping at her lips until she sought his. Only then did he press closer, sweeping his mouth across hers, accustoming her to his touch. When she answered with kisses of her own making, he teased her mouth wider until he could venture within. Then slowly, carefully, he let his tongue explore, first her lips, with tiny flickering tastes, and finally her tongue, licking like lightning over its moist surface. He caught her quick sigh in his mouth, soft with surrender.

Emboldened, he pressed her close against the bulge in his braies while his tongue plunged and swirled and tangled with hers. Moving his hand along her cheek until his fingers were entwined in her hair, he brushed his loins subtly but purposefully across her belly.

He knew what came next. She'd release one last shuddering breath of surrender and melt into his embrace. Just like all the other maidens. And when she did, he'd whisper something sweet in her ear, some endearment to reassure her that even though she may feel helpless in his arms, he meant her no harm, that 'twas safe to feel powerless, for he'd take control of her pleasure.

And so he had...until she made that sound in her throat.

'Twas little more than a faint groan. But it circled his ear like some primitive mating call, deep and savage, sending a jolting bolt of desire coursing through his body. And suddenly he felt utterly out of control.

As if bees swarmed through his brain, his head spun in a frenzied buzzing, and lust poured through his veins like hot honey. Every muscle felt shocked to life yet weak with need. He sucked a harsh gasp through his teeth and felt the air rasp through his lungs. And his hands, his capable hands, his expert hands that had caressed and coaxed dozens of lasses to pleasure and fulfillment, now trembled uncertainly.

Florie, Rane realized, was like no quarry he'd ever pursued. And what had begun as prey now became predator.

Florie's delicate hands gripped his shoulders, pulling him closer. She leaned into his chest, crushing the pillows of her breasts against him. And she began to kiss him as if she meant to devour him, opening her jaw wide to feast on his mouth and tongue, reveling in his flavor.

All the while she kept making those sounds, moans that were at once demanding yet helpless, deliberate yet fearful, expert yet artless. Sounds that were driving him wild.

Her hands slipped over his shoulders now, flattening upon his damp chest, and she arched her neck backward for his kisses, pressing her belly deliberately against the part of him that wanted her most. By Thor, he thought, he might well spill his seed in his braies if she continued.

With what was left of his wits, Rane momentarily pulled away, thrusting his thigh between hers to stop her inflaming movements. He dragged his hands down her back until he cupped her round bottom. Then he hauled her forward against his leg. She gasped as his thigh found the core of her need. Squeezing the muscles of her buttocks, he dragged her across his thigh as she writhed in wanton innocence against him.

Fortunately, not all his hunter's instincts were lost in a sensual haze. He heard the snap of branches behind him in time to salvage Florie's dignity. Or at least most of it.

Before the intruders could break through the trees, Rane tore his mouth from Florie's and pushed her away. Lord, she looked breathless and disheveled and utterly seductive, vulnerable and bewildered.

There was no time to explain his sudden retreat. She'd learn soon enough that they had visitors.

Assuring himself with a glance that Florie's disarray was not too incriminating, Rane caught up the sleeves of the linen shirt belted about his hips and slipped it up over his shoulders, forgoing the laces.

"Rane!" came a feminine cry from behind him.

Florie's eyes widened.

He glanced down. Shite! He might as well have a bloody quarterstaff in his braies. Briskly, he unbuckled his belt, allowing his shirt to float down over the blatant manifestation of his lust. Then he turned to meet the interlopers.

Florie bumped into the church door behind her, stunned silent.

She remembered when she was a lass, she and her mother had made a game of spinning in the meadow, twirling 'round and 'round, giggling with delight, until they were too giddy to stand. 'Twas how she felt now. She could neither walk nor speak nor think straight.

Her eyes felt weighted, her lips tingled, her blood seemed vitalized by the most wonderful elixir, and her body...lord, her body felt on fire. Thoroughly drunk on desire, she couldn't even muster the strength to be civil to their visitors.

Fortunately, Rane seemed to suffer no such affliction, though his voice sounded more strained than usual. "Good morn."

"Rane!" This time the voice came attached to a figure emerging from the woods.

A loud gasp ensued, followed by a second voice chiming in dramatically, "Oh, Rane! If I'd known ye were only half-dressed..."

Florie frowned and turned her gaze upon two of the loveliest creatures she'd ever seen. They had to be sisters, so alike were they in form and feature. Their skin was as pale as pearls, and blond curls peeked from their fashionable gable hoods of velvet studded with sapphires. Their twin kirtles, one of azure, one of emerald, embroidered with figures of leaves and flowers, marked them as nobility, as did the presence of a pair of servants in matching blue tabards who struggled behind them with several large timbers.

Much to Florie's consternation, she despised the beautiful noblewomen at once.

"My ladies," Rane replied, sketching a slight bow.

"Tut-tut, little sister, avert your eyes!" the first one cried, though Florie noted that the maid could not seem to look Rane over thoroughly enough herself.

The younger sister shielded her eyes with delicate fingers through which she kept peering at every possible opportunity.

"Please forgive my vulgarity," Rane apologized, laying a hand across his heart, which did little to conceal his undress. "Ye've caught me...at my bath."

He'd invented that, likely to protect her or maybe to hurry the ladies along. But he was wrong to beg their forgiveness. 'Twas they who had intruded upon him. They should be the ones begging *his* pardon.

"Oh, Rane," the young sister gushed, "ye could *never* be vulgar."

"Not even if ye were completely unclothed," the older added.

Then both sisters gasped and giggled in unison, covering their errant lips and blushing prettily. Florie nearly choked on incredulity, wondering if they'd practiced this particular speech.

Unable to listen to more of their simpering, Florie decided upon an excuse to quit them. "I'll fetch your bathwater, then," she muttered, limping awkwardly down the steps.

As if for the first time, the elder sister seemed to notice Florie. A tiny frown marred her perfect brow. "Why, Rane, is this a new servant?" she asked, her voice tainted slightly with something unpleasant.

Florie's hackles rose at that. A servant? God's eyes, she'd presented jewelry to Princess Mary in the queen's solar!

Suddenly she wished she'd already fetched the bucket of water that she might douse the sugary wenches and melt them. But then, she supposed the mistake was understandable. Florie had left her jewels within the sanctuary, and garbed in nothing but the oversized woad kirtle, she likely did resemble a servant. Still, the lady's condescending air nettled her.

Rane didn't seem to know how to answer the lady, and the truth struck Florie with the weight of a millstone. Nae, she wasn't a servant. She was less than a servant. She was an outlaw, which was far worse.

Better they should think her his maid.

Before Rane could respond, she blurted, "Aye. My ladies." She dropped into a respectful curtsy, wincing as pain shot up her injured thigh.

"Hm." The older sister cast one last appraising glare, then dismissed her, which suited Florie well. While Florie lowered the bucket into the well, the lady returned her attention to Rane. "We missed ye at Mass yesterday," she pouted.

"Aye," the younger said, aping her tone. "We missed ye, Rane."

"We fretted that maybe ye had a malady."

"Or a malaise."

"Or an ague."

The ladies regarded each other and emitted sad sighs together. Florie ground her teeth, trying in vain not to listen, and began to bring up the full bucket.

"I prayed for ye, Rane," the youngest added.

"I thank ye for your kind prayers, my ladies," Rane replied, beaming, "but as ye can see, I'm quite well."

They tilted their heads and smiled appreciatively, and Florie's fists tightened around the rope of the bucket as she hauled it to the top of the well.

"Oh, I'd almost forgotten," the older sister said, fluttering her hands. "The reason we came. Father Conan mentioned that ye had need o' timbers for a new vestry door."

Loosing the brimming bucket from the rope, Florie hefted it from the well by the bail.

"'Tis so generous of ye to offer your strong back," the younger said, her eyes dipping with transparent desire, "when the Father is so crippled."

Florie feared her fingers might snap the bail in half.

"'Tis generous of *ye,* ladies," Rane protested. "I thank ye on behalf o' the Father."

With a sharp clap of her hands, the lady in azure commanded her servants to stack the timbers at the church door.

"Actually, Rane," she confided, taking several steps nearer, "there is another reason we came."

The younger lady, at her sister's heels, nodded. "Indeed, we feared for your safety."

Rane sniffed. "My safety?"

"Aye," the elder replied, her eyes widening. "Did ye not know?"

"Know what?"

"About the..." The lady looked about her for witnesses, then hissed, "The outlaw."

To his credit, Rane remained mute.

"Aye," she whispered, warming to the subject. "There's a fugitive takin' sanctuary inside the church."

"A *dangerous* fugitive," the younger added.

Rane coughed then, though Florie was almost certain the sound concealed a laugh.

"We saw her at Mass. A horrible creature," the first continued with a shudder. "'Tis a female, but not such as my sister or myself."

"Indeed?" Rane managed a frown, but Florie thought she detected crinkles of laughter at the edges of his eyes.

"She is o' monstrous proportions," the younger breathed, "an old hag with an enormous hunched back and..." She pressed a hand to her forehead as if she might swoon.

"Oh, poppet!" the eldest said, patting her sister's arm. "Ye mustn't fret so." Then she said solemnly, "I caught a glimpse o' her face—ugly as sin."

Rane scowled, pressing his lips together, and this time Florie was certain he bit back laughter. "I appreciate your concern, my ladies."

The lass in azure sidled even closer to him. "Ye *are* our dear, dear friend, Rane, after all, and since we knew ye'd be laborin' inside the sanctuary..."

"Aye," the younger purred, fluttering her eyelashes. "We couldn't bear it if anythin' should happen to ye."

Florie feared if she clenched her jaw any harder, she'd crack it.

"I assure ye, gentle ladies," Rane said, "I can protect myself from...monstrous lasses."

Florie doubted that. This pair of monstrous lasses had him drinking up their flattery and dining from their fingers like a spoiled hound.

"Oh, we never doubted that," the older sister said with a coy grin. "After all, Rane, ye're so strong and capable..."

"And brave and cunnin'..."

Florie couldn't listen to another word. She dropped the bucket with a thud, nearly splashing water over the sisters' blue satin slippers. They gasped. In unison, of course.

"If ye need anythin' else...master," Florie drawled, "I shall be within the sanctuary." She picked up her overlong skirts. "And don't worry on my account, my ladies," she said pointedly to the sisters. "I know how to protect myself from monstrous lasses as well."

As she limped up the steps of the church she heard the ladies murmur, "Rane, how do ye put up with such an impertinent servant?" and "He's done it for charity, poppet. See? She's a cripple."

Florie slammed the church door with a satisfying bang, half hoping 'twould fall off its hinges again.

Now she'd done it, Florie thought as she hobbled toward the altar. Her leg was throbbing again. Still, when she thought about it, the pain was nothing compared to what she felt in her heart.

She knew she had no right to feel anything. After all, Rane didn't belong to her. Even if she *had* kissed him. Even if he *had* carried her to sanctuary and brought her a bath and helped her with the jordan and saved her leg from festering.

She let out a sharp sigh. In another week or so, she'd leave this place and never return. She must remember her intentions. 'Twas foolish to develop anything more than a fleeting liaison with the man.

But for the moment, she intended to make herself useful. 'Twas the way she dealt with the unpleasantness of her life. After her mother died, she'd thrown herself wholeheartedly into her work, and it had given her great solace.

The vestry, she thought. 'Twas a mess. The blind priest likely had no idea that cobwebs hung from every corner, dust lay thick upon the Christmas service, and Methuselah had made a bed for himself out of altar cloths. While the vestry door hung shattered on its hinges, she might as well trespass there and tidy the place.

The first thing she did was chase the old cat from his nest with a hiss. Then, winding her hair into a knot at the nape of her neck and rolling back her long sleeves, she got to work. Echoes of the sisters' ingratiating voices haunted her, however, the whole time she labored.

"Oh, Rane," she mimicked with thick sarcasm, piling the dirty service linens in the middle of the floor, "if I'd known ye were only half-dressed..."

She wondered if Rane was so stupid as to be gulled by such empty flattery.

The cope, maniple, and chasuble hanging on pegs she took out of the room, shaking them until dust rained down over the flagstones.

Stealing into the storage room opposite, which was in even worse condition than the vestry, Florie managed to locate a broom. She swept away the webs and the worst of the dust from the furnishings. Then she used the damp cloth to scrub the chests and table until they gleamed and the grain of the dark wood was visible again.

Next she went to work on the floor, sweeping up cat hair and mouse droppings and dead flies, chipping up globs of wax from the stones with a hoe she found in the storage room.

She'd wash the linens in well water later, when the ladies were gone, after they were done admiring their...what was it they'd called him? She lay a palm upon her bosom, sighing in mockery. "Our dear, dear friend."

She rolled her eyes, then brushed back a stray lock of hair to survey the work she'd done. 'Twas far from perfect. The wood needed a coating of tallow, burnished to a soft luster, and the stone floor could use a thorough scrubbing. But the worst of the mess was gone. And once she laundered the linens and folded them away into one of the chests, Methuselah's attempts to turn the vestry into his own opulent den would be thwarted.

She picked up the broom one last time to sweep away the dregs of the dust, wondering how much longer the ladies were going to keep Rane from his work. "Oh, Rane," she purred, "'twas so kind o' ye to offer your strong back. Ye're so brave." Then she muttered, "Stupid wenches, fawnin' over him like he was some Vikin' god."

A low chuckle told her she was no longer alone. She whipped around in horror. Curse the hunter's stealth! He'd stolen up on her again. Holy saints, how long had he been listening?

Surely long enough to hear the part about the Viking god. She bristled to think she'd said such a thing. Yet gazing at him now, as he propped one arm against the top of the vestry doorway—the contours of his chest visible beneath his thin shirt, his long hair escaping the leather tie to soften the square line of his jaw, his face washed clean and comely and swathed in an amused grin—her heart fluttered, and she found it difficult to believe he was not indeed divine.

"Ye disapprove o' my companions?" he inquired.

She tore her gaze away from his magnificent body with difficulty. She remembered how it felt against hers. "'Tisn't my place to approve or disapprove."

"Still, ye think them, what was it? Stupid?"

Nae, she didn't think them stupid. Indeed, they were brilliant. After all, they'd managed to garner a good hour of Rane's attentions with little more than the sway of a skirt and the flutter of an eyelash.

"Nae," she admitted with a sigh, "they're not stupid."

"I find them charmin'," he pronounced, proving her point.

"O' course ye do," she said, hoping he didn't notice the inexplicable bitter edge to her voice, an edge that almost sounded like...jealousy.

He did notice. "That upsets ye," he remarked, his grin widening smugly.

"Nae," she lied. "'Tis no matter to me at whom ye wag your tongue." Under her breath, she added, "Or your yard."

He choked on a laugh. "My what?"

She felt her cheeks pinken. "Nothin'."

He grinned. "Ye think I've bedded them."

"Have ye?" she blurted.

"I thought 'twas no matter to ye."

"'Tisn't." Her grip tightened on the broom.

"Yet ye're certain I have."

She shrugged. "Ye said ye found them charmin'."

"I find many lasses charmin'. I don't bed them all."

All this talk of bedding was warming Florie's cheeks. Her mind, too, was beginning to dredge up visions of that sheer linen shirt torn away, of blond hair spilled across a bolster...

"Surely with that Viking curse o' yours," she said hoarsely, "ye could have any lass ye—"

"The curse I keep tellin' ye isn't true?"

"Well, *they* obviously think 'tis true," she snipped, unable to conceal her rising temper.

He chuckled. "If 'twill smooth your feathers to know, lass, nae, I've not...wagged my yard at them." She hated to admit it, but his words did relieve her in some small measure. At least until he added, "After all, every man knows 'tis a fool who'd swive sisters."

Vexed anew, she scowled at the floor, sweeping her broom in irritated stabs at an imaginary patch of dirt and silently cursing shallow-pated men. "Maybe ye can convince the wee darlin's to give up their sisterhood, then, so ye may swive whom ye—"

His hand closed abruptly over hers on the broom, and she jumped, unaware he'd left his spot in the doorway. She stopped sweeping, and their gazes locked. His fingers were warm, cupping her hand as perfectly as the setting of a jewel, and his eyes were even warmer, their blue-green depths lit by amusement.

His nearness was intoxicating, and she suddenly longed to toss the broom aside and continue where they had left off, to lean into his embrace and taste his passion again.

But she'd learned something from the sisters this morn, something that made Rane's advances easier to resist. She'd learned she was no different in his eyes than any other maiden. He treated them with the same honor and kindness, the same sly smile and coy glances that he offered her. 'Twas evident Florie held no special place in his heart. And while 'twas what she claimed to want, the truth was Rane was special to her. Whether she willed it or not, 'twas more than mere lust that called her to him.

Yet she knew she must protect her heart at all costs. If that meant she couldn't have the liaison she desired with Rane, so be it. She'd leave his seduction unanswered.

Rane, as if spying upon her mind, retracted his hand and nodded at the broom, retreating to safer discourse. "I see ye've taken your servant's role to heart."

"I'm only earnin' my keep."

He glanced about the room, clearly impressed. "Indeed, if ye continue to earn your keep so well, the Father may decide to keep ye longer." Just then Methuselah peeked between Rane's legs, slinking possessively around his calf with a shiver. Rane reached down to scratch the old cat's grizzled head. "Though Methuselah may not be so pleased. Ye've despoiled his luxurious lodgin's."

Florie sniffed. Even the cat sided with Rane against her. "He'll have to make extreme penance for the offense he's done this holy place."

"As will I," he replied with a wink. "Come along, old man," he said to the cat. "Let's see if we can unearth an ax to split these timbers."

Florie missed Rane as soon as he left. 'Twas absurd, she told herself. She preferred to work alone. She always had. Moreover, the fact that she could possibly care for a dullard so easily gulled by a pair of scheming wenches riled her. But as she carried the bundle of linens to be laundered outside, her foolish heart quickened in anticipation of setting eyes on the handsome Viking again.

He was splitting timbers beside the church, swinging a heavy ax in his gloved hands as if 'twere feather light, his shoulders straining the fabric of his shirt, his back damp with sweat. His hair was secured once again with the leather thong, exposing his clenched jaw and furrowed brow. He took no notice of her, so she watched in uninterrupted fascination.

He truly was splendid, no matter that his wits today seemed as soft as pure gold. 'Twas little wonder the sisters pursued him like adoring pups, their tongues all a-wag. The Viking son would one day make some lass a fine husband.

Handsome and healthy.

Good and generous.

Strong.

Comely.

Kind.

"Somethin' amiss?"

Florie, enveloped in a sudden and overwhelming melancholy, only stared at him, deaf at first to his words.

"Florie," he called again, resting his ax upon his shoulder. "What's wrong?"

Everything, she thought.

Everything was wrong.

She was trapped in a strange place, accused of a terrible crime, and somehow, incredibly, falling in unrequited love with a man she'd likely never see again.

"Nothin'," she lied softly. "Nothin's wrong."

CHAPTER 13

Rane spent the entire day laboring on the vestry door, partly because it needed to be done, mostly to keep his hands busy, for they wanted nothing more than to curve about Florie's waist and haul her close for a heated kiss, to caress the thick sable masses of her hair, to awaken her warm, willing flesh. And the fact that between spates of furious cleaning in the sanctuary Florie sat on the steps of the church, watching him as he split and sawed, measured and planed, sanded and hammered, only aggravated his lusty mood.

Why he couldn't simply seize her and be done with it, he didn't know. He'd never let conscience stand in his way before. But somehow, what he felt for Florie was different from the wanton play in which he normally engaged. He wanted more from her, more than just a harmless tryst, more than just a rollicking tumble in the grass. And frankly, that alarmed him.

By the time he'd cut new hinges out of a leather purse found among the wreckage of the storage room and tapped loose the lock assembly from the old door to secure it to the new wood, evening clouds were gathering, and he was no closer to assuaging his thirst for the enchanting lass. Indeed, his desire seemed to wax with the passing hours.

As he lugged the finished door through the sanctuary, he glimpsed Florie upon the fridstool, her skirts pushed up as she adjusted her loose bandage. The sight of her bare leg nearly made him drop the heavy door. 'Twas absurd, he knew. He saw that leg every day. And yet 'twas ever like the first time.

"I'll change that when I'm done here," he grumbled.

Mere days ago, she would have snatched her skirts down in horror. Now, to his chagrin, she continued to bend her wounded leg this way and that, completely without modesty. He wondered how long that immodesty would last if she knew what corrupt thoughts streamed through his mind at the sight of all that tempting flesh.

"All my movin' about today must have loosened the bandage," she said.

He glanced about the sanctuary. She *had* been industrious. Not a cobweb remained in the corners. The flagstone floor had been swept clean, and the wooden panels around the perimeter of the church gleamed with beeswax. She must have poked about in the storage room, for a half-dozen iron holders fitted with tall tallow candles stood about the nave like guards. The apse was littered with glazed earthenware bowls of all sizes, and beneath Florie's sweetly curved bottom nestled what looked to be a brocade cushion.

How he envied that cushion.

"Rane."

He grunted, forcing his eyes to her face. She was staring

at his handiwork with a puzzled frown. He righted the door and propped it against the vestry passage. "What?"

"Did ye notice..." she began tentatively.

"Notice what?" All he'd noticed were the soft, silky planes of her thigh.

"The..." She pointed to the narrow vertical gap carved out at the bottom of the door near the hinge.

One corner of his mouth drifted up. She'd spotted his modification. "Ye mean...Methuselah's doorway?"

Her jaw fell. "Ye didn't!"

"I did." He bit back a grin. "Couldn't leave the old cat out in the cold, after all."

As slow and sweet as honey, a conspiratorial smile poured over her face. Lord, 'twas irresistible. "But the Father..."

"Is blind. I won't tell him, if ye don't."

Then, as if prompted, Methuselah trotted up to the door, sniffed at it suspiciously, and wriggled through the crack.

Florie and he laughed together, and he felt the warmth of their mated laughter waft over him like a summer breeze. 'Twas an intimate moment, this secret they shared, a closeness he'd never experienced before with a maiden. Her guard relaxed, she reacted with abandon, giggling with joy, and he felt swept along on the tide of her delight.

"What's all this levity in my church?" came the old priest's voice from the entrance to the sanctuary, which only made them laugh all the harder.

Rane was too exhilarated to resent the intrusion, especially since it came with partridge pie and cool perry sent from Gwen, the miller's daughter.

Florie, too, greeted the priest happily, raving about

Rane's excellent carpentry and pouring the Father's drink for him.

And all the rest of the night Rane felt giddy, as if he'd become drunk not on the perry, but on that one sip of shared laughter.

Florie half expected to awaken the next morn to find the priest and the archer *still* engaged in their lighthearted argument about which God created first—the egg or the hen.

But the sanctuary was quiet, lacking the jollity of the night before. The only remnant of their pleasant supper was the linen rose Rane had cleverly folded for her out of a napkin.

She smiled. Where was the archer this morn?

When she swung open the church door, 'twas onto a surprising white sea of fog, a sea that rolled across the sward to obscure all but the highest branches of pine, poking out of the mist like masts of ships. She shivered, wrapping the plaid closer about her shoulders.

Somewhere beyond the cloudy veil, a scratching like the sound of a goldsmith's filing echoed softly in the heavy air.

"Who's there?" she called, though she instantly regretted her incaution. After all, the sound could be anything—wolves gnashing their teeth, mice gnawing on bones, English soldiers sharpening their swords for her neck.

To her relief, 'twas Rane who emerged from the fog, a dagger in one hand, a couple of small wooden objects in the other. He looked even more like an invading Viking this morn as he strode toward her, his brow furrowed, breaths of mist curling about him and silvering his hair.

"Good morn," she managed, trying to convince her racing heart that Rane was neither pillaging Norseman nor seductive enchanter, but simply an ally. Never mind that he was as handsome as Lucifer, as well made as Adonis...

"Morn? 'Tis past midday." He grinned, his teeth a bright contrast to the dull afternoon. "The Father's already come and gone with bread and cheese."

Florie didn't care. She wasn't hungry. All she'd thought about upon awakening was seeing Rane again. 'Twas a sickness, she decided, one for which she had no cure. No amount of reason convinced her pulse to keep to its composed pace when Rane was in sight.

"But never fear," he continued, sheathing his dagger and reaching into his pouch for a linen bundle, "I fought Methuselah for his share and won." He offered her the parcel of food.

Florie accepted the gift, noting the way his fingers lingered on hers. She glanced at his hand. "Ye seem to have suffered no scars for your battle with the cat," she jested.

"'Twas more a battle of wits," he replied with a saucy wink.

"Yet ye won?" she teased, arching a brow.

He gave her a devilish grin. A friend, Florie reminded herself, he was a *friend*. A friend with crystal eyes the transparent shade of aquamarine...

She unwrapped the bundle of hard cheese and bran bread. For one ungracious moment, her spirits sank. She wished she were back in Stirling, where she was accustomed to supping on venison pies and sweet lemon crokain, pickled salmon and roast Warden pears. But since a beggar could not choose his own meals, 'twas what she must content herself with. And if 'twas good enough for Rane, 'twas good enough for her.

"Thank ye." Hoping her disappointment didn't show on her face, she broke off a piece of the dark bread and nodded toward the wooden pieces he carried. "What do ye have there?"

He shrugged, then said enigmatically, "A cure for boredom." At her frown he explained. "Ye'll soon tire of chasin' Methuselah, listenin' to Father Conan's sermons, and watchin' me build doors," he said, turning one of the curious carved figures between his fingers to study it.

Florie thought watching him build a door was anything but boring.

He handed her one of the pieces. 'Twas carved roughly in the shape of a man.

"A chess piece?" she guessed.

"*Hnefatafl.*"

She arched a brow.

"Hnefatafl," he repeated. "'Tis an ancient game taught me by my father. This is a *toefler,* one o' the warriors who guards the king."

She frowned at the piece, which resembled the knight of a chessboard. The figure had a sword and a rough helm, but it lacked the articulated armor and grim battle features that would bring the warrior to life. She held a hand out for his dagger. "May I?"

He handed her the knife. 'Twas not as precise as her goldsmith's tools, but 'twas sharp. The wood was less yielding than the soft gold to which she was accustomed, but she managed to gradually carve away little chips until she achieved the effect she desired.

So engaged was she that she didn't notice how close Rane had drawn until he spoke.

"By Odin," he breathed, "'tis wondrous."

She glanced up at him, knowing full well her father would disagree. He'd tell Florie her work was grotesquely coarse. Still, the genuine amazement in Rane's eyes sent a flush of pride through her. "'Tis crude," she argued halfheartedly.

"Nae." His expression was serious. "'Tis ingenious."

Flustered by his praise, she set the finished piece upon the church step. "What's the other one?"

"This is Hnefi, the king."

She studied that one as well, deciding it needed a more ornate crown and maybe a scepter. This time, she was all too aware of Rane's attention as he watched her sculpt the tiny piece. Her grip faltered, and she slipped with the dagger, pricking her finger.

"Shite!" she hissed before she thought, dropping the knife.

He seized her hand to look at it before she could pop her finger into her mouth, as was her habit when she nicked it at her workbench.

"My dagger's too large for such fine work," he muttered. Then, before she had time to be shocked, he licked the pad of his thumb and pressed it to her bloody finger. At her stunned expression he explained, "To stop the bleedin'."

It sent her thoughts reeling to think that his spit mingled with her blood. 'Twas distressingly...intimate.

When the flow ceased, they agreed that Rane would roughly carve the figures and explain the game to her. Later, when he found a smaller knife, Florie could refine the pieces.

The carving took most of the day, but when 'twas finished, Rane sat cross-legged before her, placing a plank marked with squares on the step between them.

He rubbed his hands together eagerly, placing the king in the center square of the board. "Hnefi goes here on his throne. And his warriors," he said, placing the lighter wood pieces in a diamond shape surrounding the king, "guard him. These toefler," he explained, arranging the dark pieces in a symmetrical pattern along the four edges of the table, "are the opposin' warriors. They're charged with capturin' the Hnefi before he can escape to one o' his castles." He indicated the four corners.

"But there are twice as many toefler."

"Ah, but the king's guard is quite powerful. Ye'll see."

She did see. Halfway through the first game, even though he obliged by giving her the larger dark army, his guard had surrounded and removed over half of her pieces.

Frowning, she moved one of her warriors tentatively forward, keeping her finger on the piece.

"Are ye certain ye wish to move him there?" Rane asked.

She studied the board. "Fairly certain."

"Hm."

She bit the corner of her lip, unsure whether Rane meant to assist or hinder her. "Would *ye* move him there?"

He sniffed. "Maybe not. Not yet. Not while the Hnefi advances on that corner, that *unprotected* corner."

"Ah." She put her piece back and moved another to block the Hnefi's escape.

He moved a light piece beside her dark and captured another of her men.

"Varlet!" she cried, swatting at his arm. "Ye weren't helpin' me. Ye've taken another!"

"Aye, but if I hadn't warned ye, my Hnefi would be in that far corner now."

She sighed. He was right. She may have sacrificed a piece, but she hadn't lost the game. Not yet.

"Aha!" she said, finally hemming in one of his pieces and snatching it triumphantly from the table.

He slid one of his toefler across the board and returned the favor.

"Damn!" she said, clapping her hand across the curse too late.

He chuckled, taunting her by wiggling her captured piece between his fingers.

So they continued to play the game, no sooner ending one round than they began another, advancing and attacking and seizing the wooden pieces with all the ferocity of real kings at war. 'Twas little wonder, Florie decided, that the ancient Norsemen sailed so eagerly to battle, if they played this game with half the ruthlessness Rane did. As a victor he was irritatingly arrogant, but 'twas not long before Florie, fueled by revenge, finally managed to outmaneuver his pieces and dominate the board.

Naturally, after she won a round he sought retribution, and so they continued, like warriors obsessed, hour upon hour. When the Father brought supper, they resumed the game in the sanctuary, scarcely pausing to eat and hardly mindful of the priest's attempts at conversation. Finally, Father Conan abandoned hope and left them to their vice.

Ere long the cat streaked past for his evening prowl. A distant wolf howled at the materializing stars. The half-moon rose, then peaked, finally starting its descent. And still Rane and Florie waged war by candlelight.

At last, Rane let out an enormous yawn. "Enough."

"Just one more game," Florie pleaded.

" 'Tis nigh morn, darlin'."

Florie didn't care. She wasn't sleepy in the least. Indeed, she couldn't recall having so much fun. Even working far into the night over a particularly ornate piece of jewelry didn't please her half as well as poring over these silly wooden pieces with Rane.

"But I've just conquered ye," she taunted.

"I care not."

"Indeed?" She pouted, something she'd never done before in her life. "I thought ye were the son o' fierce Viking warriors."

His grin was sleepy and unguarded, and it made her heart melt. "Fear not. The battle is far from over, sweet. For tonight, slumber. But take care ye don't oversleep, for I *will* triumph on the morrow."

She returned his grin. Curse his weary bones. The morrow seemed an eternity to wait.

Rane was engaged in the strangest dream. He was a toefler in silver armor, guarding against a vast opposing army. But instead of protecting the Hnefi, he kept vigil over Florie.

At first 'twas an easy task. Florie remained on the throne, and one by one, he picked off the dark warriors advancing on her. But then their number increased, and Florie refused to stay where she was safe. He battled fiercely, but every time he slew one knight, two more would appear, and Florie was growing farther and farther distant...

"Hist! Rane!"

The whisper shredded his dream like silk, but Rane, still

caught in its threads, awoke and spun toward the sudden sound, whipping out his dagger.

His movement knocked the board from crouching Florie's hands, scattering wooden pieces to the floor with a clatter. Startled, she gasped and scurried backward.

"What the devil?" he demanded, his dagger aimed at her breast.

"God's eyes!" she hissed. "'Tis me—Florie."

Disoriented, he shook free the dregs of the dream and lowered his blade, grumbling, "'Tisn't wise to startle a sleepin' toefler."

"A what?"

"Huntsman," he corrected irritably, rubbing at his eye. Thor's hammer, he'd never had so vivid a dream. But then, he rarely went to bed at so late an hour. He peered at Florie through one blurry eye. "Didn't ye sleep at all?"

"Oh, aye." She picked up the board and, recovering quickly from her fright, began to hum a merry tune as she replaced the pieces. Apparently, even the threat of his dagger couldn't chase the cheer from her this morn. "The sun's been up for nigh three hours now."

"Ye went to bed an hour before it rose," he accused.

Her face blossomed into a wicked smile. "Who can sleep when there's war to be waged?"

Rane was exhausted. After all, he'd been fighting all night in the land of dreams, a far direr battle than any waged on a hnefatafl board. Still, the sight of her eager face—her cheeks flushed, her eyes sparking like steel on a whetstone, her lips curving into that enticing, mischievous grin—seduced him like tender young clover seduced a doe.

He supposed 'twas his own fault. He'd introduced her to the cursed game, knowing full well how addictive it could be.

He sighed, sheathing his dagger, then sat up. He scrubbed at his gritty eyes. "'Tis your strategy, I'd wager," he groused, "challengin' me to battle when my wits are only half engaged."

She flashed a coy smile. "Maybe."

He helped her pick up the toefler pieces, stopping to examine one of the dark-colored men. Apparently, while he slept, Florie had been toiling away. The warrior he held was carved with intricate designs, scale armor, and a buckler shield, and its face bore a braided beard. Another warrior carried an ax over one shoulder, and his face was obscured by a nose-plate helm.

Rane picked up a light piece. A cloak, carved with ripples and folds, covered the man's back, the eyes were blank hollows, and he carried a cat in one arm. "Is this..."

"Father Conan."

He shook his head at the expert handiwork. It *did* look like the priest. How had she done it? How had she managed to capture Father Conan's essence in a tiny piece of wood?

"I found a knife in the storage room," she explained.

He glanced up at her. 'Twas obvious in the way she bit at her lower lip that she waited for his comments, but he hardly knew what to say. Never had he seen such craftsmanship. "How did ye... What... When did ye have..."

"I've been awake for a while now," she admitted.

"These are..." he said, snatching up the pieces, one by one, from the board, at a loss for words. "These are...magnificent. How did ye learn to..."

She shrugged but, beneath her seeming nonchalance, beamed at his words. "I'm accustomed to workin' in gold, but carvin' wood isn't so different."

He examined the priest again. "This looks exactly like Father Conan."

Encouraged by his praise, she placed a dark piece in his palm. He turned it over. A stern bearded figure in a figured doublet scowled up at him. In one hand was a broadsword. The other made a fist. And hanging about his neck was a large medallion with a crest he recognized.

"Lord Gilbert!" he shouted, laughing. She'd captured the marrow of the handsome man, from his neatly trimmed beard to the furrow that seemed to have taken up residence upon his brow since his recent marriage.

The depth of Florie's talent overwhelmed Rane. With her skill, he realized, she could create priceless pieces of art. He imagined her carving magnificent flagons for Lord Gilbert's table, making new reliquaries for the reconstructed churches of Edinburgh, fashioning chessmen for the amusement of the Scots royals themselves! With such a gift, Florie would one day be a successful artisan...

If only she weren't a fugitive bound for the gallows.

His smile faded. He didn't want to think about it. Not yet.

Several times in the last few days, dread had reared its dragon's head, threatening to incinerate the thin fabric of hope that shielded Florie. Thus far Rane had managed to relegate the nasty creature to the dimmest corners of his mind. He must eventually war with the beast, he knew, and his heart trembled at the thought. But while time was still his ally, he wouldn't dwell on the battle ahead. 'Twould serve no purpose.

Exactly when his heart had shifted, he didn't know. Maybe at the very beginning, when she'd trusted him to pull the arrow out.

Or when she'd nestled against him in her sleep.

Or sobbed upon his shoulder.

Or pressed thirsting lips to his.

Or sighed gratefully when he brought her the basin of warm water.

Or cheered when she beat him at hnefatafl.

Whenever it had happened, the wee thief had stealthily stolen his heart. And now he could hardly bear to consider what might befall her, because he'd...grown fond of her.

'Twas a curious thing, he decided, to be fond of a lass. He often *desired* lasses. They kept him amused and aroused with their soft curves and seductive glances. But never had he felt so profound a tenderness as he did for Florie.

'Twas completely contrary to reason. After all, how much affection could she bear for a man who'd shot her, scalded her, humiliated her?

Likewise, he shouldn't be attracted to her in the least. He'd seen her at her worst—bloody, sweaty, filthy, fevered. That she was a known outlaw only added to the absurdity of his feelings.

But rational or not, he admired Florie, truly cared for her, and his soul quivered with a terrible rage when he thought of the travesty of executing such a lass.

Rane glanced up at Florie just in time to see her sneaking a light-colored piece from the board. He thought he glimpsed the top of a longbow before she enclosed it in her hand.

"What's that?" he asked, nodding at her fist.

"Nothin'."

He knew instantly by her deep blush who the figure was. "Let me see."

"'Tisn't…'tisn't finished," she lied.

He seized her hand in his own, trapping her. "Let me see."

"'Twas…a mistake."

He lifted the corner of his mouth in a half smile. "We all make mistakes."

She frowned. "Let go o' my hand, then, and I'll show ye."

He knew her too well to fall for her wiles. She'd likely stuff the piece down the bosom of her kirtle as soon as he released her. "Show me. Then I'll let ye go."

"'Tis nothin'. Indeed," she hedged, "I intended to throw it away and make another."

He grinned, still holding fast to her fist. "All right, then. I refuse to play hnefatafl with ye until ye show me that piece."

Her brow furrowed so deeply that one would have thought he'd told her he was going to drown her favorite kitten. "Nae."

"Aye."

He watched her mull over his demand, but he knew she would eventually surrender. After all, once the hnefatafl flea bit, there was no soothing the itch but with another game.

With an uneasy sigh, she loosened her fingers, and he pried open her hand. There on her palm was the most detailed figure of all. A bow was slung across the archer's shoulder, and a quiver of arrows rested upon his back. His shirt was belted about his hips, and his hose were even wrinkled at the knees, above the fold of his boots. His long hair spilled over his shoulders, a stray lock falling across his brow, and the mouth had a subtle upward curve to it, as if the figure kept an amusing secret.

'Twas perfect. Indeed, 'twas so perfect that looking at it sent a strange chill through him, as if he looked upon his own soul.

He nodded, mirroring the enigmatic expression on the figure. Then, feigning perplexity, he teased, "Who is this? Your foster father? Wat, maybe?"

Her artistic hackles rose instantly to the bait. "Wat?" Suddenly she realized he jested with her. Not to be outdone, she lifted her chin and countered with a jape of her own. "Aye, 'tis Wat," she told him, her eyes calculating. "Can ye not see the ignorance in his face? The willfulness? The empty gaze that those o' lesser wit—"

His laughter drowned her words. He clapped his hand to his heart. "Ye've cut me to the quick, lass." Then he took the piece between his finger and thumb and studied it more closely, sobering. "Is this truly how ye see me?"

"I told ye," she said, lowering her eyes. "'Tis flawed."

"Nae, 'tis not flawed," he argued. "Indeed, the piece is not so flawed as the man, I fear."

Her gaze snapped back up to his. "Flawed? Ye're not..." She blushed. "That is, on so small a piece...one cannot capture all the...the intricate aspects of a person's...character."

Nae, he thought. Florie could definitely capture every last detail, down to the laces of his jerkin and the taut string of his bow. The unfortunate truth was that she *did* see him as unflawed. Which simultaneously pleased his ego and weighed heavily on his mind.

He was far from perfect. Loki's thumbs, considering all the torment he'd put her through, 'twas amazing she thought so. Surely she'd change her mind when she discovered he was Lord Gilbert's man...if he ever let her know.

"Ye won't throw this piece away?" 'Twas a question, but he said it like a threat.

She shrugged casually, but her gaze remained riveted on him.

He feigned a sigh of exasperation. "I suppose ye wish to see how he well he guards the king at hnefatafl before ye decide."

Her eyes lit up. "Aye."

"Very well," he groused. "We'll see if the archer earns his keep."

They played on the steps of the church. Bundled against a fine veil of mist through which the sun peered occasionally like a shy bride, they scarcely noticed the chill air, so hot was their blood for battle.

Under Rane's command, the little archer proved well worth his bow. Nothing interrupted their play, neither the Father, who planned to be gone all day at the home of an ill friend, nor Methuselah, who swished his tail in irritation as he stalked past, nor the repast of oatcakes, cheese, and cider that awaited them in the sanctuary, food that the priest had left the night before for their meal today.

"Oho, '*Father Conan*'!" Florie cried in victory as her Lord Gilbert piece sidled up to Rane's wooden priest, removing him from the board.

Rane clucked his tongue. "'Tis hardly fair," he complained. "The Father *is* blind, ye know." Then he slid his archer forward to seize Gilbert in turn, eliciting a gasp of shock from Florie. He winked. "Always watch your back, '*Lord Gilbert.*'"

As his fingers closed around the tiny wooden warrior, his attention was caught by a movement from the brow of the hill behind Florie. Five dark shapes slowly emerged from the fog like blood seeping through linen, a company on horseback cresting the ridge.

Oblivious to their arrival, Florie playfully rapped at Rane's knee with her captured priest. "That archer o' yours is as much a blackguard as ye are," she taunted. "I think I'll..." She trailed off, alerted by the wariness in his face. "What? What is it?"

Misgiving prickled the hairs at the back of his neck as the riders neared. Florie heard them now, and she began to turn her head to follow his gaze.

"Nae!" he hissed. "Don't turn around."

CHAPTER 14

A week ago, the stubborn wench would have disobeyed him. Now her eyes mirrored her trust. She froze as he willed, an urgent question in her gaze.

"Go into the sanctuary," he bade her. "Now."

She blanched, dropping the wooden piece onto the board, knocking over two more. "Who is it? Gilbert?"

"Mavis."

Rebellion flickered in her eyes then. "I'm not afraid o' that—"

"Go in," he warned, "or I'll never play with ye again."

Her jaw dropped.

"Go on," he insisted.

Muttering under her breath, she complied. But her skirts caught on the board as she rose, upsetting it and scattering wooden pieces over the step. He heard a soft curse as she succumbed to the urge to glance toward the approaching threat. Then she slipped through the church door, closing it firmly behind her.

As they rode up, Rane came to his feet and nodded his

head in deference to Lady Mavis, who was flanked by four of her personal guard.

"That was her—the thief!" Mavis exclaimed without preamble. "Wasn't it?"

Rane saw no reason to lie. "Aye, my lady."

"She was outside the church." She regarded Rane expectantly, as if she spoke to a slow child. "Outside the sanctuary?"

"Aye."

"Yet ye did nothin'?"

"What would ye have me do, my lady?"

"I believe my husband charged ye, huntsman, with guardin' against her escape."

"She did not escape."

Mavis snarled an oath vile enough to spook her horse. "Damn ye, huntsman! Ye're tryin' my patience. Is she close to breakin'?"

"My lady?"

"The thief, bloody hell, the thief!"

"Breakin'?"

"Aye," she said, staring at the closed church door. "She's far from home. She has no allies. Surely hunger will loosen her tongue." She smiled smugly. "I expect a confession will be forthcomin'."

"Ye mean to starve a confession from her?" Rane asked incredulously.

"I won't wait forty days."

"But, my lady," Rane said, "she's been given the protection o' the church."

"The protection, aye. Not the sustenance."

So she assumed Florie received no food. "There are those who may show her compassion, my lady.

Surely ye won't command them to withhold their mercy."

Mavis ground her teeth as if she wished she *could* command such a thing. But she was no fool. Even a noble couldn't contradict the church's doctrine of pity and absolution. She shifted angrily in her saddle. "I expect her to surrender soon."

Rane arched a brow. He expected Florie wouldn't surrender in a thousand years.

Mavis's brows converged then, and her mouth began to work, alternately pursing and thinning with the frantic, sinister turnings of her mind. The last time Rane had seen that expression on her face was two months ago, hunting game. Lady Mavis, humiliated by the fact that Gilbert had come back empty-handed after a hunt, had conspired to pass off Rane's deer as her husband's catch.

"Maybe," she muttered at last, a dark, desperate glimmer in her eyes, "there's another way."

Rane frowned. For the sake of Lord Gilbert's pride, he'd allowed him to claim the deer. But he wasn't about to let Mavis claim Florie.

Mavis straightened with sudden inspiration. "Huntsman," she said, "in my husband's absence, I can grant you leave to hunt in Ettrick."

Rane scowled. "Aye?"

Mavis's eyes flattened as her lips curved into an obsequious smile. "Let the wench escape," she said silkily. "You'll track her." Her eyes glittered. "And bring her down."

Rane blinked in disbelief. God's wounds! Could Mavis actually mean for him to chase Florie, to slay her in cold blood? She had no idea how close he'd already come to doing just that unintentionally. Nor how much it had sickened him.

His body began to tremble with suppressed rage. The idea of deliberately hunting down a maiden as if she were an animal...

Drawing himself up to his full height, he spoke through clenched teeth. "I won't commit murder for ye, my lady."

Mavis gasped at his gall. Then, spurring her horse forward and gnashing her teeth, she raised her riding crop and struck Rane hard across the cheek.

The leather whip stung like the devil, but Rane knew better than to duck the blow. Thwarting Mavis would only make matters worse.

She sneered. "If ye cannot corner this prey, archer, then perhaps my husband should find himself a more skilled huntsman."

Rane gave no answer. 'Twas oft better to be silent and misconceived than to speak and be understood too well.

With a threatening glare and a smart crack of her reins, Mavis wheeled about and rode with her men toward the road again.

Rane watched them disappear like wraiths into the mist. He glanced down at the toefler piece still clenched in his fist, the wooden Lord Gilbert that he now realized was far too kindly carved. The real man had neither eyes to see nor the ballocks to control his nagging shrew of a wife. Lady Mavis had blinded him to the plight of his own starving people, and now she sought to twist his justice as well.

'Twas clear that with Lord Gilbert away, without his tempering hand to restrain Lady Mavis, Rane's nights as a guard and Florie's days of sanctuary were numbered.

Florie dabbed gingerly at Rane's cheek. 'Twas her fault, she knew—the red welt last evening and the resulting bruise that swelled darkly under his eye this morn. He refused to explain exactly how he'd earned such a harsh blow, evading her questions with jesting, but she knew it must have been in her defense. And the thought of that wretched Lady Mavis raising a hand to strike Rane made her want to rip out the she-devil's hair.

She suppressed most of her rage, but Rane still winced as she pressed the damp linen against his tender flesh.

She flinched in empathy. "It pains ye."

Remarkably, the corner of his lip drifted up as he shrugged. "Only when ye touch it."

"I'm sorry."

His smile widened. "'Tis a jest, Florie."

His humor was lost on her. She furrowed her brow and dipped the rag in the rosemary water again, murmuring, "How men can jest at such things, I don't understand."

"'Tis only a bruise."

"Earned on my account," she muttered. "I swear, if that cursed shrew comes near ye again, I'll wrap my hands around her scrawny neck and—"

"Ye'll do nothin' o' the sort," he insisted, taking the cloth from her and dropping it back into the basin.

"But she has no right to—"

"She's the wife o' the sheriff. She has every right," he said, clasping both her hands within his. "But enough about the Frasers, eh, lass?"

Once, Florie would have felt trapped by his gesture. Now his touch was comforting. As she watched, he brought her knuckles to his lips and bestowed upon them a tender kiss.

'Twas an innocent enough gesture, but for Florie, it felt anything but innocent. His moist breath upon the backs of her fingers warmed her to her toes.

"Besides," he said, "ye couldn't get these hands around her fat neck." He smiled. "They're far too small," he whispered, tilting one hand back to look at it, stroking the inside of her palm with his thumb.

The way he was touching her soothed her, the way petting soothed a cat. Her voice came out on a soft, throaty murmur. "They're not too small. For a goldsmith...small hands are...useful."

"I can see that," he breathed, though by the smoky cast of his eyes, he was likely imagining her hands plying another trade altogether.

A hot flush stole up her cheek at the thought, and yet she made no move to withdraw from his enthralling caress.

His gaze dipped momentarily to her lips, and he flashed her a mischievous grin. "Ye know, my mother always gave my bruises a kiss. She assured me 'twould speed the healin'." He lifted his brows, affecting such a guileless, wide eyed expression that she nearly laughed aloud.

"Did she?"

"Oh, aye," he assured her with mock solemnity.

Her eyes were drawn instinctively to his mouth—his wide, elegant, sensual mouth with its seductive upward curve. Faith, she wanted to kiss him. She'd wanted to kiss him for days now, from the moment he'd first given her a taste of his passion.

But he turned his head aside, presenting his injured cheek instead, like a brave young lad trounced in his first scuffle. Though she'd hoped for more, the playful innocence in his eyes was irresistible. With a brief smile, she inclined her head to bestow upon his cheek a chaste kiss of healing.

Her lips had scarcely grazed his cheek when he captured her face of a sudden between his hands. His touch was not ungentle, but 'twas uncompromising. Gone was the childlike light in his face. A glimmer of danger gleamed in his eyes now, danger and promise.

She gasped softly. Their mouths inches apart, she felt his intent as if 'twere a living thing.

"Ye want it as well," he whispered, and there was no need to clarify. "Ye want this."

She did. There was no denying it. Deep in her heart, she had wanted to be caught, to be claimed. She knew she trod too near the hunter's snare. Aye, a part of her fell willingly into his trap.

Her breath quickened as he lowered his gaze to her parted lips, coaxing them farther open with the edge of his thumb. Anticipation sped her pulse as he eased forward with incredible stealth. From beneath weighted eyelids, she watched him moisten his lip with his tongue, and an intense craving ignited her senses as rapidly as flame touched to thatch.

She remembered the taste of him. Oh, God, she remembered. Mint and ale and rosemary. She could feel his breath upon her now, his mouth only a hair's breadth away. And still he lingered over the moment, a skillful hunter patiently tracking his prey.

Finally, when she thought she could endure no more, he touched his lips lightly to hers. Her soft gasp drew cool air between their mouths.

"Aye," he breathed in warm reply.

As if he commanded her body from that one point of contact, he gently nipped at her mouth with his lips, drawing her forward, stealing her will from her bit by inconspicuous bit, like a kitchen lad thieving silver.

Somewhere in the maelstrom of her thoughts was the vague fear that maybe she was losing control of not only her senses, but her heart. Yet she could assimilate only a growing desire for more of him.

Slowly his fingers slid back through her hair as he pressed closer and closer, forcing her mouth to his seductive dance. Then one hand lowered possessively to the back of her neck, as if to prevent her flight from what he next intended.

But flight was the last thing on Florie's mind, and though the sudden shock of his hot tongue inside her mouth startled a squeak from her, in the next moment she was replying to his ravishment with a hunger of her own.

Rane had meant the kiss as subterfuge, partly because he knew Florie's anger at Lady Mavis would only get her into more trouble, and partly because she was asking too many questions about Lord Gilbert. If she persisted in her pursuit of what had happened last evening, she might stumble upon the truth, that Rane was Gilbert's vassal. And that she must not discover.

So he had to distract her. And in his experience, the surest way to distract a lass was to seduce her.

He never doubted his qualifications. He was an expert hunter, after all. Patient. Stealthy. Subtle. Maids yielded to his stalking the same way prey did, never realizing they were vulnerable until 'twas too late.

That was the truth of what the Father called his Viking curse. 'Twas no bewitchery, but rather a natural talent he'd honed from his skill with the bow—a gift for observation, intuition, and empathy. He proposed to employ those talents now, to bring Florie slowly to the brink of yearning until she forgot all about Lady Mavis.

For a bit, he was successful. He tantalized her with his forthright gaze and practiced hands. He anticipated her every response, prolonging her passion, edging her inexorably onward.

But then the wanton lass answered his kiss with an ardor he'd never expected, and like a hungry hound unleashed, his restraint shot away, out of control.

Suddenly, *he* was the one distracted. His loins seized, flooded with simmering desire. His arms, no longer tempered by forbearance, surrounded her like a plundering army, dragging her close in conquest. And he completely forgot why he'd meant to seduce her.

Her tongue swept boldly across his, and he plunged his own deeper, reveling in the honey-sweet recesses of her mouth. Her fingers slid up along the sides of his throat, and a wave of mad pleasure surged through his skull as they found the sensitive crevices of his ears. A groan was torn from his chest, and lust roared to life in the urgent quickening within his trews. His head swam as if awash in the pealing of a hundred bells.

'Twas madness. She left him vulnerable, threatened, out of control. For Rane to feel that way with a lass...'Twas like a hunter feeling menaced by a fawn. And yet he was rendered powerless by Florie.

She moaned softly into his mouth, her moan like an elixir of desire, intoxicating him beyond constraint. His hands, unfettered by reason, pressed and caressed and explored her lovely form as a blind man's might. And

Florie, lost in her own haze of passion, granted him leave.

He traced the exquisite contours of her neck, resting his thumb lightly against the hollow of her throat, feeling her pounding pulse, an echo of his own throbbing heart. He followed the delicate bone outward, slipping his fingers beneath the edge of her kirtle and chemise to cup the perfect sphere of her shoulder, then sliding downward along her arm. All the while, their tongues coupled and their breath mingled, their passion like a wild thing set free.

He inhaled sharply as she moved closer, pressing her belly against his jutting staff so shamelessly that he feared to explode with want of her.

Holding back his own need, he let his hand come between them at the waist of her kirtle, then eased his palm down until his fingers pressed at the fabric between her thighs.

She broke from the kiss then, puffing in sweet distress against his cheek as he circled his fingertips firmly over the place he knew her yearning centered.

Lowering his head, he caught the lacing of her kirtle in his teeth, pulling the tie free, loosening the garment. He let his free hand drift from her bare shoulder across the creamy sweep of her bosom, then lower, groaning at the fawn-soft ecstasy of her flesh. His palm grazed the tender bud of her nipple, making her cry out softly, and as the responsive nubbin stiffened, so too did the restless animal in his braies.

Sweet Freyja, she'd had but a taste of his seduction, and already she was climbing toward the point of release. Never had he encountered a lass so responsive. Her breath came rapidly, she clutched at his shoulders, and such bittersweet desperation graced her face that he could scarcely keep from taking her, here and now.

Almost...

Almost...

A sudden thud on the church steps outside split them faster than a quarrel leaped from a bow.

Rane, breathless and disoriented, responded with a vile oath.

Bloody hell! Who dared interrupt them?

Odin! His ballocks ached. His blood boiled. His body burned with need.

He fought off the urge to throttle the intruder, instead raking his fingers back through his disheveled locks, wishing he could arrange his tangled thoughts as easily as his hair.

A glance at Florie told him her mind was no better ordered than his own. Her eyes were drowsy with desire, her cheeks flushed, her mouth swollen with kissing. And her brow was furrowed with bewildered frustration.

But if she was lost in lusty oblivion, he at least was accustomed to clandestine encounters. His instincts took over. He swiftly picked Florie up by the waist, plopping her down upon the fridstool, yanked her loosened kirtle back up over her shoulder, and gave her a reviving pat on the cheek. Then he scrambled a prudent distance away and flung one of her plaids over his lap, hiding the obvious manifestation of his mood.

Not a moment too soon, for when the door swung open, Carol the cooper's daughter and Velera the chandler staggered in, bearing a great wooden half-barrel between them.

Though his blood seethed with unspent lust and

227

tempered rage, he couldn't blame the intruders. And he was too chivalrous to allow the lasses to carry their heavy burden by themselves. So as covertly as he could, Rane repositioned the incriminating lump in his braies and rose awkwardly to come to their aid. Hopefully, they'd notice nothing, which was more than could be said of Florie, whose eyes had widened with horror at his bold adjustment.

"Goodwife Carol. Mistress Velera," he croaked. "Allow me." He hobbled forward. "'Tis far too heavy a thing for such delicate flowers."

"Ach, Rane MacFarland!" Carol cooed, blushing, clearly pleased by his compliment. "Always so courteous. Isn't he, Velera?"

"Oh, aye," she agreed, gladly surrendering the half-barrel to him. "Courteous." Then she narrowed suspicious blue eyes at him, and for an awful instant he feared his perfidy was discovered. "What's wrong with your eye?" She elbowed Carol. "What's wrong with his eye?"

Carol gasped. "Gads! What's happened?"

Before he could reply, her gaze traveled past his shoulder, alighting upon Florie.

"Ach!" she huffed, lowering her voice to a whisper. "'Tis that wicked, miserable, thievin' wench, isn't it? She's attacked ye. Oh, Velera, look what the wretched grig has done."

Velera pursed her mouth, tossed her pale blond tresses, and began pushing back her sleeves. "I'll blacken her eye for ye, Rane. 'Twouldn't be the first time I—"

"Ladies," he said, blocking Velera's way. "Be at ease. 'Twas no fault o' hers. I...lost my footin' in the woods and caught a branch, 'tis all."

Velera looked soundly disappointed, as if she dearly wished to beat Florie to a bloody pulp. Carol, however, wasted no time on rancor.

"Ye poor, poor man," she soothed, sidling up for a better look at his bruise. "Rosemary water's what ye need. I can fetch rosemary from—"

"There's no need. I've plenty o' rosemary," he said.

"Ach, o' course," she said with a giggle, toying with a lock of her nut-brown hair. "'Tis the scent ye wear to throw off the deer."

If only, he thought, he could throw the lasses off his scent so easily. By Thor, every fiber of his being longed to take up where he'd left off with Florie.

He hefted up the tub, which made a good shield for his still rigid staff. "What's this for?"

Carol brushed up against him. "Why, Rane, when we heard ye were laboring so tirelessly on the old church..."

"Hammerin' and sawin'...and pantin'..." Velera chimed in dreamily. "And sweatin'..."

"We wondered how the two of us might...ease your sufferin'."

"And we decided your poor achin' bones might have need of a soothin' bath." Velera dipped her eyelashes.

"And maybe two attentive maids to keep ye company." Carol ran a finger down the length of his arm.

Any other day, Rane would have welcomed the comely lasses with open arms, stripped down to his skin, and happily let them scrub his back, his chest, his ballocks, whatever they wished. But today, his desires focused solely on Florie. Indeed, he'd rather resume his thus far chaste fondling of the bewitching felon than suffer the far more sensual pleasures the pair of maids offered.

"I thank ye for your kindness," he told them, "but..." 'Twas on the tip of his tongue to decline their gift. Then he remembered Florie's fondness for bathing before the Sabbath. "I must finish this door before it grows dark. Afterward, I assure ye, I shall be very glad o' the tub."

"Then we shall be very glad to wait while—" Carol began.

"Ach, nae! I wouldn't even consider havin' ye wait for me." Carol's face fell, and he gave them his best frown of concern. "I couldn't bear the thought o' what might befall two o' my favorite lasses, walkin' home in the dark o' the wood."

"But—" Velera said.

"Nae. I'll hear none of it," he said sternly. "Ye're too precious, too temptin' a sight to outlaws who might frequent the forest at night." When they would have protested again, he flashed them a grateful grin. "But I cannot thank ye enough for the gift o' the tub. I shall treasure it and...and think o' ye two lovelies each and every time I sink my achin' body into the warm water."

They could do little but smile weakly. No doubt he'd painted a picture vivid enough to sustain their lurid fantasies.

"Sweet Carol. Precious Velera. What a pair of angels ye are," he sighed. "Hurry along now, for I won't rest easy till I'm assured ye're safely home."

Their faces befuddled with an odd mixture of pleasure and disappointment, they murmured fond farewells and left.

Now, he thought in relief. Now he'd finish what he'd begun.

But when he turned to Florie, he knew instantly 'twas

not to be. She sat on the fridstool with her good knee drawn stiffly up to her chest, her arms crossed tightly around it, her countenance bleak. In his experience, when a maid wore that stricken expression, neither reason nor cajoling nor seduction would coax her back into an amorous mood.

A moment ago, Florie had felt deliciously swept away by her passions, as if she soared on some wild charger into the heavens, where the promise of even greater ecstasy awaited. Like a starved waif, she'd feasted greedily on Rane, unable to stop her delirious craving, unmindful of the recklessness of her behavior, wanting more and more and more...

Then *they* had appeared.

She supposed she had no right to be angry. They were certainly welcome in the sanctuary. 'Twas a church, after all, a place of worship, open to everyone. Faith, Florie was the one in the wrong, expressing such carnal desires within God's house. Still, what she'd shared with Rane hadn't *felt* wrong. Indeed, nothing had felt so right in a long while.

But as she waited restlessly for the lascivious maids to leave, that destructive emotion reared its head again. Jealousy.

'Twas not as if Florie owned Rane, she reasoned. Even the priest had told her the handsome archer was...how had he termed it? Generous with his affections.

Rane offered Florie a safe way to appease her sexual curiosity, by offering her a brief, insignificant, harmless encounter she could recollect in her lonely days to come. What did it matter if he had one lover or a hundred, if Florie was only another name notched into his bow? As her foster father was fond of saying, 'twas better to drink the dregs of another's pint than to be left with none at all. She didn't require Rane's fidelity. She only craved his arms about her. Her heart had nothing to do with it. What did it matter that others found delight in his embrace?

Yet it did matter, immensely—which troubled her.

Even when Florie was a child, her mother had warned her constantly to guard her heart. Only at her deathbed did Florie learn why.

She'd placed the gold pomander in Florie's young hands, confiding that the beautiful piece had been a gift, not from her foster father, but from her mother's first love, her *true* love—a nobleman promised to another. The pomander would belong to Florie now, she'd said, for 'twas a precious reminder that had been purchased at the price of her heart.

Florie's foster father, too, had shown her the perils of loving too deeply.

Nae, she'd not make the mistakes her parents had, and the fact that she cared enough about Rane to feel jealous meant that she cared too much.

CHAPTER 15

Lady Mavis emerged from the dim dovecote, raising one hand to shield her eyes from the glare of the rising sun. On the other gloved hand perched her hooded prize merlin. Its white-spotted gold feathers fluttered as it bobbed, eager to fly. Mavis checked to see that the tiny scroll was still firmly attached to the bird's jesses.

It had taken weeks, but she'd finally managed to get rid of all the useless doves in the cote, replacing them with her modest menagerie of falcons. Marry, if Gilbert had paid closer attention, he might have noticed that her falcons had a distinct fondness for dove meat. But he was oblivious to most of Mavis's pursuits, including, thankfully, the one in which she was about to indulge.

She carefully loosened the tiny leather hood and lifted it from the merlin's head, exposing its keen, beady eyes. The bird hadn't eaten for days, not since it had feasted upon Gilbert's last dove, so 'twas hungry, which was good. Otherwise, it might become distracted.

The falcon was trained to fly at the same hour each

week to a particular spot in Ettrick Forest, a remote, shadowed grove where an English spy waited with fresh meat. After supping till its belly was full, the merlin would fly home to Mavis's glove, never knowing the great service it performed for Mavis and for England.

Mavis blew a soft breath onto the bird's breast, ruffling its feathers, and the merlin tightened its grip on her glove, not enough to pierce the leather, just enough to pinch. Then she lifted her arm and spread her fingers to release the jesses, and the falcon pushed off into the sky, winging toward the woods.

Mavis smiled in satisfaction. She'd written just two words on the scroll, a name and a town—MARY and MUSSELBURGH—but they were priceless gems, leaked to her by her loose-lipped husband. And when they were delivered, she'd once more have the English royals in the palm of her hand.

Rane picked up a long, bark-bare stick and stabbed with uncharacteristic irritability at the glowing embers beneath the steaming basin of water. He'd suffered all day from a keen sense of frustration, both mental and physical. As if their continued usefulness had come into question, his neglected ballocks ached with a sort of bewildered hunger that lodged deep in his belly. And his thoughts...

Curse him, he'd thought of nothing but Florie from the time he'd awakened. Florie, with her fiery passions and quick wit...Florie, with her brutal honesty and tender heart...Florie, with her sultry eyes, honey lips, velvet flesh...

He jabbed at the fire, cracking a black coal that squealed in protest as he exposed the flaming heart within.

What the devil was wrong with him? He wasn't some simpleton to let his loins dictate his actions. He had a brain. Not only that, but he had his choice of most any of the lasses in Selkirk...not that he let that affect his humility or his judgment. He didn't believe in the curse. And he knew that looks were fleeting and lasses fickle. But the fact remained that, for whatever reason, he could fairly well swive whom he willed.

Why, then, should he be swept senseless by a fey sprite who was too short for his liking, too dark for his tastes, and an enemy of his lord?

Frigg's arrows, he should never have touched her. For now not only did he crave her beyond reason, but 'twas clear from her reaction to their visitors yesterday, her morose mood last evening, and her pensive silence today that she suffered the pangs of jealousy. Because of that one kiss, Florie thought she owned him.

He shuddered. Possessive maids were dangerous. Rane tried to steer well away from them. But then, he'd never met a temptation quite like Florie.

He poked again through the embers, watching a bright spark rise against the violet of the twilight sky.

That kiss *had* been heavenly; the sensual play that followed, world-shaking. Her lips were soft and supple, her tongue delicate. From the first instant, he'd imagined what enchantments they might make upon the rest of his body.

She'd cleaved tenaciously to him and, like a suckling calf, responded with instinctive avarice. He could see her still in his mind's eye, her lovely breasts pillowing against him until the crevice between deepened, beckoning him to their unplumbed shadows. Then, through her skirts, the warmth of her maid's core, the sweet spot betwixt her legs that had grazed his staff and moved against his hand with earnest longing, catapulting him into realms of passion where he'd never ventured before...

His loins stung even now with raw need, and he growled in frustration.

'Twas absurd. Lust was no different than any other bodily craving. When a man needed warmth, he never questioned which cloak to wear. If a man had to piss, any tree would do. Any brewster's ale could slake a man's thirst. Likewise, when a man sought satisfaction, one lass should serve as well as another.

But the truth was that Florie was a rare lass. The desire he'd experienced with her yesterday was unlike any he'd known before. He'd never felt such a powerful bond with a maid, such a heady need to make her his and only his.

Faugh! 'Twas nonsense, he decided, crumpling a dead leaf and tossing it onto the fire, watching it flare and turn to ash. 'Twas but long-forced chastity cramping his loins and twisting his reason.

He silently cursed and frowned at a wisp of smoke curling into the night. Past its swirling veil, at the far edge of the pond, betwixt rows of bent reeds, a fat stag brazenly lowered his head to drink.

Rane grimaced. His bow, of course, was out of reach. By the time he could get to it...

He sighed. Surely the deer mocked him. Just as Frigg mocked him. Just as Odin himself seemed to enjoy tweaking Rane's destiny at his expense.

Aye, letting the temptress past his defenses had been a mistake...just as what he did now was a mistake. Kissing her yesterday had been irresponsible. Heating a bath for her today was asking for nothing but trouble.

Yet he foolishly crushed and sprinkled pungent laurel leaves into the simmering pot, then rose to his feet, unmindful of the deer that bolted away in surprise. He lifted the bail of the basin with a forked stick, already imagining Florie sluicing the warm and fragrant water over her lithe, bare limbs. Sighing in self-mockery, he trudged up the hill with all the enthusiasm of a felon headed for the dungeon.

Florie's heart pounded as she perched the cake of soap atop the stack of freshly laundered linens and rearranged the flickering candles around the half-barrel for the third time.

She'd had an entire day to think about Rane's kiss, to reflect upon her heartsick parents, to convince herself 'twas best to keep her distance from the handsome archer.

But every time she caught sight of him, her body responded of its own will, warming, yearning, remembering, as empty without his touch as a gold setting without a jewel.

Lord, she wanted him. Even if she couldn't keep him. Even if 'twas for only a day.

She could set her emotions aside. She *could*. She wasn't her mother, to engage in a hopeless romance with a man beyond her grasp. Nor was she her foster father, weak-willed and obsessive. Nae, Florie was in control of her heart. As in control as Rane.

After all, she lived in a man's world. She'd learned early on that she could do anything a man could do—set gems, keep accounts, deal with overbearing patrons. She could sweat and swear and endure pain without a whimper. Just like Rane.

And if that were true, she reasoned, then why not tryst just as freely?

Her heart skipped at the boldness of her plan. She scrutinized the stage she'd set in the narthex, praying that God wouldn't think her use of this entryway of his house as sacrilegious. Surely he'd understand. After all, was it not the Lord who created man and woman? Was it not he who said, be fruitful and multiply? Was it not he who *invented* desire?

Still, she glanced toward the distant altar of the church and genuflected quickly, reconfirming her faith in a merciful God.

The half-barrel was already partially filled with cool water to balance what simmered over the fire outside. It had taken Rane five trips to the well to make a decent bath for Florie, and though the tub was of ample size for her, she feared 'twas too small for a Viking. Surely the archer's impossibly long legs would become wedged into the barrel.

Just recalling his impressive size set Florie's heart lurching and her thoughts careening back to yesterday. That incredible kiss. Rane's massive arms wrapped about her. Her fingers filtering through his hair. His hands fondling her in places where, dear God, she'd never imagined...

She fanned a hand before her flushed face. Only a few days earlier, she would have recoiled from his possessive embrace. But what she'd once dreaded, she now welcomed. What she'd feared, she now desired. Her fingertips yearned to press into his supple flesh again. Her breasts ached to be crushed against his chest. Her mouth craved his kiss. She longed to run her palms over the sleek breadth of his shoulders, along the muscular length of his arms, over the wide expanse of his back...

A scuffling on the steps outside set her lascivious thoughts flapping off like startled doves. Her breath quickened as she hastily cast a handful of rosemary into the bath, sending pebbles of amber candlelight shimmering across the surface.

A glance assured her that her gown, stockings, and boots were out of range of any stray splashes from the bath, but though she smoothed the linen chemise that covered her head to heel, still she felt curiously vulnerable in the sheer garment and her bare feet. She clasped her hands before her, and her heart fluttered, half in anticipation, half in trepidation at what she dared, as Rane shouldered his way through the church door.

The plethora of candles seemed to alarm him, and as soon as he spied her in her chemise, he averted his eyes with a scowl.

"Hope ye like laurel," he muttered, upending the basin of fragrant, steaming water into the tub, then swirling the hot and cold, laurel and rosemary, together with his hand.

She caught her lip beneath her teeth. Now that he was here before her, real, substantial, she began to doubt her ability to carry off her plot. He *was* too large for the barrel by far. His legs would have to drape over the side. And how she'd ever manage to get him out of his garments...

He shook the droplets from his fingers and turned to go. "I'll be outside if ye—"

"Nae," she blurted, determined to finish what she had started. "Nae."

He stopped, and she could see him fighting the urge to look at her, as he had all day.

"Ye…ye needn't leave," she said.

His nostrils flared once, and his jaw clenched as he seemed to consider her offer. Then he sniffed and shook his head. "I'll wait on the—"

"Nae. Don't go. I mean…" Lord, already she sounded stilted. Her foster father was right—Florie was never more awkward than when she tried to converse. She'd meant to beckon Rane graciously, like a refined paramour, to reveal her intentions with leisurely elegance. 'Twas apparently not to be. "'Tis…'tis for ye," she said lamely.

His brow furrowed in confusion.

"The bath," she said. "'Tis for ye."

The furrow deepened.

"My lord," she added with a curtsy and a nervous smile.

His voice cracked on the reply. "I don't need a hot bath. I'll bathe in the pond come morn. And I'm not your lord."

Her smile faltered. She hadn't expected reticence on his part. "But…I want…to." Lord, why couldn't she speak properly?

He was silent a long while. Finally, he glanced down with an enigmatic smile, as if she'd made a jest only he understood. "I know."

Maybe she hadn't made herself clear. She clutched the edge of the tub. "I…want *this.*"

He let out a sigh, then lifted a brow. "And are ye accustomed to getting' everythin' ye want?"

'Twas a curious question. She answered him as honestly as she could. "Aye, most o' the time."

Laughter crept into his gaze. She knew not what he found so amusing. When you were the daughter of a drunkard, you learned to take care of your wants and needs yourself.

"Well, wee kitten, I fear I must refuse ye this time." He turned to leave.

His words took her aback. For a moment she only stared at him in disbelief. How could he turn down such a generous offer? One that promised him pleasure? She frowned. Maybe, as her foster father often complained when Florie dealt with buyers, her approach was too direct.

What should she say, then, to entice him to stay? 'Twas on the tip of her tongue to make some vacuous remark about the weather when she remembered her foster father's last words to her as she left for the Selkirk fair. *For God's sake, Florie,* he'd drawled, *if all else fails, use your womanly guile. Surely ye were born with some small measure of it.*

Womanly guile. Aye. Like the noblewomen she'd heard in the marketplace, purring to their lords to purchase jewels for them. Or the sisters who'd simpered and giggled and blushed to gain Rane's attentions. Or the pair of lasses who'd brought the tub. Womanly guile.

She blew out a calming breath and clasped her hands before her, trying to smooth her jagged nerves, though 'twas akin to pouring honey over thistles. "Wait."

Miraculously, her soft syllable made him comply. Maybe she *did* possess womanly guile, after all.

"Forgive me if I've offended ye," she murmured. "I only meant to repay your kindness."

He half turned and eyed her suspiciously from under his brows. "Repay my...to balance the accounts, ye mean?"

"Aye. Nae." She swallowed. Maybe 'twas true. Partly. But there was more to it than that. She wanted to relive what she'd felt yesterday, to be close to him, to touch him.

Her lids dipped as she glanced at his mouth, remembering the taste of his kiss.

His face darkened. "I'll be outside, guardin' the door," he said gruffly, lifting the latch.

"Wait," she pleaded. Maybe she wasn't being alluring enough. She slipped forward, insinuating herself into the space between Rane and the door, looking up at him with what she hoped were tempting eyes. "Guardin' the door?" she breathed, letting her gaze trail down his throat, where his pulse throbbed. "Against whom? A blind priest?" She lifted intrepid fingertips to toy with the lacing of his jerkin. "Nae. Stay with me. 'Tis cold outside."

His nostrils flared again, and his mouth turned solemn. "What game do ye play at, lass?"

"Game?" she whispered, puzzled. After all, she'd seen this tactic work effectively on many a lord in the marketplace. "'Tis no game."

He closed his fingers about her wrist. "I'm well acquainted with the wiles o' women, Florie."

Rane clenched his jaw. The damned lass was trying to seduce him. And succeeding. She was well aware of what she invited. She'd kissed him. She'd tasted his passion. She knew well what beast she called forth. And what 'twould lead to. The wicked wanton *wanted* him.

And, Odin help him, he wanted her worse.

The subtle smoldering in her gaze sent lust rippling through his blood. Sporting with the lass—kissing her, caressing her—was one thing, but this was no harmless play. At the moment, he had no trouble imagining taking her here, now, ravishing her before the altar on the stone floor of the church, like his heathen ancestors before him.

But he'd also realized the truth the moment he'd

walked in and set eyes on her, standing like an angel in that diaphanous wisp of a gown beside the gleaming array of candles, her eyes shining with hope. He liked Florie too well to break her heart, which he'd inevitably do. Better he should refuse her now than hurt her later. Besides, he had his own suspicions regarding the maid.

"Ye're a virgin," he murmured, "aren't ye?"

She blushed, lowering her gaze, and lied through her teeth. "Nae."

"Florie?"

She didn't answer.

He gave her a rueful smile and pointedly removed her arm from his chest. "Enjoy your bath."

Florie crossed her arms in challenge, and the enticing temptress vanished like mist, replaced by the familiar stubborn sprite. "If ye won't avail yourself o' the bath, then neither shall I."

He shrugged. "So be it."

Her jaw dropped.

He turned away.

"Wait!" she cried.

Curse his foolish heart, he did.

"Ye'd waste a perfectly good bath?" she asked in disbelief.

"Nae. *Ye'd* waste a perfectly good bath. I never asked for one."

She had no answer for that. After a moment, he stepped toward the door again.

"Wait!"

He stopped again.

"Ye drive a hard bargain," she groused, then continued with a sigh. "Very well. I concede. Ye've won." Rane didn't believe her surrender for a moment. Sure enough, she followed with, "But I pray ye don't leave yet, for I fear I may need assistance gettin' into the tub."

The only thing that kept him from laughing aloud at her transparent ploy was the vision her words inspired—Florie at her bath, slipping off her garments, baring her creamy flesh, her supple breasts, the dark tangle of curls below...

He bit down against a painful wave of longing. Nae, he had no intention of remaining in the sanctuary, within sight of her alluring curves, within hearing of her every sensual splash and sigh of contentment. His own lucid musings were torment enough. With any luck, on the steps of the church, the brisk eve would chill his heated blood, and by the time she was finished and her bath cooled, so would his ardor.

So she needed help getting into the tub, did the wee tease? Oh, aye, he'd help her.

Without a word, he whirled about and stepped forward. Ignoring the breathless expectation in her eyes and the desire parting her lips, he reached forward as if to embrace her. But instead, he clasped her about the waist, lifting her bodily, and deposited her, chemise and all, into the warm water.

Florie's mouth fell open in outrage. The breath escaped her on a huff of indignation, and her eyes flashed with disbelief. For an instant, his mouth twitched with amusement as he shook the water from his forearms.

But he should have left while he had the chance. For as soon as the water soaked through her thin chemise, making her appear as if she wore nothing at all, his mouth went dry, his humor faded, and his better judgment fled, along with his good intentions.

244

CHAPTER 16

When Florie recovered, sputtering from the shock of being dunked in the tub like a flea-ridden cat, she saw that Rane had unwittingly achieved for himself what she could not. His eyes, hooded with desire, had darkened like a stormy sea, and his nostrils fluttered as if he detected the tantalizing scent of prey.

'Twas not quite what she'd intended. She'd meant to slowly rekindle the fire they'd banked yesterday, to slip the chemise from her shoulder, to win him gradually with a tenuous touch, a kiss here, a caress there. Instead, 'twas as if he'd just set a torch to bone-dry tinder.

Faith, she might as well be naked for the modesty her drenched garment afforded. And when he regarded her with that burning gaze, his lust almost a tangible thing, she had to fight off the potent instinct to cover herself.

But she wasn't afraid. Not truly. She remembered how gentle Rane was, how adept, how patient. Nae, 'twasn't fear. Indeed, noting the way he clenched his fists as his chest rose and fell with a deep breath, she felt most empowered.

She could see him mentally weighing his choice to remain or walk out the door, the same kind of indecision she'd seen countless times on patrons' faces in the goldsmith shop. In the shop she'd do her best to display the gems in a favorable light. Maybe 'twas no different here.

Though she trembled at her own boldness, her eyes locked with his, and she reached up to slide the chemise from her shoulder. She slowly revealed the swell of her bosom above the water as the fabric rasped sensuously along her arm, low on her throat, and over one breast, catching on the taut peak. She sighed, imagining that Rane's hands did the deed.

Modestly covering her breast with one hand, she used the other to slip her chemise from the opposite shoulder. With her arms crossed over her bosom and her face burning with a delirious blend of shame and lust, she still found the courage to peel back the linen to bare her breasts fully to his view, relishing the contrast of the warm water and the cool air as the tiny waves lapped at her nipples.

Rane's mouth was tense now, his eyes dark and fierce. His fists were white with strain, and every breath he drew made his nostrils quiver. Still he came no nearer. But neither did he depart.

Her pulse palpable in her throat, she eased the chemise down farther, past her waist and the hollow of her belly, over the bones of her hips, rising slightly to free her buttocks from the swirling white cloth. The water splashed softly against the wood as she drew the chemise slowly up and over her bent knees, then slipped out her feet. With a surge of water, she lifted the saturated gown out, dropping it onto the flagstones. And then there was nothing to block his view.

But though he scowled into the water as if to boil it with his stare, still he didn't move from his spot. She could see the blatant manifestation of his lust, straining at his braies like a huge warhorse eager for battle, yet he held back his desires with a firm rein...just like a patron stubbornly unmoved by her shop full of tempting wares.

When in Stirling a patron was so intractable, Florie would make a great show of polishing the jewels till they shone like irresistible fire.

With trembling fingers, she groped atop the linens for the soap, almost knocking it to the floor. Capturing it in her palm, she wet the fragrant cake in the bath. Then, with luxuriant sloth, she began to run it over her skin. The cake glided along her throat, over her collarbone, around her shoulder, and down the length of one arm, making a slippery trail over her flesh.

Peering obliquely up at Rane, she saw her movements were having some effect. His jaw was no longer tight. Indeed, his mouth had parted slightly as he watched the path of the soap beneath lust-heavy lids.

Encouraged by his attentiveness, Florie repeated the sensual pattern over the other half of her body. Then, dipping the cake into the water again, she placed it high against her bosom and, unable to keep her eyes open for this most brazen of gestures, slipped the soap further downward. Her face hot, she proceeded to make lazy spirals around her breasts, rubbing the cake gently over her awakening nipples. Then she slid the soap down to her navel, and she flushed even hotter, remembering the way Rane had touched her. Sweet Lord, she longed to feel him there again, in her most secret of places.

But as Florie labored to breathe under the weight of her

longing, the soap chanced to slip from her hand. Before she could catch it, it coursed with unerring aim betwixt her legs.

Her eyes flew open.

Rane's hands were no longer clenched. His fingers were splayed now like a warrior's in readiness, awaiting only the command to fight. His chest heaved with great breaths of air, and his eyes focused with such intensity upon her body that she feared he might sear her with his gaze.

Her first instinct was to go after the soap. But something in Rane's eyes, some silent command, immobilized her. She could do nothing but watch as he loosened the laces of his jerkin, pulling it off and casting it aside. His steady gaze riveted her as he methodically rolled back the sleeves of his shirt, baring his muscular forearms, for what purpose Florie shivered to imagine.

The sly smile to which she'd grown accustomed was missing now. Rane's expression was one of reluctant duty, almost as if he prepared to mete out stern punishment for her wanton act.

Only when he started forward did she begin to comprehend the consequences of her boldness. Rane was a hunter, and Florie had become his prey. He was as pumped full of male energy as a charging boar. There was no turning back. What she'd begun, he would finish. Here and now.

Yet as Rane towered over her, his shadowed eyes raking down her body, taking in every inch of her, still she felt no fear, only desire. And when he dropped to one knee beside the tub, trailing his fingertips across the surface of the water, she bit her lip to silence her own whimpers of anticipation.

Without a word, he placed a finger at the spot in her throat where her pulse throbbed, sliding it down along her breastbone. Moving slowly downward, he stretched out his massive hand so that it encompassed her whole bosom, his thumb and last finger grazing her nipples. Florie moaned, tipping her head back until it rested upon the rim of the barrel, closing her eyes to relish the yearning.

When he reached her waist, beneath the water, his hand reversed, his fingertips now leading the way over the plane of her stomach and lower, dipping briefly inward at her navel, toying with the beginning of the fine black hair that shielded her nether parts from his view.

"Open your eyes," he bade her softly.

She resisted his command. Though it had been easy to expose her body to him, to lay her soul bare was another matter.

His free hand touched her jaw. "Look at me, Florie."

'Twas almost impossible, so heavy with wanting were her lids. But she managed to pry them slowly open.

"'Tis a thing to be shared," he whispered.

She gulped as his hand delved deep into the water betwixt her legs, searching. When it came up, 'twas slick with soap. He drew the cake up her abdomen, sudsing circles about her breasts in the same languid manner as before, staring into her responsive eyes like a hunter studying his cornered quarry.

Her nipples tingled now, slick with soap, roused by rubbing, stiffened with cold. And a searing flash like lightning seemed to bolt through her body, connecting those two prickling points to the sharp ache betwixt her thighs.

But she could see Rane meant to soothe her pain. The soap glided down over her nest of curls, and she clutched at the edges of the tub, arching up with a moan to meet his hand.

"Shh," he said, placing his finger across her lips. He ran the soap along the insides of her thighs, and though she tried to remain still, 'twas almost impossible when her body knew so clearly what it wanted.

Finally he slid the soap betwixt her nether lips, touching upon the core of her need, and she squirmed and cried out with the ecstasy of it. For a moment he held his hand there, letting her adjust to the white heat. His other arm came about to cradle the back of her head, and she buried her face against his shoulder.

Then he moved the soap. Slowly at first, circling and gliding and laving her delicate places with tender care until she felt as if she floated in some sensual dream.

But very soon she began to crave more, panting her wordless desire against the linen of Rane's shirt. He let the soap slip away then, replacing it with his fingers. His strokes grew firm, the pace quickened, and she couldn't help answering the beckoning of his fingers with the arch of her hips. A deep longing built inside her, less insistent, but more profound, a need to draw closer to Rane.

Clutching the fabric of his shirt in one desperate hand, Florie gasped as a huge wave of sensation built within her like an ocean wave gathering mass to break upon the shore. His arm pulled her close as his fingers played expertly upon her, summoning her release, demanding her surrender, drawing forth her most secret passions.

Suddenly something within her stilled. Like molten metal poured onto snow, she stiffened, one hand caught in Rane's shirt. Her back arched, and her forehead creased with blissful torment, while the desires within her yet roiled with increasing violence, bubbling up to the surface toward escape.

Her release came on an explosion of sound—a deep groan wrung from her chest, a great surge of water as she thrashed, out of control. Rane's growl of impassioned empathy as he held her safe was her only anchor in the storm of her emotions.

Rane shuddered as Florie sobbed out in surrender, as if he'd soared alongside her on her erotic flight, as if his soul had mingled with hers, and together they'd taken the journey. Indeed, he'd enjoyed her release almost as if 'twere his own. Almost.

There was still the matter of his bulging staff, angry with need, thick as a lance with unrequited lust.

Florie collapsed against his chest, and he pressed his trembling lips softly to the top of her head. Never had he felt so torn, caught between satiation and hunger, between blissful relief and burning need. He'd fed well on her passion, and yet he craved more. Like an arrow cocked at the ready with no prey in sight, he waited tensely.

After a long, torturous moment, Florie made up his mind. She turned gracefully to her side and, curving one dripping arm up over his shoulder, pulled herself into a more intimate embrace. Her breasts, warm and wet from the bath, seemed to steam through his shirt, and his nipples hardened against her. Her mouth closed upon his neck with grateful kisses, and he shivered as she moved higher, her breath singeing his ear.

"Lie with me," she whispered, so softly that he thought he'd imagined her voicing his own wish.

He waited with bated breath, unable to believe what he'd heard.

"Lie with me, Rane."

He closed his eyes as the dulcet sound curled into his ear, whirling his thoughts like an accomplished caress.

"I pray ye," she murmured. "I know what I'm doin'. And I trust ye'll be gentle. Please."

'Twas all the convincing his starving body needed. Let Florie claim him, he thought. Let her own him. Later he'd sort out matters of the heart, carefully, tenderly. But for tonight, he'd let her possess him, heart and soul.

In one drenching sweep, he pulled her from the bath, naked and slippery in his arms. While she clung to him, he quickly wrapped several linens about her against the chill. His gaze swept the perimeter of the sanctuary, seeking a place for their coupling. By the fierce raging in his braies, he'd be content to take her against the door of the church.

But he was neither beast nor berserker. A church was no place for trysting.

Nae, he'd take her into the forest and lay her upon a soft bed of moss, amid the sweet scent of spring clover and bay, beneath a thousand star candles. Their cries of release would be muffled by brush and branch, fern and leaf-fall.

Stopping to gather several plaids for warmth, he carried her from the church, finding his way in the shadowy night with the unerring instincts of a woodsman.

He found a place not far into the trees, a small clearing where the three-quarter moon shone softly down through the leafy elms and the grass grew thick and lush. Spreading the largest plaid, he knelt to lay Florie gently upon the forest bed, hovering close above her to keep the chill away.

'Twas tempting to take her swiftly. His body was primed for the hunt, and 'twas clear her desires were likewise inflamed. But Florie was not a milkmaid to be quickly tumbled in the hay. Nor was she a worldly noblewoman accustomed to hurried trysts.

So he took a deep, calming breath and willed himself to be patient.

She shivered once beneath him.

"Are ye frightened?" he whispered.

"Nae, only cold."

Her words were sweet invitation. "Let me warm ye," he murmured. Bracing himself on an elbow, he peeled back the layers of damp linen from her one by one until she lay naked in the moonlight. Then he dragged one of the plaids over her so that the soft wool caressed her bare skin. He quickly removed his boots, untied his hose, and pulled off his shirt, stripping down to his braies. The cold didn't begin to pierce his fiery Viking hide, but, not wishing to frighten Florie with the sight of his engorged staff, he ducked beneath the plaid before slipping his braies from his hips.

He felt the heat of her before their flesh even touched, like the radiance from a glowing iron set by the hearth.

"Let me warm ye, Florie," he breathed again.

Then he stretched atop the full length of her until their bodies kissed in the most intimate of embraces. Everywhere their flesh touched, warmth bloomed between them, petals of fire opening and spreading and bringing instant heat to the cool spring night.

Florie released an impassioned sigh, and he sucked it at once between his teeth, hissing like hot steel plunged into water. 'Twas a painful ecstasy, like searing flame in the midst of snow, yet he reveled in the fiery torment of her silken skin, urged on with nearly unbearable restraint to seek the deeper heat waiting within her.

"Ah, Florie…" He cradled her head in his hand, then let his own drop weakly beside hers.

As if the mere heat of feminine flesh upon him were not enough to tempt him to incaution, Florie began to move beneath him, luxuriating in the delicious friction with innocent impatience.

"Oh…aye," she gasped. "Aye…"

At her words, Rane's thoughts bolted like a wild beast, and 'twas all he could do to harness them. Yet somehow he managed, despite his fell frenzy of desire, to think of her needs first. He parted from her long enough to insinuate one hand between them, seeking out the soft, damp curls guarding her maidenhead. She moaned, instantly arching up to welcome his touch.

"Aye…aye…" Her voice was sultry, beckoning, irresistible.

"Nae." He needed to prepare her. She was such a wee thing. Marry, if he hurt her again, he'd never forgive himself. He needed time to ease the way.

Yet she gave him none.

"Aye," she insisted, thrusting her hips upward until his fingers trespassed into the sleek folds of her womanhood.

He groaned. Ah, faith. He'd intended to moisten her, but she was already wet, slick with lust. His staff, drenched in that same nectar, surged in anticipation.

"Aye," she gasped.

He slipped a finger within her, letting his thumb circle over the delicate bud above. 'Twas difficult keeping his desires at bay while he prepared her to receive them. But Rane was not, as Florie had once accused him, a man with no finesse. He could be gentle, even under such enormous pressure.

What he hadn't counted upon was Florie's eagerness and her unpredictability. As he pushed patiently inward, she suddenly thrust her hips up, plunging his finger deep within, impaling herself on him with a sharp cry.

Silently cursing, he did the only thing he could—remained very still, waiting for her to adjust to the invasion. "I'm sorry, love," he breathed, though indeed 'twas not his fault. After a moment, in the hopes of distracting her from the pain, he resumed pleasuring her with his thumb.

Very soon her gasps sweetened, breaking softly against his cheek. And when he finally moved within her again, she arched tentatively counter to his slow thrusts, looping her arms up around his neck in forgiveness and welcome.

"Don't be sorry," she murmured.

Her gaze rested upon his mouth, and he answered her wordless request, lowering his head to bestow a kiss upon her trembling lips.

Then he withdrew his hand to guide his aching staff where it most longed to go. As he at last slid within her, she groaned in a slow ecstasy that echoed his own. And then he was lost...

Florie had thought it couldn't get any better, but this...this union, this perfect melding of flesh with flesh like two metals blending, made her feel as if she touched heaven. He was so large within her that she should be torn in two, and yet somehow she accommodated him, stretching to a sensual tautness that left her even more sensitive to his movements. The momentary pain had vanished now, and there were no words to describe the sense of completion, of wholeness, of homecoming she felt as he gathered her against him, touching her everywhere, pulsing rhythmically into her as if 'twould make their hearts beat together.

She let her eyes drift open, looking past his shoulder into the diamond-studded ebony sky. The night was cold. Her gasps made soft puffs of mist upon the air. But the heat of Rane's body, of her own passion as she writhed hungrily beneath him, warmed her. 'Twas perfect, she decided, the cool evening, the jewel stars, the yielding bed of leaves, the scent of flower and moss and laurel. 'Twas a night she'd never forget.

And then her yearning began to wax again. Just as she'd adjusted to Rane's encroachment, accepted his full embrace, learned his dance, the hot core of her desire awakened. No longer was she the willing receptacle of his adoration. No longer did she await his pleasure. Nae, she began to strain upward of her own accord, greedily seeking, not to grant him his release, but to claim her own. Again.

She clutched at him everywhere, digging her fingers into his shoulders and back, pressing her brow against his collarbone, unable to will where she touched him, what she did. All she knew was that she hungered, more fiercely than before, that she must feed this hunger, and that Rane was the source of her sustenance.

Ah, God, she needed to be closer, closer. She wrapped her legs about his hips, drawing him into her body, into her soul.

"Florie...I can't hold on much...," he gasped. Then he began to grunt hoarsely in her ear, a groan of pure animal need that inflamed her blood and charged her senses, driving her half-mad with pleasure.

The sensation sharpened, intensifying until the

torturous craving gripped her again, leaving her wanting for air, holding her still to endure what was to come. But this time the yearning ran far deeper…

And then her body, her mind, her spirit splintered into a thousand pieces.

Rane's voice was almost a sob as he buried his face in her hair, lunging forward. The timbre of that one sound—at once sweet and bitter, powerful and vulnerable—moved her beyond the sphere of space and time, beyond the world, as if she danced on air among the diamond stars glittering overhead.

And then they tumbled from the heavens together, like jewels spilling across the velvet sky—their bodies entwined, their breath mingling, their hearts pulsing in tandem—until they lay nestled again on the soft and welcoming earth.

Slowly Florie became aware of the cool night once more, of the crisp smell of the forest. But this time the chill was diminished by Rane's warm embrace. And now the air was redolent with the musky scent of their coupling.

"Florie," Rane breathed, bedewing her face with fine mist.

"Rane," she sighed in reply, amazed and sated and happy. Gloriously happy.

'Twas a brazen thing she'd done, surrendering her maidenhood so impulsively, and yet the moment and the man could not have been more perfect. She'd remember her union with Rane, her ravaging Viking, as long as she lived.

If by chance a tear slipped out from beneath her lashes just then, 'twas surely a tear of gladness, she told herself. There was nothing to regret. Though soon Rane would go his way and Florie hers, she'd hold this precious memory in her heart forever.

CHAPTER 17

Florie could hardly think straight during Sabbath Mass. If she had, she might have noticed the telling smirk on Lady Mavis's face, the quiet, calculating expression that, like the strange peace before a storm, foretold danger. But instead, thoughts of Rane intruded upon Florie's prayers, and as she sat on the fridstool, wrapped in the sylvan scent of his cloak, the sensual remembrance warmed her cheeks, washed over her flesh, and threatened to melt her bones.

She felt...transformed.

'Twas just as well he'd gone hunting again during the service, for already she yearned for him beyond all wisdom. She missed his sly smile, his wry words, his clever touch. Her lass's body craved him again. But most troubling of all, there was a wistful longing for him where her heart resided.

So lost was she in her brooding that she took no notice at first when the Father's gentle words broke into her thoughts.

"My child."

She started, then pushed back her hood, surprised to find Mass over and the sanctuary empty. "Aye?"

"I crave a word with ye, lass." The Father leaned upon his walking staff and frowned several times, as if he didn't know how to begin. Then he said, "Ye know 'tis a serious crime o' which ye're accused."

"Aye." She straightened. "And ye know I'm innocent."

"I believe ye, lass," he was quick to assure her. Then he sighed thoughtfully. "But what ye don't know is with whom ye barter."

"Lord Gilbert?" She thought she knew him rather well. He was like a lot of the nobles she'd met—haughty, stern, domineering. But surely he was reasonable as well. After all, it took a man of some character to act as sheriff.

"Nae. Lady Mavis. She's the one who steers your fate while Gilbert is away."

Florie was used to tyrannical noblewomen as well. "I'm not afraid o' her."

"Ye should be."

"But I'm in the right, Father. I didn't steal anythin' from her. The piece was sold in error. And I returned her coin."

"Aye, lass, but ye see, Lady Mavis," he said, visibly searching his mind for the right words, "Lady Mavis is like a hound that's caught a whiff o' some choice prey. She'll give chase, lass, until she runs ye to ground." He brought his bushy white brows together. "She'll plague ye until she has what she wants."

Mavis might be persistent, but Florie was just as stubborn. "She cannot have my pomander."

Impatience twisted Father Conan's normally cheery features, and his voice was uncharacteristically harsh. "Heed me well, lass. This is no petty quarrel 'tween quibblin' sisters."

"I know that."

"Ye cannot be hopin' for witnesses. No man would be fool enough to go against Lady Mavis."

"I know that as well."

"Do ye know she'd kill ye for the piece?"

"Kill me?" Florie's eyes widened, but she kept her tone light. "But she cannot. I'm in sanctuary, and until—"

"Here's what I advise," the priest sighed. "Give her the thing and—"

"Nae!"

"Lass, 'tis but a bauble."

Never. She would never give it up. "'Tis more than that. 'Tis..."

"Aye?"

How could she tell him that her destiny resided in a chain of gold links? That the pomander represented her hope of escaping a troubled household where her drunk and delusional foster father, mistaking her for his dead wife, tried to crawl into bed with her every few nights? Faith, she couldn't tell the priest that.

She didn't even try. Crossing her arms solidly over her chest, she insisted, "She cannot have it."

Despite his blindness, Father Conan seemed to gaze down at her with displeasure, disappointment, and disgust. "'Tis not only *your* life that hangs in the balance, lass," he grumbled. "Ye've put our friend Rane at risk as well."

The priest's words stole the wind from her proud sails. She hadn't thought of Rane in that way before. Her shoulders dropped with the weight of the truth, and her arms unfolded onto her lap.

The Father was right.

Rane had already defied Lady Mavis by caring for Florie when the lady would prefer she starve. By holding him to his vow to help her escape, Florie was dragging him into her battle, making him an accomplice to her crime.

She had to let him go. This wasn't his fight. She could no longer put him in danger. He'd been too kind to say nay to her, too decent to abandon her or let her starve. But 'twas too much to ask that he aid in her flight, no matter what he'd promised.

He'd done much for her already. She could ask no more of him. Aye, she would let him go, push him away if she must.

Her heart seized with pain at the thought, and 'twas the magnitude of that pain that made her realize she *must* leave him, for whether she willed it or not, she *had* fallen in love with the cursed Viking.

"Now I've sent the lad on errands for the day," the Father told her. "He'll not return till nightfall. I want ye to think on things a while, lass. Ye're a merchant. Surely ye can see 'tis not a sensible bargain—your life for a shiny trinket."

Floried sighed. Father Conan must think her a shallow lass. But of course, he didn't know the entire story—why she'd come to Selkirk, whom she sought, why she couldn't surrender the pomander...not that it would matter if he knew. There was nothing the priest could change. Lady Mavis wouldn't care that the pomander was of utmost importance to Florie. After forty days Florie would still be tried and, according to Father Conan, be found guilty.

Nae, there was no hope but to escape...on her own.

No regrets. She said the words over and over mentally

as she tightened the laces of her bloodstained kirtle, as if repetition would make them true.

But her chest felt hollow, and unshed tears stung her eyes.

She picked up the precious gold pomander, running her fingers over the carved initials, wondering if 'twas truly worth all she risked. Should she surrender the piece as the priest suggested, give up her quest for her noble sire, return to her life of dodging the advances of the worthless foster father she was forced to support?

The image of the once talented goldsmith, unwashed and unshaven, snoring away the day while she labored at the workbench, made despair settle over her like a lead cloak. Nae, the only way she could bear the thought of going home to Stirling was if she held on to the hope that she might return to Selkirk one day and find her real father.

Before she could change her mind, she stuffed the girdle into the satchel, along with her rings—the few she hadn't given to Father Conan to buy food for the peasants, and her brooch, which, she realized ruefully, still bore a rust-colored stain from stabbing Rane.

The rest of the things she'd been given—the woad kirtle, the soap, the comb, the plaids—she left. No one would be able to claim later that she'd stolen a thing.

Indeed, it felt more like she left behind a part of her.

Her heart ached at the thought, and an errant tear seeped from the corner of her eye. Damn! She dared not weep aloud, not while the priest was working in the vestry, putting away the Sabbath service. She wiped the drop away before it could fall, but 'twas not so easy to wipe away the bittersweet memories that barraged her mind, memories of Rane's wry smile, his sultry gaze, his healing touch...

God's wounds, how could she ever bear to leave him after last night?

To her dismay, tears welled up too quickly to stem the tide, so she let them stream silently down her cheeks, let them blur her vision, soften the world, and wash the sanctuary to a vague memory of stone and wood, glass and candlelight.

She understood now. This was the feeling that had made her mother cry endlessly into her pillow, the feeling that had turned her father into a weeping drunkard. 'Twas far worse than any physical pain, worse than the arrow shot into her thigh, worse than the scalding she'd suffered. Surely her heart had cracked in two, for anguish flowed like blood from a wound, drenching her in despair.

Indeed, the only thing that gave her the strength to shoulder the satchel and place one foot in front of the other toward the church door, the only thing keeping her from throwing herself onto the stones and sobbing her eyes dry, was the knowledge that to Rane she was like any other lass he'd tumbled. He could leave her without a backward glance.

She wished she could say goodbye...and thank him...and tell him she'd never forget him. But there'd be no opportunity. And even given the chance, she knew she couldn't face him with the fact of her leaving. He might urge her to stay. And, God help her, she wasn't certain he wouldn't convince her to do just that, wisdom be damned.

Nae, 'twas surely providence that the priest had sent Rane away this day, that the only witness to her escape was blind.

Casting one cautious look back toward the altar as she reached the door, she made the sign of the cross, took a ragged breath, and crossed over the threshold...out of sanctuary.

Her heart pounding, she scanned the twilit forest for danger, half expecting a pack of Hertford's marauders to come bursting out of the trees.

But the woods were silent. She took a shuddering breath. If she could manage her fear and steal through the cover of the forest, avoiding the wolves and thieves and Englishmen that might lurk therein, maybe she'd gain enough distance from Selkirk by morn to travel safely on the main road.

She had enough gold to pay for the journey, as long as she encountered no robbers, and if she kept to the...

"Florie!"

Her heart jumped into her throat. Nae, it couldn't be.

"Florie?"

Christ's bones! 'Twas Rane, returning.

Sweet saints, he was as handsome as a Nordic prince, striding toward the church with supper as if he brought back the spoils of his latest conquest. Against her will, Florie's heart fluttered, remembering his strong body against her, around her, within her...

Ah, God, she mustn't think of such things. She mustn't. She'd made up her mind to go. She must be strong.

"Good evenin', wee fawn," he called, his face wreathed in a glorious smile, oblivious to her anguish. "I've brought a surprise for supper."

Wee fawn. The endearment was like a knife plunged in her chest. Lord, she mustn't listen or she'd be lost.

"Custard tarts," he tempted.

She bit her lip. Custard tarts. She loved them, but they'd never be as sweet, as tempting as Rane's kiss. God's wounds, how would she live without that kiss?

A sob lodged in her throat.

Sweet Lord, she must not weaken, must not veer from her course, for both their sakes.

'Twas the hardest thing she'd ever done, but she managed to tear her gaze away from him. Focusing tearful eyes on the forest ahead, clenching her fists with diamond-hard resolve, she slowly descended the steps.

Dread prickled along Rane's spine. Something was wrong.

All day long, he'd thought of nothing but the goldsmith. He hadn't even cared that his hunting was fruitless. His mind was distracted by visions of Florie with her limpid gaze, her satiated smile, her shapely body. She'd left him completely and deliciously helpless last night, beaten him at his own game of seduction.

Yet he'd surrendered happily. She'd caught him like a rabbit, in a snare of lust and trust and affection stronger than any he'd experienced before. And today his heart was full of joy, full of wonder. Full of hopeless adoration.

Aye, he'd decided at last, the mighty hunter had fallen. Rane was in love.

The confession was a relief. For too long he'd cast his net wide, sweeping up all the feminine creatures who chanced past, enjoying their fleeting company yet willing to cast them aside like undersized fish if they grew too demanding.

With Florie, 'twas different.

Though she claimed his very soul, though he was certain in his mind he'd fallen into a situation of mortal danger, still he couldn't convince his heart. Florie made him happy, deliriously happy. And if he must yield as her captive to prolong that happiness, so be it. If he must be possessed to possess her, he would.

'Twas that vow that put a skip in his step as he hurried toward the church, toward...home. Then he smiled to himself. When had he begun to think of the crumbling old sanctuary as home? 'Twas Florie who made it seem so, bringing warmth and comfort to the barren walls and shining light into the shadowy corners.

But now, as he neared the church and the lass he—aye—loved, the melancholy shadows haunting her eyes filled him with misgiving.

"Darlin'?"

She said nothing, only stared steadfastly at the path ahead and descended the steps. Her cool manner chilled him to the bone.

"Florie."

Still she didn't answer, though there was a trembling in her chin that bespoke a temptation to reply. His throat thickened. By Loki, what was wrong? Was she angry with him? Did she blame him for the loss of her maidenhood? Unaccustomed panic raced through him at the thought that she might not care for him as he cared for her, that she might regret what they'd done, that she might...leave him.

"Florie!" His voice was rough with dread this time. "Where are ye goin', lass?"

A slim part of him hoped that he misread her expression, that she stepped into the woods only to relieve herself, that she'd afterward tweak his nose and call him a silly want-wit, and they'd both laugh about the misunderstanding.

But 'twas obvious from her averted glance 'twas more than that. She carried her satchel, and she'd donned her bloodstained gown. Oh, aye, she planned more than a brief visit to the bushes. His heart thudding ominously, he watched her as, step by steady step, she walked out of his life.

Did she intend to desert him, then? Without a word? Without a farewell glance? His chest began to throb with a deep-seated ache, as if a horse had kicked him in the ribs. How could she simply walk off as if they'd never met, never talked, never, for the love of God, kissed and wept and laughed and sworn and made love together?

He wouldn't let her. He refused to stand idly by while she slipped through his grasp. Not now—now that he knew he loved her.

Thor's rod! He'd be damned if he'd let her leave.

"Florie!" he commanded. "Nae!"

The stubborn lass ignored him. He dropped the tarts into the dust and slipped the bow from his shoulder.

"Stay!"

She kept walking, her step quickening slightly. She was almost to the trees.

He bellowed an oath so foul it made her flinch, but still she stayed to her course.

Then he did what any hunter about to lose his prey would do. He swiftly slipped a quarrel from his quiver and nocked it into his bow, drawing back and taking aim.

"Stay where ye are," he warned.

Florie turned her head at the telltale creak of the bow. Her jaw slackened with amazement. Gone was the gentle lover of the night before. Rane's sweet mouth was grim, his brow furrowed, his eyes piercing. He was a huntsman now—his legs braced in an archer's stance, his bow drawn to its fullest arc, his arrow aimed to kill.

A silent scream echoed through her soul. Time slowed impossibly in her perception, and the world tilted beneath her feet. She staggered back in shock. With sudden clarity, she saw Rane's quartz-clear eyes narrowing on her. A tiny muscle jumped in his cheek, where his thumb nested, the same thumb that had brushed across her lips so tenderly once. She heard the stretch of sinew as his fingers flexed around the bow, heard herself drawing a long, jagged gasp.

Her pulse pounding like a death tabor, she turned away then, moving as if she swam through liquefying amber, forcing her legs to run, reaching forward, straining to make it to the forest.

She had no time to wonder at his betrayal, no time to question the hostility in his glare. She thought only of fleeing his savage weapon.

But as she desperately surged forward, the trees seemed to draw away before her eyes, and she felt a sob of panic rise in her throat. She'd never make it. Already she could imagine the blunt pain of the bolt shot into her back, shoving her to the ground with killing force.

But by some miracle, no shaft whistled toward her. And when she finally succumbed to morbid curiosity, craning her head around, she saw he'd dropped the bow and now pursued her on foot, closing the distance with astonishing speed.

With a startled squeak, she whipped about. Faster! She must run faster!

She could hear him now, drawing closer and closer, his normally silent footfalls pounding upon the sod with maddening regularity. The knave didn't even bother to run. He knew she couldn't match his long stride. Nor did he call after her. 'Twas clear he'd given up on that score. But they both knew her capture was inevitable. She was at a disadvantage in every way.

Still she bolted forward, unable to make herself stop, too alarmed to yield. His steps grew louder, the measured crunch of leaves sounding smug against her panicked scuffling. She could almost feel the heat of his rage burning the path behind her like wildfire.

Her heart hammered at her ribs. He was almost upon her now. Almost in arm's reach. There was nowhere to flee, nowhere to hide.

Then she found an escape.

Ahead, to her left, the land fell away, making a steep embankment that extended down a score of yards or so.

There was no time to think. She bolted toward the edge of the ravine, intending to run or slide or roll down the leafy slope, whatever it took to elude capture.

But he must have guessed her strategy.

"Nae!" he yelled, and in two strides he was upon her.

He tackled her with all the force of a falling tree. Thankfully, as she went down he turned with her, taking the brunt of the fall upon his own back. But her wind and her dignity were knocked from her as she dropped, sprawled across his body as if he were a great pallet, inches from the edge of the ravine.

There was no chance of escape now, not while he trapped her in his strong Viking arms. She squirmed in vain against his powerful body, her heart fluttering as wildly as a fledgling's wings.

"Hold still," he muttered against her ear.

"Nae! Let me go!" she screamed. "Let me—"

His palm covered her mouth, silencing her cries, and she struggled desperately, fearing he would suffocate her with his hand.

"Hush," he murmured. "Quiet." His voice was surprisingly gentle for someone who had just aimed a loaded bow at her. "I wouldn't have shot ye," he muttered against her ear, almost as if he convinced himself. "I wouldn't have. 'Twas only my damned instincts."

She didn't believe him. She'd seen the intensity of his hunter's gaze, and she didn't want to see it again. At the very least, she'd not go down without a fight. Her arms trapped, her dagger out of reach, she resorted to the only weapon she had. Baring her teeth, she bit down, catching the meat of his thumb between her jaws.

He cried out, snatching back his injured hand, and for one victorious moment Florie thought she might escape.

But he rolled to his feet, dragging her with him, and, before she could get her bearings, hefted her up and slung her across his shoulders like fresh kill.

The temptation to yell for help was strong. But 'twould avail nothing. No one in Selkirk would come to a felon's aid, not when a brawny huntsman stood in their way.

So she tried her last weapon—reason. All the way back to the church, she tried to explain. 'Twas dangerous for her to stay any longer. She had to return to Stirling. She even promised that she'd disavow any knowledge of Rane, so none would know he aided in her escape, if only he'd let her go.

He turned a deaf ear.

Her hopes fell as he climbed the steps and pushed his way through the door, returning her to where she'd begun, to sanctuary.

"Florie!" Father Conan was shouting when they entered. She had the sense he'd been calling her for some time.

"She's here," Rane answered, his voice stern.

"Ah, lass!" the Father sighed in relief, clapping a hand to his bosom. "I wondered where ye'd gone off to. I feared maybe Lady Mavis or—"

"Father!" Florie seized the opportunity for an ally. "Help me, Father!"

"What is it, lass?"

"He tried to kill me!" she shouted in a rush, despite Rane's tightening grasp. "Rane tried to kill me!"

With a sigh of exasperation, Rane swung her off of his shoulders, setting her on her feet none too gently.

"Rane?" the priest asked.

"I told ye, Florie," Rane said, "I wouldn't have shot ye. I only wished to stop ye."

"I didn't wish to be stopped."

"Ye put yourself in grave danger by fleeing. Ye're an outlaw. Do ye know how long ye'd last in the forest, alone, at night?"

The priest's brows rose. "Is this true, lass? Were ye fleein' sanctuary?"

She couldn't lie to a priest. "Maybe."

"Well then, lass," he said with a puzzled frown, "what else would ye expect o' the lad?"

'Twas an odd statement indeed, not at all what Florie anticipated from the affable priest.

"What do ye mean?" she asked.

"What did ye think Rane would do?"

"I...I expected he might...protect me."

The Father straightened suddenly in surprise, turning his head toward Rane. "Did ye never tell her, lad?"

When Rane didn't answer, Florie turned to look at him. His face had darkened into an inscrutable scowl.

"Tell me what?" She glanced back and forth between Rane and the priest.

Rane's expression reflected a confusion of rage and shame and frustration. With a growl, he turned on his heel and swept back through the door of the church, slamming it so hard that it echoed in the sanctuary and knocked dust from the ceiling timbers.

Florie felt dread steal along the back of her neck. "What is it, Father?" she ventured. "What did he not tell me?"

"Lass," he said, reaching out to squeeze her shoulder. "Rane is huntsman to Lord Gilbert. He's not here to protect ye. He's here to prevent your escape."

ChAPTER 18

Florie felt sick. She couldn't speak. She couldn't breathe. Shaking, she staggered back, fumbling her way to the fridstool.

"Lass," the Father said, "are ye well?"

Nae, she was not well. She would never be well. Rane's betrayal tasted like bitter poison.

"Fine," she managed to choke out, straining to draw breath into her lungs.

"Do ye not see, lass?" the priest said in soft concern. "Ye cannot leave. If ye do, Rane will pay the price o' your crime. He'll hang for thievery."

Against her wishes, images flew through her mind, nightmares of Rane swinging, gaunt and limp, from a gallows, and then bittersweet visions of the past few days—Rane's laughing eyes and flashing white teeth, his protective arms and gentle hands. She heard his voice in her head, soothing and warm, smelled his woodland scent, felt the power of his embrace.

Had it all been a lie? Had he played her false only to

keep her docile? To keep her in captivity? Or worse, only to coax her into his bed?

She felt as if her heart had been kicked from her breast, that her chest lay empty, her soul hollow. Only a deep-seated nausea lingered to remind her she was mortal.

Later, she'd be furious. Later, she'd rail and cast aspersions and curse his offspring for all eternity. And after that, she'd accept what she'd learned from her parents—'twas a fool who'd surrender her heart.

But for now, she was stunned and aching. Unable to cease trembling, she hunched over her knees and fought the urge to retch.

What words of solace the priest offered she didn't know. The outside world faded from her awareness as a slow, killing frost crept into her bones.

Rane didn't come back. But Florie was certain he stood guard outside the church, his lord's obedient huntsman to the end.

At suppertime she refused sustenance from the priest, having lost her appetite, though she was tempted to drown her hurt in the bottle of cider he brought. But that was her foster father's way, and Florie was not her foster father. Nor would she weep pitifully like her mother. Instead, as the night closed like a burial shroud over her dying spirit, Florie huddled in the dark, trying to escape into sleep.

Later she would gather the shreds of her trust and confront what lay ahead. But for now, her broken heart would let her do nothing but wallow in profound sorrow as she tried valiantly to fade into the oblivion of slumber.

Mavis bit her lip as she gazed out her sunny window in the direction of the decrepit old church, tapping the rolled missive on the sill. If she managed to pull off this bit of subterfuge, she'd be restored to her former status as the English Crown's most valuable spy.

Her contacts had grasped the significance of the cryptic message she'd sent by falcon. According to their reply, they intended to make their way in numbers to Musselburgh to intercept Princess Mary before she could take refuge there. The return missive in Mavis's hand requested she keep Gilbert's men-at-arms occupied for the next few days so that the English troops could safely steal across Fraser land to claim the princess.

Two birds with one stone—King Henry had taught her that expression, and it seemed apt now. She turned from the window with a smug grin and tossed the parchment onto the fire, where it smoldered and unfurled, glowing orange before it went up in flames.

She knew exactly how she was going to keep the Fraser soldiers busy.

Rane hitched up and tied his braies, then ran both hands back through his tangled hair. He bit out a weary curse, pounding the side of his fist against the oak tree he'd just pissed upon.

Two days had passed since he'd spoken to Florie. Two long days and three interminable nights. God help him, he'd slept horribly for all of them. Dawn had never come this morn, unless one could call the roiling spring storm clouds visible in the east proof that the sun was somewhere in the sky. He felt as miserable as the bruised heavens looked, and even the expectant peace of the forest could not cheer him.

He'd wanted to hurt Florie, to repay her for playing maliciously with his heart, for leaving him. But he hadn't meant to threaten her with his bow and arrow. And he'd certainly never meant for her to find out about Lord Gilbert's orders.

Now she'd never trust him.

If she had harbored regrets about their tryst before, surely now she wished she'd never met him. If before she questioned her affections, now she must loathe him.

For two days they'd eaten their meals apart. For two days he'd seen only glimpses of her when the Father passed in and out of the church. 'Twas driving him mad.

He picked up a stone from the path and cast it into the bushes. There was only one way to regain her trust, he knew. One way he might enter into her good graces again.

He'd promised to take Florie home to Stirling. Maybe 'twas time to make good on that promise.

'Twas a great risk. Lord Gilbert would blame Rane for Florie's flight and hold him accountable for the loss. If the lord felt merciful, Rane would be lucky to escape with his life and a lifetime of debt. But if Lady Mavis was of a mind to steer Gilbert by the ballocks, as she often did, Rane might hang.

Not that that would stop him. He'd be happy to save Florie's life even at the cost of his own. But he also wanted to prove to Florie that he'd never betrayed her trust.

Would she believe him? Did she even care for him any longer? After everything they'd shared, it seemed impossible that she could have feigned her love for him all this time.

She'd seemed truly charmed by his company, pleasured by his kisses, gloriously thrilled by their moonlight lovemaking. They'd soared into the night together, howling their passion at the moon like kindred wolves, mated for life.

How could she walk away from it all, turn him aside as if nothing had happened, as if their hearts had never entwined, as if their souls were not melded?

'Twas inconceivable that she didn't love him, he decided—that as they'd consummated their lust beneath the stars she hadn't experienced the same joy, the same passion, the same perfect oneness of mind, body, and spirit. That bond was undeniable, the magic between them unquestionable. After all, he thought with a self-mocking smile, was he not irresistible to all Scottish maids?

'Twas obvious, then. Florie wasn't guided by her heart. 'Twasn't her heart that whispered in her ear, *abandon him*. Her heart was too kind, too gentle for that. Nae, that insidious advice came from her head.

And her head could be reasoned with.

Rane squared his Viking shoulders. If he wanted the lass, he'd just have to fight for her like his ancestors before him. Fueled by hope and iron resolve, he lengthened his strides toward the sanctuary.

He couldn't have been absent from the steps more than a few moments. Yet as he emerged from the wood and glanced at the church, he saw that in this brief time everything had changed. His bow and quiver were no longer propped against the wall, and the door to the sanctuary stood open.

He halted in his tracks. From the dark doorway emerged the silvery tip of a quarrel. 'Twas aimed at him, though it strayed frequently from its mark. And squinting behind the wavering shaft nocked into his own half-cocked bow stood Florie.

"Don't come any closer," she called hoarsely.

He didn't intend to, not with the way that arrow dipped and bobbed in her unsteady grip. If she let fly the shaft, there was no telling where 'twould end up. In his experience, an unpracticed archer was far more dangerous than a seasoned one. At this distance, at least, he was in little peril. Florie hadn't the strength to draw the bow completely. She'd be fortunate to send the quarrel flying more than a dozen yards.

"Stay there," she said, her voice trembling almost as much as the arrow.

He didn't move a muscle. He wondered what Florie intended. Surely she didn't mean to kill him. On the other hand, if she truly believed he meant to hold her in sanctuary until Lord Gilbert came for her...

She took a hesitant step across the threshold, kicking the door shut behind her, then made her tense way down the steps. Rane gulped as the bow swung toward him. Her full satchel hung from one arm. 'Twas apparent she meant to succeed this time. And 'twas apparent she wouldn't hesitate to shoot anyone who stood between her and escape.

Anyone but the man who loved her. Surely she wouldn't shoot him. He had to believe that.

Silently praying for the first time that there was truth to the ancient Viking curse, Rane drew himself to his full height and called her name softly. "Florie."

"Nae!" Florie cried, her agitation making the bow wobble wildly.

She'd waited all morn to steal away, listened at the door since dawn for sounds of Rane's daily trek to the woods to empty his bladder. The bow and arrow had been an afterthought. She thought she'd be gone before he could come after her, before he'd even realized she'd left. But when she found his weapon on the threshold, she'd decided to arm herself as a precaution.

Never had she imagined she might have to use it.

She'd devoted hours over the last few days to despising the duplicitous archer, imagining fearsome punishments for his treasonous soul. She'd even carved reliefs of tortured figures into the wooden beams of the church to keep her hands busy, telling Father Conan they were depictions of martyred saints. She'd convinced herself she would be well rid of the lying coward. Indeed, she almost hoped he *would* be hanged in her stead.

But now that he stood before her in the light of day...

Against the gray mist of the forest, his flesh looked golden and warm and alive. His voice sounded deep, sweet, and impossibly tender. His eyes were dewy with... It must be the cool morning air. But 'twas so painfully easy to imagine they shone with love.

A sob lodged in her gullet. Her limbs quaked like a newborn foal's. God help her, despite his cruel betrayal, despite her broken heart, she couldn't fire the arrow.

He took a step toward her.

"Nae!" she shouted, needing to bluff, even if she hadn't the will to shoot.

"Florie."

"Don't." She clenched her jaw so tightly it hurt, and her breath came in shallow gasps. If he took another step...

"Wee fawn."

"Nae," she sobbed.

"I would never have let him take ye."

She tightened her grip on the bow. Even now the bastard lied to her.

"Ye must believe me," he said.

"Why?" she burst out, anger rising to drown her pain. "So ye can ply me with more empty promises?"

"Nae." His eyes slowly traced the length of her, as if he memorized every curve. She shuddered under his perusal, as if he touched her everywhere he looked. "Ye must believe me...because I love ye."

Florie's chin began to tremble. She clamped her lips together to still it. Hell, Rane did not fight fairly. 'Twas unspeakably cruel to taunt her so. Aye, she may have been stupid enough to believe him once, but no longer.

"I love ye, Florie." He took another step.

"Nae."

"I love your laughter. I love the way your hair shines in the sunlight." Another step. "I love your sleepy eyes in the mornin' and your soft breathin' at night." Another. "I love the way ye sulk when ye lose at Hnefatafl, and the way ye crow when ye win."

Florie cursed the tears of misery that filled her eyes. If only he meant what he said... If only he truly loved her... But 'twas all deception.

"I love the passion ye have for your craft," he continued, advancing slowly, "and the way your shoulders straighten with pride when ye speak o' your work."

She could shoot him now. He was close enough that she was fairly certain not to miss. But her eyes were so flooded with moisture, she could hardly take aim.

"I love your strength in the face o' pain, and Odin mock

me for a fool, I even love your stubborn spirit." He was so close now that he needed only to murmur. "I love the way your hands disappear within mine."

Her arms shuddered dangerously on the bow, but still he came toward her, unafraid.

"I love your breath upon my neck."

He stood not three yards away now. If she released the arrow, 'twould kill him.

"I love the way ye taste," he whispered.

He was staring at her mouth, and she swore she could almost feel his kiss.

"I love the welcome in your arms," he breathed, "and the warmth o' your body."

He stopped directly before the bow, his chest a perfect target for the arrow.

"Kill me if ye will," he said, "for if I don't have your love in return, I'm better off dead."

A tear spilled over, escaping down her cheek. Like gold over flame, her resolve melted, reducing her to a formless pool of emotions. Maybe she *was* bewitched, for despite the warnings in her head, despite every shred of sense that told her she was mad to trust him, her heart yearned to believe.

With a soft cry, she let the bow slip from her fingers. As the arrow clattered harmlessly upon the dirt, he stepped toward her, his arms open and welcoming. And, God curse her for a fool, she fell willingly into them.

Their kiss was sweet and savage and desperate, filled with the hunger of their lonely nights apart. Florie let herself drown in his pacifying embrace. 'Twas as if Rane's lips sucked the very will from her, infusing her lungs instead with the elixir of desire. She drank it of her own volition, letting it numb her reason and assuage her fears. Their tongues spoke the language of love together, and a heady rush of desire coursed through her, humming in her ears, sizzling in her veins. Before long, her senses were spiraling out of control, like a whirlpool dragging her down to her doom. And still she let it happen.

"Oh, Florie," he growled against her mouth, weaving his fingers through her hair. "Don't leave me. I couldn't bear it."

"Rane," she gasped, her lips at last revealing what her mind had so long denied. "I love ye so."

As if her words were an incantation breaking a curse, he pulled abruptly away from her, his chest heaving, his nostrils flaring, his eyes piercing her with such intensity she feared she'd go up in flame.

"Indeed?" He looked as if his fate hung upon her answer.

"Aye, God help me."

He closed his eyes in relief, and when he opened them again, they were filled with an emotion that made her knees weak. "God help us both."

Then there was no time for words, for he drew her into another embrace, and his mouth swept down to claim hers once again. She no longer cared that she was foolish, no longer cared that she'd wagered her heart. All she knew was how divine Rane made her feel, how precious, how cherished, how beloved.

Casting aside propriety as easily as a cloak, she leaned into his arms, resting her hands upon his massive shoulders, arching back to let him deepen the kiss. His hand eased up her side, catching her under the arm, his thumb brushing over her gown, awakening the nipple beneath. She jerked at the lightning shock of his touch, and her senses began to rise as quickly as a raging river in a storm of passion.

She moaned as he cupped her bottom, squeezing gently, pulling her forward against the firm evidence of his lust with an answering groan. Her body tingled in memory, in anticipation, and she writhed greedily against him. Saints forgive her, she wanted him again. Inside her.

Blithe pleasure and sweet frustration warred within her as she sought to touch more of him. She stroked and kissed and lapped at what delicious skin was bared to her, but 'twas not enough. She clawed at his garments, seeking access to the supple flesh underneath, like a wild animal feeding on prey, until she grew near feverish with longing. Then she let her fingers trace his ribs, his abdomen, and lower, until she finally pressed her bold palm against his trews.

He gasped. Then he grunted deep in his throat, opening her mouth with his tongue, invading with almost violent thirst until she grew dizzy with desire.

"I need ye," he muttered against her mouth.

"Then take me," she breathlessly replied.

Without a word, he swept her off her feet and carried her into the wood.

She would have let him savage her like a plundering Viking, so keen was her desire. And he would have done so, she sensed, were it not for the short walk into the forest that cleared his thoughts and tempered his need.

He found their soft, grassy meadow and spread his cloak for her. Then, instead of claiming her quickly, Rane lingered over each moment, as if each precious jewel of time was to be enjoyed for its own sake. He forced her to an almost painful leisure, and yet that made their lovemaking all the more poignant.

He laid her atop the cloak and undressed her slowly, unlacing her kirtle and peeling back the edges. He sighed lightly upon her skin, making her shiver in anticipation. Then, with the wicked hint of a smile, he slowly bathed her with his tongue. She moaned, arching toward his kiss.

He let his hand follow a wandering path up her leg then, caressing the back of her knee, leaving tingling traces of his touch along her skin, easing her skirts higher and higher. He contacted the nearly healed scar left by his arrow on her thigh and, moving down her body, placed a gentle kiss there, then one higher, then one higher.

Dear God, she thought, her heart drumming, if he continued...

'Twas precisely what he intended. He slipped her hem up an inch and kissed her, then another inch, then another. Her face burned as she wondered where he would stop, imagining what 'twould be like if he didn't.

He didn't. Higher and higher his kisses progressed until she squirmed in discomfort, tempted to say nae to him yet biting her lip to keep from uttering the words.

Then he dragged back her gown completely, and Florie, simultaneously ashamed and aroused by her own wanton urges, burrowed her head in the folds of his cloak.

"How beautiful ye are," she heard him say.

She squeezed her eyes tighter. She'd seen herself down there. 'Twas nothing but a nest of black curls. And yet the ragged edge to his voice told her he spoke the truth. He thought she was beautiful.

She felt a warm current of air then as he blew gently upon

her, and she quivered as her body responded, tightening and swelling and straining toward him.

"Let me touch ye," he murmured.

Her eyes still shut, she nodded.

He parted her legs slightly, stroking the insides of her thighs with the backs of his fingers, then spanned her waist with his hands. He ran his thumbs side by side from her navel down to the beginning of her downy hair, parting her gently, then gliding inward along her sleek recesses.

She brought her hand up to her mouth, biting at her knuckles as her body strove upward on its own, seeking more and more contact.

As if he knew what she craved, he slid a finger inside her. 'Twas her own body that made the motion, rocking insistently against his hand.

"Ah, wee cricket," he said, his chuckle low and seductive, "ye tempt me beyond reason."

God, she hoped so, for she had left reason behind long moments ago.

"Let me taste ye," he whispered.

She gasped. Surely he did not mean...

Before she could fret and say nae to him, indeed before she could even tell him aye, he spread her legs wider. Then he lowered his head and covered her with his mouth, searing her flesh with his warm lips in the most wicked kiss. She tossed her head back, making fists of her hands. Never had she felt so alive, so awakened.

And then he feasted upon her.

His tongue was like fire and honey and lightning all at once, burning her, soothing her, shocking her. She moaned, thrashing her head across the cloak in mindless ecstasy. As his tongue circled and stroked and suckled at her, desire rose so rapidly within her that she could scarcely catch her breath.

Higher and higher she climbed, her muscles straining, her mouth open in disbelief. And when she at last crested the pinnacle, she plummeted from the cliff so gracelessly and with such abandon that surely only Rane's steadying hands kept her from crashing to the earth.

She should have felt mortified. After all, she'd completely lost control. She lay mostly naked before a man she'd known but a fortnight, splayed in the sunlight in wanton disarray for all the world to see. She should have hidden her face in disgrace.

Instead, she felt strangely free of shame and gloriously content. Indeed, she hadn't the strength to feel anything but quiet satisfaction.

Eventually she found the will to open her eyes. When she did, Rane was looking upon her in a sort of fond wonder that warmed her heart and her bones and her soul.

"Ah, Florie," he sighed, "what ye do to me..."

She managed to rise up on her elbows to see exactly what she did to him. Aye, there was his proud staff, stretching his braies as if they were a banner announcing his desire.

And as miraculous as it seemed, her own passion was already rising again. She wanted him...now.

"Come, huntsman," she bade him softly. "Come claim your prey."

He came into her gently, slowly, gazing into her eyes, as if to make the moment last forever. He coiled his fingers through her hair, brushed his lips across her forehead, whispered endearments in her ear, all the while keeping up a leisurely rhythm that belied the storm to come. His nostrils flared with restraint, and sweat beaded his forehead as he eased deeply into her body.

Florie didn't mean to take command. 'Twas only that her body began to move on its own, at a quicker pace. She wrapped her legs about his hips and writhed upward, seeking his length, pulling back only to take more of him inside.

He didn't seem to mind. Indeed, he shuddered in pleasure, sucking air between his teeth as she forced him to a faster gait. She felt his buttocks flex beneath her heels as he took up the chase, and suddenly she was careening toward release again.

No longer did she pay heed to his movements. Burying her head against his shoulder, she clung to him, giving her body free rein. As her desire focused more and more intensely upon the place where their bodies joined, she became dimly aware of his rasping breath against her ear, in tandem with hers. Then she heard him gasp out, "Let me look at ye, Florie."

'Twas almost impossible, but somehow she managed, even in the throes of ecstasy, to open her eyes, to meet his wondrous gaze. What she saw there was almost indescribable, a joy so intense, a torment so fierce, a knowledge so clear that it touched her very soul.

She didn't remember falling. Nor could she clearly recall receiving his seed. What impressed itself upon her memory was the look in his eyes as they drank passion together, the look of pure love. Never would she forget that look.

She must have dozed a while, for when she woke, Rane had laced her gown and snuggled her into his cloak. He was fully dressed now, reclining upon his elbow, watching her. For once, there was not a glimmer of a smile in his eyes.

"What?" she whispered.

"We need to talk," he said, lifting the satchel she'd unwittingly dragged along, "about this pomander."

She swallowed, gathering the cloak about her and sitting up. Of course. 'Twas naive of her to imagine their lovemaking had solved everything, that she could bask in the warm afterglow of their coupling forever and forget her cares. Of course Rane would try to talk her into surrendering her heirloom.

"'Tis mine by rights."

He frowned thoughtfully, replacing the satchel. "'Tis a piece o' jewelry, Florie. Would ye truly throw away..." He tenderly clasped the back of her head, touching his forehead to hers, commanding her gaze. "This." Lord, his eyes were so beautiful, so cherishing. "...for a bauble o' gold?"

'Twas tempting to yield to him. Nae, she'd not barter what she felt for Rane for a hundred gold pomanders. But this pomander was not just a bauble. 'Twas her past and her future.

"Ye don't understand," she said.

He lowered his hand. "I understand that ye cannot abide the injustice of it," he told her. "'Tis one o' your qualities I admire. But there are times when a man prizes somethin' above justice, when somethin' is more dear to his heart."

"Oh, Rane, ye *are* more dear to my heart than all the gold in the world."

"Then you'll—"

"Nae."

He cursed. "'Twill cost one of our lives. Ye know that now. At the end o' forty days, either ye or I will hang from the gallows."

She sat up straight. "Then we'll leave. Both of us. This very night. I have my things. We can—"

"Leave behind the starvin' crofters? Who'll hunt for the nobles? Who'll care for Father Conan?" he said gently. "Would ye let them perish as well for your precious gold?"

She hung her head. She couldn't let Rane believe she was so selfish. Not after all they'd shared. Not after all he'd promised. She knew she took a great risk, telling him her secret. But he'd earned the right to know.

"'Tis more than just a trinket," she told him softly. "'Tis the key to my real father." At his silence, she took a shuddering breath, then told him the full story. "In Stirlin', long ago, a young merchant lass lost her heart to a nobleman, her heart and her maidenhood. The man claimed to love her. He bought her velvet gowns, ribbons for her hair, and had commissioned for her the most amazin' gold piece—a pomander with a heart-shaped lid that hung from a girdle of chased links."

She swallowed. "Ere long, he got her with child. 'Twas then she discovered he couldn't take her to wife, for he already had a betrothed. For days she wandered the streets, outcast and heartbroken. 'Twas by pure chance that the goldsmith who'd crafted the piece recognized his own handiwork hangin' from the girdle about her swollen waist and, takin' mercy upon the distraught and abandoned young lass, offered for her hand."

Florie lowered her eyes to her hands in her lap. "He said he'd marry her and claim her bastard child as his own. But he was never the child's true father. Her true father was the nobleman, the one who'd commissioned the gold piece, a man who came from Selkirk."

Rane's eyes softened. "'Tis ye. Ye're the child, the daughter o' the nobleman," he murmured. He gave a low whistle. "And ye need the piece to prove your birthright."

She nodded.

"Do ye know his name?" he asked.

"My mother never told me, and my father...my foster father...didn't wish for me to seek him."

"Why did ye not tell me sooner, lass? I might have taken the piece, sought out your sire for ye."

"And brought my father here to meet me—a common outlaw taking sanctuary in an abandoned church?" She shook her head. "He'd believe I was a thief, that I stole the piece...like everyone else does."

Rane squeezed her hand. "Not everyone."

She gave him a smile of gratitude, then stared down at his hand enclosing hers. "Ye know, I offered the lady a fortune in gold to give it back to me of her own free will."

"'Tisn't about the value o' the thing. Mavis is an arrogant, greedy, stubborn wench. And ye've given her pride a crushin' blow."

"I couldn't surrender it," she said. "I still cannot. As long as I keep the pomander, I can return to Selkirk one day." She sighed. "If I lose it..."

"Ye'll lose your father forever."

"Aye." She met his eyes. "Ye understand, don't ye?"

He nodded.

"Then ye'll...let me go?"

He was quiet a long time, and she began to worry that he didn't understand, after all; that he would insist she sacrifice the pomander. But he finally bowed his head in agreement. "We'll leave at first light."

Hope flickered in her heart. "We?"

"Someone has to keep the wolves and Englishmen at bay," he said, sighing in feigned annoyance. "And I've seen *ye* with a bow."

CHAPTER 19

Rane bedded down beside Florie that night in the sanctuary, but his sleep was troubled by doubts.

He wasn't worried about the crofters anymore. Florie had unfastened the gold pendant about her neck, taken off her bracelet, removed her rings, one by one, and dropped them into his palm, insisting he give them to Father Conan. She'd said they should bring in enough to see the crofters fed through winter.

Nae, what kept him tossing and turning half the night was the knowledge that Florie was the daughter of a nobleman.

Rane understood well why Florie desired to claim her heritage. Doing so would elevate her to a life of privilege. She'd wear velvet and silk. Servants would bow and scrape to her. She'd never have to blister her hands with menial labor again. Eventually her noble father would wish her to marry, and when that time came, he'd find her a rich, powerful, titled, suitable husband.

Certainly one more suitable than a huntsman.

That was what wrenched at his gut.

Yet what else did he expect? If Florie was indeed a noblewoman, what right did he have to lay claim to her heart, much less her hand? Nae, he loved Florie, and because of that he wanted to see her content. If being embraced by noble kin and welcomed into a highborn family made her happy, who was he to destroy that happiness?

He sighed resolutely into the quiet nave. Father Conan had oft told Rane he was too self-sacrificing, generous to a fault. He supposed 'twas too late to change now. Aye, he'd bear up and escort Florie to Stirling. And then he'd set her free.

One day she might return to Selkirk to seek out her father. Maybe by then Rane would be recovered from his heartbreak. He hoped so, but he thought it unlikely.

As the full moon crawled past the window, it cast a pool of colorful light onto the floor, slowly dragging it across the stones like a stained-glass carpet. Only when it reached the far wall and began to climb upward did Rane at last succumb to exhaustion.

But his slumber was short-lived. In the dim hours before dawn he awakened to a curious noise outside. Instantly alert, he raised his head to hear better, his hand on the hilt of his dagger. The sound must have roused Florie as well, for she struggled up beside him.

"What is it?" she murmured sleepily, scrubbing at her eye. "Time to go?"

He shook his head, hushing her with a finger to her lips.

There were men outside. He could hear scuffling and the metal clink of weaponry, and light flickered faintly through the windows. What the devil was going on? He checked to see his bow and arrows were within reach.

"The English?" Florie hissed.

Rane shook his head. He doubted it. Hertford's men preferred chaos to stealth. But as he strained to hear, a diabolical possibility curled its way into his brain.

"Stay here," he murmured to Florie.

"Nae," she whispered back.

He knew 'twas fruitless to argue with the imp, but to his satisfaction, from beneath her pillow she withdrew a sharp knife, gripping it before her in both hands. He trusted she'd use it if she had to. After all, she'd managed well enough before, armed with only a brooch pin.

With a conciliatory nod, he rose to his feet and stole toward the door with Florie close at his heels.

By quietly easing open the church door just a crack, he could see a sliver of the outside world. As he'd feared, a dozen well-armed soldiers milled about by the light of a single flaming brand. Thus far, no weapons were drawn.

He closed the door softly.

"Who is it?" Florie whispered.

"The Frasers."

She swore under her breath.

Rane rubbed thoughtfully at his chin. "In the lord's absence, Mavis is in command o' the men-at-arms."

Her knuckles whitened around the knife, despite her steady voice. "Can they take me forcibly from this place?"

Her calm and her courage caught at his heart, calling forth an intense protectiveness in him. "Nae," he said, gently prying the knife from her hand and tucking it into her girdle, "not while I draw breath."

"But they'll try?"

He didn't think so. After all, a church was sacred, and

Lord Gilbert's men feared God at least a little more than they feared Mavis.

He shook his head. "It looks like they're layin' siege. I think she means to starve us out," he told her. Then he patted the pack of supplies, winking to put her at ease. "Lucky for us, we're well provisioned."

"But for how long?"

"Lord Gilbert should return in a few days. He'd never allow such a travesty, even by his wife. 'Tis a blatant violation o' the right o' sanctuary."

Rane hoped he was right. Not only did he not know when Gilbert would return, but lately he wasn't even sure he knew his lord at all. Mavis seemed to have blinded Gilbert to a lot of things. Rane prayed she hadn't blinded him to mercy.

Florie wanted to scream in frustration. If only they'd left yesterday while they had the chance...

Now, with nearly half of her time in sanctuary elapsed and only enough provisions to last a week, they might not get another opportunity. She felt so damned helpless.

She forced herself to swallow the panic that was wont to rise in her throat. If she and Rane were to face a siege together, she must be completely honest with him. And herself.

Though she'd held out a slim hope of deliverance, she realized there was about as much chance of her drunken foster father riding to her rescue as there was of an angel coming to save her.

She took a deep breath. "There's something I must tell ye." Ashamed, she couldn't meet his eyes. "My foster father won't be comin' for me."

He sighed, turning to sit beside her. "I know."

Startled, she glanced up. "How could ye know?"

He rested his arm across his upraised knee. "I don't believe that fellow Wat returned to Stirlin'."

Florie gulped. That possibility, too, had nagged at the back of her brain for days. Hearing it voiced made it all the more real.

He explained. "He dared not stay in Selkirk, for fear o' being charged as an accomplice to your crime. Yet he could hardly return home, havin' failed in his mission to protect ye."

"Ye think he fled with my goods."

Rane nodded.

Of course, Wat had fled. But even if he *had* gone to Stirling, even if he'd alerted her foster father, Florie knew her foster father would never have been able to crawl out of his cups long enough to come free her...if he even remembered he had a daughter.

"We'll be fine," Rane told her, wrapping a consoling arm about her shoulders. "We have a roof over our heads. We have food and drink aplenty. If we grow cold, we have each other." He arched a mischievous brow. Even such grave circumstances could not destroy his good humor. "And if we grow bored o' the company, I seem to recall a hnefatafl board around here somewhere."

She could not help being coaxed into a smile. Indeed, were it not for the serious intent of the men outside, she might enjoy being imprisoned with her handsome archer.

Though 'twas yet early, falling back to sleep was impossible, particularly when Rane kept constant surveillance, getting up to listen at the various windows and peering out the church door. Even Methuselah sensed the tension, slinking from the vestry with flattened ears before climbing with uncharacteristic affection onto Florie's lap.

As edgy as the cat, despite his reassurances to Florie, Rane finally decided to speak with Gilbert's men, to learn their purpose, begging her to stay well back from the door for safety's sake.

What he'd guessed was true. Mavis had ordered the men-at-arms to surround the church. 'Twas of some comfort that they did so reluctantly. The captain of the guard was apparently well acquainted with Rane, and he thought laying siege to a church an outrage, particularly with English troops ranging the Borders and threatening the tower house. But the man was also loyal to Lord Gilbert and, in his lord's absence, to Lady Mavis, and so was compelled to carry out her orders.

According to Rane, no one was to be allowed in or out until Florie surrendered herself.

Understandably, Florie lost her appetite. After a sip of ale and a long time spent in prayer, she tried to keep herself preoccupied, using the knife to amend the vengeful carvings she'd made in the church beams, altering the gruesome saints to look less like Rane. Meanwhile, Rane rummaged through the storage room, though Florie doubted he'd find much. Surely no one had set aside provisions for the event of a siege on the church.

But 'twas not supplies he sought. He searched for an exit. Sometimes old churches had secret passages leading from them. She joined him in the hunt, hauling rusty tools and rotting cloth away from the walls, scraping at crumbling mortar, feeling for drafts of air.

After several hours, Florie's hands were scratched and raw, and she sneezed for the twelfth time as a puff of mold exploded from one of the damp bags. Despite their enterprise, they were no closer to freedom. Obviously, the builders of the church hadn't anticipated a need to ever have to escape from it.

Halfway through the day they shared one of the capon pies Rane had packed for the journey, and Florie couldn't help but think how much better 'twould have tasted in the shade of an elm along the road to Stirling. Still, 'twas sustenance, and she wondered grimly if there might come a day when even a morsel of oatcake would seem a welcome banquet.

Rane passed her the ale, and though she was thirsty, she took only a swallow. After all, it might have to last a long while. As she handed the costrel back, she heard a disturbance outside the sanctuary—angry voices erupting. Rane shot to his feet and went to listen at the west window. Florie followed him. The men were shouting all at once, but interspersed with their barks were the high-pitched voices of maids.

With a puzzled frown, Rane motioned for her to stay while he went to the door. But Florie was not content to wait, so she listened from a dark corner of the apse, well enough out of harm's way, close enough to hear the conversation between Rane and the captain of the guard.

As Rane opened the door, a great feminine cheer arose.

"Nae!" a man-at-arms was bellowing. "No one may enter the sanctuary, my ladies. Lady Mavis has forbidden it."

"Then let him come out to us," one maid suggested.

The others joined in with enthusiasm. "Aye! Aye!"

"He's done no wrong!"

"Let him go free!"

"Rane, save yourself!"

Florie saw Rane raise his hands in apology, quieting the crowd. "Ladies, thank you, but I couldn't leave this place in good faith, even were the guards to allow it."

Guilt laid a heavy hand on Florie's shoulder. If 'tweren't for her, she realized, Rane could march free, straight into the adoring arms of any of the dozens of maids cheering outside.

"I've promised to protect the lass in sanctuary," he declared, "and I intend to do so as long as I have breath in my body."

Florie's throat swelled. No wonder half the burgh had shown up to come to his aid. Rane was their champion. No minstrel had spoken nobler words, no knight a more gallant vow. She sighed and heard her sigh echoed on several maids' lips.

"But Rane, what can be done?" a lass called. "We couldn't bear to lose ye." The other maids voiced their distraught agreement.

"I'll save ye, Rane!" a tiny voice intruded. "I have a claymore!"

Florie blinked. The voice belonged to a lass who couldn't have been more than four summers old. Lord, was no Scotswoman safe from that Viking curse? The lass swung her miniature wooden sword, narrowly missing the captain's kneecap, and was hastily disarmed by her blushing guardian.

'Twas then Florie slowly realized the true meaning of Rane's amorous curse. Aye, she and Rane might be two individuals alone, under siege, but the well-loved archer had a whole army of soldiers at his disposal. He had the maids of Selkirk.

As if they heard her thoughts, the lasses all chimed in with offers to help.

Rane hushed them with an upraised palm. "My thanks to all o' ye. But if ye wish to lend me aid," Rane announced, "find Lord Gilbert. Send word to him that he's needed at home. At once."

Florie smiled at his genius.

"Aye," the captain of the guard added, clearly condoning Rane's strategy. "Run along and fetch the lord, then. He'll put the matter to rights."

'Twas obvious no one was very loyal to Lady Mavis, save perhaps her own obsequious ladies. 'Twas also apparent that Rane the huntsman was held in high esteem, not only by the Scotswomen, but by everybody, from the gruff captain of the guard to an innocent child, from a blind priest to...a goldsmith's apprentice. And that made her heart fill with pride, admiration, and, aye, love.

Florie realized she hadn't truly loved anyone since her mother was alive. Oh, aye, she'd cared for her foster father, but that was far more pity than love. The truth was she was afraid of love. After all, she'd loved her mother, and her mother had died. Her mother had loved a nobleman, and he'd deserted her. Her foster father had loved too well and, deprived of that love, had become destitute.

Love had always seemed a destructive force. And Florie, who'd once told Rane she feared nothing, had been secretly terrified to open her heart.

Yet love had served Rane well. She could tell by the cheer that arose when he blew a kiss and waved a fond farewell to the devoted crowd.

Because of Rane's love, the crofters' bellies were a little less empty.

Because of his love, the Father's faith had been restored.

Because of his love, dozens of burghers came to his aid.

And now Florie found herself willing to trust, willing to risk her heart...because of his love.

Despite the horde of beautiful lasses gathered in his name, when Rane turned away from the door, his eyes shone for Florie alone. "Naughty lass," he accused, clucking his tongue, "listenin' at doors again. I suppose ye still have a low opinion o' my friends?"

"Nae." She grinned up at him. "And I don't believe it anymore."

He brushed the hair back from her forehead. "Don't believe what?"

"I don't believe in the curse."

He lifted a brow, then shook his head. "Now would be a good time to believe in it. After all, I'm countin' on those 'enthralled Scotswomen' to come to our rescue."

She smiled and nestled into his embrace, her ear against his chest, listening to the strong, steady pulse that beat there. She had to say the words now, while the feeling was powerful, before she lost the courage, before she resorted to mumbling them against his chest.

"Rane."

"Mm."

With a hard swallow, she drew back enough so that she could gaze up into his eyes, his darkly crystalline eyes that were far more beautiful than any gemstone. She took a slow, shaky breath, and then she told him.

"I want to marry ye."

Rane felt the world stop. He'd heard those words countless times from countless adoring mouths. Lasses proclaimed their marriage intentions to him all the time. He knew 'twas meaningless, inspired by fleeting infatuation or spoken in the heat of passion. But Florie's sweet lips gave the phrase new meaning. 'Twas not easy for her, and that made it all the more precious.

He wanted to sweep her up into his arms with joy, ravish her mouth, kiss every strand of her hair, run his hands over every inch of her body until she had to beg for freedom.

He wanted to, but he resisted.

She didn't belong to him. She'd never belong to him.

Aye, they'd trysted, and it seemed to Rane that he'd never loved so deeply, so completely, never soared so close to heaven. Far beyond mere affection, far beyond lust, their very souls had mated. At the time it had felt like a marriage of their hearts, as though their spirits had become eternally entwined.

But that was when she'd been Florie the goldsmith's apprentice.

When Florie the noblewoman went hunting for love, lasting love, she'd surely aim for more prized prey.

Somehow he managed to smile through his pain. Somehow he summoned the strength to reply, even though his heart felt fractured into a thousand shards. "Don't worry," he said with a wink, his light tone belying the bitterness of his words. "I'm sure you'll be free o' the curse once you're free o'—"

Interrupted by a loud thunk upon the church door, Rane was saved from witnessing the disillusionment in Florie's eyes. And when the door swung open he instantly became her guardian, hauling her behind him and drawing his dagger.

But 'twas only Father Conan who barreled in, muttering and shoving the door shut behind him. "Keep me out o' my own church, will they?" he huffed.

"Father!" Florie called.

"They let ye in?" Rane asked.

"I'll be damned if I'll be barred from my own house," the priest said, pausing to make the sign of the cross so the Lord wouldn't take him too seriously about the damning.

He dusted off his sleeves and hobbled forward faster than Rane had seen him do in a long while. The priest's blood was obviously heated for battle.

"Layin' siege to a church!" he grumbled. "What in the name o' the Holy Mother is goin' on?"

Rane put away his blade. "Lord Gilbert's been delayed. In his absence Lady Mavis—"

"Mavis?" He stopped, his snowy brows shooting up. "Mavis! O' course!" the priest fumed. Rane had never seen him quite so full of wrath. "Who does she think she is? The bloody queen?" Resuming his pacing, he nonetheless began genuflecting again, mumbling words of contrition between bouts of cursing.

"Father," Rane said gently, "until this is over, I think 'twould be best if ye stayed away from here, out o' danger. 'Tis no place for an old man. Go home," he urged.

"Nae!" the priest roared, as much of a roar as his feeble lungs could muster. "I'll not stand by while this travesty o' sanctuary continues. A siege indeed! 'Tis an abomination in God's eyes! Nae, my work is here, and by God—"

He gasped, clutching one hand against his chest, and staggered back against the wall. Rane rushed forward, Florie close behind him.

"Father!" she cried. "Are ye all right?"

Rane grasped the man's bony shoulders, holding him upright. He didn't look well. His face was red, he wheezed, and his limbs trembled with agitation.

After a harrowing span of time, he finally calmed, blowing out a few long breaths. "I'll be fine."

Rane was not convinced, and from her meaningful look, neither was Florie. "Father," he said, "I pray ye go home. Ye should go somewhere...safe."

"But that's just it, lad," the priest rasped, lifting his quaking hand to place it over Rane's heart. "If one cannot be safe in a church..."

Rane clasped his hand over Father Conan's. The priest was right, of course. No mere mortal should be able to challenge God's authority.

"Besides," the priest continued, with a trace of a twinkle in his milky eyes, "ye're the one who dragged me back into this forsaken place. Are ye goin' to shoo me back out, then?"

Rane sighed, patting the Father's hand. He'd already appointed himself guardian to an outlaw. He supposed he could watch over a blind priest as well. "All right."

"Ye may be happy to know," the Father added with a sly grin, reaching into his robe to pull out a bulging satchel, "I've brought a little siege relief."

Rane gaped in amazement. The blessed Father had sneaked in a bundle of provisions.

"From the good folk o' Selkirk," Father Conan explained.

The four of them dined well that night, the three humans and Methuselah, despite the threat that surrounded them like a dark cloud. While Rane sipped at the smooth mead Dame Margaret had sent along, prayed softly with the priest by candlelight, and, after Father Conan dozed off, played at hnefatafl with Florie, he could almost imagine 'twas a pleasant, peaceful evening they enjoyed in their own cottage.

But 'twas only fantasy. And that was made clear when the peace was shattered sometime in the hours past midnight.

Rane's nose twitched. He was dreaming of venison roasting over the fire, a fat three-point buck he'd shot with a single well-placed arrow. The night was warm, the sky sprinkled with glittering stars. A gentle breeze tickled the flame higher, and Rane's mouth watered as the sweet wood smoke filled his nostrils.

'Twas Father Conan's coughing that woke him fully.

Rane opened his eyes. The sanctuary glowed with strange light. He craned his head to glance up at the candle, but it had gone out. He eased up on an elbow. The smell of his dream lingered, and for one brief instant he wondered if he was still asleep.

Then he saw the tendrils of flame curling beneath the door.

He sat bolt upright.

The church was on fire!

Grotesque shadows danced along the lower edges of the windows, and by the eerie yellow light Rane could see the rafters filling with smoke.

"Florie!" he yelled. "Father!"

Florie scrambled to her feet at once. "Oh, God!" she gasped. "Fire!"

The Father awoke and began wheezing, unable to catch his breath.

"We have to get him out," Florie said, mastering her panic, echoing Rane's thoughts.

Rane nodded. In his condition, the Father would not last long in the smoke.

He frowned. Where the bloody hell were the Fraser men?

'Twas impossible to leave by the door. 'Twas entirely enveloped in flame.

He glanced at the windows. He'd have to break one and hope he could lift the Father over the ledge and safely drop him onto the ground.

In an instant he swept up his bow, fitted it with an arrow, and shot through a brilliant blue pane.

But as soon as the window burst, the fire roared in like a dragon unleashed, lapping at the plaster with its fiery tongue as if it tasted ambrosia.

Rane cursed. The fire had been burning for some time, and the smoke was thickening with startling speed, the yellow cloud dropping lower and lower in the sanctuary. He snatched up the woolen plaids and handed them to Florie, indicating to her to cover her mouth, to breathe through the fabric. She nodded and helped the Father with a plaid.

Whether 'twas wise or not, Rane had to shoot out the other windows to see if there was a possible escape. He couldn't let them become trapped inside.

Thor's hammer! Where were the Frasers?

His five arrows quickly found their marks, splintering the glass. Just as swiftly, five snarling beasts of fire entered in through the portals. There was no exit.

Rane lowered his bow. Without help from the outside, there was no water to quench the fiery dragon's thirst, only wood and plaster to feed it.

And there was no escape but through the dragon's belly.

They were doomed.

CHAPTER 20

It was Florie who thought of the storage room. Soon it, too, would fill with smoke, but for a while at least, the closed room would protect the Father, who coughed uncontrollably now.

"Aye! Go!" Rane shouted, yelling to be heard above the ungodly howl of the fire.

They stumbled toward the haven of the storage room, and Rane hurried them through the passage. The ax he'd used to split wood for the vestry door leaned against the wall. He scowled at it, his thoughts racing. If he could hack open the church door before smoke overwhelmed the sanctuary, they might have a chance at escape.

"Where are ye goin'?" Florie asked in panic, somehow sensing he meant to leave them.

He hefted up the ax. "To kill the beast," he said.

"Nae!" she screamed.

Her cry clawed at his heart, but he couldn't afford to heed it. Every instant was precious.

He sent her one last look of fierce determination and fiercer love, a look that told her he was doing what he had to do. "I love ye, Florie," he said. "Never forget." Then he closed the door and squinted through the roiling smoke toward the fiery foe at the far end of the sanctuary.

He stalked toward the door like his fearless Viking forbears, letting rage fuel his advance until he was almost at a run. The orange dragon roared and bellowed in challenge, its fervor so intense that rivulets of sweat poured down Rane's face as he neared.

Then, gathering all his fury, all his outrage, all his strength, he charged the burning door, swinging the great ax with such force that when it struck, it shook the foundations of the church.

The door should have burst. The fact that it didn't meant that someone had sealed it shut. Someone meant for them to burn alive.

He shuddered with rage. The fire seared his skin, but he held on to the ax handle. He worked the blade free and backed away from the door, coughing as the ubiquitous smoke filled his lungs. 'Twas impossible to tell what damage he'd done. The door was so engulfed in flame that it flared brighter than the sun.

Again he rushed toward the door, blindly chopping at the burning oak. This time he thought he felt the wood yield, but as the beast sampled his flesh again, blistering his hands and scorching his brows, he was forced to retreat.

He doubled over with the force of his coughing. Tears streamed from his eyes as he blinked back the stinging smoke. He sank low, seeking whatever sweet air remained near the ground, took a deep gulp, then came up once more with the ax.

This time when he buried the ax in the door, sparks

scattered, like teeth punched from the dragon's maw. Several of them lodged in his shirt, smoldering and burning tiny holes there.

The walls wavered in the unbearable heat like demon children taunting him, growing blacker and blacker as the smoke curled up against them. Then, over his head, an ominous rumble slowly ran the length of the sanctuary, as if the church itself groaned in anguish. Rane's gaze followed the sound as it traveled toward the altar.

"Nae," he choked out. Despair thicker than the ocher smoke smothered him. He couldn't even see the altar now. 'Twas completely enveloped in the dense cloud of Loki's breath. Surely Florie and the Father would suffocate.

He'd failed. Bloody hell, he'd failed.

His hair crisp, his clothing smoking, his skin charred, with one last bitter oath and the last of his failing strength, Rane stormed toward the door and embedded the ax deep into the wood.

'Twas the last thing he remembered.

"Rane. Rane. Wake up, Rane."

Sweet Valkyrie were calling him.

He wanted to wake up. Their voices sounded so soft, so gentle. But he had no strength.

Something poked at his side. He grunted. It jabbed him again, harder.

"Get up, ye worthless bastard."

Rane frowned. That was no Valkyrie. 'Twas Lady Mavis. He'd recognize her caustic whine anywhere. Even in Valhalla.

Nae, he decided, it must not be Valhalla, after all. Lady

Mavis could never steal through the gates of the Viking heaven.

He felt a sharp blow to his ribs then, followed by several feminine gasps. He groaned, rolling onto his side in pain. Slowly he opened his eyes. They stung, and his throat stung, and against his will he began coughing, an ugly, hacking cough that rattled his bones.

"Where is she?" Mavis sneered.

Frigg, where was *he?*

He wheezed in a breath of cool, moist air. He was outdoors. He knew that much. The smell of wet earth permeated his nostrils. But his eyes were so dry, he could hardly see. A few raindrops struck his cheek and forehead. There must be clouds overhead. But the sky seemed so bright. Odin's wounds, he longed to close his eyes and return to blessed oblivion.

"Where is your doxy?"

She kicked him again, and this time he rolled onto his belly, fully awake and aware and in agony as memory rushed back too swiftly.

Florie. The fire. Bloody hell.

"Where is she?" he cried hoarsely, struggling to rise.

"Ye fool!" Mavis snapped. "Don't pretend ye don't know."

He peered through burning eyes at the fuzzy crowd of people gathered beneath the trees, then turned to see what was left of the church. The roof had collapsed. Someone must have dragged him to safety. But all that remained of the structure—the vestry, the altar, the nave, the storage room—were smoldering black beams and cracked stone. His heart seized. Had Florie survived the fire? Could they have possibly escaped the destructive inferno?

"Rane!" one of the maids sobbed. "Tell her what she wants to know."

'Twas the ladies of the burgh, keeping a safe distance from Lady Mavis, but present nonetheless. He staggered to his feet. Maybe one of them knew what had happened to Florie. "Have ye seen—"

"Answer me now, huntsman," Mavis barked, "or I'll string *ye* up in her stead!"

The ladies gasped and sobbed and carried on at Lady Mavis's words. But her threat was meaningless to Rane. If Florie was dead, he didn't care if she tore him limb from limb.

He turned in a slow circle, perusing the faces of the onlookers, searching for her familiar countenance. His gaze landed on the captain of the guard, who shifted uneasily from foot to foot, twisting his doffed coif in his fists.

"Did ye..." Rane asked him, squinting in confusion, "did ye set the church afire?"

"Nae!" he replied vehemently, casting a wary glance toward Lady Mavis, rushing to explain before she could hush him. "We were lured away by a pair of English spies. 'Twas...somebody else who did her biddin'. 'Tis unholy, *unholy* to do such a thing, to set fire to a—"

"Silence!" Mavis screeched, her eyes wild like a frightened mare's. "Ye'll hang beside him, ye treasonous patch!" She was breathing heavily now, as if simultaneously excited and terrified. "Besides, 'twas likely...lightnin' that started the fire."

Rane's mind might be dazed, but he could read Mavis's crafty eyes well enough. The rumble he'd heard last night might have indeed been thunder, but the fire had been no accident. Mavis had ordered it set, which meant...

She'd intended to kill Florie.

His heart sank into his gut like a lead weight. Were it not for the kernel of rage burning at the pit of his belly, he might have dropped to his knees in surrender, let himself drown in a mire of despair. But as he narrowed his eyes at the spoiled, simpering witch who had violated sanctuary, who had set fire to a church, who had—Thor curse her— slain his love, anger and injustice smoldered inside him, sparking, then flaring, then exploding into a conflagration to rival last night's blaze.

With a bellow of blinding fury, he charged toward the evil hag.

His scorched fingertips grazed her worthless neck, leaving black marks, but that was all. Before he could throttle her, the men-at-arms came at him from all sides. To his credit, it took several of them to subdue him, despite his diminished strength. But subdue him they did, much to the captain's regret. They tackled him to the ground, splaying him on his back in the mud. While they held him down, the rain spattered his cheeks like scornful spittle.

And his only gratification, one for which he'd undoubtedly pay later, was witnessing the ugly grimace on Mavis's face as she staggered back in shocked horror.

After that, he put up no resistance. He had neither the strength nor the heart for it. They shackled him and forced him to trudge to the tower house in the mud while all around him the heavens wept, soothing his burns but not drowning his pain.

Nothing could do that.

Between the black storm clouds and the dim interior of the

tower cell where Rane was chained, 'twas impossible to tell the time of day. Chill air whistled through the tiny slit in the outer wall, bringing with it slashes of wind-whipped rain. It must have been a squall like this that had extinguished the fire and saved his life two—or was it three—days ago. If only it had come an hour earlier... If only...

He squeezed his eyes shut and bowed his head over his bent knees. 'Twas pointless wondering what might have been. He'd already spent hours racked by remorse. Remorse for not letting Florie go while she had the chance. For persuading the Father to come back to a church that was, Rane was convinced now, indeed cursed. For being unable to save them from a fiery death.

He'd go willingly to the gallows, for 'twas the only way to unburden himself of his torturous guilt.

A rattle at the door made him lift his head. The captain of the guard stepped in, his jaw set in bitter disapproval even as he let Lady Mavis into the cell.

Though every bone ached with the effort, Rane struggled to his feet. He might be chained to the wall, but he'd be damned if he'd let Mavis play lord over him.

Indeed, to his satisfaction, her smug countenance faltered perceptibly as he towered above her, looking down his nose with loathing and silent domination.

"He can't get loose?" she asked uncertainly, and Rane relished the note of fear in her tremulous voice.

The captain yanked on the chains to assure they were secure. "Nae, my lady."

Her lips curved then into a tenuous smile he supposed she thought was alluring. But he knew a whore's bait when he saw it.

"I've decided to forgive ye," she said, indicating her throat with trembling fingers, "for that bit of knavery ye engaged in."

Bit of knavery? If the men-at-arms hadn't prevented him, he would have strangled her with one fist.

"I think we can be civilized about this, now that ye've had a few days to think it over," she said, pacing back and forth in the tight space, her heels clacking on the wooden floor. "Ye have somethin' I want. And I have somethin' *ye* want."

He looked at her sharply. Something he wanted? Against his better judgment, a hopeful thud started in his chest. Florie? Had she captured Florie? Was she yet alive?

Shite, he couldn't breathe.

"Ye know where that girdle's hidden," Mavis purred, "and if ye give it to me, I'll grant ye your life."

His hopes crumbled. His life? What did his life mean without Florie?

Mavis stopped pacing and waited expectantly.

"Nae," he said under his breath.

She blinked. "What? What's that? I didn't quite—"

"Nae," he stated clearly.

He saw the temper simmering just behind the thin slash of her tightly compressed lips. But he didn't care. He had nothing to lose by angering her.

Somehow she reined in her anger and began pacing again. She flashed another smile. "Ye don't seem to understand. Maybe the smoke or hunger has fogged your brain."

"Why do ye want it so badly?" he blurted, startling her to a halt.

He could see her itching to backhand him for his

impertinence. But she dared not. For one thing, that would put her dangerously within his reach. For another, she was still counting on striking a bargain with him.

She gave him a fleeting, insincere smile. "I owe ye no explanation. However, if 'twill make our negotiations more palatable, I'll tell ye." She glanced briefly at the captain of the guard, as if committing his face to memory, and 'twas then Rane realized that whatever she was about to reveal, she intended to leave behind no witnesses. "I was wed to your lord for practical reasons—he needed an heir and a dowry, and I needed a place to live." She made a moue of disgust. "But I find the poverty here insufferable. Selkirk is drainin' my coffers at an alarmin' rate." She twisted the ring upon her finger. "I simply won't have it. I was in the queen's court. I'm accustomed to livin' with certain comforts, and I intend to have them always." When she turned to him, her fists were clenched like an overindulged child's. "I want that girdle. And when I want a thing, I get it."

"Even if it comes to murder?" he said quietly.

Mavis looked away. "The waif was a thief. She should have surrendered herself. 'Tis her own fault if she was cowerin' in a church when God decided to let lightnin' strike—"

"God!" Rane shouted, rattling his chains with his vehemence. "God had nothin' to do with it, and well ye know it. Who set the fire? Who did ye get to do your biddin'? 'Twasn't the Fraser men. And it sure as hell wasn't the burghers."

Mavis retreated a step at his outburst. "Ye've no proof of anythin'," she said as fear flared momentarily in her eyes. "Tell me where the thing is hidden, and I promise ye a quick death."

The corners of Rane's mouth turned down. At least she was being honest now. She'd never intended to let him live. But she hadn't won. She'd never win.

"Ye crack-brained trull," he said with a wicked smile. "Ye probably destroyed it yourself in the fire."

He expected to be clouted for his insult. But the blow wasn't going to come from the captain of the guard, whose gaze was fixed upon the ceiling. And Mavis—her jaw clenched, her eyes full of sparks, her face purpling with slow building rage—fled the room, slamming the door before he could witness the full force of her temper.

It took a full hour of beating pillows for Mavis's fury to subside, and now feathers littered her solar like fallen snow. But at last she'd regained control, enough to command the English bastards who'd bungled the task in the first place to fix their mistake by day's end.

Why could nothing ever go according to her plans? She'd ordered the imbeciles to trap the wench, not *in* the blaze, but as she *fled* the blaze. Their stupidity meant that Mavis's only hope was to find evidence that the piece had truly been destroyed.

Now, watching the cloudy sky blacken like a bruise as the sun set, Mavis dug her nails into the stone sill. Surely she'd heard wrong.

"What did ye say?" Her voice faltered, and her blood chilled as she turned to face the monk who wasn't a monk at all.

He shrugged. "Didn't find nothin' in the ashes. Not a trace," the man repeated in his slow English drawl, perusing with suspicion the feathers strewn about the room. "No girdle. No pomander. No gold at all. Not even bones."

A laugh of hysteria escaped her, startling her visitor, who stepped back a pace. "Not even bones?" His words seemed like a cruel jest.

"Nay, my lady."

She nodded, feeling the ice in her veins slowly beginning to melt and boil.

He frowned. "Mind you, we still expect to get paid—if not from—"

Mavis screeched at him, her patience at an end, her fury returning in full force. She snagged her fists in the front of his cassock, hauling him roughly toward her. "Paid! Paid? I paid your masters when I told them where to find Princess Mary. And what did ye do for me? Nothin'!"

He straightened, indignant. "We set the fire just like you asked," he whined.

"Ye doddy-poll!" she spat in his face. "I wanted that girdle. I told ye that!"

Suddenly she felt the sharp point of a dagger beneath her chin, and the monk's dull eyes turned dangerously dark. "I told you we looked for the thing. We didn't find it. Now unhand me, and I'll be out of your way."

Mavis quivered with rage and fear. While King Henry was alive, no Englishman would dare speak to her like that. But things had changed. And now she had to choose her battles carefully.

Reluctantly, she released the man and stepped back. He gave her an insolent look, wrinkling his nose at the feathers strewn about, then wheeled and made his exit. Only when he was gone did she collapse in tears of frustration.

Dear God, what was she going to do? No gold in the ashes? No bones? Gilbert would return soon, and that cursed wench was apparently still out there somewhere with her prize. Mavis had to find the whelp before her husband did.

But how? She'd just alienated a valuable English ally, and his fellows were on their way to Musselburgh. Like one of Henry's mistresses, she'd been used and discarded. And now, when she needed aid the most, there was no one left to help her.

She pressed her fingertips to her aching brow and peered through her fingers and her tears past the shutters, toward the gathering clouds.

'Twas truly a miserable place—this patch of land with its stony fields and biting cold and sudden storms. And its people were no better. How could she hope to bend them to her will when they had such a bullheaded will of their own?

A flash of lightning pierced the clouds, casting harsh light across the stark knoll, startling a flock of crows and silhouetting the naked tree on Gallows Hill.

The rain began to pour from the sky like well water from a bucket, drowning the land. But Mavis paid no heed to the drops that drenched her sill, for inspiration had struck as abruptly as the bolt of lightning.

She sniffed back her tears.

She knew what to do now.

She might not be able to hunt down the slippery wench, but she knew how to lure the brat to *her.*

Night transformed into morning so subtly 'twas almost

imperceptible. A faint gray bar of light from the window slit provided the only illumination to the bleak tower room. 'Twas as dark as the woods. As dark as the grave.

Rane would die today. He was sure of it.

'Twould be ugly. He didn't delude himself. After the insults he'd handed out, Mavis would spare no instrument of torture, he was certain, to make his dying a most slow and painful ordeal.

But he consoled himself with the fact that at the end of it, when his body was broken and he gasped out his last earthly breath, he'd be reunited with his beloved Florie.

He smiled ruefully. She'd told him that she loved him, that she wanted to marry him. And he'd been too afraid to answer her. Too afraid to lose her to another. Now he'd lost her to death. In heaven, he vowed, he'd tell her he loved her with every breath.

When the executioner came for him, the skies were raging with unseasonable wind and biting rain. The distant trees thrashed beneath the onslaught, and the ground, already drenched from a spate of spring storms, seemed to bleed the excess water. 'Twas as if Thor himself, angered by the unjust execution of one of his sons, had unleashed the furious maelstrom.

Six men-at-arms, their gold tabards turned the color of clay, slogged across the spongy sod, escorting the blackened cart that would convey Rane to Gallows Hill. Beside the road huddled at least twoscore lasses from the burgh, shivering and sobbing in the rain.

He knew them all by name. 'Twas strange to think he'd never see them again, never kiss them upon the cheeks, never wrap an arm companionably about their shoulders.

An ornate, heavily draped litter borne by eight squires

accompanied the procession, and Rane didn't have to look to know that Mavis sat within it, warm and dry and no doubt contemplating inventive ways to extend his suffering.

When they stopped at the crest of Gallows Hill, Mavis's beringed hand reached out from the heavily embroidered curtain to summon the executioner. The hooded man hastened to her, listened to her request, and bowed over her hand, then returned to Rane.

"Ye're to be disgraced," he grumbled, likely annoyed at anything that made him spend more time in the pouring rain.

Stepping forward, the executioner took hold of the top of Rane's shirt and tore it down the middle, wrenching the fabric down off his shoulders and arms, baring him to the waist.

If 'twas Mavis's hope to humiliate him before the lasses of the burgh, she failed. Most of the maidens had glimpsed his naked body at one time or another. Nae, if anything, she invited their sympathy. They wept and moaned as he was lifted into the cart, and as he scanned the faces he saw wee Josselin Ancrum in her guardian's arms, her wooden claymore drooping in her hand, her sweet child's face twisted into a mask of uncomprehending sadness.

He frowned. He didn't want Jossy to see him like this. He didn't want any of them as witness. 'Twas not a pretty thing, to watch a man die. And they were too kind, too innocent to sully their eyes on such ugliness.

He wanted to send them home, to tell them to remember him as he was. But Mavis had something else in mind.

"Do ye wish to see him live?" she called from within the litter.

The ladies stilled, then answered with a chorus of ayes.

"I'll spare him on one condition. Surrender the wench with the gold pomander. I know one o' ye must be harborin' her."

Rane knew then that the lady was mad. Florie hadn't survived the fire. And he'd told Mavis the pomander was destroyed. Yet she still sought it, like a hunter obsessed with a mythical beast.

"Tell her I'm about to hang her lover," Mavis continued, "and she'll come to me of her own accord to bargain for his life."

The ladies of the burgh murmured among themselves in despair, but of course, none of them could do Mavis's bidding. They knew nothing about the pomander. Most of them had never seen it. And they didn't know what had become of Florie.

"Nae?" Mavis barked in a fit of pique. "Well, perhaps watchin' him suffer a bit will change your minds!"

The ladies gasped, and Jossy began to wail.

"Take her away, Will, please," Rane bade Jossy's guardian.

"Nae!" Mavis shrieked. "She'll stay until I get that pomander. *All* o' ye will stay."

Rane compressed his lips. While the rain dripped off of his nose and made icy rivulets down his chest, he gazed up at the ominous black oak, leafless and solitary and stark against the pale clouds. Few corpses had twisted from its great limb in the last few years. Gilbert ruled with an iron fist, and his reputation for harsh justice had kept most lawbreakers at bay.

He glanced up at the dreary sky. No birds dared fly in such miserable weather. He prayed the storm would pass and the crows would find his body quickly. He didn't wish to frighten the lasses with his grisly remains.

CHAPTER 21

"**B**loody storm!"

True, 'twas the same kind of downpour that had thankfully doused the fire before it could burn the church *all* the way to the ground, but enough was enough. Now it slowed their progress as Florie rode with the Father along the marshy road, in the company of the most unlikely allies.

Hurry, she wanted to scream. Hurry! God knew how long Mavis would wait before she...

Florie squeezed her eyes shut and gripped the reins more tightly as the Father clung to her waist, and the horses' hooves smacked and slipped in the mud. She couldn't bear to think of what was happening.

It had nearly killed her to leave Rane. Even now she wondered if she'd done the right thing. 'Twas the Father who had convinced her they should steal away while they could from the smoldering ruins of the church, who'd assured her that Rane was alive and could take care of himself while they sought help, and who'd warned her that even if she surrendered the girdle now, with Gilbert away, 'twas likely Mavis would see both her and Rane hanged just for spite.

She brought a shaky hand to her throat.

The last time she'd seen Rane, he was lying helpless on his back before the steps of the smoking church. Several maids had pulled him from the wreckage. She'd longed to go to him, to see for herself that he yet lived. But Lady Mavis had ridden up just then, and now, knowing he was in that evil shrew's clutches...

She shuddered. If it weren't for Florie overhearing the maidens' plans to fetch Lord Gilbert, they'd still be on their way to the court at Stirling, assuming the royals were in residence there. But Florie knew that Princess Mary had been secretly transported to Dumbarton months ago for her safety.

Still, it had taken two precious days for Florie and a dozen of the most intrepid burgh maids to reach the castle, even with the horses the Fraser men-at-arms lent them. After all, despite their determination, they were for the most part inexperienced riders.

When the motley group rode awkwardly but boldly up to the shores of the firth surrounding Dumbarton Castle, the queen had been so astounded by the sight that she'd released Lord Gilbert from her service at once to see to his affairs.

And when Florie and the Father, exhausted and reeking of smoke, told him the full story—the significance of the gold piece to Florie, the truth about the theft, how Rane had been torn between his obligation to his lord and his protection of Florie, and how Lady Mavis had set fire to the church and taken Rane captive—Gilbert decided 'twas time to take his unruly wife in hand.

Florie pulled her wet hood closer about her head and peered at the lead rider. 'Twas a very different man she saw now in Lord Gilbert. He was stern, aye, but away from the influence of his wife he seemed more civil, more reasonable, more just. Still, he'd set his huntsman as a guard against Florie's escape, and that she'd never forgive.

Nae, she amended. She'd forgive even that.

If they arrived in time.

If he saved Rane from Lady Mavis.

Like a cruel taunt, thunder cracked overhead, and the rain increased until blinding sheets of it pummeled the earth, hitting with such force that the drops bounced back up to make a mist along the ground.

Florie cursed silently, cradling the miserable, mewling cat closer within her cloak. If only the rain would stop, she wished. If only they could see Gilbert's tower house over the next rise...

But three more hills obstructed the horizon before they finally spotted the tower. Smoke rose from the various hearths within the house, only to be shredded like sendal as soon as the wind caught it. If Florie shielded her eyes against the storm, she could see the tiny figures of guards manning the wall. But more significantly, she saw a cluster of people gathered along the narrow road leading from the tower house, around what appeared to be a nobleman's litter. Florie straightened in the saddle.

An eerie shiver that had nothing to do with the storm slid along her spine. She leaned forward, as if 'twould help her discern what she saw. The cat meowed in complaint.

"What ails ye, Florie?" the Father asked, sensing her unquiet.

"Is that..." She forgot that the priest couldn't see. "Is that a...a black cart?" Black carts were what they used to transport criminals.

Before the Father could reply, Florie, her heart skipping a beat, kicked at the horse's flanks. It lurched forward, nearly unseating the poor Father. When she was even with Lord Gilbert, she caught at his sleeve.

"My lord! Up ahead, is that not a blackened cart?"

Gilbert frowned in irritation at her impropriety but followed her gaze. Then his eyes narrowed, and he held up a hand, halting the company. "Mavis's litter," he said, more to himself than anyone else. "What the devil would she be doing out in a storm like this?"

"Oh, God," Florie breathed. "She's hangin' him. She's hangin' Rane."

The lord's scowl deepened, and he clamped his lips together until they were white. "My huntsman? Not while I am lord here."

A wave of relief rushed over Florie as she glimpsed the determination in Gilbert's stony eyes. Before she could send up a prayer of thanks, the lord was calling out the names of his best men, commanding them to break away from the company, to follow him and make haste for Gallows Hill.

Florie wasn't about to be left behind.

"Hold on. Tightly," she murmured to Father Conan. She didn't have to warn Methuselah. His claws were already firmly embedded in her gown.

As the men urged their horses forward, Florie smacked her mount with the reins and bolted after them. Mud flew everywhere, kicked up by flying hooves, and the cat drew blood from Florie's throat in its panicked bid for escape. But when her hood fell back, and she felt the cold wind in her hair and the stinging rain upon her cheeks, as the thundering steeds swallowed up the ground at breakneck speed, she at last felt a faint glimmer of hope.

Rane meant to die bravely. And to do that, he had to remove himself from his body. He had to leave behind earthly pleasures, earthly pain, and focus on Valhalla, the heaven that awaited him.

He let the precious images of his life slip through his mind one last time.

He thought of his mother, small and lovely and full of mischief. Of his father, tall and handsome as a Viking prince.

He thought about his first kill—how he'd felt sick at heart when he looked upon the dying stag, until his father showed him the family of hungry peasants its meat would sustain.

He thought about the first lass he'd lain with, how soft and wondrous she'd felt beneath his untried body.

He thought of Father Conan and his long-winded tales. Of a younger Lord Gilbert who boasted tirelessly of his expert huntsman.

He thought of cold winter nights spent drinking ale with his fellows around a roaring hearth. Of hot summer afternoons bathing naked in the pond while giggling lasses spied upon him.

He thought of the glory of a full silver moon hung in a star-shot sky. The vibrancy of the first green shoots springing up through the last season's leaf-fall. Twilight breezes caressing his hair. Swallows of clear, cold stream water slipping over his tongue. Sunlight warming his face...

And he thought about the burgh maids, etching each face carefully onto his brain. Dimpled Kate. Sweet Miriam. Freckled Alyce. Shy Elizabeth. One by one he kissed their faces farewell, until one shining image remained.

Florie.

He forcefully swallowed the lump that lodged in his gullet. Florie he'd never forget. Indeed, 'twas her face he'd carry with him to sustain him through whatever torment his body endured. For at the end of his suffering, he was certain 'twould be Florie who welcomed him with open arms at the gates of Valhalla.

Lost in his thoughts, he scarcely noticed when the executioner took his arm to lead him from the cart.

"I'd give ye opium wine," the man muttered apologetically as he guided Rane to the huge tree, "but m'lady says there's to be nothin' to numb the pain."

Rane nodded. He'd expected as much.

A steel spike had been driven long ago into the wide tree trunk, about seven feet above the ground. One of Rane's shackles was removed, his arms looped about the rough tree as if in an embrace, then both wrists secured to the spike by the chain.

Despite the chill weather, despite his resolve to be brave, an icy sweat formed at the back of his neck as he rested his brow against the trunk, pondering the sinister possibilities for his torture.

Apparently, making him ponder those possibilities was the first of his tortures, for nothing happened for a long while. He could see from the corner of his eye that the executioner rummaged in the cart, looking for the weapon of Mavis's choice, but he heard nothing from the lady herself.

Then there was a stirring among the men-at-arms.

"Lord Gilbert!" someone shouted. "Lord Gilbert comes!"

The ladies began chattering excitedly.

Strangely, Rane's mind resisted comprehension. After all, he had accepted his death. He had accepted that he was beyond help. He was past hope, past pain. He now devoted all his thoughts, all his strength to venturing unafraid into that dark realm. And the men's interruption was only delaying his journey.

He wished they would cease their prattle. He was ready to go. The sooner he passed, the sooner he'd be reunited with his Florie.

Aye, he *wanted* to die.

"Do it!" Mavis shrieked suddenly. "Do it now! Hang him!"

"But m'lady—" the executioner said.

"Ye heard me!" she screamed. "Make haste!"

But the executioner didn't seem in a hurry at all. He dropped the shackle key twice in the mud. He couldn't find the rope and, when he finally did, had trouble winding the knots properly.

All the while, Mavis was near hysteria, popping her head out of the litter to curse his stupidity and nag him to hurry.

By the time the men-at-arms managed to move Rane, position the cart beneath the hanging limb, throw the rope over, and secure the loop about Rane's neck, he began to hear the rumble of horse hooves coming closer.

"Ye dolt!" Mavis screeched at the executioner. "Do I have to do it myself?"

"Sorry, m'lady," the executioner mumbled.

But the man had trouble controlling the cart horse well

enough to command it forward. Indeed, were it not a mortal sin, Rane might consider jumping off of the cart himself, just to end the suspense.

The downpour ceased abruptly, as if Thor's wine barrel had been tapped to the dregs. Yet the stormy slosh and rumble continued as the riders advanced. Mavis's shrill squalling was a constant barrage now, and Rane thought 'twas a shame that hers would be the voice he took to his grave.

He swallowed once beneath the rough knot under his chin and closed his eyes, trying to drown the sounds of her clamoring beneath his own silent bid to Odin.

"Cease!" Lord Gilbert's voice came like a boom of thunder.

Rane squeezed his eyes more tightly shut. He didn't want the lord's interference. Damn Lord Gilbert! Rane wanted to die. He *wanted* to die.

"Take him down!"

Nae, he thought in desperation. He couldn't live. Not without Florie. He opened his eyes to slits. The edge of the cart beckoned. 'Twould take but one step into air to end it. One step. And then he'd join his beloved. Then he'd be with Florie…forever.

He leaned toward the edge of the cart.

One…short…step…

"Rane!"

He faltered then, jerking back. He silently cursed his cowardice, his brow crumpling in distress. Like Loki, his mind deceived him, for he thought he heard Florie calling him. If he could just find the willpower to take that step…

"Rane! Nae!" she screamed. "Nae!"

She sounded so painfully real…so close…

Then he turned his head.

The hoarse cry came from the depths of his soul. "Florie!"

She was alive! Alive and beautiful. Even ashen and soaked and muddy, her lips blue with cold, tears and rain streaking her face, her hands clinging to a pathetically singed creature that might be Methuselah, come through hell. By Odin, she was the most beautiful sight he'd ever seen.

Somewhere in the distance he could hear Mavis's petulant whining, but 'twas submerged beneath a loud tumult as everyone—men-at-arms, Gilbert's guard, Father Conan, Florie—cheered. Even the executioner, his mission thwarted, let go of the horse's bridle to applaud.

Then the mare, startled by the sudden noise, bolted forward, taking the cart with her.

CHAPTER 22

Rane felt the knot jerk and tighten around his neck as he dropped off the cart. For a nightmarish moment, the strangling tension about his throat was intense, unbearable.

But an instant later, his feet hit the ground.

Stunned, he simply stood there in disbelief, choking. No one moved. Or spoke. Or breathed. Then someone prodded the executioner, and he rushed forward, grabbing the rope.

Someone snickered.

As the executioner loosened the knot about his throat, Rane coughed reflexively.

A few onlookers giggled.

Rane glanced dazedly down at his feet, planted solidly on the earth, then up at the oak branch.

Soon the entire assemblage was roaring with laughter. He glanced at the executioner.

"Ye're a tall one," the man said with a sheepish shrug. "I must have measured wrong." He winked, sending everyone into gales of helpless mirth.

Only Florie wasn't laughing. She was as white as

alabaster, and her eyes pooled with unspilled tears. With a decisive sniff and wiping at her nose with the back of her hand, she passed Methuselah to Father Conan. She opened the satchel at her hip, and Rane knew, without ever seeing it, what was inside. And what she intended.

Florie licked the raindrops from her lips, looking pensively at the girdle of gold links, her heirloom, her legacy. She took a quavery breath. The very meaning of her existence resided in that girdle.

But because of it, she'd almost lost Rane. She'd almost lost the chance at a future filled with love. And what could possibly be as meaningful as that? Certainly not a piece of gold that had never been hers to begin with, the relic of a love that was no more and a bloodline that made no difference.

Aye, she would cast away the promise of prosperity and wager her fate upon this untamed son of Vikings. For love.

Giving Rane a tremulous smile, she turned toward Mavis's litter and knelt in the mud.

"Nae," he called hoarsely to her, knowing all that she was about to sacrifice.

She glanced back at him, smiling again. "I *want* to, Rane. I want this."

Then, bowing her head before Lady Mavis, who was near apoplectic with dismay at her foiled spectacle, she offered up the gold girdle in both hands. "My lady, I wish to buy the life o' your prisoner."

Mavis didn't think twice. Her eyes wide with alarm, she reached out, planning to snatch the prize before anyone could see it.

"Wait!" Gilbert barked.

A panicked whimper escaped her as he gestured angrily toward the girdle. "Ye'd kill a man over this trinket?" he demanded. "Ye'd execute my best huntsman to put another bauble about your hips?"

Mavis, her eyes fixed on the pomander, her fingers itching to seize it, answered him as calmly as she could. "Nae, Gilly. I'd execute the thievin' *wench* who stole it from me. But *he* let her escape and—"

"Escape! Escape? Ye mean from the fire ye set?"

The crowd gasped, and Mavis felt fear clog her throat. Her mind whirring, she tried to think of something, anything, that would distract Gilbert from the pomander long enough for her to wrest it from the wench.

"Ach, Gilly," she said on a feigned sob, pressing a hand to her bosom, "how could ye think such a thing? I'd never set fire to a church."

"Nae!" he spat. Then, so softly that only she could hear, he bit out, "Ye likely left that task to one o' your English friends."

"Wha—?" Her heart plummeted.

With one hand, Gilbert tore the curtain from her litter, and Mavis recoiled with a squeak, feeling as if he'd ripped the clothing from her body.

"Free my huntsman," Gilbert commanded the executioner over his shoulder, his cold stare never leaving Mavis. "Lady, ye've been nothin' but trouble from the time I brought ye home to wife."

Mavis glanced about at the gawking peasants, wishing she could banish them with a wave of her hand, the way King Henry always had. "Gilly," she said between her teeth, "this is hardly the proper time and—"

"I indulged ye, knowin' ye weren't happy here. I allowed

ye to spend your coin freely, hopin' to keep ye entertained. I gave ye servants to order about, prize falcons for your amusement, gold for ye to squander at the fair. I see now, however, that ye're no happier. I've only let ye become an even more spoiled child."

"I'm not a child," Mavis protested, unfortunately sounding just like a child.

He hauled her swiftly up against him, burying her face in his doublet, holding her there in the crook of his arm. To onlookers, it likely appeared to be a lover's embrace. To Mavis, 'twas suffocating.

"And now," he whispered in her ear with deadly calm, "I've proof ye've been consortin' with the enemy."

Mavis stiffened. She'd feared Gilbert might discover the truth about the lass and her trinket. She'd never expected he'd discover the truth about *her.*

"Ye've been passin' messages to the English," he hissed, "tellin' them the whereabouts o' the Scots soldiers. Givin' them information about my comin' and goin'."

"Nae," Mavis breathed.

"The queen feared ye were disloyal. She'd hoped to curb your spyin' by sendin' ye away to the Borders. But it didn't cure ye, did it?" He lowered his voice to a deadly growl. "Ye told the English that the princess was bein' moved to Musselburgh."

Mavis swallowed, her thoughts racing. What had happened? Had the ambush worked? Had Hertford's men found Princess Mary? Had they finally brought the stubborn Scots queen to her knees?

Gilbert chuckled humorlessly. "There's just one problem. I lied to ye. The princess isn't there. Ye sent the English into a trap this time."

Mavis, who'd spent a lifetime deceiving men, wasn't about to confess to a crime for which she might hang. "Gilly, my love," she said, turning a stricken gaze up to him, "I don't know what ye're talkin' about."

"I'm not your love," he snarled. "Ye never cared for me. Ye only hoped to use me."

"'Tisn't true, Gilly. I love ye," she choked out. "I want to give ye sons and grow old with ye."

"Aye, that ye do. Like that bastard Henry, ye'd do anythin' to secure your future," he said, shaking his head, "includin' stealin' away the future of another. Do ye even know what ye're takin' from this lass, or is it only another costly bauble for your amusement?"

Mavis pressed her lips together to keep them from trembling.

Gilbert released her and gestured toward the wretched girdle, which winked in mockery now as the sun filtered through the clearing clouds. "This piece was never for the sellin'. The lass said it belonged to her father, her *noble* father, whom she seeks. So ye see, Mavis, the lass may be as highborn as *ye* are."

Mavis blinked. Gilbert didn't know the whole truth yet, then. His words had given her one last slim hope. She sighed in feigned exasperation and fluttered her hands in surrender. "Oh, very well. The lass can have it back, then. Now that I see the piece again, I find I don't like it all that well anyway." She placed her palm on Gilbert's chest and stared sweetly into his eyes, willing him to look at her. "Come, Gilly, let's just put all this nonsense about spyin' and fires and hangin' behind us, and..." She trailed off as she saw she'd failed to gain his attention.

Florie was too busy staring at her beloved Rane to notice that the lord sheriff had grown silent and was studying the girdle in her hands.

Rane's weary eyes were rimmed with red. His hair hung like wet, charred twine over his face. His neck was raw where the rope had throttled him, and his chest was covered with scrapes and bruises. But faith, he was the most beautiful man in the world. And, thank God, he was alive to hear her say it. Which she intended to do, from this day forward for the rest of her life.

His lips lifted in a grateful smile as he returned her stare, but then he glanced up at Lord Gilbert, and his brow furrowed.

She followed his gaze.

The sun had pierced holes in the gray clouds like arrows shot through silk, and in her hands the gold girdle glittered in the brilliant light. Lord Gilbert's eyes narrowed upon the pomander, and he spoke so softly that surely only Florie could hear him.

"I know this piece."

Florie blinked. Maybe he'd seen it at the fair. Or one similar. Aye, the pomander was unique in all the world, but in her experience, most men couldn't discern the difference between rubies and red glass.

He slowly drew his gaze upward to look at Florie's face, as if he sought something there. "Ye said your mother gave it to ye?"

"Aye, my lord, upon her death," she said. "She said it belonged to..."

Suddenly 'twas as transparent as the rain-washed air. The same dark hair that, in her mother's words, seemed nearly black but shimmered like claret in the sun. The same fair skin. The same tilt of the eyes. Why hadn't she noticed it before?

"My father," she breathed.

He was still staring at her, but his gaze had gone to another time, another place, maybe to memories he wished he could revisit, sorrows he wished he could repair.

Florie's thoughts raced and tumbled one over the other as she considered the import of her discovery. Was her search truly over? Had she found her father? 'Twas a most astonishing miracle.

Now that she'd found him, she realized she could begin her life anew. She'd never have to return to Stirling. She could remain in Selkirk and live in a tower house, her *father's* tower house. She could have a hundred servants at her beck and call. She could wear the finest silks and have a daily bath if she so desired. Best of all, she could be free of the burden of her foster father, of toiling long hours over a worktable to ensure he was steeped in enough ale to keep him numb.

'Twas such a temptation.

Yet if she stayed, if she revealed that Lord Gilbert was her true father, if she embraced a new life, she'd also inherit the hindrances of that life. Noblewomen didn't sully their hands on common labor. Could she bear to give up her craft entirely? Would she have to curb her forthright tongue for propriety's sake? And, God's wounds, did she truly want Lady Mavis for a foster mother?

Such thoughts gave her pause. But the one that brought her to her senses as swiftly as a splash of cold water, the one that convinced her to hand the pomander to Lord Gilbert without a word and only the slightest indication in the meeting of their eyes that they shared a secret, was the realization that if she chose Gilbert, she would lose Rane.

Her father glanced down at the pomander, tracing his fingers over the letters—F and G—and Florie suddenly realized they didn't stand for Florie Gilder, but Gilbert Fraser.

"Ye're certain ye wish to give this up?" he murmured.

Though he spoke no further word, his message was clear. If Florie wished him to acknowledge her as his daughter, he would. She could see now why her mother had loved the handsome nobleman. Florie supposed she'd only half believed the tales her mother told, suspecting her real father had used the young, naive, pretty lass to ease his lusts, then cast her aside on a whim. Indeed, she sometimes wondered if in seeking out her father, she wished to punish him in some way by giving a face and a name to his sin.

No more. Now she believed. Now she saw Gilbert's dilemma. Just as he was caught now in a miserable second marriage to a demanding shrew, a union ordained by the queen, so he'd been caught before. Abandoning her mother hadn't been a choice. It had been an unavoidable tragedy. She couldn't blame him for the machinations of royalty.

Nobles, she thought, were like the warriors in hnefatafl. They had no will of their own. Their destiny was controlled by their overlord. They moved about the board of life, advancing and losing ground, making sacrifices, living and marrying and dying according to the wishes of another.

Nae, she decided, she wanted no part of it.

"Ye keep it," she said, smiling gently, a smile that told him she forgave him for the past.

"Is there..." he began, pausing to clear his throat,

obviously deeply affected by the fact that, unlike his current wife, Florie yearned for neither his land nor his title. "Is there anythin' else I can do for ye?"

"Aye," Florie answered, coming to her feet as Gilbert held out his hand. "There is one thing."

The burgh maids had straggled up now, having scrambled after the racing horses as quickly as they could to see what transpired with their hero on Gallows Hill. Now, gasping and clasping their hands to their pounding hearts, they whispered among themselves, utterly baffled by the curious turn of events.

Rane set his hand upon her shoulder, and Florie covered it with her own, swallowing hard. 'Twas a reckless thing she dared, a petition that went against all her parents' warnings, a wager on which she staked everything. 'Twas foolhardy and audacious and ill-considered. But for the first time in her life, she intended to listen to her heart, to close her eyes and step off the cliff of reason.

"I wish to marry your huntsman, my lord," she said, her heart throbbing. "And I wish for your blessin'."

Gasps sounded all around them. But Florie held her breath. There was only one response she awaited, and 'twasn't Gilbert's. Fortunately, she didn't wait long. In the next instant Rane's chuckling sigh of consent blew past her ear, sending a relieved shiver through her.

"'Tis agreeable to ye, Rane?" Gilbert asked.

She could almost feel his grin. "Oh, aye, my lord."

At once, plaintive feminine weeping filled the air—the burgh maids, Florie realized, mourning their loss. She almost pitied them—almost. But the soft sound was more bittersweet than sad, and soon the enthusiastic cheering of the men-at-arms overshadowed their sniffling. Florie grinned. Later, without a doubt, the men would be more than happy to console the grieving lasses.

After a space, Gilbert held up a hand for silence. "I grant permission for this marriage, then. We'll have the weddin' feast at the tower house. May ye both enjoy the blessin's o' true love." His voice was tainted with sadness at the end, and Florie felt sorry for him. Gilbert had had to walk away from his true love, and he knew the price he'd paid.

"Gilly," Mavis ventured meekly, aware of her tenuous position. "Let them keep the piece as a weddin' gift."

Gilbert's jaw tensed, but he turned a grim smile on his wife and said in a deceptively friendly tone, "Nae, I've decided to give ye your prize, after all, since ye worked so hard to earn it." He weighed the piece in his hand. "Only since ye don't like its design, I'm goin' to give it to the armorer to melt down into a new one." He spared a wink at Florie, then thoughtfully stroked his beard. "I'm goin' to have him fashion it into a collar o' sorts for ye," he continued, "the kind the hounds wear, permanently fitted with a leash o' gold links."

Mavis's eyes went as round as her mouth.

"A very short leash," he added, "to remind me to keep ye obediently at my heel until the queen decides what to do with ye."

With a mortified squeak, Mavis flung herself back into the farthest corner of the litter, where she sat in cowering silence, subdued for the moment.

But though Mavis surely deserved such punishment and more, Florie was strangely dissatisfied. She'd treasured the girdle for such a long while, and to see the gold carelessly melted down...

"Ye don't approve?" Gilbert asked her gently.

"'Tis only that the gold might be put to better use, my lord," she said tentatively.

"And what use would that be?"

She wet her lips. Dared she tell him? "The crofters are starvin'," she blurted. "Meat is scarce, and there's nothin' but what can be coaxed from the few wheatfields the English have left unburned. The ale's so weak 'tis little more than water, and they must make bread from weeds." She glanced over at the Father, who was nodding in approval. "Sell the piece, my lord," she bade him, "and use the coin to purchase food for them."

Lord Gilbert said nothing but lifted his eyes, scanning the faces of the humble burghers surrounding him. Finally he sighed, and when he spoke, 'twas to himself. "I've been blind to their needs these past months," he muttered. "Aye, they shall be fed. Rane." He clapped the archer on the shoulder. "Are ye fit to hunt?"

"Fit enough, my lord," he bravely replied, though Florie saw to her dismay that the backs of his hands were red and blistered from fighting the blaze. "Though I lost my bow in the fire."

"I'll have a new one made," Gilbert told him. "Till Midsummer's Eve, Rane MacFarland, Ettrick Forest is yours. All game hunted therein shall belong to the crofters."

Another great cheer arose from the burghers, and it seemed at that moment that God smiled upon Gallows Hill. The sun suddenly streamed down, warm and healing and full of promise.

But Florie hardly noticed. For Rane had immediately swept her into his arms, hugging her so closely against his bare chest that she thought she might gladly suffocate there. He swung her around until she was giddy and giggling, and even after he set her feet upon the ground again, her head spun wildly.

With no thought for shame or propriety, he ran his bold hands over her everywhere, as if ensuring she was substantial, and just as improperly, she allowed him, smiling all the while. He tipped her head back in his hands and kissed the tip of her nose, then her brow, then each cheek, covering her face with so many enthusiastic kisses that soon she was squirming in unabashed delight.

"Rane," someone called distantly.

He cradled Florie's face between his great Viking hands, tipping her head to press warm lips to hers. Lord, his kiss left her breathless. He tasted of smoke and rosemary and desire...

"Rane," came the insistent voice.

Florie groaned in complaint, standing on tiptoe to deepen the kiss, lifting her hands to place them brazenly upon Rane's wide warrior chest. Her blood warmed and thinned and raced through her veins like molten gold poured into a mold, and her ears sang with the harmonies of yearning...

"Rane!"

He tore his mouth away in irritation. "What?" he snapped.

Florie's dazed annoyance vanished as soon as she saw the wee, pale, heart-shaped face frowning up at them. The lass was undaunted by Rane's bark and only tugged harder at his braies.

"Ach, Jossy," he said in chagrin as ripples of light laughter coursed through the crowd. He hunkered down to speak to the lass. "What is it?"

Florie stifled a grin as the tiny lass spoke to him in a voice loud enough to be heard in the next barony.

"No more curse?" She stuck out her lower lip in a vexed pout.

Rane took her tiny hand. "Jossy, poppet, there never was a—"

"No curse?" Florie interjected. "But o' course there's a curse." She peered solemnly down her nose at Jossy. "Ye still love Rane, don't ye?"

The lass glanced at Rane, then returned her gaze to Florie and nodded.

"And even if he marries me, ye'll still love him?" Florie asked.

Jossy nodded.

Florie scowled intently. "Even if he gives me bairns?"

Jossy eyed her belly as if gauging that possibility. So, to her amusement, did Rane. Then the wee lass nodded.

"Even," Florie intoned, "if he swears his undyin' love to me every day for the rest of his life?"

Jossy pursed her lips, thinking for a moment. Then she jutted out her chin and soberly nodded.

Florie affected a heavy sigh full of regret. "Then I'm afraid there's nothin' I can do to break the curse."

With a smug smile, Jossy gave Rane an impulsive hug. Then she scrambled back to her disgruntled guardian, a man Florie feared would have his hands full when the spirited little lass grew to womanhood.

Rane's lopsided grin as he rose to tower over her again made her pulse race. "My undyin' love?" he murmured as the crowd began to disperse. He lifted her chin and brushed his thumb across her lower lip, sending a delicious tingle through her that made her knees go weak.

Then he narrowed his twinkling eyes. "And what do ye bring for barter, merchant?"

She thought she'd tell him. Her heart. Her life. Her soul. But there were no words to fully answer Rane. 'Twould take a lifetime to say.

So instead she said only, "This." And she gazed tenderly into his chrysolite eyes shot with spikes of aquamarine, more precious than any gemstone. She tucked an errant strand of sooty hair behind his ear and lowered her eyes to his mouth, his luscious, seductive, irresistible mouth. Then, sliding her palms along his strong jaw, she cupped his face and rose up to bestow upon him a kiss he'd never forget.

A kiss full of yearning and blessing and promise.

A kiss of surrender and victory, of faith and honor, of untold adventure and blissful homecoming.

A kiss the lasses of Selkirk would be talking about for years.

epilogue

Florie straightened on the cushioned fridstool, one of the few remnants left from the fire, and pressed a hand to her aching back. She shouldn't have remained for so long in one position, especially in her condition. But the work was almost complete, and once the bairn was born she'd likely be too busy for such diversions. Besides, 'twas the best gift she could think of to give Father Conan.

The craftsmen Lord Gilbert had commissioned to rebuild the sanctuary at Mavis's expense had spared no effort to make the otherwise modest church as beautiful as a jeweled crown, with vivid stained-glass windows from Paris, richly painted wood panels from Flanders, and the most stunning glazed enamelware from Majorca for the font and basin.

Now that Princess Mary had been whisked away to France to live with her betrothed, out of the reach of the English army, Scotland might stand a chance of recovering from Hertford's devastating attacks. Lady Mavis could no longer orchestrate his raids, for she'd been stripped of her

351

wealth and exiled to a convent. For the time, at least, the Church at the Crossroads could be rebuilt without fear of vandalism.

The intricate gold cross at the altar Florie had fashioned herself. 'Twas replete with twining vines set with pearl roses and a crown of topaz thorns for the Christ, enameled at the base with the likenesses of the four Evangelists and their symbols—the man, the lion, the ox, and the eagle. Indeed, so cleverly had she crafted the cross that the guildsmen of Selkirk had awarded it the status of masterpiece and welcomed her into the guild as a goldsmith in her own right.

But though Florie was well pleased, she knew such treasures meant nothing to a blind priest. And so she now endeavored to employ her decorative skills to create an embellishment he could appreciate.

Biblical scenes graced the new pillars of the church now, carved in deep relief, scenes of the birth and baptism and resurrection of Christ and figures of all the various saints, with special places of honor for Saint Hubert—the patron saint of hunters; Saint Dunstan—the patron saint of goldsmiths; and Saint Valentine—the patron saint of lovers.

When she ran out of sacred themes, she carved depictions of animals—deer and doves and wolves and lions, roaring and resting and romping in spirals up the posts. And to her gratification, the Father had wept with joy when she guided his fingers gently over the carvings.

But now she worked on the lesser figures at the base of the last pillar, and for this final scene she departed from saints and animals and biblical fare. She squinted as she leaned forward again to put the final touches on the scene. The tall Viking huntsman, his bow over his shoulder, his quiver of arrows upon his back, curved his arms affectionately about his wife's swollen belly. She rested her head back upon his shoulder, gazing lovingly up at his smiling face. At the lovers' feet, forgotten, its pieces scattered, was a hnefatafl board. In the distant background, the lasses of the burgh stopped at their labors to gaze fondly upon the couple, and from between two trees peered mischievous wee Josselin Ancrum.

But the focal point of the scene was the tiny brooch perched over Florie's heart. 'Twas fashioned in the shape of an archer's arrow, an arrow she painstakingly covered now with gold leaf.

"Florie."

She turned toward his voice. Faith, even after all these months, Rane still had the power to make her heart throb when he entered a room. His shirt was open, revealing the golden chain and antlered pendant she'd promised to craft for him. His tawny skin glistened, and though she knew 'twas but perspiration from the spring heat, in her mind's eye he was suddenly a marauding berserker, swimming from his dragon ship onto the English shore, emerging from the sea, naked and golden and dripping. She smiled at him, her eyes dipping languidly, and she thought 'twas a wonder that she could feel such desire for him in her present state.

"I thought I'd find ye here," he said, flashing her a dazzling smile.

"I'm almost finished." Eager now to be done, wondering in the back of her mind how indecent 'twould be to make love to him in their favorite copse of the wood by the light of day, she bent forward again, coaxing the thin sheet of gold onto the wooden arrow.

He walked toward the altar with a frown. "They still haven't scrubbed the bloodstain from the flagstones."

"I told them not to."

"Why?"

She shrugged. "I like it. It represents sacrifice. And sanctuary. And it marks the place where I first fell in love with ye."

"Fell in love with me?" he said in mock disbelief, a coy twinkle in his eye. "Ye mean while ye were stabbin' me with your brooch? And jabbin' me with your pointy elbows? And cursin' me for dressin' your wound?"

She grinned and returned to her work. "I do not have pointy elbows."

He chuckled, and as she worked he ambled about her, circling the pillar to inspect the menagerie of beasts and saints and people she'd carved upon them. "These are amazin'."

His praise made her blush with pleasure. She pressed the gold leaf over the arrow tip, trimming it carefully to preserve the remnants of precious gold, and glanced up at Rane. He carried a wrapped parcel. "So what did Lord Gilbert give ye?" She'd almost forgotten. The lord had summoned Rane to the tower house to give him a gift in honor of their firstborn.

He smiled, that secretive, mischievous smile she'd come to both adore and be wary of, and then he held forth the package.

She put away her tools and took the parcel upon her lap, or what was left of her lap. "What is it?" she asked, untying the cord that bound the thing.

But he only grinned, crossing his arms over his chest like a conquering hero.

When she first spied the gleam of gold, she was surprised. Why would the lord give Rane a gift of gold when he was married to a goldsmith? But as she unwrapped the lovers' cup, the breath caught in her chest.

'Twas an exquisite piece. Yet there was something familiar about the work, the intricate designs about the rim, the cabochon rubies around the base, the style of the figures circling the bowl of the cup.

She studied them more closely. On one side was carved a perfect rendering of Rane with a deer slung across his shoulder and Florie cradling an aquamanile of gold in her arm. Lord Gilbert's crest figured subtly into the tower house in the background.

But, to her amazement, on the other side of the cup was a reproduction of her goldsmith shop in Stirling, and standing hand in hand were the figures of her parents, her foster father with his once proud stature, her mother with her shy beauty.

'Twas impossible. Who could know…?

And then she saw the stamp at the bottom. Her foster father's mark.

Her heart stuttered. "How came ye…"

She lifted her eyes, and suddenly 'twas as if the figure on the cup had come to life. There he was, walking toward her through the nave, with Wat shuffling behind him. His beard was trimmed, his eyes clear, his jaw held rigid to keep his chin from trembling with emotion.

"Father?"

She hadn't seen him sober since her mother died, hadn't heard from him since she'd left long months ago for Selkirk. Yet here he was, strong and hale and as handsome as she remembered from her childhood. And curse her frail condition, seeing him thus brought instant tears to her eyes.

Rane softly explained, "Lord Gilbert said to tell ye that he owed your foster father a debt, that bringin' him to Selkirk and carin' for him was the least he could do to repay him for guardin' his dearest possession for so long."

Florie saw her foster father's eyes were filled too as he left Wat and came forward to take her hand, helping her up from the fridstool. Too moved for words, he tucked her arm beneath his own and then, with a sniffle, escorted her toward the altar.

"I hear this altar cross is somethin' to behold," he said. "A masterpiece, I'm told."

A sob caught in her throat, and she could hardly speak. "'Tis not as expert as...as my father's work."

"Nae, your talents were always far superior," he told, "and your eye far more ingenious." He indicated the detailing at the feet of the Christ. "Ah! See how ye've used tiny rubies here to represent the blood o' Christ. Brilliant."

He continued in his praises, but Florie couldn't absorb them all. Her heart was too full of love and hope and joy. As he rambled on, his arm was for once steady and supportive beneath hers.

Even Wat ventured forward to admire her work, mumbling in contrition, "I'm sorry I couldn't save your goods, m'lady."

Her foster father explained. "Wat limped home after thieves ransacked the cart." He clapped Wat on the shoulder. "He was lucky to escape with his life."

Florie nodded. "That's all right, Wat. 'Twas only gold." The bairn stirred within her, and she absently rubbed her belly. "I've somethin' much more valuable now."

The poor child, she thought, smiling—'twas already restless. 'Twas likely a boy, then, who'd no doubt share the Viking curse of his father.

She turned to glance at her irresistible husband. He gave her an endearing crooked grin and a seductive wink. Her breath quickened and her heart melted as she let her eyes roam over the magnificent Scots archer who'd hunted and tamed her, the gentle Norseman who'd claimed her body and touched her soul, a man more precious than all the gold in the world.

The End

тhAПK you FOR READIПG my BOOK!

Did you enjoy it? If so, I hope you'll post a review to let others know! There's no greater gift you can give an author than spreading your love of her books.

It's truly a pleasure and a privilege to be able to share my stories with you. Knowing that my words have made you laugh, sigh, or touched a secret place in your heart is what keeps the wind beneath my wings. I hope you enjoyed our brief journey together, and may ALL of your adventures have happy endings!

If you'd like to keep in touch, feel free to sign up for my monthly e-newsletter at www.glynnis.net, and you'll be the first to find out about my new releases, special discounts, prizes, promotions, and more!

If you want to keep up with my daily escapades:
Friend me at facebook.com/GlynnisCampbell
Like my Page at bit.ly/GlynnisCampbellFBPage
Follow me at twitter.com/GlynnisCampbell
And if you're a super fan, join
facebook.com/GCReadersClan

Excerpt from

ϻᴀᴄᴀᴅᴀϻ's Lᴀss

The Scottish Lasses Book 2

QUEEN MARY'S CORONATION PROCESSION
EDINBURGH, SCOTLAND

Drew grumbled under his breath. He didn't know why he'd come. He usually avoided crowds like the pox. Already he'd been jostled by drunks, elbowed by peddlers, pushed aside by filthy urchins trying to get a better view, and aye, even patted on the arse by a wench looking for a bit of business.

But he was currently staying in Edinburgh, and the whole city seemed to be in a feverish fervor over their new monarch, Queen Mary. He hadn't been able to persuade any golfers to play today, even with the offer of weighting the game in their favor. So he'd decided, since the links were deserted, and since he'd missed the coronation of his own Queen Elizabeth three years ago, perhaps he'd venture down to the Royal Mile to see what the clamor was about.

So far, Queen Mary had been nothing but an inconvenience to him. Her early arrival at Leith Harbor had interrupted one perfectly good golf game, and her homecoming festivities today prevented another. True, he'd been paid handsomely for the forfeit of his match with Ian Horn. But lately, he was driven as much by his love of the sport as by coin.

He frowned, beginning to regret his decision to come. The hubbub was inescapable. The crowd was packed in at Lawnmarket as tightly as herring in a barrel. People were cheering and singing and shouting and laughing in a deafening commotion. And the queen hadn't even arrived yet.

He scanned the crowd with an uneasy scowl, wondering how quickly the Scots would string him up if they found out he was English. Fortunately, he'd played the part long enough to be fairly certain he could convince even the most dubious Lowlander that he'd been born and bred in the Highlands. And the rare Highlander who ventured this far south had never heard of his hometown of Tintclachan—which was no surprise, since Drew had invented the village and placed it in a vague, remote part of the country.

'Twas a necessary deception. Traveling as a Highlander along the eastern coast of Scotland, he could steal from the purses of those who'd stolen his father from him, exacting a fitting but bloodless revenge.

His uncles, of course, would have preferred he join the English army and kill every Scot in sight. Drew considerable skill with a blade, thanks to his uncles' training. But like his father, he'd never had the heart for violence. Besides, with King Henry dead and Queen Elizabeth on the throne, battles along the Borders were rare. Still, to keep his uncles content, Drew let them believe the coin he earned was won on the English tournament circuit with a sword rather than on the Scots links with a golf club.

He thought his disguise was reasonably convincing. He'd let his hair grow a bit shaggier than was fashionable, and he usually went a day or two without a shave. He owned a pair of sturdy knee-high boots and a long, belted saffron shirt with a short leather doublet, beneath which he wore dark tartan trews, even in summer, for he'd never quite accustomed himself to the Highland habit of going bare-arsed. When the weather grew cold, he tossed a Scots plaid over one shoulder.

He'd spoken so long with a brogue that he could hardly remember how to speak proper English. After three years of living the lie, he almost believed it himself.

"And ye have the ballocks to call yourself a Scotsman!" cried the lad beside him unexpectedly.

Drew stiffened.

But the lad was yelling at someone else, a half-drunk redbearded fellow who was carrying on about the new queen in a loud bellow. "I'm more Scots than some Catholic tart who's been livin' in France all her life!"

The lad gasped, then spat, "Ye take that back!"

"I won't!" snorted the redbeard.

The lad gave him a hard push.

The man stumbled back a step, spilling a few drops of his ale, but continued his tirade. "What gives the wench the right to sail into my harbor and tell me how to say my prayers?"

The youth raised a puny fist and spoke through his teeth. "Ye'd *better* say your prayers."

The redbeard was too drunk to recognize the threat. "I won't be takin' orders from ye, nor from that French trull."

The lad growled a warning.

Drew groaned inwardly. The last thing he needed was

to get caught in a brawl. This wasn't his fight. He wasn't Scots. And he didn't care a whit about the queen. He was already having a miserable day. He didn't need to make it worse.

But the lad was half the redbeard's size. A strong wind would blow him over. Drew couldn't just stand by and watch the young pup get his arse kicked. He laid a restraining palm on the lad's shoulder. "Easy, half-pint."

"He's right!" a third man chimed in from Drew's other side, suddenly placing Drew squarely in the middle of the battle. "No Scot should have to kiss the derriere of a French wench."

The lad shrugged off Drew's hand. "Mary was born here, ye lobcocks!" he insisted, his voice breaking with his vehemence. "She knows our history. She speaks our tongue."

"Ye're a daft grig!" the redbeard crowed, raising his cup of ale. "No sensible Scotsman would let a hen rule the roost, eh, lads? Even John Knox says so!"

Drew grimaced as the surrounding men cheered in accord.

He could practically feel the heat rising off of the angry youth beside him as the lad ground out, "John Knox is a bloody blockhead."

Drew had heard the preachings of John Knox, who was an infamous misogynist, and he had to agree with the lad. But he couldn't afford to be trapped in the midst of a rabid pack of battling Scots. He leaned down to murmur a few words of friendly advice to the reckless youth. "Careful, lad. Ye're outnumbered."

The lad whipped his head around, facing Drew directly, and answered him with all the fearless passion of youth. "I'll gladly fight them all in Mary's defense."

Drew recoiled, not from the youth's bold boast, but from a startling revelation, a revelation that the men surrounding him had not yet had.

All at once, the crowd began cheering wildly, and the debate was forgotten as everyone turned toward the road. The procession had arrived at last. People clapped and shouted and waved their arms. Some chanted—whether in welcome or mockery, Drew couldn't tell.

Nor did he much care. He was far more interested in his new discovery. He stepped back a pace and let his gaze course down the back of the youth beside him. 'Twas hard to tell with the ill-fitting shirt and the oversized hat, but Drew would have wagered his putting cleek that the brazen half-pint standing beside him, making bold threats and swearing like a sailor, was a lass.

Josselin was so caught up in the excitement of Mary's arrival that she forgot all about her quarrel with the drunken redbeard. She stood on her toes to try to get a better view as a loud fanfare sounded to announce the procession through Lawnmarket.

This was what she'd come for—to see the Queen, to lay eyes on the ambitious lass who, though not much older than Josselin, had already forged for herself a powerful legacy.

As Alasdair had explained to her, Mary, the descendant of both King Henry VII of England and King James II of Scotland, had not only been wife to the Dauphin of France, but would also now be Queen of Scotland, and might well inherit the English crown from Elizabeth.

Josselin admired Mary's spirit and ambition, for she knew what 'twas like to be a woman, fighting for a significant place in the world of men. This new queen was going to change things. She was sure of it. And Josselin wanted to be a part of that change.

As she peered over the shoulders of the people in front of her, she spied the first wave of the procession. Dozens of yellow-robed Scotsmen disguised as Moors—their limbs blackened and their heads covered with black hats and masks—cleared the way through the flowers the townsfolk had strewn in the wide street. Behind them came the Edinburgh officials, who carried aloft a purple canopy embroidered in gold with French lilies and Scottish unicorns.

French soldiers and Scottish lairds made up the bulk of the impressive entourage. Behind them, four lasses of Josselin's age rode shoulder to shoulder, and she knew they must be the Four Maries. Seeing their lavish velvet gowns and rich jewels made Josselin curse her guardian all over again for forcing her to disguise herself in his drooping trews and baggy shirt.

Then, beneath the canopy, riding upon a white palfrey, came Queen Mary herself, more magnificent and beautiful than Josselin had imagined. Though Mary had recently lost both her mother and her husband, today she'd discarded her white mourning shroud in favor of a more festive gown of purple velvet with gold embroidery. Jewels twinkled from her neck, waist, and wrists, but they couldn't outshine the charming sparkle in Mary's eyes. As Josselin looked on in awe, the queen nodded regally to the crowd, her face lit up by a serene smile.

A huge, brightly painted triumphal arch had been erected across the road at Lawnmarket, and from the gallery above, a choir of children began to sing. Riding forward, Mary waved to them in greeting.

As she passed beneath the arch, a mechanical globe painted like a cloud slowly opened to reveal a child dressed as an angel. Josselin watched in amazement as the angel was lowered on a rope to hand the queen the keys of the gates.

Then the child began to recite an eloquent welcome to Mary in verse. But as the words became clear, the Catholic queen's smile faltered. Buried in the prose was a thinly veiled reference to the Reformation.

Some in the crowd gasped, and some, including the men Josselin had been arguing with, sent up bellows of approval.

Josselin's blood simmered. Who dared insult the new queen with such obvious blasphemy? She rounded on the redbearded oaf who'd earlier called Mary a tart and shoved him.

Someone gripped her elbow. "Not now, lass," a man murmured into her ear.

It didn't occur to her that he'd called her "lass" at that moment. Her hackles were up, and she was itching for a fight. She wrenched her arm free and shot him a scathing glare over her shoulder.

Then she cast her gaze back to the spectacle before her. The child angel was handing the queen two purple velvet tomes now, a Bible and a Psalter, and Josselin knew without a doubt that they were Reformer books.

"A fittin' gift," the redbeard muttered to his friend, "for the Whore o' Babylon."

"Aye," another added. "'Twill show her she'd best leave the Pope in France."

"Shut your mouths, ye jackanapes!" Josselin fired back, her blood now seething.

Once more, the man behind her seized her arm, this time more forcefully, hissing in a strong Highland accent, "'Tisn't worth it, lass."

Again, she twisted away.

John Knox must be behind this travesty, she decided. 'Twas rumored the Reformer meant to meet with the queen personally very soon in order to challenge her faith. That might be, but by God, Josselin didn't intend to let anyone humiliate Mary today.

"Refuse the books, Your Majesty!" she shouted in encouragement over the crowd. "Go on! Toss them away!"

The Highlander made a choking sound. "Cease, lass. Are ye daft? Don't draw attention—"

The redbeard yelled up at the child suspended from the arch. "'Tis no use tryin' to court Mary, wee angel! She's already wed to Rome!"

The men nearby howled with laughter.

Josselin had had enough. 'Twas bad enough that the new queen had to hold her own against the bloody English without having to deal with detractors among her own countrymen. With a roar, she unsheathed her dagger and faced the redbearded dastard. "Defend your slander with a blade!"

Behind her, the Highlander swore in exasperation.

But the redbeard took one look at her dagger, threw down his cup of ale, and went for his weapon.

"Aye, that's it," Josselin goaded, beckoning him with the fingers of her free hand. "Come on!"

The Highlander stepped suddenly between them to address the drunk. "Ach, man, ye don't want to be doin' that."

"Out o' my way!" the redbeard bellowed.

"Aye," Josselin agreed. "Out o' the way, Highlander, unless ye want to get skewered."

The Highlander turned to her then, filling her vision and sternly commanding her gaze, and for one stunned instant, she couldn't breathe. She hadn't paid much heed to him before, but now she saw he had the face of a dark angel—strong yet sweet. His eyes were the clearest blue she'd ever seen, like the sky on a warm spring day.

His heavy brows lowered as he said pointedly, "Ye can settle this...later."

The redbeard shoved him aside. "Stay out of it, man. 'Tis between the lad and me."

Rattled, Josselin nonetheless managed to raise her knife and face her opponent, eager to resume the duel. "No one insults my queen, ye traitor. Ye'll answer to me for your offense."

"Oh, I'll answer ye," the redbeard assured her. "I'll carve a cross into your flesh to remind ye o' your misbegotten faith."

"Ye won't get the chance," she promised.

"Put your blades away, both o' ye," she heard the Highlander mutter. Nobody paid him heed.

They faced off, and the crowd gave them room.

"Sheathe. *Now*," the Highlander insisted.

She ignored him, waving her dagger at the redbeard like a taunt. But before she could get off a good swipe, the Highlander stepped toward her.

"Fine," he said.

She half-wheeled in his direction, thinking he meant to attack her as well. Instead, he snatched the hat from her head. She gasped as her curls spilled over her shoulders like honey from a crushed comb.

The redbeard's eyes widened, and he retreated, dropping his knife.

Josselin tossed her head, angry that her secret was out. But she wasn't about to call off the fight. Her heart was pounding now, and she was primed for battle.

"What, ye sheep-swiver?" she sneered at the redbeard. "Are ye afraid to fight a woman?" She twirled the dagger once in her fingers. "Pick it up, coward! Pick up your knife."

The crowd had suddenly grown quiet.

"What's wrong with ye?" she challenged. "Is there not a single champion among ye poltroons?" No one moved. "And ye call yourselves men!" she scoffed. "Who stole your tongues and cut off your cods?"

No one answered. There was nothing but tense misgiving and wide eyes in the faces around her.

She frowned in sudden confusion. Then she realized the entire street had grown silent. 'Twas more than a silence of surprise. 'Twas a silence of warning.

The back of her neck began to tingle with apprehension. Slowly, cautiously, she lowered her dagger and turned toward the procession.

Staring at Josselin from atop her noble white steed, a curious, inscrutable half-smile playing upon her royal lips, was Queen Mary herself.

Josselin gulped. As she stood there, breathless, the queen gave her a thorough inspection, perusing her from her tangled blond hair to her dusty leather boots. After what seemed an eternity, Mary finally passed the Bible and Psalter to her captain, then waved her fingers in a beckoning motion.

Josselin instinctively started to step forward, but the

Highlander dug his fingers hard into her shoulders, holding her back.

Mary's gesture hadn't been meant for her, but for one of the royal officials. The distinguished-looking man approached the queen, who bent to whisper something in his ear, nodding toward Josselin.

While Josselin watched with bated breath, Mary gave her a slight dismissive nod, then urged her mount onward down the road, and the procession resumed.

Meanwhile, the official straightened his belt and strode directly toward Josselin. The crowd parted to make way for him.

He was French, tall and thin, perhaps a dozen years older than Josselin, and he looked mildly displeased. He had perceptive brown eyes, a neatly trimmed beard, and a long nose that he probably found useful for looking down on people.

With a curt nod, he introduced himself. "I am the queen's secretary, Philipe de la Fontaine. The queen has commanded that you make yourself known to me. You and I are to have a rendezvous today at The White Hart. You know the place?"

Josselin tried to speak, but her voice refused to come out. Faith, she'd received a command from the queen herself!

The Highlander answered. "I know the inn."

"Very well," the secretary said. He gave Josselin a belittling frown. "I expect to see you there this afternoon, Madame...?"

"Josselin," she managed to croak.

"Zhos-a-lahn," he repeated, using the French pronunciation. Then he gave her a brief, contemptuous inspection. "See if you can stay alive long enough to make the appointment."

The secretary hastened off to catch the royal entourage, and gradually the crowd resumed their chattering. But Josselin's pulse was still racing when the Highlander gently pried the dagger from her white knuckles.

"Ye aren't from around here, are ye, lass?" he murmured.

"Nae," she answered in a daze. "I'm from Selkirk. Holy saints, did ye see that? Did ye see how she—"

"Who brought ye to Edinburgh?"

She stared in wonder after the procession. "I came alone."

"Alone?"

"My da said I could," she said dreamily. The queen was well down the road now, but Josselin kept watching. "As long as I don't talk to strangers. Or go to taverns. Or lose my temper." She smiled. "Ach! Wait till I tell Da that the queen herself—"

"A piece of advice, lass," he confided. "Hie home to Selkirk straight away." He scooped up her hat, dusted it off, and pressed it into her hands. "Ye could be halfway there by afternoon."

She snapped out of her stupor and frowned up at the man with the dark hair and the clear blue eyes, who really was quite handsome...for a Highlander. "Home? Why would I want to go home?"

He looked at her as if she were barmy. "Ye aren't thinkin' o' keepin' the appointment?"

"O' course I am. The queen herself commanded it." The sound of that sent a shiver of excitement through her. "The *queen*." She couldn't wait to tell her guardians.

He arched a stern brow. "Look, lass, before ye get your trews in a twist, I don't expect ye're bein' invited to supper."

Supper! That idea hadn't even occurred to her. Was it possible? She tucked the corner of her lip under her teeth, imagining it. Then she recalled, "She smiled at me."

"Royals always smile whilst they're sharpenin' their swords."

She lowered her brows. The damned Highlander was ruining her good mood. "Ach! What would *ye* know?"

"I know ye brought the procession to a halt." He shook his head. "I don't imagine the queen's too pleased about that."

She bit the inside of her cheek. He had a point. Josselin had made an impression on the queen. But what if 'twas the wrong impression?

"I did draw a blade," she admitted.

"Aye."

"And I *was* brawlin' in the street."

She looked at him uncertainly.

"I've heard in the French courts," he said, eyeing her garments, "they even have strict laws about dress."

She looked down at the overlong hem of her linen shirt, clutching a fistful of it. "Do ye think I offended her?"

He gave her a maddening shrug.

Her shoulders sank. "I didn't mean to offend her."

Then she narrowed her gaze at the Highlander.

"This is all *your* fault!" she decided, swatting his chest with her hat. "If ye hadn't stolen my hat, none o' this would have happened."

His lips curled into a smirk that was half-smile, half-frown. "Oh aye, lass. Instead ye'd be wheezin' at me through a knife-hole in your chest."

She scowled at him, jamming the hat back over her head. "Ye've obviously never seen me fight with a blade."

"I've seen enough to know ye've got a hot temper that likely ruins your aim." He handed her dagger back to her, hilt first.

She snatched it from him in irritation and slid it back into its sheath. Her Da Angus had told her the same thing a hundred times. She didn't need to hear it from a bloody Highlander, no matter how handsome he was.

The crowd began to disperse. Mary's procession was moving toward the Tollbooth. Drew could easily make his escape now, retreat to the comfort of his lodgings, settle in front of the fire with a frothy pint of ale, and forget about the whole upsetting debacle.

But something prevented him. Something with flashing green eyes, wild honey hair, and a filthy mouth. Something that was quickening his pulse and rousing the beast in his trews.

As a rule, Drew kept his distance when it came to exchanges with the natives. The less they knew about him, the better. His dark scowl kept most people away. For those to whom he had to be civil, he'd learned to affect Highland charm to steer the conversation away from personal matters. As for intimate encounters, he employed discreet wenches who charged for their services and their silence.

Why he felt drawn to engage a wee, fiery-tempered, trews-wearing lass who was a danger to herself and others, he didn't know. Surely it had nothing to do with her rosy pink lips, the rough whiskey timber of her voice, or the thought of what bewitching charms might lie beneath that baggy shirt.

Lord, he thought, shaking his head, he'd spent too many days of late on the links and not enough feeding his carnal appetites.

The lass might be beautiful, but she was trouble. 'Twas a mistake to intervene in the affairs of quarrelsome Scots. And the last thing Drew needed was to draw the notice of their queen.

But he supposed he was obliged to help the maid. She was partly right—it *had* been his idea to expose her. The queen might never have noticed her had it not been for the waving pennant of her dazzling curls.

Besides, be they Scottish or English, he'd never been the sort who could walk away from tiny, helpless creatures. Especially those with sparkling eyes and tempting lips. He'd at least get the lass out of immediate danger and on the road home. He owed her that much.

ABOUT THE AUTHOR

I'm a *USA Today* bestselling author of swashbuckling action-adventure historical romances, mostly set in Scotland, with over a dozen award-winning books published in six languages.

But before my role as a medieval matchmaker, I sang in *The Pinups,* an all-girl band on CBS Records, and provided voices for the MTV animated series *The Maxx,* Blizzard's *Diablo* and *Starcraft* video games, and *Star Wars* audiobooks.

I'm the wife of a rock star (if you want to know which one, contact me) and the mother of two young adults. I do my best writing on cruise ships, in Scottish castles, on my husband's tour bus, and at home in my sunny southern California garden.

I love transporting readers to a place where the bold heroes have endearing flaws, the women are stronger than they look, the land is lush and untamed, and chivalry is alive and well!

I'm always delighted to hear from my readers, so please feel free to email me at glynnis@glynnis.net. And if you're a super-fan who would like to join my inner circle, sign up at http://www.facebook.com/GCReadersClan, where you'll get glimpses behind the scenes, sneak peeks of works-in-progress, and extra special surprises.

Made in the USA
Middletown, DE
05 September 2018